ADVANCE PRAISE FOR

wish you were here

"Beth Vogt hits a home run with her debut novel, *Wish You Were Here*. Quirky, snappy, and sweet, it's a story of finding true love that will leave you sighing and smiling."

—RACHEL HAUCK, bestselling and award-winning
author of *The Wedding Dress*

"What a delightful story! From the first line to the last page, Beth captivated me with her voice and this charming, funny yet poignant story about letting go of your life and finding the love that's been waiting all along. A fabulous first novel . . . I can't wait for the next by this talented new author!"

—SUSAN MAY WARREN, Rita Award–winning,
bestselling author of *The Shadow of Your Smile*

"I was swept away to the splendor of the Rockies in *Wish You Were Here*, a lovely debut by Beth K. Vogt. This perfectly paced love triangle has endearing characters and plot twists that kept me turning the pages deep into the night. I loved it!"

—CARLA STEWART, award-winning author of
Chasing Lilacs and *Broken Wings*

"Beth K. Vogt creates character, paints personality, and defines drama within a romantic comedy that sparkles with fun. *Wish You Were Here* will tickle your fancy from the first misplaced kiss to the kiss that lands exactly on the right spot in the end. This could only be the first book of many to come from a sensitive and talented new fiction author."

—DONITA K. PAUL, bestselling author of
the Drago̱n̲ ̲K̲e̲e̲p̲e̲r̲ ̲C̲h̲r̲o̲n̲i̲c̲l̲e̲s̲

"Beth Vogt's *Wish You Were Here* is a heartwarming story of reconciliation and second chances. Her characters charmed me from the first page and had me tearing up by the end of the novel. Beth weaves in spiritual truth that massages the soul while sprinkling in LOL moments to tickle the funny bone. Definitely one for the keeper shelf."

—LISA JORDAN, author of *Lakeside Reunion*

"Vogt's writing shines in this contemporary take on a timeless theme. She excels in portraying vibrant characters who grapple with vital questions. *Wish You Were Here* provides a postcard-perfect glimpse of the courage it takes to really be who you are."

—SIRI MITCHELL, author of *The Cubicle Next Door* and *She Walks in Beauty*

"Beth Vogt is a sparkling new talent whose *Wish you Were Here* brims with life, fun, and depth. Allison has acquired the wrong wedding dress, but worse yet, she may have grabbed the wrong groom. I hope you enjoy this book as much as I did. It's always refreshing to find a new voice in Christian fiction that shines!"

—KRISTIN BILLERBECK, author of *What a Girl Wants*

"One kiss can change everything! *Wish You Were Here* takes the reader on an emotional journey with Allison Denman as she struggles to find her place in this world. Allison comes to grips with the truth that playing it safe is not the same as living to the fullest—a good lesson for all of us. Beautifully written, *Wish You Were Here* is a lovely debut novel by Beth K. Vogt that illustrates the plans we make may not be God's choice for us. A fun and satisfying read!"

—MEGAN DiMARIA, author of *Searching for Spice*

wish you were here

A NOVEL

BETH K. VOGT

HOWARD BOOKS
A DIVISION OF SIMON & SCHUSTER, INC.

New York Delhi

Howard Books
A Division of Simon & Schuster, Inc.
1230 Avenue of the Americas
New York, NY 10020

First Howard Books trade paper edition May 2012

HOWARD and colophon are trademarks of Simon & Schuster, Inc.

For information about special discounts for bulk purchases, please contact Simon & Schuster Special Sales at 1-866-506-1949 or business@simonandschuster.com.

The Simon & Schuster Speakers Bureau can bring authors to your live event. For more information or to book an event, contact the Simon & Schuster Speakers Bureau at 1-866-248-3049 or visit our website at www.simonspeakers.com.

Designed by Jaime Putorti

Manufactured in the United States of America

10 9 8 7 6 5 4 3 2 1

Library of Congress Cataloging-in-Publication Data

Vogt, Beth K.
    Wish you were here : a novel / Beth Vogt.
      p. cm.
    I. Title.
    PS3622.O362W57 2012
    813'.6—dc23
        2011027560

ISBN 978-1-4516-5986-3
ISBN 978-1-4516-5997-9 (ebook)

For my husband, Rob: Together we've discovered the true meaning of happily ever after, with God's lavish grace woven through all the joys and sorrows. You are my most favorite person in the whole world— and my hero. (Song of Solomon 6:3)

wish you

were here

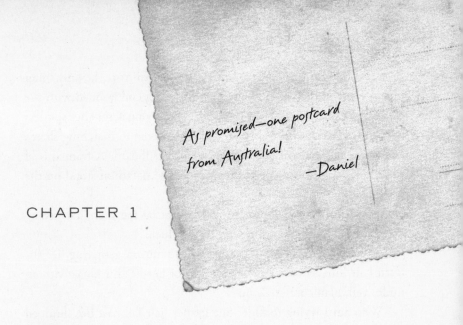

As promised—one postcard from Australia!

—Daniel

CHAPTER 1

*S*he never should have said yes.

Allison smoothed the bodice of the wedding gown, the fitted lace sleeves clinging to her arms. Waves of material billowed out from her waist, threatening to overwhelm her like a silken tsunami.

The style was all wrong.

She'd known it months ago—the moment the saleswoman released the dress from its protective plastic covering. Allison doubted all those layers of ivory lace and silk, bows and beads would ever fit back into such a small bag.

Securing the myriad of tiny pearl buttons marching down the back took precedence over her request for something simpler. She'd been instructed to stand on a round carpeted platform in front of a wall of angled mirrors. Encouraged to turn this way and that for the assembled critics—her best friend, Meghan; her mom; her younger sister, Hadleigh; and Seth's mom. Her future mother-in-law's breathless "Perfect" sealed Allison's fate.

While her mother paid a price as outlandish as the dress, the bridal shop attendant stressed the "no returns/no refunds" policy. And now . . . well, Allison couldn't do anything about her decision five days before the wedding.

Allison moved toward her standing beveled mirror. The only thing out of place in the room was the garment bag emblazoned with the elaborate, oversize initials of the bridal shop lying across her spotless white matelassé bedspread. Four pillows covered in matching shams and arranged just so lined the open-rail headboard. A framed oval photo of a triumphant Seth after winning a marathon stood on the bedside table.

Allison turned the photo around so it faced the wall. "No seeing the bride before the wedding day. It's bad luck."

She leaned toward her reflection in the mirror, gathering her auburn hair into a haphazard pile on top of her head. Maybe with an updo, veil, manicure, makeup—

"Who am I trying to kid?" She let her hair fall past her slumped shoulders. "Nothing can turn the wrong choice into the right one."

She should have spoken up, insisted she have the chance to try on a few more gowns. But if there was one thing she'd learned during the six years she'd dated Seth Rayner, it was how to go along with what someone else wanted.

Turning away from the irrefutable evidence, she fought to move past her bed as the gown swirled around her legs. The partially buttoned dress gaped open in the back, causing the sheer sleeves to slip off her shoulders.

She wouldn't wear the dress forever. Just for the ceremony. The reception. The limo ride to the hotel. Six hours, tops. Once it was dry-cleaned and stowed in the cavernous walk-in closet in Seth's town house, she'd never have to see the designer debacle again.

Except in the wedding photos.

"Scat, Bisquick." Allison lifted the material as her cat swatted the delicate hem. "I am not wearing a pricey cat toy."

Undeterred, her yellow cat stalked her out of the bedroom, menacing sounds warning Allison the game was still on. She sidestepped down the hall to her living room, keeping a watchful eye on her marauding feline. The five-foot train followed her like a guest who had overstayed her welcome.

She paced around her couch and matching chairs, upholstered in soft white suede. She was careful to avoid snagging the gown on her cognac-colored coffee table as she swished by. She hated the thought of storing the items in her parents' attic, but it couldn't be helped. There was no place to put her furniture at Seth's.

Maybe she should practice walking down the aisle. Practice made perfect, right?

Allison closed her eyes. Took a deep breath. Sang the words "Here comes the bride . . ."

Just step forward. One foot in front of the other. One. Two. One. Two.

Her eyes flew open. "I'm flunking the wedding march five days before my wedding. If I can't walk down a pretend aisle in my apartment, how am I going to manage the real thing?"

She collapsed on the couch, waves of material swelling up around her like a hot air balloon. It wasn't that she didn't want to get married. Seth was perfect for her. She was just tired of talking about the wedding and thinking about the wedding . . . and what came after. Most of all, she was tired of this dress—and she hadn't even worn it for real yet.

She needed a diversion. Maybe Meghan would be up for a movie. Something happy, like . . . *An Affair to Remember*. She'd give her a call and then escape the bridal gown nightmare.

And the sooner the better. If they had a fire in the building, she'd perish under five thousand dollars' worth of lace, beads, pearls, and silk. As if to emphasize the ugly truth, someone rapped on her door. Meghan, reading her mind? Or the local fire marshal, ready to declare her a walking fire code violation?

Shoving the skirt aside, she pulled the door open with a welcoming smile. "Hey, Meggie—"

Or not Meggie.

Seth's older brother, Daniel, leaned against the doorjamb. "Hey, yourself, Kid." His mismatched eyes—one blue, one green—skimmed over her bridal frenzy. "Am I interrupting an elopement?"

A lazy grin slid up his face, as if he'd like to help with that adventure. Of course, Daniel's motto might be "Grab Your Backpack and Follow Me," thanks to the miles he'd logged in his hiking boots over the years. He appeared straight off some mountain trail, dressed in cargo pants and a LIFE IS GOOD T-shirt under his brown leather bomber jacket, chin unshaved, brown curls tamed by a baseball cap.

How he and her starched, spit-polished fiancé happened to be kin baffled her.

"O-of course not!" She gathered the open back of her gown in one hand, shoving the ivory fabric back over her shoulders. "What are you doing here?" And why now, when she wore the fire hazard? She debated grabbing the coat hanging on the rack near the door, but knew a layer of hunter green wool wouldn't improve her appearance.

"Seth asked me to help move some of your stuff to his house this week, remember? I thought I'd pick up a few boxes."

"Boxes?"

"Books. Kitchen supplies. Knickknacks. Whatever you've packed." He stepped into her apartment, his larger-than-life persona managing to shrink even her dress down to size. But Allison still had to part the waves of material as she backed up.

"Uh, is that the dress?"

Was he choking back a laugh? Confirmation the dress was a nightmare.

"Yes. Please, no comments." Allison ran her hands along the flowing skirt as if she could tame it. Not going to happen.

"It's impressive."

Allison blew a wisp of hair out of her eyes. "Are you kidding me? I look like Bridal Fashion Disaster Barbie."

"Hey, all brides are beautiful on their wedding day." Daniel tucked the strand of hair behind her ear, the warmth in his eyes offering encouragement. "Seth won't be able to take his eyes off you."

"He'll be trying to find me somewhere in all this fabric."

As Daniel stepped around Allison, she caught the sound of his chuckle. She imagined his glance skimming the stack of assorted packing boxes piled in the living room of her otherwise immaculate apartment.

"You *are* planning on moving in with Seth after the wedding, right?"

"Of course I am. I've just been busy with deadlines and . . . and things . . ." She hated how the unused packing boxes made her feel guilty of some unnamed crime.

"Okay, so show me where the *packed* boxes are, and I'll get out of your way."

She longed to provide proof that she'd packed something. Say a few magic words and conjure up some boxes under the dress. *Abracadabra, I do, I do.* "I-I haven't packed anything yet." She shrugged, causing the lace to slip a few inches.

"Too busy playing dress-up?" The disarming grin Daniel tossed over his shoulder took any potential sting out of his question. "I really do like the dress, by the way."

"You're a liar, but thanks." She tugged the fabric back in place. Stupid dress.

Daniel turned back and wrapped an arm around her, pulling her close. Allison's dress crunched in protest even as his embrace wrapped her in the scent of leather and remnants of the brisk November night air. "Listen, Alli, you don't have to explain to a master procrastinator like me. Let's just consider helping the bride pack a best man's duty. Besides, what's a future brother-in-law for? We can order Chinese and tackle a few boxes. Deal?"

"You sure you've got time? I'd have to change."

"I hope so. Or I'm hopelessly underdressed." He turned her in the direction of her bedroom, his hands warm on her shoulders. "Need help with the buttons in the back . . . ummm, that would be a no."

Allison fled to her room, her laughter mingled with the heat of a blush that coursed across her face and all the way down her spine.

That Daniel—he knew how to make her laugh. She couldn't wait until he was actually her family.

. . .

Daniel sat back on his heels, his hands braced on his thighs. "How many boxes is that? Six?"

"That makes eight." Alli wrote LINENS across the top in block letters with a black Sharpie.

"I've never known anyone to color coordinate a linen closet." Daniel stood and offered his hand to Alli. "Your über-organization makes it easy to pack your stuff. DVDs filed by genre and alphabetized by title?"

"It makes life easier. I don't like wasting time looking for things." She wrapped her fingers around his and stood, rubbing her neck with her other hand. "You know what they say: 'A place for everything, and everything in its place.'"

"Yeah, well, this is why you're marrying my brother, Mr. Clean. I'm more of a 'let everything go all over the place' kind of guy." Daniel placed his hand over hers where she kneaded her shoulder. "Muscle spasm?"

"Just a little one." Allison stilled as he worked to ease the tightness. "Too much time hunched over my computer, trying to finish up projects before the h-honeymoon."

Somewhere in the midst of her detailed retelling of a recent graphic design deadline, Daniel realized he'd stopped listening and let himself focus way too much attention on the curve of Alli's neck and the softness of her skin as he massaged her shoulder. He patted her back—a nice brotherly gesture—and stepped away. "All better?"

"Y-yes. Thanks." She turned, pulling at the hem of her oversize Air Force Falcons sweatshirt and then smoothing it against her black yoga pants. "So . . . interested in dessert? I mean, something other than fortune cookies? I've got some ice cream."

"Sounds great."

Shoving his hands into his back pockets, he followed her to the kitchen. She'd decorated in basic black and white—white towels, black ceramic containers on the countertops, a white KitchenAid mixer. Even her cat's dishes were color-coordinated, one black, one white. The only splash of color was the large bulletin board displayed on one wall. He stood in front of it, realizing it was a pictorial travelogue of his past. An assortment of "Wish You Were Here" postcards threatened to overflow the frame's borders. Almost all of the fifty states. Canada. Germany. The Bahamas. Turkey. Kenya. He went through passports the way some people went through credit card balances. He shook his head. "I can't believe you kept all these."

"Some people collect antique paperweights." Alli came to stand beside him, a metal ice cream scoop in her hand. "I collect postcards from my future brother-in-law."

"Isn't this the first one I ever sent you?" He touched a postcard in the middle of the collection.

"That's the one. And nice guy that you are, you kept sending them. Thanks. I liked seeing all the exotic places you were visiting while I slogged through midterms and finals."

"I remember that trip to Australia. You and Seth were—what?— juniors in high school. You begged me to send you a postcard—"

"I did not beg!"

He deflected her well-aimed jab with the spoon, wrapping his hand around hers. "Were you already dating my little brother back then?"

"Barely." Allison withdrew her hand and went to the freezer to get the ice cream. "He'd asked me to homecoming, and we just kind of started dating after that."

"Kind of started dating?" Daniel gave a snort of laughter, watching her scoop mounds of fudge ripple into a white ceramic bowl. "You know Seth better than that. He had every step planned out to get you to fall in love with him."

And he accomplished that goal, just as he gets everything he sets his sights on.

Daniel leaned against the counter, snagging a spoonful of ice cream. "Aren't you going to have any?"

Alli stashed the carton back in the freezer. "I'm the one who has to fit in a wedding gown in five days, remember? I thought I'd share a bite of yours."

He held a spoonful of fudge ripple in front of her. "I suppose this counts as another best-man duty—saving you from not fitting in that gorgeous gown of yours?"

"Very funny, wise guy." She paused before handing the spoon back to him. "Hey, there's a thought! If I can't fit into the dress, I can't wear it, right? Quick, I need more ice cream!"

She dashed toward the fridge, but Daniel was there ahead of her, blocking her way.

"Come on, Daniel. Move."

"I'm saving you from a very rash decision, Alli." He marched her back into the living room, directing her to sit on the couch. "I told you that you look beautiful in that dress."

"And I told you that I don't believe you." Alli pulled her legs up and wrapped her arms around her knees.

Daniel started piling boxes by the door to carry them down to his truck. As he turned from depositing a box by the door, he caught Alli smothering a yawn. "That's my cue to leave." He moved Bisquick from where he lay snoozing in a chair—on top of Daniel's ball cap. "Stupid cat."

Allison followed him to the door, watching him slip on his boots. "I'll ignore the 'stupid cat' remark because you didn't laugh out loud when you saw my wedding gown."

"Don't worry about the dress, Alli. You'll take Seth's breath away." He ran his finger along the line of doubt etched between her eyebrows. "Trust me."

"I can help carry the boxes to your truck—"

"Don't bother, bride-to-be." He leaned down to place a quick good-night kiss on Alli's cheek just as she tilted her face up. His lips brushed hers, halting her thanks with the lightest of touches. The slightest bit of contact.

Not a kiss. Not really.

Just enough for Daniel to capture the softness of Alli's lips and the hint of chocolate that lingered there.

He would never kiss his brother's fiancée.

He looked up—and lost himself in Alli's eyes, their gray-blue depths reminding him of a cloudless expanse of sky. The light citrus scent that always lingered in her auburn hair lured him closer. "Alli . . ."

He placed his hand against the curve of her back, drawing her against him. Caressed the side of her face, watching as the cloud of confusion in her eyes changed to a spark of startled awareness. Their lips touched again. He closed his eyes, his hand sliding through her hair to the nape of her neck, just enough to let her know that yes, he meant every moment, every gentle touch of this kiss.

And to his shock, Alli kissed him back.

Instead of slapping his face.

Just as he began to lose himself in the kiss, an incessant tone jarred Daniel's senses, pulling him back to reality—away from Alli. What *was* that?

Alli stared at him, confusion once again clouding her eyes. She cut short the whisper of his name when she covered her lips with trembling fingers. "Y-your cell." She shook her head as if clearing her thoughts and stepped out of his embrace. "You probably need to answer that."

"Alli, wait." He reached for her hand as he dug his phone out of his back pocket and flipped it open. "Daniel here."

"Hey, it's Seth. Did you go by Allison's tonight like I asked? I've tried calling her, but she's not answering her cell."

"Seth." Alli's eyes widened, the lips he'd just kissed forming his brother's name. Their eyes locked, and Alli seemed to hold her breath, waiting to see what he would say. What was he supposed to do? Add lying to his sins? "Yeah, I'm just leaving Alli's. I grabbed a load of boxes. I'll drop them by your house tomorrow."

"You want to bring them by tonight?"

"No, it's later than I realized." He faced away from Alli, putting distance between them.

"How's Allison?"

"She's fine." Not that Daniel was asking at the moment. "She'd tried on her dress when I showed up. Counting the days until the wedding."

"I can't wait to see it. Mom said it's stunning."

Daniel managed some noncommittal reply. Their mom was right—and wrong. The dress *was* stunning, but it wasn't right for Alli. Didn't matter. Alli would be a beautiful bride for his brother.

After signing off, Daniel shoved his cell into his back pocket. Took a deep breath and faced—an empty room. Where did Alli disappear to?

The kitchen?

Empty.

Daniel walked down the hallway to Alli's bedroom. Her cat lounged in front of her closed bedroom door like a sorry excuse for a watchdog.

"Not necessary, cat."

He eyed the door, debating. Beat a hasty retreat or face Alli like a man? The cat stared him down through half-closed eyes.

He rapped his knuckles against the door. "Alli, come on out."

Silence.

"Come on, Kid. We need to talk."

When he leaned close, he heard her muffled response: "Go away, Daniel."

"This is ridiculous. We can't have a conversation through a closed door."

"We're not having a conversation—"

"What do you call this?"

Silence.

"Alli?" Daniel stared at the door, unsure if he wanted her to open it or keep it closed.

She pulled the door open so fast that he took two steps backward. He missed trampling on the cat, who hissed and darted back down the hallway to the living room.

"You want to talk? Fine. What do you want me to say?" She raked her fingers through her hair. "How could you . . . how could we . . ." Her voice broke off as she choked back a sob.

"Don't cry, Kid—"

She stomped her foot. "Don't you dare tell me not to cry, Daniel Rayner! You're not the one getting married in five days! You're not the one who just made the biggest mistake of her life!"

He held up his hands. "Hey, I don't think what happened is the biggest mistake of your life."

She glared at him. "I am not going to stand here and discuss all my mistakes with you, letting you decide where k-kissing you ranks—"

"That's not what I meant, and you know it."

More silence.

"Look, I got ahead of myself, wanting to kiss the bride." Daniel figured if he downplayed the whole episode, Alli would too. "Let's not make a big deal out of it."

"N-not make a big deal out of it?" She stared at him, looking as shocked as if he'd suggested they kiss again.

"It was just a kiss, not a one-night stand." Daniel's lie tore him apart. The kiss had mattered to him—not that he could admit it. How many lies had he told tonight? "You're not the first woman I've kissed, Alli. You won't be the last." He forced a laugh that sounded fake, even to him. What was that verse his scoutmaster used to quote? *Even a fool, when he is silent, seems wise.* Daniel needed someone running a teleprompter with that verse on it.

Alli's words were a strained whisper. "How could we do something like that?"

"It was my fault, Alli. Not yours." He longed to take her in his arms and comfort her, but he didn't dare touch her again. No more mistakes tonight.

She wiped away her tears with the back of her hand. "I-I need you to leave. Please."

"I'll load the boxes in my truck and lock your front door, okay?"

"Fine."

Okay, then. His work here was done. The sooner he left, the better. He needed to put some distance between himself and the temptation of his brother's fiancée.

Allison twisted the shower handles. *Come on, hot water.*

She tilted her head so the water streamed across her face and down her shoulders, waiting for the warmth to ease the tension from her body.

It was late for a shower—more like early—but she knew she'd never go to sleep. Every time she closed her eyes, she saw Daniel's face right before he kissed her . . .

Shampoo. She should shampoo her hair. One less thing to do when she got up for work in a few hours. She'd French-braid her hair before she went to sleep.

She lathered her head, savoring the familiar mandarin-orange scent of her favorite shampoo. Scrubbing her hair reminded her of how Daniel's hand slipped through her hair as he pulled her close . . .

Rinse. She needed to rinse and condition.

And she needed to stop thinking about Daniel Rayner.

Massaging the cream from scalp to ends, she conjured up a mental to-do list.

One: Send off the PDFs of the magazine layouts she'd completed.

Two: Make sure Lori knew what deadlines would come up while she was on her honeymoon.

The honeymoon. She and Meghan were going shopping tomorrow—*today*—for some last-minute must-haves. She still needed a beach cover-up and some sort of hat. And maybe she could find a new dress for the wedding rehearsal.

The rehearsal.

Well, that was a huge number three on her list.

How would she survive seeing Daniel at the rehearsal? How would she survive being his sister-in-law for the next who knew how many decades of wedding anniversaries with Seth?

"Why did I kiss him, God? Why? Why?" Allison leaned her forehead against the shower tile. "What was I thinking?"

No answer.

Instead, Daniel kept interrupting her attempts to organize the upcoming day. The strength of his arms wrapped around her. How his lips coaxed an unexpected response from her. How he whispered her name right before he kissed her the second time.

The cold spray forced Allison to turn off the water. She'd emptied her hot water tank. Shivering, she grabbed her faded green robe and wrapped it around her still-damp body. She grabbed a towel off the rack and gathered her wet hair into the soft cotton. Turning, she caught a glimpse of herself in the mirror over her sink.

Don't you look great?

Not.

Gray streaks of mascara marred her pasty white face. She looked like she had the twenty-four-hour flu. She certainly felt sick. The Kung Pao chicken and beef and broccoli she'd shared with Daniel threatened to come back up her throat.

"What have you done?" Allison whispered to her reflection.

Again, no answer. Apparently, both she and God were out of answers tonight.

She walked into her bedroom, toweling her hair. The pristine white designer gown hung in front of the window, the moonlight making it seem iridescent. It loomed like a silent judge, declaring her guilty. She ought to stitch a scarlet "K" across the bodice. If anyone asked about the last-minute embellishment, she could say, "Oh, this? I somehow managed to kiss my fiancé's brother."

Allison climbed into bed, too tired to care about dropping the towel on the floor. She removed a wide-tooth comb from the bedside table, worked out the snarls in her hair, and began braiding it.

How long would she and Daniel have kissed if his cell phone hadn't rung? Did the caller have to be Seth? It was almost as if he'd caught her in Daniel's arms.

As hard as she tried to avoid them, Allison knew she'd made some mistakes in her life. And now she could no longer lie about her feelings for Seth's adventuresome brother. Part of her wished Daniel hadn't answered his phone. The harmless first not-really-a-kiss had surprised her. But she hadn't resisted when Daniel kissed her again. During her impressionable teen years, she'd imagined what it would be like to kiss Daniel. Now she knew.

She'd always admired Seth's older brother—his love for the outdoors, his independent streak, his ability to make her laugh. Until tonight, she'd convinced herself that her mixed-up emotions for Daniel were remnants of an adolescent crush. Now she wasn't sure what she felt for her fiancé's brother.

But she was engaged to Seth. She'd dated him for six years. He was perfect for her. Reliable. Safe. Her dream come true.

How could she betray him like this? What kind of person was she to kiss her fiancé's brother? Did she even deserve someone as good as Seth?

With a groan, Allison slipped under the blankets, rolling onto her stomach. How was she going to tell Seth?

Shame caused her to bury her face in her pillow, her prayer a broken plea. "I can't tell him, God. I can't. He won't understand. I don't even understand how it happened."

Tears scorched her face as she imagined standing before Seth, confessing her sin. He would be so hurt.

Allison pressed her hand against the ache in her chest.

Could he hurt any worse than she did?

Shoving the pillows away, Alli turned onto her side, staring at her wedding gown.

What if Daniel told Seth?

CHAPTER 2

*D*aniel considered tonight a warm-up. If he survived the rehearsal at the church and the dinner, he could survive the wedding.

And all the rest of Seth and Alli's happily-ever-after.

Daniel stood inside the door of the restaurant's private dining room. Some guests still relaxed at the round tables covered in crisp white tablecloths, finishing their selection of either stuffed Rocky Mountain trout or filet mignon. Others lingered by the dessert table, which displayed a selection of mini tarts, cheesecakes, and assorted chocolate truffles. Daniel didn't even remember tasting his meal.

He shoved up the cuff of his wrinkled dress shirt and glanced at his watch. So far he'd endured exactly one hour and thirteen minutes of the rehearsal dinner. How soon could he slip away unnoticed?

Avoidance had worked so far. He'd continue evading Alli until after the "I dos" tomorrow night. Less than twenty-four hours to be the "stealth" best man. He'd managed the previous four days by leaving town. Sure, Seth hadn't appreciated his impromptu camping trip right before the wedding, but he'd shrugged off Daniel's decision. What had Seth said? *Just like you, Daniel—avoiding responsibility.*

There was no way his little brother could know Daniel was avoiding Seth's future bride by throwing on a backpack and hiking as fast and as far from Alli as he could get. And other than being there for the rehearsal and the ceremony, he had no real responsibilities. Seth had made sure everything went off without a hitch. Being such a micromanager, Seth didn't like the idea of his best man being outside of cell phone range this close to the wedding.

After three cold days and long nights tramping around Mueller State Park, Daniel got to the rehearsal with barely enough time to shower and no time to shave. Seth scowled at him. Alli ignored him, playing with her bracelets or staring at the minister as if enthralled by his instructions.

Caught by the sound of Alli's laughter, Daniel glanced toward the happy couple.

Across the room, the soon-to-be Mr. and Mrs. mingled with family and friends. Right after all the guests were served the main course, Seth had stood and asked for everyone's attention. Then he surprised Allison with a wedding present—an expensive pair of diamond earrings that coordinated with her engagement ring. His little brother enjoyed the guests' oohs and aahs as much as Alli's exuberant kiss.

Now Alli smiled up at Seth, her long, loose ginger curls cascading down her back. Seth looked relaxed, even in a pair of dark pants with a crease sharp enough to almost cut through Daniel's anxiety, a conservative navy blue blazer, white shirt, and blood-red power tie.

Was Alli wearing a new dress, or was he just having a hard time not looking at her? The deep red material of the wraparound design clung to her body in all the right—make that all the *wrong*—places. What happened to Alli the Kid, the high-schooler who wore long-sleeve T-shirts, jeans, and flip-flops? Why couldn't she pick a style in a boring neutral color?

Seth placed an arm around Alli's waist and pulled her close. Tired of watching his brother and Alli celebrating, Daniel turned away, only to confront their reflection in a mirror on the nearby wall.

He was a glutton for punishment.

He'd been surrounded by images of Seth and Alli all night. Sterling-silver-framed photographs of Seth and Allison from the past six years decorated the tables. Allison as a shy seventeen-year-old standing quietly in Seth's shadow. Both of them at high school graduation, huge grins on their faces as they held hands and showed off their diplomas. An exhausted Seth celebrating winning different marathons, Allison by his side at every finish line. Their college graduation, where Allison wore a three-quarter-carat engagement ring.

As Daniel exited the room and strode down the hallway, he slipped his hand into his coat pocket. His fingers touched one photo he'd removed from the collection. It had been taken during Seth and Alli's youth-group snowshoeing trip during their senior year of high school. With his experience planning outdoor trips, Daniel had organized and helped chaperone. Once again playing big brother to Seth and Alli, who were eight years younger than he.

In the photo, Alli stood between him and Seth. Both brothers had their arms around her shoulders. Alli was laughing—and looking at Daniel. He'd made some wisecrack as the camera's automatic timer counted down, and Alli couldn't hold back her giggles.

"Where ya off to?" Daniel's best friend, Jackson, slung his arm across Daniel's shoulders, causing him to slow his pace.

"Looking for an exit."

"Partied out?"

"It's Seth's party, not mine."

"Exactly. He's getting married tomorrow—not us." Jackson's grin creased the freckles spanning his face. "There are a lot of single ladies in there, Danny."

"Not interested."

"So I noticed." Jackson loosened his tie. "Something bothering you?"

"Just not in a party mood, I guess."

"Aren't you happy for your brother?"

"Couldn't be happier for him. Alli's a great girl. They're perfect for each other."

"All right, then. Your time will come, my man. You'll fall in love with some woman and get married. Settle down—"

"I don't think so, Jackson."

"I didn't realize you were such a skeptic about love."

"Not everyone grew up in a family like yours. Your parents loved each other, and they loved being parents. Loved their kids—all five of them." Daniel huffed out a breath. "I like my life, but it doesn't fit well with marriage. And I'm good with that."

Jackson walked beside him in silence for a few moments and then gave Daniel's shoulders a shake. "What are we doing out here, talking about getting married? You ready to go mingle with somebody besides me?"

"In a minute, Jackson. I'm going to step outside for some fresh air."

The parking lot was a contrast of shadows and light. Daniel kept to the darkened corners, skirting cars and avoiding even casual greetings. He hunched his shoulders against the cool night air, hoping it would clear his head, ease the tension pressing against his temples.

Except for the major slipup a few nights ago, he had never violated The Code. Rule #1: You don't go after another guy's girl—especially if the other guy is your little brother and he's marrying the girl in less than a week.

Even though he and Seth weren't close, guilt tainted every moment of the wedding rehearsal. Alli and Seth had been together forever. She was so much younger than Daniel. What had he been thinking when he forgot all that and kissed her?

He lasted all of one circle around the front parking lot. Enough was enough. He'd go grab his leather jacket and head home. As he'd told Jackson, this was Seth's party, not his. He was done watching Seth and Alli's almost-wedded bliss. Nobody would notice if he disappeared. He strode into the hotel lobby—and found himself face-to-face with Alli.

She put her hand out to stop him from running into her. "Daniel—"

"Alli." He took a step back. He'd decipher the look in her eyes if she'd look at him.

"I'm trying to find Hadleigh. She wandered off with my camera."

"Haven't seen your sister since dinner."

"I'll keep looking, then." Alli moved to step around him.

"Alli, wait." He reached out and clasped her wrist, forcing her to stand still. She stared at the carpet. "About the other night."

Silence, just like the other night. Alli knew how to shut him out.

"We both know it was a mistake, right?"

Alli stared at the carpet as if memorizing the multicolored floral pattern. Then she met his eyes. "Yes—a huge mistake."

"I'm sorry."

"I'm sorry too." Alli tugged against his hand still encircling her wrist. "I need to go—to get back to Seth."

He released her, stepped back. Nothing more needed to be said.

"Hey, you two!" Hadleigh's voice echoed in the brittle silence. "Ready for your photo shoot?"

"I'll pass, Hadleigh." Daniel shoved his hands in his pockets, shaking his head.

"Aww, come on." Alli's younger sister came to stand in front of them, aiming the camera at their faces. "Alli put me in charge of getting lots of photos. I haven't gotten one of you two yet."

"That's okay, Leigh." Alli rubbed her wrist.

"Don't move!" Hadleigh stepped in front of Alli, blocking her sister's departure. Her exuberant grin cajoled them from beneath her short black hair, highlighted with red streaks. "I'm the photographer, and I want a picture of you and Daniel. Go stand by your future brother-in-law. *Now.*"

Daniel glanced at Alli, who twisted her hand around her wrist and stared at her sister. Might as well do what Hadleigh wanted and get it over with. He moved next to Alli, placing his arm across her shoulders. When she tried to move away, he smiled down at her, speaking through clenched teeth. "Let's humor her, shall we? Get this over with."

A hint of lightning sparked in the depths of Alli's gray-blue eyes. She tilted her chin and faced her sister.

"Oh, come on, you guys." Hadleigh motioned at them in disgust. "You act like you don't even know each other. Put your arm around him, Allison!"

"I know this guy better than you think, Leigh."

Alli's words were so quiet, Daniel knew they were spoken for his benefit alone. Alli placed her arm around his waist. When Daniel pulled her closer, she stiffened. He offered her an apologetic smile. "Gotta make the photographer happy."

Hadleigh adjusted the camera's focus. "Okay, on three . . ."

Daniel grinned like a madman, trying to ignore Alli's closeness. Hurt, mingled with anger, radiated off her.

The second the camera flashed, she stepped away. "Seth is probably wondering where I am." She tossed the words over her shoulder.

"Sure. I'll see you tomorrow—at the wedding."

Daniel turned in the opposite direction, heading for the parking lot. He'd text Jackson to get his coat.

Allison glanced at her microwave's digital clock. Three A.M. She should be asleep, enjoying sweet dreams about Seth, not sitting in her kitchen sipping a tepid cup of jasmine tea.

At least she was wearing a veil with her wedding gown. No one would see the bags under her eyes.

Since the wedding was in the evening, maybe she'd sneak in a nap before she went to the day spa with Meghan and the bridesmaids.

She'd probably doze off during her pedicure. Why didn't she listen to her mom and dad and sleep at their house tonight? Or Meggie's loft?

Allison stood and wandered over to the postcard-covered bulletin board. "Wish You Were Here." What she really wished was that she could stop thinking about Daniel. Stop remembering their kisses. She'd made a mistake, and she wanted to forget it ever happened.

Seth had been furious when his brother took off for the mountains right before the wedding. She'd been relieved, saying, "It's not his wedding." Allison hoped Seth didn't notice how her hand shook as she checked the seating chart for the reception.

"But he is the best man."

In name only.

"He'll be back in plenty of time. Don't worry." She'd pulled Seth close and kissed him.

And thought of Daniel.

She stared at the multicolored photographs, all the places Daniel had explored. All the places she imagined visiting one day. *With Seth.*

It was past time to retire the postcard collection.

Before she could talk herself out of the decision, she pulled the coordinating decorative thumbtacks out of the corners of each postcard. One, two, three, four. Repeat. One, two, three, four. Repeat. In a few minutes, a jumble of tacks and a tall pile of cards lay on her kitchen counter.

What now?

The tacks were easy. She deposited them in a container on her desk. Everything in its place. Where should the postcards go? She stared at the stack. She couldn't bring them to Seth's. She should throw them out. The movers would come and pack up her furniture while they were honeymooning. Hadleigh was looking forward to getting the bedroom furniture. The rest of her stuff would be stored in her parents' attic or sent to her aunt Nita's in Estes Park.

Just throw the silly things out.

She grabbed the cards and stuffed them in the bottom drawer of her desk, back behind her files. Out of sight, out of mind. Like Daniel.

She'd keep telling herself that.

Allison wandered out to her living room, her cat pacing behind her. "One of us should be sleeping, Bisquick."

Tucking her feet beneath her, she curled up in one corner of the couch, grabbed the remote, and started channel-surfing. There had to be something on TV that would put her to sleep.

Black-and-white images played across the screen. *Bringing Up Baby,* one of her favorite classic movies. Why did things always work out between Cary Grant and Katharine Hepburn? Or Cary Grant and Deborah Kerr? Cary Grant and any woman he fell in love with?

"Why can't life be in black and white, God? Why won't you give me a happy ending?" She drew her knees up, resting her chin on her folded arms. "I'm trying to do the right things—shouldn't that guarantee me happiness?"

On the drive home, Seth declared the rehearsal dinner a success, but then he always enjoyed being center stage. He also liked the new dress she'd splurged on at the last minute, insisting she bring it along on the honeymoon. Meghan had been on the mark when she said, "The style's not over the top, just a little more . . . umm . . . provocative than you usually wear. Seth will want to fast-forward to the honeymoon."

By staying close to Seth, she'd avoided Daniel—almost. She hadn't known what to say when they'd met in the hallway. *I'm sorry I let you kiss me? I'm sorry I wanted you to kiss me?*

Looking down, Allison noticed the angry red scratches on her wrist. Again and again, she'd raked her nails across her skin.

How many times would it take before she bled?

Jumping up from the couch, Allison rubbed her arm against the soft material of her robe.

No. *No.* Nothing was worth that.

She paced around her living room, circling the couch half a dozen times, breathing in and out.

Calm me down, God. Help me do the right thing. Calm me down.

No matter how Allison tried to soothe her irritated skin against her robe, her wrist tingled. She forced herself to take slow, measured steps to her bedroom, where she grabbed a tube of lavender-scented lotion off the dresser. Squeezing out an ample amount, she slathered it on her hands and wrists.

Over and over.

Again and again.

Good morning, Kid—
although I'm hitting the
sack right after I mail this
card. The water really
is this green in Destin—
that's why they call it the
Emerald Coast.

—Daniel

CHAPTER 3

"I do."

Allison whispered the words as she stood at the back of the church.

I do.

That's all she had to say.

Two words.

Two syllables.

Like a pair of invisible hands wrapped around her throat, the thought of saying those words choked Allison.

The scent of dozens of burgundy roses adorning the altar and the pews saturated the sanctuary. Identical blossoms nestled among stephanotis in the bouquet held in Allison's trembling grasp. She stared at the sprays of purple blossoms Seth insisted be included in the arrangement. No explanation. Seth said it needed to be done, so she agreed.

Forgetting her hair was ensnared in a classic French twist, Allison reached up to smooth it back behind her ears. Seth also insisted she wear her hair up for the ceremony. Said he liked the way the few loose tendrils framed her face.

Allison avoided looking at the 350 guests waiting for the procession to begin. She couldn't think that far ahead. Her stepfather, Will, stood beside her, waiting to escort her down the aisle. He'd supported her for fifteen years. Once again, he was a tangible sense of security in Allison's life when she most needed it.

The church was as she'd always imagined. Candlelit. White satin carpet unrolled at her feet to guide her to Seth. The guests a blur of smiling faces. Family and friends of the bride on one side of the aisle. Family and friends of the groom on the other. Everyone and everything in its place. Seth had conceded to her wish for a string quartet to play before the ceremony started. Allison tried to let the poignant sound of the violins, cello, and viola soothe her frayed emotions.

She caught sight of Seth waiting for her at the front of the church. The black cutaway morning tuxedo accented his tall, lean frame. He smiled as if to say, *This is our day.*

Next to him stood Daniel, staring at some distant spot over her head.

Probably planning his next backpacking trip. What kind of postcard would he have sent her?

She needed to pay attention. Look at Seth. Smile at her husband-to-be.

The first of her three bridesmaids walked down the aisle in a long champagne-colored gown. Allison had wanted a smaller ceremony, but Seth wanted a "celebration to remember." So besides Hadleigh as her maid of honor, she'd asked Meghan, Lori from work, and Jessica, the wife of one of Seth's business colleagues.

Allison glanced back and forth at the two brothers. So alike. Yet so different. Seth was an inch taller than Daniel and wiry. Both were athletic and had spent years playing sports. Now Seth focused on training for marathons, always determined to cut seconds from his time. Daniel preferred to hike and canoe and snowshoe. Both men had the same dark brown hair, though Seth wore his short and controlled, and Daniel's curled at the nape of his neck. Haircuts were low on his priority list. Seth's eyes were brown, like his father's. Daniel's eyes were that striking blue–green; he carried off the genetic oddity with a laissez-faire attitude. Seth's seriousness had propelled him up the corporate ladder to second in command at Rayner Construction. Daniel's easy manner was seen in his smile as he charmed his way around the world for both pleasure and business. He loved being his own boss, developing or updating outdoor activities—snowmobiling, ski runs—for resorts.

Daniel wasn't smiling today.

And she wouldn't remember his appealing grin on the night he kissed her.

What kind of woman thought about kissing one man minutes before she married his brother? Thank God her thoughts weren't broadcast live for all her wedding guests to hear.

God, please, please, help me do this. Help me do the right thing. I do love Seth. I do.

Breathe in, breathe out. Smile. What's that trick to keep yourself from crying? Grit your teeth while looking up at the ceiling. Take a long, slow breath. Blink once. Twice. Repeat.

Maybe Seth wouldn't see her tears through her veil. If he did, maybe he'd think they were tears of happiness. All brides cry on their wedding day, right?

Now it was Meghan's turn to walk down the aisle. Meggie was a natural, all long-legged grace and poise. She was thrilled to be in Alli's wedding. What was her motto? *Always a bridesmaid, never the bride. That's fine with me.*

Really, she should be the bride. Meghan would march down to the front of the church and face a firing squad without flinching.

Allison glanced at the Rayner brothers again. For one brief moment, she thought Daniel looked at her. Then he rubbed his hand across his face and looked away.

After Hadleigh gave her a quick wink and did a slow one-two-one-two glide down the aisle, the musicians played the first notes of Vivaldi's *The Four Seasons,* "Autumn: III. Allegro." Seth hadn't wanted the traditional Wedding March.

Will squeezed her hand. Leaning close, he whispered, "Here we go, Allison," adding with a chuckle, "unless you've changed your mind?"

He had no idea. But Allison couldn't disappoint him. Or Mom. Or Seth. Marrying Seth was the right thing to do.

Her stepfather moved forward, then paused, waiting for Allison to begin her walk down the aisle.

I do.

I can't.

I must.

Daniel swore he could hear his Swiss Army watch, each tick-tick-tick bringing Alli one step closer to Seth.

Not him.

Seth.

Alli entered the sanctuary in an explosion of lace and satin. Her bouquet of deep red roses was the only splash of color he saw when he allowed himself to look at her. Alli's face was a pale blur underneath her veil.

Look anywhere but at her.

He refocused on the EXIT sign stationed above the doorway Alli had stepped through. The white letters bled into the bright green. No exit for him. He would not watch Alli walk toward his brother. If only he could plug his fingers in his ears so he wouldn't hear the vows. Maybe he should practice the toast he was supposed to say for Seth and Alli during the wedding reception.

All he could do was wonder how many times he could read the word "exit."

Shifting his stance so he turned away from Alli, he watched his brother. Seth's eyes never left Alli's face, and he wore a smile of pure pride. Why shouldn't he be proud? In less time than it took to run a 5K, he and Alli would be Mr. and Mrs. Seth Rayner. Tag, the little brother who'd tried to follow him everywhere when they were younger, would never know his big brother kissed his fiancée—and that Alli kissed him back.

E-X-I-T.

Daniel would not allow himself to remember holding Alli in his arms. How he hadn't wanted to let her go.

E-X-I-T.

But he had kissed Alli a mere five days ago. Too late to change anything—like the groom. Besides, Alli didn't want him. She was in love with Seth.

What did other brides think about when they walked down the aisle?

Allison counted her steps. One. Pause. Two. Pause. Three. Pause. Four.

Could anyone guess she was afraid she was marrying the wrong man? But how could Daniel be the right man?

Allison tried to swallow. How would she say her vows with her tongue cleaving to the roof of her mouth? What would oh-so-proper Seth say if she paused by Aunt Nita's pew and asked if she had a mint or a piece of gum?

Being the focus of attention caused Allison's steps to falter. Did everyone have to stare at her as if there were an actual scarlet "K" stitched on the bodice of her gown?

"Easy does it, sweetie." Will tucked her hand more securely in the crook of his arm. "One step at a time."

"Right, Dad. One step at a time." Allison focused on the white runner at her feet.

Will stopped next to the front pew where her mother stood, smiling. It seemed as though everyone was smiling today.

Except her. And Daniel.

The musicians played the final notes of the processional. She heard Seth's minister begin the ceremony—something about being gathered here today in the sight of God—and then he asked, "Who gives this woman in holy matrimony?"

Will squeezed her hand again, causing her engagement ring to press against her fingers. He cleared his throat and announced, "Her mother and I." He lifted her veil, removing the fine lace that had shielded her face. Kissed her on the cheek. "I wish you so much happiness, Allison."

As Will stepped aside, Allison's mother leaned over and embraced her. Allison clung to her, crushing her veil against her mother's shoulder.

Would God bless her if she married Seth after kissing Daniel less than a week ago?

It was time to step forward and stand next to Seth. To take his hand and promise to love, honor, and cherish him.

For all the days of her life.

Allison moved away and turned toward Seth. He held his hand out to her, his smile welcoming.

Allison took one step toward him.

Another.

Stopped.

"Seth . . ." She tried to force her voice above a whisper. "I'm so sorry . . . I can't do this . . ."

Seth's smile faltered.

Allison couldn't repeat her words. Instead, she dropped her wedding bouquet and turned away from Seth. The excessive material of the dress impeded her steps. Grabbing fistfuls of lace, she lifted it off the floor and ran back up the aisle.

Out of the church.

Away from Seth shouting her name.

Away from Daniel.

She wouldn't be happy—but she wouldn't be living a lie.

Hey, Kid—Everybody needs a postcard of a Jackson Hole jackalope, right? Here's yours!

—Daniel

CHAPTER 4

*A*llison dragged the veil off and threw it onto the car's passenger seat. The delicate lace slid off the leather onto the floor.

She should have taken the dramatic cathedral veil off hours ago.

No wonder people stared at her as they passed on the highway. They probably wondered if she was going to a costume party. Or if she was cruising, looking for her lost groom. Allison's crack of laughter morphed into a choked-off sob.

Maneuvering through traffic prevented her from running her fingers through her hair, hunting for all the hidden pins. She squirmed in the bucket seat. The dress bunched up around her thighs, overflowing onto the console and into the backseat. She couldn't see the speedometer, thanks to the mounds of lace and silk billowing around her.

Her driver's ed teacher never tested her on this ridiculous automotive situation.

Tears blurred her vision and cascaded down her cheeks, trailing warm, wet lines down her neck.

Who did she think she was, a Julia Roberts wannabe starring in *Runaway Bride Revisited*?

How many hours had gone by since she'd raced back up the

aisle—past the photographer with a camera frozen in front of her face, past the rows of staring, no longer smiling guests—into the church foyer? She'd stood still for a few seconds before scrambling down the stairs on her way to the safety of the bride's dressing room. She'd tripped over the front hem of the gown and just avoided falling flat on her face.

Looking around, she spied Meghan's magenta hobo bag in a corner of the room, tossed in a pile with her best friend's black jeans and cashmere black sweater. She could almost hear Meghan warning, "Don't even think about it, girlfriend!" With a whispered "Sorry, Meggie," she grabbed her leather messenger bag and Meghan's keys, ran from the church, and hijacked her best friend's MINI Cooper.

What are friends for, right? If Allison had her own car, she'd have taken it, but Meghan had insisted on chauffeuring Allison to the church.

Now what?

Allison stared at the taillights in front of her. All of those people knew where they were going. Even the guy driving the tandem UPS truck barreling past her had a destination mapped out. But she was caught in an endless loop on I-25, counting the mile markers and crossing under the green exit signs. Her beautiful evening wedding had become a haze of billboards, fast-food signs, and watching the white stripes that ran down both sides of the front hood of Meghan's MINI.

The muffled rings of her cell phone from within the depths of her messenger bag caused Allison to bang her fist on the steering wheel. Over and over again, she heard Seth's ring tone. "Stop calling me, Seth. Please. Just stop."

Grabbing the strap, she slung her purse into the backseat.

She should toss it out on the highway.

There was no sense in answering. Seth would demand she come back and marry him. And she couldn't do that.

She also couldn't go back to her apartment. That was the first place Seth would look for her.

She couldn't go to her parents' house. That would be Seth's second option.

Meghan's?

Nope.

She clenched the steering wheel, her engagement ring glinting in the glow of the streetlights. Mocking her. She twisted the ring backward, causing the diamond to dig into her skin. At least she wasn't looking at the oh-so-expensive diamond Seth had insisted on buying her three years ago.

Allison's words were a broken whisper. "God, help me . . . I know. Same old prayer. Help me. Seems like I've been praying it since I was seven . . . but could you fix things one more time?"

She shoved her overflowing wedding gown lower, battling to see the clock on the dashboard. Ten P.M. She'd driven from Denver to Colorado Springs and back again for almost three hours. Up Monument Hill, past Park Meadows Mall, and turning around before she headed all the way to Wyoming to repeat the trek in reverse. If she passed the Broncos' stadium one more time, she might pull over in the parking lot and sleep there for the night.

She was beyond exhausted. There was a time when she loved living a map-free, go-where-you-will life. Not anymore. She liked having a plan. But she'd just tossed her carefully planned future into the air like a wedding bouquet. Only no one was there to catch it.

The welcome sight of a hotel beckoned her from the side of the highway. Time to stop running and find some place to rest. Somewhere Seth couldn't find her.

"Don't you have Allison on speed dial?"

Daniel watched his brother pace in the living room of his town house, redialing Alli's number again and again.

"What?" Seth stared at his iPhone, his hand poised to input Alli's phone number. Again.

"Speed dial. Why do you keep redialing Alli's number?"

"I didn't even realize what I was doing. How dense can I be?" Seth scowled as he hit redial and listened to Allison's voice mail. Again. "Where *is* she?"

Good question.

"This isn't like Allison at all. Why would she do something like this?" Seth looked at Daniel as if he knew the answer.

Maybe he did.

His head ached from the one question haunting him since Alli disappeared. Had his stupidity five days ago caused Alli to run out on Seth? Daniel shrugged. There was nothing he could say. Once again, he'd made a mess of things.

There's no rewind button on life. Only forward. And this was not the time for any grand confessions.

His brother continued pacing, tapping his phone against his leg. "What do I do now? File a missing person report?"

"Seems a bit drastic, don't you think?"

"I don't know what to think! I keep seeing Allison walking toward me—and then she turns and runs out of the church!" Seth threw his phone down on the tempered-glass coffee table. It skated across the top and landed on the cream Berber carpet. "Now my fiancée's missing! No call to tell me she's okay. No messages. She won't answer her phone. This is crazy!"

Seth had that right. The last three hours had been an insane nightmare. Thank God for the wedding coordinator, who kept everyone calm. Seconds after Alli bolted, the redheaded dynamo in a black sheath dress and four-inch heels had directed Meghan to go after Allison. Meghan came back and reported that her best friend was gone—and that she'd made her getaway in Meghan's car.

The guests watched the goings-on, shifting in the pews and whispering after Allison's unexpected display of bridal shock and awe. After forty-five minutes, the coordinator declared the wedding indefinitely postponed. A few at a time, the 350 guests left the church, deprived of the planned sit-down dinner.

Allison's mother remained stoic, gripping her husband's hand, pacing in the back of the church. She didn't shed a tear. When Seth asked where she thought Allison could be, she said, "I have no idea. No idea."

In true Rayner fashion, Seth and Daniel's father stormed out of the church, their mother trailing behind him, pleading with him to wait. He was probably on his second tumbler of Scotch in his study.

Daniel paid the limo driver. Called the restaurant and canceled the wedding reception. Best-man duties he'd never imagined. The maître d' told him not to expect a refund. Then he handed the minister a check and followed Seth over to Alli's apartment and back to his town house. Why, he didn't know. He had no idea where Alli could be. She wasn't at her parents' or Meghan's.

She'd vanished.

Where does a woman in a barely used wedding dress hide?

"Do you think she's ill, Daniel? Should I call hospitals?"

"She didn't look sick. Don't start thinking the worst." Daniel watched his brother take another loop around his living room. Like Daniel, he still wore his tux, although he'd pulled off the tie in a moment of frustration.

"Did she plan this? Did I miss something? Not see that she was unhappy?" Seth threw himself down on his tobacco-brown extra-long leather couch. "But why would she be unhappy? We've been together for six years. We've never had a problem. No fights. No disagreements. We're a perfect match. She likes everything I like. Same food. Same books. Same music."

"Seth, I don't think you're going to be able to figure this out—"

"She said she couldn't do this . . ." Seth sat up and rubbed his eyes with his palms. "Maybe the size of the wedding upset her. Early on she said she wanted a smaller wedding. Maybe that's it. She didn't say she didn't love me. Just that she couldn't do this."

By the time Daniel left an hour later, Seth had it all figured out, as usual. Allison had run because of a major case of stage fright. Seth had his answer, and he was sticking to it.

Daniel convinced Seth to go to bed, assuring him that Allison wasn't in any danger. "She'll call you tomorrow. You'll talk this all out and reschedule the wedding." Daniel stood, his hands on Seth's shoulders. He gave him a shake. "And if she wants a smaller ceremony, Tag, then go with a smaller wedding."

Even though he persuaded Seth to be reasonable, Daniel couldn't stop himself from driving to Alli's apartment again. He needed to know she was safe. Maybe, just maybe, she was home and not answering her phone.

He found himself taking the side streets through Colorado Springs, looking for the MINI. Why did he think he'd find Allison parked by Ute Park? At her complex, he got out of his F-150 and walked toward Alli's building. No lights in her second-story window. No Bisquick sitting on the sill.

Where was she?

He walked to her door and knocked. Once. Twice. Was she hiding in her dark apartment?

"Alli. You in there, Kid? It's me, Daniel."

Nothing.

If she was there, would she even open the door for him?

Not likely.

Allison left her veil in the car, but there was nothing she could do about the gown. It was the only outfit she had at the moment. She watched the hotel clerk tuck a paperback underneath the counter and eye her as she walked across the polished marble floor to the front desk.

"I'd like a room for the night, please."

"Yes, ma'am. I assume you'd like something special for you and your husband, Mrs.—"

"It's Miss. Miss Denman." Allison took a deep breath, willing her voice not to tremble. "And no one will be joining me tonight. Any room will be fine, so long as it's nonsmoking." She grabbed her wallet from her bag, fished out a credit card, and slid it across the wood counter.

"All right then, Miss Denman. Give me a moment to get you registered. How long will you be staying with us?"

"Just for tonight. I think. Tonight is fine." Realizing she was drumming her fingers on the counter, she forced herself to step back and wait while the clerk selected a room for her. No need to ruin a perfectly good manicure.

She'd ruined a twenty-thousand-dollar wedding. Why should she worry about a manicure?

"Here's your key, Miss Denman." The clerk handed her a folder, told her where she could park her car, and asked for her signature. "We've got a great complimentary breakfast buffet, and you're welcome to use our exercise room or pool. Can I have someone get your luggage?"

"No, thank you. I don't—I'm fine." Her luggage waited for her in a suite at the Broadmoor back in the Springs.

"I'm J.R., Miss Denman. If there's anything else you might need—"

"No. Nothing." The clerk looked as if he was just out of college. Probably hadn't been briefed on how to handle an unaccompanied bride. She couldn't worry about him—and he couldn't unravel her complicated life. With a weary sigh, she went to park the car before finding refuge in her room.

Minutes later, she slipped into the farthest corner of the elevator and held her breath until the doors closed. No one else inside. Just an overdressed fugitive whose reflection stared back at her from all sides. Good thing. Her wedding gown spread out, threatening to engulf every spare inch of the elevator.

The candlelight in the church probably accentuated her dress and complexion better than the dim light in the elevator. Now she resembled an aged wax figurine of a bedraggled bride. A bride with a decidedly wrinkled gown, no veil, no bouquet—and no groom.

Allison offered a silent prayer of thanks when she stood in the darkness of her hotel room. She switched on the desk lamp, giving enough light to glimpse the queen-size bed covered with a deep blue duvet and piled high with coordinating pillows. Cherrywood octagonal-shaped tables stood on either side, matching the small table flanked by two chairs upholstered in the same blue brocade material as the duvet. An impressive armoire probably hid a TV and—she hoped—a small refrigerator.

She walked over to the bathroom area. Leaning over the glass mosaic sink, she dampened a washcloth, wrung it out, and then patted it over her face. She spied a complimentary toothbrush standing in a water glass, and felt thankful she didn't have to resort to scrubbing her teeth with the washcloth.

Now to get out of her dress.

She reached around to the back, fumbling with the small satin-covered buttons running from the top of the neckline down the length of the dress past her waistline. There were dozens of the irritating little things. After several frustrating minutes and some rather uncomfortable gyrations, Allison sank onto the bed, covering her face with her hands.

Trapped in a bridal nightmare gone viral.

She would be sleeping in her wedding gown.

She kicked off her heels, tossing them across the room, and collapsed against the down-filled duvet, her arm flung across her eyes. So much for a wedding night to remember. She certainly wouldn't forget tonight—but there would be no hanging the DO NOT DISTURB sign on the brass doorknob, no blushing-bride memories of Seth unfastening her gown one button at a time, trailing kisses down her neck. No whispered "I love yous."

Tonight it would be her and the wretched, wretched dress.

Sitting, on the edge of the bed, she opened the refrigerator door and scanned the contents. Red wine. White wine. Seagram's 7. No, thanks. Obscenely priced bottled water and soda. She grabbed a plastic-wrapped ham and Swiss sandwich and—thank you, God—a ginger ale.

She crawled to the top of the bed, rearranged the mound of pillows, and leaned back against the headboard.

Not quite what she had planned for her wedding night. Cruising I-25 for hours, the green mile markers keeping track of her journey to nowhere. Alone in a hotel room. Eating a prepackaged sandwich. Imprisoned in her wedding gown.

Questions bombarded her. What was Seth doing? What had they done about the reception? What do you do with an uneaten wedding cake? Was there someplace to donate five tiers of white cake with raspberry and lemon filling? Maybe Seth had taken the dark chocolate groom's cake—decorated with a miniature marathoner crossing a finish line—and stashed it in his refrigerator for some late-night snacking.

She closed her eyes, but Seth's face danced across her mind. He smiled at her . . . and then his face twisted into bewilderment. She'd put that look on Seth's face.

What was he doing right now? What was he thinking?

Did she really want to know?

Allison yawned and placed her half-eaten sandwich and empty soda can on the side table. Lying down, she kicked at the wedding gown, which had wrapped around her ankles. Then she gathered a round tasseled pillow into her arms.

Too tired to think.

Too tired to even get up and turn out the light.

She'd face her now-unknown future tomorrow.

Hot tears slipped past her closed eyelids. She turned her face into her pillow, hoping it would muffle her sobs.

CHAPTER 5

$\mathcal{S}$eth bent at the waist, feet spread wide apart, hands on his hips. Sweat dripped off his face and drenched the long-sleeved Under Armour shirt clinging to his torso. He took slow, measured breaths in and out, then stood and walked up the sidewalk to his front door.

After a twenty-mile run, he knew he should take the time to stretch his legs. But he needed to be home in case Allison called. He'd hoped running would relieve the tension that prevented him from closing his eyes for longer than half an hour at a time throughout the night. But as he'd settled into his pace, scenes from his humiliating wedding day replayed in his mind.

Breakfasting with his parents and Daniel at the Garden of the Gods Club yesterday morning. Enjoying the view of the massive redrock formation known as the Kissing Camels, as well as the friends who stopped by the table to congratulate him. His father's look of pride. His mother's assurance that Allison looked breathtaking in her wedding gown.

Finalizing the honeymoon details one last time. Reservations at the Broadmoor. Airline tickets for today's flight to the Turks and Caicos Islands. Confirming their Grace Bay Club penthouse reservations. Storing the traveler's checks and passports in his leather satchel.

Getting ready for the ceremony with the other men—all except Daniel, who insisted on changing at his own place and meeting them at the church. Daniel had brushed off Seth's reminder to bring the wedding bands with a gruff "Got it covered, Tag."

And then—*finally*. Standing at the front of the church, watching Allison, his Allison, walking down the aisle. He couldn't stop smiling. The dress *was* beautiful, all shimmers and lace. He watched her walk toward him, anticipating Will lifting her veil so he could finally see her face. Their eyes meeting. Sharing the knowledge that they were meant to be together.

What had she said?

"I can't do this."

And then she'd run. From him. Even though they'd dated since they were sixteen. Whispered "I love you" when they were barely seventeen.

Seth drew his arm across his forehead, wicking away the sweat. How had all he'd worked for, all his dreams, ended up like this?

He walked into his town home, stopping to unlace and then pull off his running shoes. Allison's wedding bouquet lay on the granite breakfast bar next to his cell phone.

No messages.

Seth stared at the flowers Allison had dropped at his feet. The rich burgundy blooms hadn't begun to wilt. The pure white stephanotis nestled among the buds, interspersed with a few tiny sprays of gloxinia.

Allison didn't know why he'd insisted the florist include the tiny purple blossoms edged with white. He'd planned on explaining the symbolism at the Broadmoor over a champagne toast. Red roses for respect—and desire. Stephanotis for happiness in marriage. And gloxinia symbolizing love at first sight.

Allison had discarded the floral representation of his feelings for her on the white satin carpet.

"Where are you, Allison?" Seth banged his fist on the countertop, almost smashing the bouquet. "How can I fix this if I don't even know where you are?"

Hey, Kid—Can't decide what I like best about Switzerland—the skiing or the chocolate. Oh, wait! Now I know. It's the skiing!

—Daniel

CHAPTER 6

"*B*isquick . . . get off my feet!"

Still more asleep than awake, Allison shoved with her left foot. Why did Bisquick insist on sleeping on top of the blankets, anchoring her feet to the mattress?

"Move, cat!"

Allison jerked her foot again—and woke up.

No Bisquick smothering her toes.

No familiar bedroom.

She lay across the queen-size bed in a dark hotel room, her head buried under a pillow. The delicate material of her overabundant wedding gown twisted around her ankles like lace and satin shackles.

"Ugghhh . . ."

In a futile attempt at freedom, Allison thrashed her feet like a drowning woman, tossed the pillow off the bed, and then rolled onto her back.

Alone.

Still held hostage in a five-thousand-dollar, full-length designer straitjacket.

Pushing her hair out of her face, she squirmed to a sitting position against the headboard.

Time to take stock of the post–wedding day situation.

Know your assets and liabilities, that's what Seth always said.

Seth.

Would he ever forgive her? Could she forgive herself for making a mess of his life—of her life?

Maybe she should have married Seth.

The digital alarm clock's red numbers shone 6:12 A.M. Too early to think about yesterday. Allison plucked the tiny gold bobby pins from her hair, releasing it from its disheveled state. So much for the $150 salon updo.

Liability: She'd managed a mere six hours of sleep.

Asset: She'd never been one to sleep in.

Liability: She was tummy-rumbling starving, and the leftover ham and cheese sandwich looked less than appetizing.

Asset: She could take advantage of the hotel's complimentary breakfast.

Liability: She was still stuck in her wedding dress—and it wasn't releasing her without a fight.

Asset: There was a luxurious white cotton robe, compliments of the hotel, that she could throw over her gown while she made a dash for some food.

No time like the present. You have nothing to fear but missing out on all the fun, that's what Daniel always said.

Daniel.

Definitely a liability.

Probably tossing his duffel bag over his shoulder, already gearing up for his next adventure.

She wouldn't expect a postcard from him while he was on this trip.

Daniel had no idea how her mixed-up feelings about their kiss— about him—figured into her running away from his brother.

Better that way.

Allison swung her legs over the side of the bed, stood, and then shook out the long folds of her skirt. Where was her maid of honor when she needed her?

Probably wondering where Allison—and her car—were.

She pulled the robe over her dress, drawing the front closed and tying the belt. Allison frowned at the unkempt reflection in the mirror over the dresser. Her once-stylish hair tumbled about her shoulders. The robe bunched up over the layers of her dress, a feeble attempt at best to hide the fact she was a bride on the run.

"Let's get this over with," Allison whispered as she walked down the quiet hallway. "The sooner I go, the sooner I'm back. And how many people can be up at this time of the morning . . ."

At least thirty.

All high school boys.

To judge from the logos on their matching gray and red T-shirts, they were members of a sports team in town for some sort of competition. Allison wasn't asking.

She corralled as much of her gown as she could with one hand, grabbing a strawberry yogurt and a banana in the other. Snagged a spoon with her pinkie.

The gown fighting her all the way, Allison double-timed it back to her room.

Which was locked.

And she didn't have the key.

Brilliant, Allison. Just brilliant.

Knowing she had to go back downstairs, she banged her already aching head on the door. She set her breakfast outside the room, gathered the gown in her hands, and trudged to the elevator. Refused to make eye contact with the two immaculately groomed businesswomen who gave her—and the dress—a wide berth as she huddled in a corner.

J.R., still manning the front desk, looked like a long-lost friend. "Good morning, Miss Denman. I hope you had a pleasant night."

He must be trained to say that to everyone, even a woman who slept trapped in her wedding gown.

"Can I get another room key, please? I locked myself out when I came downstairs to get some breakfast." Might as well clarify she hadn't been running on the treadmill in the exercise room.

On the way back to the elevator, Allison sidestepped into the breakfast room and grabbed a bagel and a packet of cream cheese. The athletes had plowed through the buffet like locusts on a wheat field, leaving a few boxes of bran cereal and an overripe banana for any guests who wandered in after seven A.M.

Allison gathered her three-course breakfast at the round table in her room. She wouldn't think about the scrumptious wedding dinner she'd missed last night. She and Seth spent months selecting everything from the cheese-filled-date appetizers to the after-dinner coffee bar. Allison shook her head. All that food—wasted.

After slathering cream cheese on the bagel, she dug through her messenger bag until she found her stash of Tylenol and her cell phone. After downing two tablets, she deleted her messages one by one.

An even dozen from Seth.

Another ten from Meghan.

Five from her mother.

And one from Daniel.

Tempting. She tapped on the OK button with the French-manicured tip of her fingernail. Once. Twice. Then she pushed OK.

"Hey, Alli—where are you, Kid? Seth's worried sick. Call him. Or call Meghan. Let someone know you're—"

Allison deleted the message. Why did she think Daniel would say something personal? Stupid. Stupid. Stupid. She didn't have to call anyone. She could figure this out on her own.

She needed to get out of her wedding dress and into regular clothes.

Think, Allison, think!

She could run by her apartment, grab some jeans and T-shirts, and head—where? Where could she hide that no one would think to look for her? She nibbled on the bagel, praying for inspiration.

Meghan's parents' cabin up in Divide.

She knew where they put the spare key. And she was pretty sure no one was using the cabin right now. Worth a try.

An hour later, Allison parked Meghan's car near the entrance to her apartment. She leaned back against the seat and scanned the lot. She didn't see Seth's Lexus. And, of course, she had Meghan's MINI.

"Okay, here's the plan." Talking out loud helped Allison focus. "Go to the apartment. Get changed. Make sure Bisquick's okay. Get out of here. It can't get any easier than that. I can text Meggie later about still watching Bisquick and tell her where I left the car."

Allison grabbed her bag and clutched the keys as she stepped out of the car. Casting furtive glances left and right, she headed up the stairs, the train dragging behind her. As she neared the second landing, she stopped.

Seth stood facing her door.

Back up, back up, *back up.*

Gripping the railing, Allison moved down the stairs. She held her breath, praying Seth hadn't heard her—and that she didn't trip over her wedding dress and break her neck falling down. In the silence, she heard her door open and close. Seth must have gone inside her condo, giving her time to retreat to the car and run away—again.

She was getting good at this.

She turned, gathering the skirt into her fists, and bolted onto the sidewalk, running straight for Meghan's car. Just as she reached the driver's side, someone grabbed her arm, halting her escape.

"Going somewhere?"

The sound of Daniel's voice jerked her around, the wedding gown swirling against her legs like a silken tornado. She'd manage to avoid one troublesome Rayner—and run into the other.

"Y-yes. I'm going to my . . . to the car."

Daniel kept a hand on her arm, nodding toward the entrance to her apartment. "You didn't happen to run into my brother back there, did you?"

"I saw Seth, but . . ."

"But?" Daniel arched an eyebrow, his face grim, and waited for her answer.

"But he didn't see me. I'm not ready to talk to Seth yet." Allison pulled against Daniel's grip, twisting away from him, and stepped toward the car.

"Are you kidding me? He's worried, Alli. Talk to him. At least let him know you're all right."

Allison brushed her hair out of her face so she could see to unlock the car door. "I will, but not today."

"Why not today?" Daniel placed his hand over Allison's, stopping her from opening the door.

Allison snatched her hand away. "I-I can't. I'm just not ready."

"Would it help if I came with you—"

"No!" Allison pressed back against the car, her clenched fists buried in the folds of the dress. "I don't need you to help me fix things. Just get out of the way."

"No can do, Alli." He grabbed for her hand, pulling her back toward the building. Toward Seth. "You're going to talk to my brother."

Allison gripped the car's door handle, digging her two-inch heels into the ground. "I told you, I *can't*." She looked over Daniel's shoulder, afraid she'd see Seth walk outside. Her voice dropped to a desperate whisper as her eyes filled with tears. "Please, Daniel. I n-need some time."

Daniel hesitated, his eyes searching hers before he released her from their ridiculous tug-of-war. "Please, Alli, no tears." He rubbed his unshaven chin and heaved an exasperated sigh.

"I-I'm sorry." She looked away, smoothing the bodice of her gown. "Rough night."

"I can imagine." A rueful smile tilted the corners of Daniel's mouth as he took in her unbrushed hair and rumpled dress. "You've looked better."

"No comment." She noticed Daniel's wrinkled T-shirt and torn jeans. Exhaustion and concern dimmed the normally friendly look in his eyes. "You don't look so great yourself."

"Didn't sleep well. Seth called me every hour on the hour."

"Oh." Allison didn't want any details of those phone calls. Not yet. "I really do have to go."

"On one condition." Daniel stepped toward her.

Allison clambered into the car, dragging the dress's train with her. "Like you have any right to make conditions."

"You're forcing me to aid and abet a runaway, Alli. Reason enough."

She started the car, watching Daniel as she rearranged the waves of lace. "What?"

"Promise me you'll contact Seth within twenty-four hours."

Was there some sort of expiration date on making things right with Seth?

"If you promise me that you won't tell him I was here." She revved the engine, easing the car backward a few inches, aware that Daniel stood close to the car.

"Fine." He stepped back.

"Fine." Allison focused on backing up, ignoring the look of frustrated concern on Daniel's face. She glanced into the rearview mirror as she drove off. "I'll call Seth when I'm ready to call him, Daniel Rayner—and not a minute sooner. Promise or no promise."

Allison shifted in her seat, shoving her dress up past her thighs.

It was long past time to escape the dress's death grip.

Sure, she had developed a certain knack for driving Meghan's stick-shift, bucket-seated MINI Cooper while barefoot and drowning in yards of voluminous lace. But she'd never imagined wearing her wedding dress overnight, much less making repeated trips up and down I-25 in it.

The sooner she got out of the dress, the better. Escape demanded drastic action—and some assistance.

She drove thirty minutes north of the Springs to the outlet shops just off the interstate. It wasn't as if she'd blend in with the Sunday crowd—not in wedding attire. But she probably wouldn't run into someone she knew. Most of the people looking for her wouldn't expect her to go shopping in wedding regalia.

She cruised to the far end of the shopping center. J. Crew. Perfect.

As she walked across the asphalt, she gained a new understanding of the phrase "stopping traffic." Cars and pedestrians came to a complete standstill as she paraded by in her wilted wedding finery.

Head held high, Allison marched into J. Crew, which was already decorated with tinsel and jumbo cardboard ornaments for the Christmas holidays, and up to the nearest racks of jeans. Grabbed two pairs. Maneuvered her double-wide gown through the narrow aisles to the display of V-neck sweaters. Grabbed three sweaters. White. Red. Brown. As she passed the register, she said, "I need a dressing room and some help—now, please."

A young petite Asian woman quickly stepped up behind her, unlocking a room and asking, "How can I help you?"

Allison appreciated that the salesgirl didn't smirk, but wasn't her dilemma evident? "Help me get out of this dress. Please. There are hundreds of buttons . . ."

Allison welcomed the seclusion of the dressing room, closing her eyes to block out her road-weary reflection. For this she'd spent yesterday morning at Veda Salon?

She exhaled as first one button and then the next were undone. She lost count at forty-six.

"That's the last of them. Would you like me to put this in a bag for you?" The salesgirl struggled to gather the material in her arms. "I think we have one large enough."

"Most definitely put it in a bag."

Allison didn't ever want to see that never-should-have-said-yes-to-the-dress again. For just a moment, she debated telling the salesgirl to throw it away. Or telling her to keep it. But then she remembered how much her mother had paid for the gown. She couldn't give it to a stranger—or toss it into a Dumpster behind an outlet store. While Allison was no longer a captive in the dress, she was stuck with it.

She shut the dressing room door, relishing the delicious coolness of air on her skin. After savoring her newfound freedom for a few moments, she slipped on a pair of jeans and the red sweater. They would do. She looked at her reflection again. The clothes would do, but she needed to make a quick stop at the Jockey store to buy new undergarments. What was appropriate with a wedding gown certainly didn't work under casual clothes.

A knock sounded on the door, and Allison heard the salesgirl say, "Our leather flats are on sale. I brought several sizes for you to try." She handed Allison three shoe boxes. "Your dress is hanging up at the counter."

"Thanks. Do you have headbands or clips for my hair?" Allison slipped on a pair of brown ballet shoes. "And maybe a coat of some kind?"

Ten minutes later, Allison lugged the bags containing her dress, heels, and new clothes out to the car.

Much better.

She ran back and grabbed cash from an ATM, purchased an iced tea and a sandwich to go at the food court, then filled the car with gas. Before heading toward Meghan's family's cabin, she had a few phone calls to make.

Meghan's phone went right to voice mail, so she left a message. "Hey, Meggie, it's me. First, I'm sorry I stole your car. I know I owe you big-time. I know I've made a mess of everything. I-I just couldn't do it—"

A recorded voice interrupted, asking if she was satisfied with her message. For now that would have to do. If she were any type of daughter, she'd call her mom and Will. But the thought of that conversation made her feel as if she were standing at the back of the church, preparing to walk down the aisle to Seth. Instead, she typed a quick text message to Hadleigh, asking her to tell their parents that she was okay and that she would call soon. And that she was sorry.

How many apologies loomed in her future? Would she ever be able to fix the mess she'd made? Would people always see her as the woman who'd run out on Seth Rayner? She hadn't thought of all the consequences when she'd left Seth at the church—how many people she was hurting. For so long, marrying Seth had seemed so right—until the day she had to say "I do." There was no undoing the choice she made yesterday. She could only go forward and face the future she'd chosen for herself.

Hey, Kid—Apologies for the generic photo of Banff. I snagged this postcard in between ski runs!

—Daniel

CHAPTER 7

*A*llison's cell phone sat on the butcher-block counter in the cabin's kitchen, next to a stack of used mugs, spoons, and empty Splenda packets. Intermittent beeping signaled more unanswered voice messages and texts.

Seth.

Her mother.

Seth.

Meghan.

The relentless electronic beep grated on Allison's exhausted mind. If she hadn't been so responsible and plugged her phone into Meghan's car charger, it would have been dead by now—and silent. With a muffled groan, she shoved the chair away from the table, stalked over to the counter, and stuffed the phone in the silverware drawer. As it clattered among the mismatched spoons and forks, she glanced at the steak knives—and slammed the drawer shut. Allison rubbed her wrists and then tugged the sleeves of her sweater down over her hands.

No.

"Lead me not into temptation, God. Help me."

She paced over to the table, sitting and wrapping her hands around her mug of jasmine tea, holding on to it like a life preserver.

She should be at the resort with Seth. Lounging by a pool. Searching the beach for shells. Taking those snorkeling lessons Seth signed them up for.

But that would mean they were married.

Instead, she hid out in Meghan's family's rustic cabin, decorated in early-American moose and bear. She felt like an outlaw with a price on her head, ignoring her voice mails and text messages—and the world.

Her wedding gown languished on the back of the bedroom door, yards and yards of ivory lace and satin stuffed into a too-small plastic J. Crew bag. Her veil decorated the wrought-iron headboard of the bed she'd been unable to sleep in. She'd almost left them in the car, but guilt prodded her to bring the items inside. She'd been doing the right thing for so long, even now—after committing a monumental mistake—she found herself reverting back to what was expected of her.

For the past two days, she'd tossed and turned on the lumpy couch, praying for sleep to banish the memory of running from the church, abandoning Seth and her future. At times the sound of Seth calling her name jolted her from a restless sleep. Piles of wadded-up tissue littered both the old wooden chest that served as a coffee table and the kitchen counter, a testament to her crying jags.

Hearing a metallic scraping noise, Allison took several cautious steps toward the living room.

What was that?

She stumbled back against the faded corduroy couch when the cabin's front door swung open and Meghan walked in.

"Okay, girlfriend." Her best friend stood with her hands on her hips, her brown curls wind-tossed. "Time to talk."

"Meghan, you scared me to death."

Meghan shrugged out of her bright red coat. "Yeah? Well, you scared me too. Running out of the church. Not answering your cell phone after leaving me half a message. I've been taking care of your cat, waiting for you to show up or call again or send up a flare— something!"

Allison sank to the couch. "How did you figure out I was here?"

"You've got a smart best friend, sweetie. This cabin was always our 'I'm going to run away from home' choice when we were teenagers." She motioned outside. "I finally borrowed my parents' spare car— their twenty-five-year-old Cadillac, thank you very much!—and decided to visit our old getaway. Thanks for leaving me stranded at the church, by the way."

"Did you get any groceries on your way up?" Allison stood and headed toward the kitchen. "Maybe an extra box of tissues?"

"I've got a couple of root beers, some chips, and a mostly eaten bag of jelly beans." Meghan surveyed the cabin. "You've had a good seventy-two hours to sulk by yourself—"

"I am not sulking! I'm trying to figure out what I'm going to do!" Allison hated how close she felt to crying again. Would the tears ever stop?

"You mean besides not marrying Seth?" Meghan followed her into the kitchen. She walked over to the 1970s avocado-green refrigerator and helped herself to a carton of blueberry yogurt.

"Be my guest," Allison muttered, slumping back into her chair.

"Hey, you're hiding out in my parents' cabin, remember?" Grabbing a spoon, Meghan joined Allison at the table. "Come on, girlfriend, talk to me."

"Oh, Meghan . . ." Allison wiped away the tears spilling over her face. She grabbed a box of tissues. Empty. "I've made such a mess of things."

"Maybe. Maybe not."

"What?"

"I'm going to ask you a question. All you have to do is give me an honest answer." Meghan's kohl-rimmed brown eyes locked on hers, making Allison feel like she was part of a grade school stare-down.

"Have you considered that maybe you did the absolute right thing when you ran out of that church three days ago?"

"What?"

"You sound like an idiot. What? What?" Meghan's husky laugh softened her words. She wrapped her hand around Allison's. "You were marrying Mr. Right for all the wrong reasons. Leaving Seth Rayner at the altar—while lousy timing—was one of the few smart things you've done in your relationship."

Allison stared at her friend. What did she mean? "Meghan, if you thought Seth and I were so wrong for each other, why didn't you say something?"

"Like you'd listen to me? Love is not only blind, sweetie, it's deaf." Meghan ran her long fingers through her disheveled curls. "Even if I had said something, you wouldn't have heard me. You convinced yourself that Seth was the best man for you. He's so, so—perfect! Just the way you like things. He fit perfectly in your perfectly ordered world."

"Meghan, you make it sound like I don't love Seth!"

"I think you love what Seth offers you. Security. Safety." Meghan shook her head. "Seth's the only guy you ever dated! How safe is that? With Seth around, you never had to think."

Allison grabbed her cup of tea, jumped up from the table, and dumped the amber liquid into the sink. "My relationship with Seth wasn't some sort of parent-child thing."

"Think about it. You let Seth make all the major decisions, from what dress you wore to our high school prom to where you were going for your honeymoon." Teal polish glinted off Meghan's nails when she pointed an accusatory finger at Allison. "You're a smart woman—except when Seth Rayner's in the picture. And he's been hogging the picture since you were sixteen."

Allison moved around the kitchen, refilling her mug with hot water from the copper teapot and ripping open another packet of tea. Could Meghan be right? "Are you saying I let Seth boss me around?"

"Listen, Seth Rayner has redeeming qualities, don't get me wrong. I'm not trying to paint him as some big, bad villain here." Meghan rapped her spoon on the wood tabletop. "But he's a guy who likes to be in charge. And you let him. I know some of your past, Allison—and I also know you decided not to tell Seth any of it."

"There was no need to go back there, Meggie. No need to rehash my past."

"Aren't husbands and wives supposed to know each other intimately? Shouldn't you feel so safe with Seth that you can tell him anything?"

"I do feel safe with Seth."

"Not safe enough to marry him."

Ouch. Meghan wasn't pulling any punches.

"I think Seth was part of your carefully planned happily ever after. Enter Seth, Mr. Straight and Narrow. You can set your watch by Seth. Even his fun activities are all about running times and being the best."

"Is it so wrong to want security, Meghan?"

"No-o. But do you want to marry Safety Patrol Boy, or do you want to find out if there's someone else out there who is really your Mr. Right?"

"That's so risky, Meghan."

"Exactly. And you don't want the risk—not even with Seth, it seems." Meghan got up from the table and dumped her spoon in the sink. It clattered against the porcelain, jarring Allison's strained nerves. "You know what, Allison? Maybe when you ran out of the church, it was because, in your heart, you wanted more. And you weren't willing to settle."

"What am I going to do now?" Allison slid down to sit on the floor, her back resting against the scarred kitchen cabinets.

"You're going to clean up the soggy tissues all over my parents' cabin. We're going into Woodland Park and get something decent to eat before we head back to your apartment. Then you're going to pack away your wedding dress." Meghan knelt beside Allison, wrapping her in a comforting hug. "I'll help you. Get some carbs in you, and you'll be ready to face your future."

"For the first time in a long time, I don't know what my future is, Meggie." Allison rested her head on Meghan's shoulder.

"If you can stop controlling your life, maybe God will finally have a chance to get a word in edgewise and be able to tell you want he wants for your life."

Alli, almost missed my train in Venice. That's what I get for having that second helping of stracciatella gelato!

—Daniel

CHAPTER 8

Allison stood in the grocery store aisle, pushing the cart back and forth beside her, trying to ignore the squeaky front wheel while she stared at the stacks of frozen dinners. Did she want something exotic, like low-carb potstickers and seasoned rice, or low-sodium turkey and mashed potatoes?

Did she feel like eating anything at all?

Pulling open the cold glass door, she grabbed lasagna, two turkey dinners, and a sweet-and-sour-chicken meal. She had to eat something, sometime. Maybe later tonight one of the entrées would appeal to her. Tossing the boxes in the grocery cart on top of the package of paper towels and a six-pack of ginger ale, she turned the corner, heading for the produce section.

One advantage to midmorning shopping—the store was quiet. Allison usually shopped in the evenings with all the other harried just-off-work-but-my-cupboard's-bare customers. Now she had no reason to go to work, thanks to getting all her projects done so she could jaunt off on her honeymoon. She had an abundance of time to grocery shop. She had an abundance of time to do anything she wanted. And lots of time to do things she'd rather avoid.

Like return bridal shower and wedding gifts.

Discuss bills with the wedding coordinator, who'd been much friendlier when she helped plan the wedding.

Avoid Seth.

One week after their nonwedding—seven whole days—and she still hadn't fulfilled her promise to Daniel to contact Seth. Maybe Daniel figured since she'd broken her promise, he could tell Seth that he'd seen her. Or maybe Meghan had told him that Allison was home.

No matter who told him what, her determined ex-fiancé made his presence known. Every day elaborate bouquets arrived at her apartment. Leaving the arrangements on the landing outside her door, Allison called Meghan to come pick them up. She stuck Seth's unopened notes in the top drawer of her bedroom dresser. Why, she didn't know. She had no intention of reading them.

As Allison bagged a bunch of purple grapes and mused over ways to get Seth to cease and desist, someone tapped her on the shoulder.

"Allison? Allison, is that really you?"

Allison wished she could deny her identity. Oh, no. She wasn't that Julia Roberts wannabe. Though she'd been told they looked alike.

Why, oh why did it have to be Amanda, the ever-curious wife of one of the executives at Rayner Construction?

Amanda pulled Allison into an awkward embrace, the plastic bag of grapes lodged between them. If the woman hugged her any tighter, Allison would have juice stains all over her pea coat.

"Allison, how are you? Are you feeling better?"

"I'm fine. Fine."

"I can't tell you how relieved I am to see you!" Amanda hugged her again as Allison tried to toss the fruit into her cart. "I've been imagining all sorts of horrible things since your wedding day."

*Non*wedding day.

"I've asked Christopher every day if he knows anything, but he says Seth is staying pretty quiet. Men. You know how they are." Amanda rolled her eyes and waved a dismissive hand in the air, her charm bracelet jangling. "I told Christopher you must have gotten sick or something, to postpone the wedding like that. I thought maybe it was your appendix. Christopher did say Seth sent an interoffice memo about the wedding being postponed. Do you have a new date set?" Amanda pulled out her iPhone. "I want to get it on my calendar."

Allison clutched the handle of the grocery cart and took a deep breath. "The wedding isn't postponed, Amanda. It's canceled. Permanently. I'll be returning your shower gift—"

Amanda's hand remained poised over her phone. "But Seth's memo—"

"Was wrong." Allison attempted to soften the harsh words with a smile, but the action felt like a parody of politeness.

How could Seth put her in such an awkward situation?

Why blame Seth? She'd walked out on him. This whole mess was her fault. Not his.

Amanda continued to ask who-what-where-when-why-and-how questions for ten minutes. Allison felt like a celebrity cornered by an unwelcome reporter. Only when Amanda realized she had a spray-on-tan appointment did she give Allison a final hug and leave.

Remorse weighed Allison down, slowing her steps. She might as well be wearing her wedding gown as she pushed the grocery cart toward the checkout line.

She and Seth had planned the wedding for months, and in a moment of panic, she'd thrown all his carefully orchestrated efforts back in his face. She'd disappointed her parents, his parents, and the 350 wedding guests who watched her sprint past them like an overdressed marathoner.

There was no going back and fixing the wedding fiasco. No way of knowing how many more uncomfortable moments were waiting around the corner.

Allison tried to put the Amanda encounter into perspective.

Pro: Amanda would waste no time spreading the news that the

wedding was off—not postponed—saving Allison some time and effort.

Con: There was no telling how she'd embellish the story.

Pro: Amanda wouldn't be surprised when Allison returned the set of etched water glasses.

Con: Allison liked those goblets.

Pro: One less person to explain things to.

Con: Only slightly more than three hundred people left to go.

As she climbed the steps to her condo, Allison dreaded finding another floral offering from Seth. "Please, God, no flowers today." Allison chanted her plea as she mounted the last three steps to the landing. Despite Meghan's encouragement to let God tell her what he wanted for her life, she and God weren't talking much. She shot up multiple "please" and "thank you" prayers but couldn't seem to get past that to anything more intimate. Guilt and God didn't seem to go together.

She lifted her eyes from watching her feet and spotted Hadleigh cradling a bouquet of multicolored tulips.

"Hey, sis! Special delivery." Hadleigh held the flowers up like a torch.

Allison lifted a grocery-bag-laden hand in acknowledgment. "Seth didn't ask you to deliver those, did he?"

"Nope. I got here and found them outside your door." She stepped to the side, allowing Allison to slip the key into the lock. "I was getting ready to text you to see when you were coming home."

Hadleigh trailed behind her into the kitchen, dumping the tulips on the kitchen counter before starting to empty the grocery bags. "Cat food, cat food, more cat food, a bag of grapes . . . frozen dinners . . . more cat food." Hadleigh snickered. "Next time let me take you grocery shopping. This is pathetic."

"I don't have much of an appetite these days."

"No joke. What are you on, the cat-food diet? Does it cleanse your colon and get rid of guilt too?"

"Funny. Take your act on the road, Leigh." Allison opened a cupboard and snagged a white three-ring binder containing an alphabetical file of take-out menus. "Here. Pick something and we'll order dinner."

"I'm not staying long enough to eat dinner, sis."

Allison paused, the collection of menus suspended between them. "Oh?"

"I, uh, I told Evan he could pick me up here tonight."

"Evan?"

"Yeah." Hadleigh snatched the binder and walked past Allison to place it back in the cupboard. She faced away as she continued talking. "He's a friend of mine from school."

"Uh-huh."

"We're going to the library to study."

Allison's laughter erupted, the sound filling her with a glimmer of hope. Too bad the return of her sense of humor was at her kid sister's expense.

Hadleigh whirled to face her, her green eyes snapping with anger. "What's so funny?"

"Study at the library? You?" Allison snorted. "That is the lamest excuse in the book, Leigh. First off, you never study. *Never.* I don't think you even know where the local library is."

"Evan's driving, not me. I don't need to know where the library is." Hadleigh stuck her tongue out like a toddler.

"What are you studying?" Allison carried the bag of grapes to the sink and dumped them into a colander to rinse them off.

"History. We've got a midterm."

"Where's your textbook—or did you plan on digging out my old notes?"

No response from Hadleigh.

Allison stayed turned away from her sister, giving Hadleigh some space. "Why don't you tell me what's going on?"

Hadleigh sighed. Closed the cupboard door. Walked over to the kitchenette table and sat. "Mom and Will don't like Evan. They think he's a troublemaker."

"Why would they think that?" Allison finished rinsing the grapes and turned to face her sister.

"I don't know."

Allison glimpsed the stubborn lines bracketing Hadleigh's mouth. "Don't know or don't want to say?"

"Evan's nineteen." Hadleigh rushed on, not giving Allison time to comment. "And yes, he's a junior like me. He got held back a couple of times. School's hard for him."

"So you're tutoring him?"

"I'm not going to lie to you. I like Evan. I want to go out with him. But I want to help him with his studies too."

"You're not going to lie to *me,* but you're going to sneak around behind Mom and Will's backs?"

Hadleigh jumped to her feet. "I knew you wouldn't understand."

"I do understand—"

"Then don't say anything about Evan picking me up tonight. Mom and Will don't have to know."

"No can do, Leigh."

Her sister stormed out of the kitchen with Allison following her. "I knew it, I knew it, I knew it." Hadleigh grabbed her black-and-white houndstooth sweater coat from the couch, dumping Bisquick on the floor.

"Knew what?"

"I knew you wouldn't help me. You're so narrow-minded."

"Had-leigh!" Allison stepped in front of her sister, leaning against the door to block her escape. Her sister glared at her from beneath choppy black bangs. "Look, I can't let you see Evan on the sly." She raised her hand to halt Hadleigh's next verbal assault. "But how about if you invite him to study over here?"

"What?"

"Text Evan. Tell him to pick up whatever we order for dinner and come here for a study-dinner date."

"You'd do that for me?"

"Yes, your narrow-minded sister would do that for you—*if* you call Mom and tell her you and Evan are studying over here tonight."

Hadleigh launched herself into Allison's arms. "You're the best sister ever!"

"Even if I am narrow-minded, right?"

"Forget I said that. I was just mad."

"I know." Allison turned to go in search of the menus. "And Leigh?"

"Yeah?" Hadleigh's fingers were flying over her cell phone.

"Make sure Evan brings his history book and his notes."

Daniel thanked the airport barista and wrapped his hand around the insulated cup of hot coffee. Plain black coffee. No extra shots of espresso. No fancy flavors of cream or extra foam. Black, bitter coffee—that cost him four dollars.

He pulled his cell phone from the side of his backpack and glanced at the time. Still an hour and a half before the plane boarded. He took a slow sip of his coffee as he wandered the airport shops. *Hot.*

Why wasn't he surprised when he stopped in front of a rack of postcards?

Keep moving.

He glanced at the glossy photos. Day shots of Banff. Night shots of Banff. Now, there was one Alli would love for her postcard collection—a sunrise over Lake Moraine.

His store-wrapped wedding gift for Alli and Seth still stood in his hallway, markedly out of place next to his dinged-up, mud-splattered mountain bike. He'd found the stunning photograph—Thomas Mangelsen's *Maroon Bells Daybreak*—while waiting for a delayed flight in the Denver airport. Bought it, ignoring the damage it did to his savings toward a new snowboard and boots. The wedding was the one time he could splurge on Alli and no one would notice. Everyone would think the extravagant gift was for Alli *and* Seth.

Perfect.

Except now the perfect gift sat unopened in his apartment.

Daniel grabbed the postcard off the rack. While he was at it, he selected one that blared WISH YOU WERE HERE. He'd bought Alli postcards for six years. Why stop now, even if the postcards ended up stuffed in his backpack?

"Idiot." Daniel berated himself under his breath as he handed the cashier the postcards and a twenty-dollar bill.

"Excuse me?" The cashier's dreadlock-covered head snapped back as she stopped gathering his change.

"Nothing. Talking to myself." Daniel grabbed the brown paper bag and the cup of coffee and exited the store, heading for his gate. As he dumped his backpack on the floor, his cell phone rang.

Seth.

"Daniel here."

"Where exactly is here, Daniel?"

"I'm waiting for my flight back to Colorado. Just finished backpacking around Banff." Daniel shifted in his seat so his outstretched legs didn't trip up a passenger running to catch a flight.

"Do you ever do any *real* work, Daniel?"

"I scoped out the site of a future ski resort, Tag. I work as often as the bills demand."

Seth huffed in disbelief.

"So, why'd you call? Certainly not to check up on me. Not even Dad does that anymore."

"I need some advice. I'm getting nowhere with Allison."

"Why are you calling me? I'm not exactly Dr. Phil." Daniel took a swig of his now-cooled coffee.

"You've had your share of relationships, Daniel. And even if you aren't married, I figure you might know some things I don't. I've only dated Allison."

"Maybe that's the problem. Maybe you should have dated more."

"Are you suggesting I date someone else to make Allison jealous?"

"No!" Daniel startled the older gentlemen reading the sports section across the aisle. "Do you even listen when I say something? Maybe this is why you and Alli had problems."

"We don't have problems."

"Could've fooled me." Daniel eyed the trash can across the way, wondering if he could toss his coffee cup into it without splattering himself and the carpet. "Or maybe you can explain to me why Alli didn't go through with the wedding."

Silence echoed on his brother's end of the phone. No surprise. His words sounded harsh even to him. But give advice to Seth about how to get Allison back to the altar? Hardly.

"Forget I said that. Or at least forget the way I said it." Daniel watched a young woman in a coordinated gray, blue, and red business suit step behind the counter and start notifying passengers on the waiting list. No time to waste.

"Seth, you may not be able to fix this. And if you don't even admit there's a problem, you're certainly not going to get anywhere with Alli."

"I've been sending her flowers every day. *Every day.* She doesn't even call me to say thank you."

"Frankly, Seth, this isn't just about you." Was his brother even thinking about Alli? "Maybe you need to give her some breathing space. Don't send flowers. Don't call. Give her some time. In a couple of weeks, try again."

"I don't know." Daniel could almost hear Seth mentally assessing the pros and cons of his suggestions. "I always like the straightforward approach. Let Allison know I mean business—that I'm not giving up."

"This isn't business, Tag. This is your relationship with Alli." Daniel stood and wandered over to the trash can, tossing his coffee cup onto the stack of newspapers. Returning to his seat, he dug his boarding pass out of his jacket pocket. "Look, Seth, back off a bit. That's my advice. Take it or leave it. I've gotta sign off. It's almost time to board."

He shut his phone and leaned back in his seat.

Pathetic, Danny boy. Giving your brother advice about handling his love life. Next thing you know, you'll be setting Alli up with blind dates.

CHAPTER 9

Hey, Kid, camping on the coast of Turkey near some old castle ruin. The Mediterranean Sea is just a few feet outside my tent. I'm at a spot called Kizkalesi, which means "Maiden's Castle."

—Daniel

*A*llison stared at the row of thimbles lining the back edge of her desk like miniature pewter sentries. One by one, she picked them up, cradling them in her palm.

A carousel horse.

A teapot.

An apple.

A turtle.

An owl.

A unicorn.

No real rhyme or reason to why she bought a particular design. The only significance was the timing of her purchase. Her desk calendar declared mid-November—time to add to her collection.

Maneuvering her mouse, Allison clicked the Web address of her favorite online shop and scanned the latest offerings. A festive green Christmas-tree thimble adorned with tiny crystal ornaments caught her eye. Within minutes, she placed her order, requesting the package be gift-wrapped.

Why not? It's a celebration, right?

No one knew why she'd circled December 4 in bright red marker on her calendar every year for the past six—almost seven—years.

Fine with her. She preferred a private celebration. She hoped to still have something to commemorate in a couple of weeks.

Her fingers rested idly on the computer keyboard.

One more thing to do.

Do it.

Time to put her wedding dress up for sale on eBay. She dreaded seeing it lurking in her walk-in closet every morning when she got dressed.

Half an hour later, Allison admitted defeat. Setting up an account, taking a photo of the dress, much less uploading a photo, figuring out how much she wanted to sell it for—it was all too much at the end of an overly long day that spilled over into the next twenty-four hours. Maybe she should hang the beleaguered gown outside her apartment with a sign: FREE TO A HAPPY BRIDE-TO-BE. Meghan was already rescuing her from Seth's floral attacks, so she couldn't ask her best friend to post the gown on eBay by saying it was an overlooked maid-of-honor duty.

She managed to handle the question of where she was going to live without Meghan's help. Sure, her savings account was a shambles. There were so many consequences to not marrying Seth, including the fact that not marrying him meant she wasn't living with him. She had to scramble to renew her lease, handing back both her security and pet deposit.

"Tomorrow. I'll think about it tomorrow." Allison powered down her computer. "Great. Now I sound like Scarlett O'Hara. My life is becoming a collection of movie sound bites—but not the movies with happy endings."

She stood and stretched, walking through the apartment toward the bedroom. Spotless. No remnants of the impromptu burrito-fest and study session with Hadleigh and Evan. Was it really almost two A.M.? She'd listened to her sister and her—what was Evan? a study buddy? a boyfriend?—wrangle with Civil War dates and names for four hours. Thank God her years of memorizing facts were over.

She'd let Hadleigh and Evan take over the living room, retreating to the relative quiet of her study. Whenever she checked to make sure they had an adequate supply of munchies, Hadleigh surprised her by being in charge of the textbook and notes. Evan stretched out on the floor, his eyes scrunched closed in concentration, using two pens like drumsticks to beat a nonstop staccato rhythm on the carpet.

Since when had Leigh become a scholar, much less a tutor? Would she help Evan? Or would his history of poor academic performance take any hint of shine off of her sister's already lackluster grades?

Several days later, Allison parked in front of her parents' house. She turned off the heater, the radio, and finally, the Subaru, just as her stepdad taught her.

It wears on the engine to have all that stuff turned on when you first start the car, Allison.

She could hear Will's instructions from way back when she had braces, a learner's permit, and no boyfriend. Will had told her braces were no big deal, and neither were boys. He'd also taught her to change a tire and the oil, as well as how to parallel park and make a three-point turn. He'd shown up when she was all of eight years old, desperate for a daddy. He'd embraced both her mother and Allison—and her then-unborn sister—assuring them that he loved both mom and daughter.

She touched the car key in the ignition, tempted to start the car and drive away. She hated confrontation. Would they want to talk about the wedding day again, or could she steer the conversation to something safe, like holiday plans? She was a master at varied styles of avoidance.

She had stayed in a relationship with Seth for too long, just because it was easier than facing the truth that they weren't the ideal couple the way everyone thought. She ignored her feelings for Daniel because . . . well, you couldn't be in love with your fiancé's brother. Nice girls didn't do things like that.

"And more than anything, God, I want to be a nice, normal girl living a nice, normal life."

She leaned back, her head pressed against the headrest. She'd given up any hope of people thinking she was a nice girl the day she jilted Seth. Now she'd always be the woman who was foolish enough to walk—make that *run*—away from Seth Rayner.

Cold seeped into the car, forcing her to shut down her thoughts and walk to the house. She'd handle whatever her parents decided they wanted to talk about. Right?

Why wasn't Mom waiting for her, asking why she was late? She expected a quick hug and a motherly admonishment to hang up her coat and wash her hands before dinner. Some things never changed no matter how old she got.

"Hey, where is everybody?"

Stashing her coat in the closet, Allison moved through the living room and family room, waiting to be decorated for Christmas. Both empty. Hearing voices, she turned to the left and stepped into the kitchen. Her mom and Will must be chatting while she finished tossing the salad or stirring the soup.

"Sorry I'm late, Mom—"

Allison stumbled backward when she realized two men were in the kitchen with her mother. Her stepdad—and Seth.

"Wh-what are you doing here?" Allison blinked in surprise, her glance moving from Seth to her mother and then back to Seth.

"Hello, Allison. Your mother invited me to dinner." Her ex-fiancé moved toward Allison as if expecting a welcoming hug. Just like old times. Allison retreated farther into the hallway, backing up against the wall lined with family photos.

"Why would she do that?" Without waiting for his reply, Allison spun away from Seth and dashed back through the house to the foyer, pulling the front door open.

"Allison, what are you doing? Where are you going?" Her mother followed her while Will, wise man that he was, stayed in the kitchen.

What had her mother been thinking, inviting Seth for dinner?

"I'm leaving, Mom."

"Now, Allison, there's no reason to overreact. Stay and have dinner." Seth stood off to the side, sounding like he was trying to coax a child to eat all her vegetables.

Dinner with him, as if she hadn't left him standing at the altar?

"Tell Dad I'm sorry." Allison couldn't even acknowledge Seth's part in the conversation. "I'll call."

"Why won't you stay?" Allison's mother put a restraining hand on her arm. "It's just dinner. Seth called and asked for a chance to talk to you. Will and I thought it would help if we were there the first time you two talked."

"I know I need to talk to Seth. But I'm not ready. I'm not sure when I'll be ready." Allison stepped outside, the cold night air enveloping her. Maybe it would cool her emotions. She stood with her back to the door, arms wrapped around her waist as if to hold herself up, waiting for the frantic beating of her heart to slow down. When she heard the door open and close again, Allison figured her mom or Will had returned, bent on cajoling her into the house. Instead, Seth's quiet voice broke through her jumbled thoughts.

"Won't you please come eat dinner?"

Allison stared straight ahead, refusing to be drawn in by Seth's calm tone. How many times in the past had he used it to get her to agree to do things his way?

"No, Seth."

"It's just dinner."

"So everyone says." Allison rubbed her hands up and down her arms. "We can't just sit down at the table like nothing's happened."

"Then let's talk."

Allison closed her eyes, shaking her head. Seth sounded so reasonable. Why not go back inside and talk? Let her parents referee? Finish this once and for all?

But that would be ignoring her feelings, as she had for so many years, and doing what Seth wanted her to do. Old habits die hard. She needed to learn how to speak up for herself, starting now.

"Seth, I know we need to talk. But not tonight." She forced herself to turn and face her ex-fiancé. "I was expecting to have a nice, quiet dinner with my family, not hash out our relationship."

Seth stepped forward, standing so close that Allison inhaled the scent of the expensive cologne he preferred. "What about what I want, Allison? Are you even thinking about me?"

"Believe it or not, I was thinking of both of us when I didn't go through with our wedding."

"I don't think so. If you'd been thinking of me, you'd have married me."

Allison drew a ragged breath. So much for not talking about what had happened. She wanted to scream and cry at the same time. "I can't do this—hash out what happened standing on my parents' porch. Good night."

Aware that Seth watched her, Allison forced herself to walk to her car. She would not run from him again. There was no need to run. But there was also no reason for her to stay.

Halfway home, she realized she'd left her coat at her parents' house.

Stupid, stupid, stupid.

She pounded the steering wheel with her fist.

No. Stupid was having your parents ambush you with your ex-fiancé. And where was Hadleigh? Was her sister a part of the scheme?

She choked back a sob. If she started crying, she'd wreck the car. That would be really stupid. With a jerk of the wheel, she pulled into an empty bank parking lot and turned off the car. Then she rested her head on the steering wheel, waiting for the release of tears.

Nothing.

Just an ache in her chest that wouldn't go away. A burning behind her eyes. And the realization she might never get past being a runaway bride.

• • •

It wasn't cutting if she didn't bleed, right?

Allison touched the edge of the razor blade against the inside of her thigh.

Just a scratch. Not an actual cut. Just a scratch. Or two. Something to relieve the stress—

The blade clattered into the tub as her cell phone rang.

Meghan.

Saved by the bell.

Or rather, by Meghan's ridiculous "Don't Worry, Be Happy" ringtone.

Allison stepped out of the tub and grabbed her phone off the bathroom counter with one hand as she reached for her robe. "What is it?"

"Well, hello to you too. Did I catch you exercising? You sound out of breath."

"N-no. I'm good. I'm not working out." Allison shrugged one shoulder into her robe and pulled it around her trembling body.

"I wanted to tell you what I did with the most recent rejected bouquet."

"What do you mean?"

"It was time to stop all the flower folderol. So, I delivered the bouquet back to Seth."

"You didn't—"

"I most certainly did." Meghan's husky laugh was unrepentant. "I don't know who was more surprised, Seth or his prim and proper secretary. Talk about a control freak. She and Seth make a perfect team."

"What did you do? What did Seth say?" Switching hands, Allison tightened the belt around her waist as she walked from the bathroom over to the bed, collapsing onto it.

"Stop asking questions and I'll tell you. Yesterday I marched myself and that bridal bouquet re-creation past Seth's secretary and into his office. He was a bit surprised, I'll admit. I told him, and I quote: 'Stop with the flowers. She doesn't want them *or* you.' End quote."

"You didn't."

"Yes, I did."

"Meghan, how could you?" Allison crawled under her covers and pulled the blankets up to her chin.

"I can't keep picking up your unwanted flowers. I do have a life, Allison. I'd rather you say something, but until you're ready to talk to him, I decided to stop wasting my time and tell him myself. You should thank me."

"I-I don't know what to say." Allison bit her lip to keep her teeth from chattering. Her body shook underneath the blankets.

"I told you, say thanks. Are you okay? You sound funny. Did I wake you up?"

"No. Actually, I'm just going to bed. I'm tired, that's all. It's been a long day. A long week." Allison twisted onto her side, moving her legs back and forth, trying to create some body heat.

"I can only imagine the stress of putting your life back together after canceling a wedding. I'm only on flower duty. Are you going to be okay? Do you want me to come over?"

"No. I'm good. It's late. We'll talk tomorrow. 'Kay?"

"All right. Tomorrow it is, then."

"And Meggie?"

"Uh-huh?"

"Thanks."

"What are best friends for? Talk to you tomorrow."

Allison flicked her phone shut and tossed it onto the end of her bed. She turned her back toward her bathroom, wrapping her arms around a pillow.

Just stay in the bed. In peace I will both lie down and sleep . . . in peace I will both lie down and sleep . . . just stay in the bed . . .

Believe it or not, Kid, I visited a convent in Luxembourg! I've got photos to prove it! They had blind nuns there who make baskets. Watch your mailbox for a package.

—Daniel

CHAPTER 10

*A*llison rearranged the silverware surrounding her china plate for the third time. Salad fork there. Dessert fork there. Spoon there.

Why had she let Meghan convince her to talk to Seth face-to-face? She'd told her best friend about the family dinner fiasco, expecting sympathy, and ended up with a lecture.

"Do the right thing," Meghan insisted. "You don't date someone for six years, say yes when he proposes, bolt on your wedding day, and then not have the decency to give the guy closure by talking to him in person."

Knowing Meghan was right didn't make the showdown with Seth any easier. First she'd run out on him on their wedding day. Then she'd walked out on him at her parents'. Thanksgiving dinner a few days ago had been a strained mix of her parents' attempts at reconciliation and Hadleigh's denying any knowledge that Seth planned to ambush her. Allison hadn't tasted much of her mother's turkey stuffed with chestnut dressing, or the surrounding dishes of green beans, sweet potatoes covered with maple glaze, or her favorite sour cream-and-chive dinner rolls. She doubted she'd eat much tonight.

No matter what happened, she wasn't leaving.

When she called, Seth quickly one-upped Allison's suggestion to meet at Starbucks, recommending they have dinner at the Craftwood Inn, where they'd eaten the night he'd proposed. When Allison balked, he recommended Mataam Fez, a Moroccan restaurant where they'd celebrated their college graduation. They finally settled on the Summit, one of the Broadmoor's smaller restaurants. Funny how she'd forgotten Seth's masterful way of getting what he wanted in such an "I'm just being a gentleman" way.

She checked the time on her phone, slipping it back into her messenger bag. Seth wasn't late. She'd been twenty minutes early. Seth was Mr. Punctual.

Did she have time for a strategic trip to the ladies' room?

"Hello, Allison."

Allison jumped, her leg knocking into the table and causing the stemware to rattle back and forth. She settled back into her seat as Seth sat across from her. His brief nod felt like a dismissal, not a greeting.

"S-Seth. Hello." Allison bent to retrieve the starched white napkin that slid from her lap to the floor. She smoothed it over her linen pants. Anything to avoid making eye contact for as long as possible. What would she see in his eyes?

When she glanced up, Seth held a gold-embossed menu. The waiter handed one to Allison. She glanced down the list of entrées as Seth ordered a bottle of his favorite red wine.

"Would you like an appetizer, Allison?"

"No. I'll just wait for the salad."

"Fine. We'll have our orders ready in just a moment." Seth waved his hand, letting the waiter know he wasn't needed. "So. Allison. How are you?"

"I'm good, Seth. And you?" She rubbed her wrist with two fingers. Back and forth. Back and forth. Realizing what she was doing, she clasped her hands around her napkin.

"I'm doing well, all things considered. I'm busy with a new

project—we got the contract for the hospital in Arizona." He leaned back in his chair, never glancing away from Allison.

"Congratulations. I know how hard you worked for that."

Silence stretched between them. Six years together, and she didn't know what to say to the man sitting across from her. Usually, she'd ask him all about his newest project, but it seemed forced, the expected thing to do. She'd done that for too long.

"Seth, I'm sorry for wh-what happened five weeks ago." Allison struggled to control the quaver in her voice. Any sign of weakness and Seth might think she doubted her decision.

"I expected an apology, Allison, but what I want is an explanation. What I'd like you to tell me is *why*." Seth's eyes narrowed. "Why did you decide you couldn't marry me?"

"I'm not sure I can explain why—"

Seth leaned forward, his hand raised to stop her. "You can't tell me why? Are you telling me you don't have a reason?" He quirked an eyebrow, a habit Allison used to find intriguing. Now it felt condescending. "You just decided to run? To leave me standing in the front of the church, in front of all our family and friends, *and you don't know why*?"

The waiter came back and, oblivious to the tension swirling around them, opened the wine, pouring some into a glass for each of them with a flourish. Seth sat looking out the window, pressing his lips together. Allison felt the table move as he jiggled his leg up and down, a telltale sign of frustration. As the waiter left, Seth centered the salt and pepper shakers on the table.

Allison reached for her glass of water, hoping to ease the tightness in her throat. Seeing how her hand shook, she left the glass untouched. "Seth, I have my reasons . . . my reasons why I can't marry you. Discussing them isn't going to change anything." She twisted the napkin in her lap. "I'm sorry. Terribly sorry. That's all I can say."

"Allison, how can we work this out if we don't discuss what happened?"

Work this out? Seth wanted to work things out?

"That isn't a good idea, Seth."

"I realize the ceremony was larger than you preferred, Allison. Maybe we should have planned something smaller." Seth leaned forward, his brown eyes alight as if an idea had occurred to him. "We can always reschedule something more intimate, like a destination wedding. Combine the wedding and the honeymoon. The cost doesn't matter. Don't walk away from six years together because of nerves."

So that was his explanation—he thought she had an extreme case of cold feet.

"Seth, it's true we dated for a long time." The napkin was a knotted mess. "But we started dating awfully young. Getting married would be a mistake."

"You waited until the absolute last minute to decide marrying me was a mistake." Uncharacteristic sarcasm laced Seth's voice as he leaned back in his chair.

The waiter reappeared. Out of habit, Seth ordered for them both, not even asking Allison what she wanted.

It doesn't matter. Just let him order.

"Would you consider counseling, Allison?"

"What?" Allison pushed a lock of hair behind her ear. The man was nothing if not persistent. "No, no, Seth. I think it's best if we accept . . . if you understand . . ."

"You're saying you don't love me anymore." Seth scanned her face as if trying to find the truth there. "Is there someone else, Allison?"

Allison stilled, willing herself not to look away from Seth's scrutiny. She wrapped her hand around her wrist and dug her nails into the skin.

What could she say? *Seth, you see, I ran away because I kissed your brother a week before the wedding.* She didn't think so. "No, Seth. There's no one else. I j-just can't marry you."

Seth leaned forward in his chair, fingers steepled together, his gold signet ring glinting under the lights. "Let me see if I understand you, Allison. You ran out on me on our wedding day. You can't tell me why. You say there's no one else. You think we started dating too young—that our getting married would have been a mistake." Seth ticked off the statements like a checklist. "That's the only reason you've given me—we were young. That may be true, but we dated for a long time. Six years. Isn't that long enough to know whether you loved me enough to marry me?"

One by one, Seth's words backed Allison into a corner. Abandoning him in the restaurant seemed more and more appealing.

Relief washed over her when the waiter brought their salads and a basket of rolls. Staring at the mixture of chicory, crisp applewood bacon, blue cheese crumbles, and garlic croutons, Allison knew she'd merely move pieces of the salad around her plate.

"Allison, I'm going about this all wrong." Seth reached over, covering her hand with his. "I should have told you that I still love you. I still want to marry you."

His gentleness caught Allison off guard. Tears pricked at the corners of her eyes. For so long Seth had been her Prince Charming, but now he felt like an unwanted anchor holding her to her past.

"I want you back, but I need to know why you did what you did." His fingers caressed the back of her hand. "And I need you to understand how I felt that day."

"Seth, I came here tonight because I owed you this time face-to-face. To tell you I'm sorry." She took a deep breath, trying to control her tears. "B-but I don't . . . we can't go back."

Seth's face hardened, and he clenched his jaw as he withdrew his hand from hers. "That's it, then? You're throwing away our relationship for no good reason." His voice was wooden, distant, and yet Allison could see the pain shadowing his eyes. "Do you realize how you embarrassed me in front of our family, our friends, my colleagues?"

"I'm so, so sorry, Seth," Allison whispered. She reached down and fumbled in her purse, searching for the black velvet boxes containing her engagement ring and diamond earrings. She set them on the table, close to Seth's glass of wine. "I need to give you these. This is best—for me and for you. If we got married—I don't think we'd be happy."

Seth ignored the boxes, pushing his chair back to stand beside the table. "Allison, this isn't like you. I have to admit I'm angry." He spoke with grave deliberation. "I love you. You're confused, and you've let something upset my—our—plans."

"Seth, I *have* thought about this."

His gaze flickered to the ring box and then returned to her face. "No, Allison, I disagree. You can't be thinking clearly if you're willing to throw away our relationship. We can work this out. I'm willing to try." He picked up the jeweler's boxes. "I'll keep these. I know I can convince you that you've made a mistake." He leaned down and, before she realized his intent, pressed a kiss to her lips. Turning, he strode from the restaurant, leaving her sitting alone at the table.

Allison buried her face in her hands. *Oh, God, that was awful.* But then what did she expect? For Seth to understand? She didn't even understand herself.

She brushed her hair back from her face, ignoring the stares of the other people in the restaurant. She fought an odd desire to laugh and cry at the same time.

Well, she kept her promise. She hadn't walked out on Seth. She let him do the honors this time.

CHAPTER 11

$\mathcal{S}$eth flung the two jeweler's boxes onto the dashboard of his Lexus.

"I can't believe it." He braced his arms on the steering wheel and stared out the windshield into the dusky evening. "Why is she acting like this?"

He leaned back against the leather seat, reaching for one of the boxes. When he lifted the lid, the diamond in Allison's ring glinted under the parking lot lights. He touched the cool stone, remembering how she'd requested something smaller, simpler. But he'd worked overtime at his job between going to college classes in order to buy what he knew was just the right ring—this ring.

He snapped the lid closed.

His plan to woo her back with flowers failed. He'd spent several hours with his favorite florist, discussing the different bouquets to be delivered to his runaway bride. Red chrysanthemums meaning simply "I love you." Blue hyacinths representing constancy. Orchids for a beautiful lady. Even variegated tulips symbolizing beautiful eyes. Every offering returned. But re-creating her bridal bouquet—that had ended in the ultimate floral fiasco.

He'd been sitting at his desk, going over architectural plans for a new state-of-the-art hospital on the West Coast. He loved the challenge of designing a stunning building while emphasizing energy-saving elements.

The door to his office swung open, disrupting his thoughts.

"Michelle, I asked not to be disturbed—"

"I am not Michelle."

Allison's best friend, Meghan, descended on him, a mop-topped avenging Valkyrie in a pair of purple UGGs, the duplicate wedding bouquet dangling from her fingertips. His assistant stood in the doorway, a look of icy disapproval marring her flawless features.

"What can I do for you?" Seth stood and couldn't stop himself from stepping back as Meghan leaned across his glass-topped desk, dropping the flowers on top of the plans.

"Just returning something of yours."

"Those flowers were meant for Allison."

"I know that—just like all of your other come-back-to-me arrangements." Meghan planted her hands on either side of the bouquet. "Allison doesn't want your offerings. And she doesn't want *you*."

The woman was nothing if not direct. Well, she was a lot of things. Flamboyant, with her neon-orange nails and her deep brown eyes outlined in vivid purple. And tall. If he took her on, he'd be nose to pert-and-pierced nose with her.

"Why doesn't Allison talk to me directly?" Seth moved the bouquet to one side and stacked his papers in the center of the desk, squaring off the corners so they were even.

"She doesn't feel like the last attempt to communicate went well, what with being ambushed at her parents' house."

"Really?" Seth quirked an eyebrow. "And Allison told you this herself?"

Meghan's own pierced brow rose. "Yes, *really*. You know Allison and I talk about everything."

The door clicked shut. Had Michelle witnessed the verbal

sparring? So much for maintaining his reputation as a calm, cool, and in-control boss.

"You've delivered your message, so you can leave."

Meghan nodded and moved toward the door. After a few steps, she turned back. "Listen, Seth, don't misunderstand me—"

"I understand you fine."

"Don't interrupt me, either." Meghan marched back to the desk. "I've already told Allison you're not some heartless villain. I think you think you love her."

"I do."

Again, the eyebrow piercing rose.

"My apologies for interrupting."

"Just because you love someone doesn't mean you're meant to be together forever."

That sounded like a line from one of the romance movies Allison liked to watch.

Meghan's voice softened. "For what it's worth, I think my best friend had lousy timing—leaving you at the altar like she did. But I also think she was courageous, not stupid. Marrying you would have been stupid."

"Well, thanks."

"For *both* of you." Meghan shoved her hands in the pockets of her white coat trimmed with fur. "You know what they say—'Don't shoot the messenger.'"

"The idea hadn't entered my mind."

"I'll leave before it does."

His assistant scurried through the door scant seconds after Meghan left. "I'm so sorry, Mr. Rayner. That woman insisted she see you, even after I told her you didn't want to be disturbed."

Seth stared at the abandoned flowers on his desk. "I understand. She's . . . determined, I'll grant her that."

"Is there anything I can do for you, Mr. Rayner?"

"Yes." Seth picked up the roses. "Throw these away, would you? And then hold my calls. I don't want to be disturbed."

Michelle held the bridal arrangement at an awkward angle. "Yes, sir. Anything else?"

"This time make sure no one—and I mean *no one*—bothers me. Especially my fiancée's best friend, determined to give me another piece of her mind. Is that clear?"

"Yes, Mr. Rayner."

Seth sat back in his chair, swiveling around to stare out the window at the view of Pikes Peak. Clouds obscured the top of the mountain. By tomorrow morning the peak would be snow-covered.

What did historians write about Zebulon Pike when he first saw the incline? The explorer had believed the mountain would never be conquered. But Pike had no vision. It was said he'd even lost his way as he traveled through Colorado.

Pike had been both unprepared and wrong. Cars drove up and down the mountain in a day. The cog railway chugged back and forth, weather permitting. Runners scaled its heights, and even race car drivers took the hairpin turns at audacious speeds.

Unlike Zebulon Pike, Seth Rayner knew he could accomplish whatever he set his sights on. He ran in any kind of weather, conditioned to ignore cold, rain, even snow. He'd convinced his stubborn father to see beyond business as usual, helping him to embrace structures that were examples of conservationism and artistic elements.

"Allison Denman, I've loved you since the first time I saw you." Seth turned back to his desk, rearranging the architect's design. "I asked you to marry me, and you said yes. This isn't over yet."

Interesting view of the Dead Sea from Masada. I ran all the way up with Israeli Special Forces guys. They were great about letting me tag along.

—Daniel

CHAPTER 12

Daniel lifted his mountain bike out of the back of his truck, laying it on the ground while he grabbed his helmet and slammed the tailgate shut. Rolling the bike to his patio apartment, he lifted it over the concrete wall and then leaned it against the other side. He hopped over the wall, brushed off his hands, and let himself in through the sliding glass doors.

One of the advantages of living in a ground-floor apartment: no hauling the bike up and down flights of stairs.

He snagged a brown cotton towel off the back of the couch. Sniffed. Not too bad. Rubbed it through his sweat-soaked hair before slinging it across his shoulders.

Hydrate first. Then shower.

He strolled toward the galley kitchen, ignoring the stack of mail splayed across his dining room table. Plenty of time to figure out who was ahead: his checking account or the bills waiting to be paid.

All five of his glasses were piled in the sink, waiting to be transferred to the dishwasher. All four of his plates and what was left of the silverware set he'd bought a year ago too. First he needed to buy dishwasher soap. Maybe he should go the paper-plate-and-cup route.

Daniel opened his fridge, hoping to find a bottle of cold water. No luck. Turning on the faucet, he let it run for a minute, then ducked his head and drank from the tap. At least he lived alone. Of course, a roommate might be the responsible one and remember to get groceries or pay the bills or do the laundry. Maybe he needed a maid service or a personal assistant. Or both.

He headed for the shower, stripping off his orange and black cycling jersey, tossing it in the general direction of his laundry basket. Close enough to find when he decided to do laundry. Or went for another bike ride.

As he sat on his unmade bed to remove his shoes, his cell phone beeped, signaling a voice mail. He threw his shoes into a corner, peeling off his socks, and walked over to his bureau. His phone sat in front of the photo of him, Seth, and Alli—the one he'd smuggled out of the rehearsal dinner—on the snowshoeing trip. Flipping open his phone, he waited for the message.

Seth.

What was the deal? The guy hardly ever called him. Now Alli ended their relationship, and Seth thought his brother was the Answer Man.

Blah, blah, blah. Tag's voice droned on and on as Daniel walked into the bathroom and started running the water for a shower. Seth was still frustrated. Daniel ended the message before Seth finished talking.

The shower eased the tension in his muscles, but Daniel's mind stayed focused on Alli. Should he help Seth figure out how to get Alli back? Was that really the best thing for either of them? Maybe now was the time for the high school sweethearts to find out there were other fish populating the dating pool. They both needed to meet new people, expand their relationship horizons. Then, if they did get back together, at least they wouldn't wonder about what—or whom—they had missed. Besides, Daniel had his own history of failed relationships, thanks to his commitment to work—or what several past girlfriends called an overcommitment. Would his advice even work?

According to The Code, he wasn't a candidate to date Alli. He couldn't deny he was attracted to her, but he could control his actions. He'd put the mental DO NOT TOUCH sign back in place and crisscrossed it with imaginary yellow DO NOT CROSS tape. That should do it.

Daniel wrapped a blue-and-green-striped beach towel around his waist and sat on the edge of the tub.

So, if he couldn't date Alli, he'd assign himself the role of master planner of blind dates. Who was a possible candidate? Alli was almost like a little sister to him. The kid deserved somebody decent. A guy more laid-back than Seth. Who could Daniel—as an objective but concerned outsider—trust to treat Alli right and show her a good time?

He'd toss the idea around with Jackson tonight when they met for dinner.

Daniel paused on his way to the bedroom to get dressed.

Jackson.

Why not? He could set Alli up on a casual date with his best friend—and keep an eye on her at the same time.

Genius. Absolute genius.

Every single table and chair in Starbucks was taken. Several women sat in one corner, holding identical books and sipping from insulated cups. A book club? A group of teens huddled over laptops. One couple held hands and leaned across a table, talking to each other with their eyes more than with words. A line of customers—men, women, parents with antsy children who'd probably get their own Starbucks treats—snaked toward the barista at the register.

Allison eased around the tables, trying to catch a glimpse of the time on her iPhone. Slow-moving rubberneckers watching the aftermath of a rollover on I-25 had delayed her, but surely she wasn't over ten minutes late.

In the back corner of the room, someone stood and waved.

Jackson.

She tucked her bright red gloves in her coat pocket as she walked toward him.

"Hey, Allison. Good to see you." Jackson pulled a chair out for her to sit next to him. "I was beginning to think you'd stood me up."

Stood him up? This wasn't a date.

Allison slipped out of her coat, hanging it on the back of the chair. "An accident snarled traffic. Everybody wanted to see the EMTs in action."

"Let me go get our orders. You like the nonfat no-whip pumpkin-spice latte with two Splendas, right?"

"Um, yeah. How'd you know?"

Jackson shrugged. "I guess Daniel mentioned it."

Okay, then.

Allison reached for her messenger bag. "Let me get you some money—"

"No need. This is on me."

As Jackson worked his way to the back of the line, Allison wondered again why he had invited her out for coffee. He was Daniel's friend, not hers. She usually saw them together when they were heading out on some adventure—or just finishing one.

She assumed he wanted to talk about some kind of business project. What did he do again? Had Daniel ever mentioned that? He hadn't brought any folders or notebooks. Allison laced her fingers together. *Patience, girl.*

A few minutes later, Jackson slid an insulated cup in front of her and folded his lanky frame into a chair. "So, how's it going?"

"Life's finally getting back to normal, thanks. Just in time for the holidays."

"Yeah, Daniel tells me you've had a rough go of it since calling off the wedding." Jackson grimaced. "My bad. That topic is on the NFD list."

"Excuse me? What's the NFD list?"

"Well, when Daniel suggested . . . I mean, when I talked to him about asking you out, he suggested I not mention the wedding." Jackson wrapped his large hands around his cup.

Oh, really?

"So NFD stands for?"

"Not for discussion."

Allison ran her thumb back and forth along her wrist. "What other topics did Daniel put on the NFD list?"

Jackson chuckled. "Now, if I told you, I'd be talking about them, wouldn't I? Surely we can find other things to talk about on our first date."

"Is that what this is, Jackson? A first date?" She found herself glancing around the coffee shop, looking for Daniel. Was he hiding somewhere, watching all of this and laughing?

When she looked back at Jackson, she couldn't help but notice the tips of his ears were bright pink. Had she embarrassed him? He'd get no apology from her—she hadn't even realized this was a date!

"Daniel thought—"

"Stop. Right. There." Allison leaned closer to Jackson, having to fight back a giggle when he leaned away from her. "I only see you and me sitting at this table. But Daniel's name keeps coming up. Why is that?"

"Okay, hear me out." Jackson shifted in his chair. "And I'm going to have to mention Daniel again."

"Why am I not surprised?"

"Daniel and I were talking about you the other night." He held up his hand when Allison started to interrupt again. "I'll never get finished if you keep asking questions."

Allison closed her mouth, covering her lips with her fingers.

"Anyway, we were talking about you, and he suggested I ask you out. He thinks you and Seth need to discover the other fish in the sea, or something like that. I figured why not? I mean, you're not interested in getting back with Seth." Jackson paused, running his hand through his thick blond curls. "Are you?"

Allison stared at Daniel's best friend, trying to comprehend the question.

"Are you?" he repeated.

"Am I what?"

"Are you interested in getting back with Seth?"

"No!"

"Then what's the harm in us dating?" Jackson gave her a wink. "It's not like I'm Seth's brother."

With a groan, Allison buried her face in her hands. Somebody, somewhere, had to be filming this.

"Allison, you okay?" Jackson rested a hand on her shoulder. "Maybe it's better we've got this all out in the open. We can start the date over. I was thinking we could have coffee first and then maybe check out a movie—"

"No."

"No?" Jackson shrugged. "Okay, no movie. You want to get something to eat?"

"No, Jackson. No movie. No dinner. No date."

"Come on, Allison, relax." Jackson covered her hand with his. "Daniel's going to ask me how tonight went, and I want to give him a good report."

Allison stood, shoving her chair back. "Oh, I'll make sure Daniel Rayner gets a report about our little everybody-else-knows-this-is-a-date-except-me event." She dug a five-dollar bill out of her bag, throwing it on the table. "Tell him we went dutch. Tell him the date lasted less than twenty minutes. Tell him I can get my own dates, thank you very much."

Ignoring the stares of the baristas and the assembled customers, Allison stalked out the door to her car.

Daniel Rayner had better stay out of her way—and stop messing with her life.

She was so not sleeping.

Allison turned her head and faced the reality staring back at her from the alarm clock: 2:27 A.M.

She'd retreated to her bed four hours ago and tossed, turned, tossed, turned for every minute of those hours.

"Daniel Rayner, you owe me one cup of coffee I didn't get to drink and one good night's sleep." She pulled herself up to lean against the headboard, gathering her hair into a haphazard knot. "Well, more than one night's sleep."

Through one half-open eye, Bisquick watched her from his position stretched out across the bottom of the bed.

"Sorry to disturb you, cat. Must be nice to sleep away all nine of your lives."

Moonlight filtered through the curtains pulled across the window, casting her room into diluted darkness. If it weren't so late—make that *early*—she'd call Meghan for a heart-to-heart talk. Allison couldn't seem to see her way clear to tomorrow, much less to next month or the next year. Meghan, on the other hand, was settled in a high-paying job that funded her cute orange sports car and her twice-a-month mani-pedi addiction.

What had her wise best friend said when she'd interrupted Allison's nonstop crying jag in the mountain cabin? "If you can stop controlling your life, maybe God will finally have a chance to get a word in edgewise and be able to tell you what he wants for your life."

Want to weigh in, God?

After abandoning Jackson in Starbucks, Allison had wandered into a local bookstore. She found herself staring at rows and rows of books, hoping one would jump off the shelf, proclaiming, "Here! I've got all the answers you need!"

There were self-help books about dating the wrong guy, being the wrong girl, how to strengthen a relationship, how to end a relationship, getting over a breakup, reinventing yourself, discovering your true self.

She'd browsed the religious section because, well, she was a believer, wasn't she? After that one summer-camp experience when she was fifteen, she'd gone to youth group and church with Meghan . . . at least for a while.

Allison pulled her comforter up around her shoulders, trying to recapture the feeling of that long-ago night in July. Several weeks earlier, her sophomore English teacher had confronted her about her secret after noticing a fresh mark on Allison's wrist. The shame at being discovered stalked Allison, threatening her with unspoken words.

She recalled the bonfire, the youth pastor's zeal about Jesus and discovering his will for your life—he'd called it "a great adventure." Her heart yearned to grasp something bigger, stronger . . . something lasting. Something true. But how could God want someone like her . . . someone who made such awful mistakes?

When the pastor led the group in prayer, she bowed her head with everyone else. Whispered the words "I'm sorry, I'm sorry," over and over again, her eyes pressed closed. But the reality of her life managed to find its way past the flimsy barricade.

Then the crackle and pop of the bonfire faded away. She no longer heard the sound of the high school boy strumming on a guitar or sensed anyone sitting around her. And somewhere in her heart, she heard a whispered *Forgiven.*

She clutched the word like a desperate child, letting the echoes of it wash over her, bring her hope.

She returned home with a brand-new Bible to match her brand-new faith. For months afterward, she attended youth group and a weekly girls' Bible study with Meghan.

And then Seth came along.

She found herself intrigued by the self-assured, lanky young man who seemed to be everywhere she was, always ready to offer her a ride, or to help her with math homework. How could someone so good be interested in her? Then he'd asked her to homecoming. Before she knew it, Seth was the top priority in her life. Everything and everyone else had to take a number.

Even God.

Allison shifted against her pillows, a weary sigh deflating her shoulders. "Well, God, it's just you and me. I'm back where I was in high school—telling you I'm sorry. Sorry about a lot of things. I'm sorry I hurt Seth and that I kissed Daniel and that I've made a mess of everything. Why can't I get it right? I'll try to figure out what you want me to do before I make any more major decisions, okay?"

Allison sat huddled under the blankets for a few minutes. Nothing. No whispered word in her heart. No spiritual pat on the back or high five. She snuggled back down into the bed, wrapping her arms around the pillow. It was a start. Tomorrow she'd go looking for her old Bible. And maybe God would decide to jump into the conversation.

Surf, sand—and sunburn.
Ouch! Next time, remind
me to bring sunscreen,
okay, Kid?
—Daniel

CHAPTER 13

"There's a parking space right there, sis!"

Allison looked in the direction Hadleigh pointed and spied the compact space between a yellow Hummer and a black four-by-four. She maneuvered her car between the two automotive behemoths. "Since when were these compact cars?"

She snared her messenger bag from the backseat and eased out of the car. Heavy clouds hung in an overcast sky, threatening snow. Cold air crept past the warmth of her coat, causing Allison to dig in her pockets for her gloves. Cars crawled through the overcrowded parking lot of the open-air shopping center as too many holiday shoppers searched for too few parking spaces—the customary last-weekend-before-Christmas madness.

'Twas the season to go crazy trying to finish—make that *start*—her Christmas shopping. Somehow the "want to" had the reality of "had to" this year.

She followed her sister, trudging past people lugging purchases, parents pushing strollers carrying cranky toddlers, couples laughing and holding hands while checking off their gift lists and probably maxing out their credit limits. Christmas music floated out of speakers hidden in greenery planted in cement containers, adorned with wire and ivy-covered reindeer sculptures.

"Why did I let you talk me into this, Leigh? Couldn't we have gone to Chapel Hills Mall—an enclosed, climate-controlled mall?"

"You've got to do your gift shopping sometime." Hadleigh looped her arm through Allison's. "Besides, if I'm with you, I can show you what I want for Christmas—and to do that, we have to shop here."

Allison cracked a laugh, pulling her hair out from inside her coat collar. "You circled that purple sweater in the Limited catalog in orange highlighter. Sent me a link via e-mail. Put an ad up on my bulletin board—"

"You need something up there—the board's so empty!" Hadleigh stopped to look at the Ulta window display of glitzy holiday-themed gifts of makeup and hair products. "What happened to your post-card collection?"

Allison ignored the question. "So you decided to start a new collection of 'This is all my little sister wants for Christmas'?" She resisted as Hadleigh pulled her down the sidewalk toward Panera Bread's front door. "We're shopping, *not* eating."

"Oh, come on." Hadleigh pouted and pulled on her arm. "Evan got a job here last week. Let's get coffee to go."

"You don't drink coffee—and I don't, either." She grimaced, think-ing of the blind-date fiasco with Jackson. "Unless it's a pumpkin-spice latte."

"So order tea." Her sister grinned as she opened the door and ush-ered her into the café. "I just want to say hi."

"Oh, all right. Tea to go. Got it?"

"Got it—but I want a chai latte."

Hadleigh dumped their coats at a table while Allison stood in line. She watched as her sister looked around for Evan. What did he do, anyway? Cashier? Cook? Bus tables? She glanced over her shoulder— and stopped breathing.

Daniel and Seth sat in a booth across the room, lunching on sand-wiches, soup, and extra-large drinks.

She hadn't seen the brothers together since her ill-fated wedding day. Once again, she noticed how different they were. Seth wore a white dress shirt and a dark tie, his classic tan trench coat laid across a chair he'd pulled up next to the table. Daniel had on a gray fleece pullover and jeans, a baseball cap turned backward on top of his wayward curls, his legs stretched outside the booth.

And he was looking right at her with his intriguing mismatched eyes.

What? Wake up, girl! He was looking right at her.

When the line moved forward, Allison turned away without acknowledging Daniel's smile. She wanted to walk out of the shop without ordering anything.

Don't overreact. She had every right to be here. They all lived in the same town. She couldn't avoid Seth or Daniel forever.

She could do this. *Order tea. Get Hadleigh and leave.* Easy, right?

She kept her eyes focused on the menu board, reading and reread-ing the lists of bagels and drinks. By the time she placed her order, she felt as if she'd memorized the entire assortment of bagels and bread selections.

As Allison turned, she scanned past the section where the Rayner brothers sat. Still there. And Daniel still watched her. Only this time he waved, causing Seth to look at her too.

Thanks, Daniel.

Near the front of the restaurant, Hadleigh chatted with Evan. Al-lison handed her an insulated cup of chai and picked up her coat. "Let's go, Leigh."

"What's your rush?" Hadleigh set her cup on the table. "Say hi, why don't you?"

"Hi. Sorry, Hadleigh can't stay to chat. We know you're working, and we wouldn't want to get you in trouble with your boss. Bye." She motioned for her sister to follow and headed for the exit.

Cold air laden with the hint of a coming snowstorm wrapped

around her. She should have stopped to put on her coat rather than carrying it over her arm. But her immediate concern was escape, not warmth.

"Do you mind?" Her sister stomped up behind her, the tone of her voice cooler than the winter air causing Allison's teeth to chatter. "That was just plain rude."

"Sorry, Leigh." Handing her sister her cup of tea, Allison slipped into her pea coat, buttoning it with stiff fingers. "I didn't want to meet up with the Rayner brothers."

"Both of them?" Hadleigh turned and peered back inside the plate glass windows.

"Yes, both of them." She pulled her sister away from the bagel shop. "Let's go shopping."

Hadleigh shoved her hands in the pockets of her pink down vest. "I can understand why you don't want to see Seth, but Daniel's an okay guy, right?"

"Sure. Daniel's fine." Had she lied to her little sister? "It's just that he's Seth's brother, and since I've broken off the engagement—" She shook her head, not sure what else to say.

"Don't you mean since you jilted him?"

Allison groaned and gave her little sister a playful shove. "Thanks for clarifying that for me, Leigh."

Hadleigh walked beside her in silence for a few seconds. "Do you want to leave?"

"To be honest, the thought crossed my mind." Allison straightened her shoulders. "But hey, I circled the lot five times before we found the parking space. We shouldn't let it go to waste, right?"

"True, true. And there is the purple sweater . . ." Hadleigh grinned.

"As if I could forget the purple sweater." Allison looked back but didn't see either Seth or Daniel in the crowd of shoppers behind them.

"You going to be doing that all afternoon?"

"Probably, Leigh. Probably."

• • •

"I agreed to lunch, not to prowling the women's clothing stores look-ing for Alli." Daniel followed Seth out of Coldwater Creek, glad for the fresh air. He preferred the outdoors—even surrounded by asphalt and concrete—to Chico's, Ann Taylor, and Banana Republic.

He sidestepped a double stroller overflowing with identical twins and assorted shopping bags. The mom looked triumphant but ex-hausted.

"You ready to leave yet?"

"If you had told me sooner that Allison was at the restaurant, I wouldn't be searching for her now." Seth opened the glass door of a store filled with makeup products.

"No. Absolutely not." Daniel stopped so quickly that a teenage girl wearing skintight jeans tucked into knee-high black leather boots almost ran into him. "I draw the line at lipstick and eye shadow, little brother."

"Fine. Wait outside."

What now? Go take a nap in the car? Pulling his cap farther down on his face, he moved up the sidewalk outside the stores. He pre-ferred hikes where he didn't have to dodge strollers and shoppers and even a troupe of Christmas carolers. He walked the entire length of the shopping center, weaving in and out of the mass of must-find-the-best-deal humanity, before turning around and heading back to where he'd left his brother.

As he neared Williams-Sonoma, he spied Seth talking to Allison. Good. His brother's mission was accomplished. Should he slow down to give Seth a few extra minutes before interrupting? As he got closer, he realized Allison refused to make eye contact with Seth, and that her shoulders were hunched over, as if she were protecting herself. Had he really expected the conversation to go well? Why hadn't he stopped himself before he waved hello when he saw Allison at Panera?

"I've got to go . . ." Allison took a step away from Seth.

Seth, who faced away from Daniel, reached out and grabbed Allison's wrist. "Let me come with you. I can carry your purchases. Remember how much fun we had last year when we did our Christmas shopping together?"

"I've already told you no." Allison pulled against Seth's hold.

"What could it hurt if we spent a little time together?" His brother refused to relinquish Allison's hand.

"It could hurt me." Daniel watched Allison twist against Seth's grip on her wrist. Watched her brush trembling fingers across her lips when she realized they were attracting attention.

"You're being unreasonable, Allison." Seth placed his other hand on Allison's free arm and jerked her toward him.

Enough was enough.

Daniel stepped up behind his brother, clamping his hand down on Seth's shoulder.

"Seth."

Under the increasing pressure of Daniel's hand, his brother tensed and then let go of Allison. He stayed facing forward, jamming his fists into the pockets of his coat.

Before either brother could say anything, Allison pushed her way through the small crowd that had assembled and dashed in front of an SUV, disappearing among the cars crowding the parking lot.

Daniel dropped his hand away from his brother's shoulder as Seth spun around to face him. "What was that for? I had everything under control!"

Daniel leaned close to Seth, keeping his voice low and speaking through gritted teeth. "If you think manhandling a woman is having everything under control, Tag, you're an idiot."

Daniel's glare silenced Seth's response.

"Don't worry about taking me home." Daniel shook his head and sighed. "I'll find my own way back."

Hey, Kid—Ate lunch sitting on the rim of a volcano. The guide said it's inactive. I'd hoped for a little bit of action.

—Daniel

CHAPTER 14

Allison inhaled the buttery scent of popcorn as she carried the red ceramic bowl filled to the brim with the just-popped-and-salted snack to where Meghan sprawled across the couch. She moved aside the napkins and glasses of soda on the coffee table to make room for the bowl.

"You bring some DVDs?" She sat on the other end of the couch, kicking off her flats and tucking her feet underneath her.

"An even dozen for you to choose from. Action. Mystery. Comedy. A couple of chick flicks." Meghan grabbed a bowl and dipped it into the popcorn. "What do you want to watch while we wait for the New Year?"

"Can we talk first?"

"What's on your mind?" Meghan nestled the bowl and a soda in her lap, an expectant look on her face.

"My aunt Nita called today."

"Oh, really? What's your adventuresome aunt up to these days? Beekeeping? Organic farming? Mapping out what fourteeners she wants to climb come spring?"

"She's rescuing llamas."

Meghan sputtered on a sip of root beer. "Never say something like that when I'm taking a drink, girlfriend." Her eyes watered as she coughed and giggled. "Why would a llama need to be rescued?"

"I guess just like other animals, llamas can be neglected and abused." Allison shook her head, releasing her long hair from its high ponytail. During the hour-long phone conversation, her aunt had done most of the talking. "Aunt Nita's home in Estes Park is now a halfway house for rescued llamas. She rehabilitates, ummm . . . problem llamas."

"That I would love to see. Or not."

"That wasn't the only reason she called." Allison reached over and grabbed a handful of popcorn.

"Do tell."

Allison waited until Meghan swallowed her soda. "She invited me to come live with her."

"What, you're suddenly some sort of llama whisperer?" Meghan stared at her friend as if she'd announced plans to move to Peru and become an alpaca herder.

"Aunt Nita called to talk to my mom last week—"

"Nice of her, even though she's your dad's sister."

"Don't go there, Meggie. Please."

"Sorry. Continue with Aunt Nita, the amazing llama trainer."

"Well, Mom and Will weren't home, so she talked to Hadleigh. And Hadleigh just had to tell Aunt Nita about my last run-in with Seth—the whole Christmas-shopping fa-la-la-la-la."

"So, now Aunt Nita wants to rescue you too."

"I guess. In her words, I might want to get out of town for a while. Give Seth a chance to get over me." Allison couldn't hold back a sigh. "But Aunt Nita also said she could use my help. She's taking care of two llamas right now, and the state organization asked her to temporarily shelter a third. She's afraid that's going to be too much work for her, especially since she started a part-time job at the local hospital."

"She has a real job?"

"Believe it or not, yes. She's using her nurse's training and helping out at the emergency room admitting desk."

"I would so love to see your aunt Nita handle some of the people who show up in an ER. I remember how she almost took down the trucker who made a pass at you when you were visiting her the summer after high school. He probably didn't walk upright for a week."

"Let's just say if she told me to go and fill out paperwork, I wouldn't argue with her about it." Allison grinned. "Knowing Aunt Nita, she probably hands out llama-shaped pens with the hospital clipboards."

"So she wants you to come live with her as an apprentice llama caretaker?"

"Yep." Allison munched on some popcorn, savoring the buttery-salty flavor. "Since I started working as an independent contractor, it's doable. Have computer, can travel. Aunt Nita said she'd put me up in her furnished basement—and I can bring Bisquick. Apparently, llamas love cats. Not sure what Bisquick is going to think about llamas."

"Imagine that." Meghan's maraschino-cherry-red nails plucked popcorn from the bowl a kernel at a time. "She may have a point."

"You think I should run away? Again?"

"I think you should make a tactical retreat. That's different from bolting from Seth in an overpriced wedding gown."

"Tell me how you really feel about my dress, Meggie." Allison tossed several pieces of popcorn at her.

"The dress wasn't you. I knew that. You knew that. You just didn't have the guts to say so." Meghan winked at her. "You looked beautiful—but you didn't look like you."

Allison buried her face in her hands. "I am so over that dress. Can we please not talk about it? If I ever get married—*if*—I might just wear a pair of yoga pants and a plain white cotton top."

"What, no veil? Stranger outfits have shown up in wedding albums, sweetie."

"What do you think I should do?"

"What do *you* think you should do?"

"I asked you first."

"And I'm not telling you. You're a big girl. Decide for yourself. Ask yourself what you want to do. Better yet, pray about it. Ask God what he thinks about your moving to Estes Park."

"I have been praying about it, Meggie. I'm just not hearing God saying anything back."

"What, are you waiting for God to send an angel—or maybe a talking llama?"

"I'm serious. I'll be the first one to admit I haven't been as strong a Christian as you—"

Meghan held up her hand. "That is not the point, girlfriend, and you know it. Faith is not a game of comparison."

"I know I put God on the back burner and spent most of my time focusing on Seth in the last six years. I'm trying to do what you told me to do—get my priorities straight, pay more attention to God. I even found the Bible from youth camp."

"And?"

"And I'm a little rusty. I tried to start in Genesis and got bored. Then I flipped to the back and tried Revelation—and I got lost. Bowls, scrolls, plagues . . . So I found a section that was divided into categories. Things like: verses to read if you're worried, verses to read if you're angry, verses to read if you're tempted."

"What section did you settle in?"

"I just keep flipping back and forth between verses about peace and verses about worry."

"Can I make a suggestion? Park your brain on one verse a day—or even for a whole week. Don't jump all over the place."

"That's it? No getting up early and reading for hours and hours?"

"I know people who do, but I have a bad habit of falling back asleep and waking up an hour later, hoping I haven't drooled all over my Bible. So I focus on staying awake and remembering one piece of God's truth for the day."

"I'm desperate for some sort of direction. It would be nice to not stress out about seeing Seth and Daniel—"

"Seth *and* Daniel? Is Daniel causing you problems too?" Meghan scooped up another bowl of popcorn. "Surely he's not pulling the protective-big-brother act for Seth?"

"No, it's not that." Allison sighed, wishing she'd manage to make it through the night without mentioning either of the Rayner brothers. But she hadn't made it through a day without thinking of one or the other in weeks. "Things are just a little . . . strained between Daniel and me right now."

"You, my dear, are being vague. V-A-G-U-E."

"I know how to spell 'vague,' Meggie."

"If Daniel's not up in arms about you calling off the wedding, what's the problem?"

Allison grabbed a pillow and buried her face in it, muffling her answer. When Meghan tugged on the pillow, Allison held on tighter, refusing to let go or to look up at her friend.

"Allison, this is ridiculous. Give me the pillow *now* and look at me."

With a groan, Allison released the pillow. She glanced at her friend and then looked away.

"Repeat what you mumbled just then."

"I said, 'Daniel kissed me.'"

"All-i-son."

"Yes?"

"Details. Now."

"Remember the night five days before the wedding when Daniel came over to pick up some of my stuff to move it over to Seth's? Only I didn't have anything packed, and I was trying on my wedding dress and hating it?"

Meghan nodded.

"Daniel said helping the bride pack was a best man's duty. So we ordered Chinese and packed boxes and talked and . . . you know how Daniel is, he's so casual and fun. It was nice to relax after being so stressed about the monster dress and all the wedding details. And then he was saying good night and somehow . . . somehow we ended up kissing."

"That's one way to help you relax."

"This is not funny, Meghan!" Allison grabbed another pillow from the back of her couch and buried her face in it. Sat there. Waited for Meghan to say something. And waited. She risked peeking at her best friend. "Aren't you going to say anything?"

"I'm torn between asking who's the better kisser—Seth or Daniel"—Meghan dodged the pillow Allison threw at her—"and asking the obvious: Why did you kiss Daniel?"

"I didn't kiss Daniel. *He* kissed *me*."

"And you didn't respond? You didn't kiss him back?"

Allison reached for the bag of DVDs sitting beside the couch, dumping them in her lap. "How about a nice action movie?"

"Okay, then. That tells me all I need to know." Meghan set her bowl and can of root beer on the coffee table and began helping Allison separate the movies by genre.

"I've replayed what happened over and over again, Meghan. I don't know how it happened. One minute he's saying good night, and the next minute he's kissing me like . . . like . . ."

"Like you've never been kissed before?"

"No. He's kissing me like he meant it. Like the kiss . . . meant something." Allison realized she was touching her lips, remembering. "But it couldn't mean anything. Could it?"

"I have no idea what Daniel was thinking." Meghan stacked *Bringing Up Baby* on top of *The Proposal*. "What were you thinking?"

"I wasn't."

And now she couldn't stop thinking about Daniel.

She rested her elbows on her knees, cradling her head in her hands. "You know, maybe Aunt Nita's offer to come hang with her and the llamas isn't such a crazy idea after all. Maybe I need some distance from Seth and Daniel."

"And I thought I lived dangerously because I took up rock climbing."

"Are you talking about living with llamas or . . . my mishap?"

Meghan snorted. "Oh, that's what you're calling it now?"

"It's not like I planned on kissing Daniel!"

"That's what surprises me. You've got spreadsheets to keep track of your spreadsheets, for goodness' sake." Meghan waved her hand around the room. "Your apartment is immaculate because you clean it by day of the week *and* by area. Don't say you don't—Tuesday is the day you clean your bathrooms. Wednesday is your bedroom. Thursday is—"

Allison waved the pillow like a white flag. "Fine. You're right. What does this have to do with Daniel and Seth?"

"If I were a counselor, I would be asking what made you abandon all your carefully made plans with Seth for one kiss with his brother."

"And since you're my best friend?"

Meghan's luminous grin had all the wattage of the Cheshire cat's. "I'm asking the same question."

"I wasn't thinking. I reacted."

"Okay. Makes sense. Now tell me what you *felt.*"

Allison picked up the salt shaker from the coffee table. "Do you think the popcorn needs more salt?"

"Ah, an evasive answer. Ve-ry revealing." Meghan giggled. "You wouldn't want to tell me which Rayner is the better kisser, would you?"

"I think it needs more salt." Allison tossed salt into the bowl.

"Okay, then. It's amazing how much you tell without saying a word." Meghan tapped a DVD case against her knee. "I'll let you be evasive, girlfriend—but only for a while. What movie do you want to watch?"

"Anything but *The Wedding Planner.*"

"Or *27 Dresses.*" Meghan tossed the case back in the bag.

"*Seven Brides for Seven Brothers.*"

"*Sabrina.*"

"While You Were Sleeping."

Allison found the movie she'd been searching for. "And most definitely not . . ." She held the movie up so that Meghan could read the title. The friends spoke in unison, barely getting the words out before collapsing in laughter.

"Runaway Bride!"

*Alli—Shouldn't have tried
that last run down the
mountain. The doc says I'll
be in this blasted walking
boot for six weeks.*

—Daniel

CHAPTER 15

The move would do her good. Start the New Year in a new place.

That's what Allison kept telling herself. She'd repeated "You're making the wise choice" as she shut down her life in the Springs—sublet her apartment, toted boxes of stuff from her cupboards and closets to the thrift store, and hummed "Let's Start the New Year Right" while filling out change-of-address cards.

She'd prayed about it, talked it out with Meghan, and finally decided the best thing she could do was to put 139 miles between herself and Seth Rayner. If it just so happened that she also distanced herself from his handsome older brother, so be it. Moving in with Aunt Nita was the smart thing to do.

Now Allison wasn't so sure. The movers ignored her carefully devised color-coded labeling system. An overwhelming assortment of clothes and miscellaneous boxes lined the walls of her basement apartment. Boxes marked KITCHEN were stacked in the bathroom. Boxes marked BOOKS blocked the tiny kitchenette area. Bisquick prowled from bedroom to bathroom to the combo living and dining room, his tail swishing in annoyance. Could he detect the presence of the wide-eyed llama duo grazing in the backyard?

One thing was certain: Allison wouldn't be bored.

Between her looming deadline and getting organized, she'd have plenty to do. She wouldn't be seeing much of the mountains surrounding Aunt Nita's home on the outskirts of Estes Park, but she'd be busy.

Too busy to think.

Maybe so busy that she'd fall into exhausted sleep at night and not dream of Seth. Or Daniel. Or Seth finding her wrapped in Daniel's arms.

"So, what do you think of the apartment?" Her aunt's trademark voice, echoes of Ethel Merman, startled Allison from her reverie of staring at the mountain of boxes surrounding the bed.

"Once everything gets put away, it'll be great." Allison surveyed the chaos. "Of course, this is when I wish I could blink or wiggle my nose and magically make things fall into place."

"Take it a box at a time, honey, a box at a time. I can help until it's time for my shift at the hospital." Aunt Nita placed her suntanned hands on her hips. "Where do you want to start?"

"Let's go unpack the kitchen—but that means we start in the bathroom." Allison retwisted her hair into a ponytail. "I don't think the movers listened to a word I said."

"They were too busy fighting over who was going to ask for your phone number."

"Please, Aunt Nita. I am so not interested."

"Oh, I put a stop to that foolishness." Her aunt carried a box marked POTS AND PANS out of the bathroom. "I told them they weren't getting paid to practice pickup lines on my niece."

"I appreciate that. Believe me, I am not looking to get involved."

"Still getting over Seth?" Her aunt's intense blue eyes studied her over a pair of white-and-black-checked reading glasses.

Allison hefted a box marked UTENSILS onto her hip and headed for the front room. "That's not an easy question to answer. I mean, I'm not proud of how things ended with Seth. Jilting your fiancé is a lot funnier when you're sitting at home eating popcorn and watching

Julia Roberts hop onto a FedEx truck." She rubbed the tension building in her forehead. "But I know not marrying Seth was the right decision."

"I got to tell you, honey, when you came charging back up that aisle, I didn't know whether to tackle you or block anybody coming after you."

Allison realized it was the first time she'd talked to anyone about her almost wedding day without cringing in embarrassment. "I can see people's faces—the surprise, the shock. I know everyone was thinking, *What is she doing?* Funny thing is, I was wondering the same thing."

"Well, what's done is done." Aunt Nita dropped sheets of crumpled packing paper into a haphazard pile at her feet and reached over to wrap Allison in a warm hug. "And what's not done is not done. You know what I mean?"

Allison leaned her head on her aunt's sturdy shoulder and found herself wrapped in her aunt's familiar cocoa butter scent. "I guess. Truthfully, while I regret how things happened, I'd had doubts for months, but I didn't know how to say anything. We'd been together forever. Everyone just expected us to get married. And Seth was so . . . safe."

Her aunt held her away, her hands resting on Allison's shoulders. "It's understandable that you'd value safety—your childhood left you with some insecurities."

"Please, Aunt Nita, let's not talk about that." Allison pushed back from her aunt's embrace. "That's in the past. Like you said, what's done is done."

"Honey, something may have happened a long time ago, but it can still affect you today."

"End of discussion, okay?" Allison walked back toward the bathroom, dodging Bisquick, who seemed determined to pace his new home all day long.

"You and he are a lot alike, you know?"

"End of discussion."

"Both stubborn."

"I repeat, end of discussion."

After three days, the only boxes left to unpack were books and photo albums. Allison had divided her time between searching the iStockphoto website for photographs of circus performers and hanging up her clothes. Her unwanted wedding gown had made the trip, despite Allison's desire to leave it behind. She needed to deal with it—post it for sale on eBay or find a local thrift store to donate it to. For now the gown hung in her closet like a lace albatross, a daily reminder of her wedding-day fiasco.

With her apartment almost settled, she decided to get acquainted with the llamas, Kuzko and Pacha.

"Really? The characters from *The Emperor's New Groove?*" Allison had watched her aunt feed the almost-six-foot-tall llamas. "The owners couldn't come up with more original names?"

Aunt Nita leaned against the wooden fence enclosing the bad-boy llamas. "What would you name them?"

"Starsky and Hutch."

"Too eighties."

"Robin Hood and Little John."

"Double names are tricky."

"What was the name of that two-headed llama in *Dr. Dolittle?*"

"Pushmi-Pullyu." Her aunt scratched the thick white fur along Kuzko's long neck. "But we are not renaming these guys. We are rehabilitating them and then finding them new homes."

"*You* are rehabilitating them. I am merely helping you manage them—and the new guy when he gets here." Allison leaned forward as Pacha paced toward her, coming to stand nose to nose and blowing a soft breath in her face. "I guess there are worse ways to say hello."

"Most definitely. Llamas are more civilized than dogs, if you ask me." Aunt Nita turned back to the house. "When are you going to introduce Bisquick to the boys?"

"Let him get used to our new home before he comes face-to-face with those two, okay? Llamas may like cats, but I'm not sure Bisquick is going to be all that thrilled with llamas."

After spending another two hours setting up the photographs with the copy, Allison was ready to walk away from her computer. She left the boxes of books unopened while she put DVDs in order by title and genre. She hung her bulletin board in its customary spot in the kitchen. She debated digging out the postcards again but knew each photo of faraway places would remind her of Daniel. How many times had she gotten through studying for exams by reading the messages scrawled across the backs of each postcard? Silly details about Daniel's trips. Where he'd eaten. Sights he'd seen. Mountains he'd climbed. Or skied.

Did he really wish she'd been there with him?

Not likely.

Allison attacked her books. Nonfiction on the top shelves. Fiction on the bottom shelves. Hardbacks with hardbacks. Paperbacks with paperbacks. No mixing. Everything in its place. Daniel used to tease her, occasionally switching books from shelf to shelf when he dropped by with Seth. Sometimes he even put them in upside down and backward.

Nothing left but the photo albums.

Most of her photos were stored on her computer—by date, cross-filed by event. She always put certain photos in albums she arranged on her coffee table. Though she wasn't a Creative Memories whiz, she devised basic layouts and captions. It was a relaxed form of graphic design without the stress of deadlines. She had a heart connection to the faces and places in these photos.

Allison huffed out a breath, admitting to herself that she was stalling. She could fix a cup of jasmine tea. The light floral scent always soothed her. She slipped a mug in the microwave, missing the custom faucet in her old apartment. It dispensed boiling water— no waiting on a microwave or a teakettle to boil. Seth and Daniel installed it for her one Saturday; Seth read the instructions and Daniel did the labor. For such opposites, they were a good team . . .

Ding!

She grabbed her mug, immersed a tea bag in the hot water, and dumped in two packets of Splenda. Then she wandered back out to the living room.

Time to tackle the albums.

She sliced open the top of both boxes with a sharp knife, then cradled the knife in her hand. She rubbed her finger along the sharp blade. With an abrupt shake of her head, she walked back to the kitchen and replaced the knife in the appropriate drawer.

She hadn't been tempted since right before Christmas. One day at a time; she wouldn't slip up again. So far, so good.

Allison ran her fingertips over her wrist and then pulled her sleeve down over the faded marks on her skin. Some mistakes couldn't be undone.

"Am I interrupting anything, honey?" Her aunt rapped a quick staccato on the doorframe as she stood on the bottom step leading into the apartment.

"No, just unpacking the last few boxes. Come on down."

"I haven't seen much of you the past few days, what with working those extra shifts at the hospital." Aunt Nita settled on the couch and pulled a box over to her. "Are you settling in okay?"

"No complaints. Pacha and Kuzko are quiet, except for those 'nerk' noises. And their staring is a bit disconcerting." Allison began lifting photo albums out of the box.

"Can I help?"

"How about if I hand you these in the order I want them to go on the shelves?"

"Sounds good." Her aunt dug a pair of pink polka-dotted readers out of the pocket of her jean shirt and positioned them on the bridge of her nose. "What are they?"

"Photo albums—mostly from high school and college days."

Her aunt flipped open the first album and scanned the pages. "When was this?"

Allison settled on the couch next to her. "High school. Probably sophomore year." She ignored the fact that in too many of the photos, she wore long-sleeve T-shirts while the other girls wore slinky camisoles or sleeveless tops.

Couldn't be helped.

"Oh, there's Meghan and her dye job gone wrong! That girl was so not meant to be a blond bombshell!" She could almost hear Meghan's shrieks when she saw her first attempt at platinum hair. "Our mothers grounded us for a week when they found out what we'd done. And then Meghan's mom made her pay to go to a salon and fix the whole fiasco."

As she turned the pages of the album, she caught glimpses of herself from long, long ago. Seth started showing up in some of the photos, at first in a few shots. Then he moved from being just one of the faces in the youth group to front and center.

Her aunt caught her looking at a series of homecoming photos. "Not all bad memories, are they?"

"No, not all." Allison closed the album, shutting the memories away. "Seth and I started out well. We just finished badly. Not all high school sweethearts get married."

She shelved the book and pulled another album out of the box. A four-by-six print slipped from between the pages and landed at Aunt Nita's feet, facedown. Her aunt reached over and picked it up, turning the snapshot back over. "You kept this?"

"Kept what?"

"This picture of your dad."

Allison continued to place albums on the shelves. She checked the date on the spine of each to make sure they were placed in chronological order.

"Are you taking the Fifth?"

"I forgot I even had that photo of him." She wiped her hands on her jeans and stood up. "Do you want a cup of tea?"

"When was this taken? You look like you were about—"

"I was seven. It's the last photo I had taken with Dad before . . . before . . ."

"Why don't you put it in a frame or something?"

"Why would I want to do that?" Allison walked over to the kitchenette and took a mug out of her cabinet. "Tea?"

"No, thanks." Her aunt sighed, taking off her glasses. "You don't miss him?"

"No. Why would I?"

"You don't ever wonder—"

"No. I don't." Allison turned around, bracing her hands against the counter. "Aunt Nita, I love you. We've always had a great relationship. But one of the reasons we've always had a great relationship is because we don't talk about my dad."

"He's my brother too."

"I know that. If my being here is going to make it too hard for you, then maybe this wasn't a good idea."

Her aunt crossed to where Allison stood and pulled her into an embrace. "I wanted you here. Having you here is like having a piece of Randy back in my life."

Allison found she couldn't lean into her aunt's embrace. Not this time. "Look, why don't you take the photo? I don't want it. I honestly don't think about him anymore."

"You could put it back in the album. Forget I found it."

"It's okay. The photo means something to you. It means nothing to me. Go ahead and take it."

Ducking her head, her aunt forced her to make eye contact. "Are you sure?"

"Would I lie to you?"

"I hope not. If you did, I'd sic the llamas on you!"

"If that threat doesn't keep me honest, I don't know what will."

CHAPTER 16

"Mrs. Denman, this is Seth Rayner." Seth snugged the Bluetooth into position as he held on to a bag of takeout and shoved open the front door with his other hand.

"Hello, Seth."

He heard hesitation in Allison's mother's voice. Not good.

"How are you? Did you have a good Christmas?"

"We're all fine."

Definitely reserved. She didn't even bother to ask how he was. She probably already knew he was frustrated. Might as well drop the niceties and get to the point.

"When I tried to call Allison earlier, I got a recording that said she changed her cell phone number."

"Yes. Yes, she did."

Little help here, please. You're going to be my mother-in-law, remember? Seth tossed the bag of chicken on the kitchen counter and opened a cabinet to get a dinner plate. He hated takeout—all the plasticware and paper napkins.

"Would you mind giving me her new number, please?"

Silence. Then an awkward moment as Mrs. Denman cleared her throat.

"Mrs. Denman?"

"I'm sorry, Seth, but Allison asked me . . . asked us not to give you her new number."

Seth paused, his hand wrapped around a fork and knife. "Excuse me?"

"She mentioned things were, um, tense between you and said she didn't want you contacting her." Seth heard voices in the background. "Allison said she'd get in touch with you when—if—she thought it was a good idea."

"I see." Seth placed the silverware back in the drawer. "You know where Allison is?"

"Yes."

"Is she still in town?"

"I-I really can't say . . ."

Seth slammed the kitchen drawer shut. He'd asked a simple yes-or-no question. A muffled voice in the background interrupted the conversation, and then Allison's stepfather was on the phone.

"Seth, Will Denman here."

"Good evening, sir."

"I understand you're looking for Allison. There's no easy way to put this. She doesn't want to talk to you. She told us not to give you her phone number or to tell you where she's living now."

"I see."

"I'm not sure you do." It sounded like Denman was pacing the room. "I'm sorry about how things ended between you and Allison. But that doesn't give you the right to get physical with my daughter. Do I make myself clear?"

Seth closed his eyes, searching for a way to make amends. "Look, Mr. Denman, Allison and I had a bit of a disagreement before Christmas. I assure you that I didn't hurt—"

"The only thing you can say at this time is 'Yes, sir.'"

Seth gritted his teeth. "Yes, sir."

"That may have been hard for you to say just now. But believe me, it would have been a whole lot harder if I'd come over there and dealt with you like I wanted to after Hadleigh told me what you did—and after I talked to Allison. Do I make myself clear?"

"Yes."

"All right, then. This conversation is over. Good night, Seth."

"Good night."

He stared at his phone for a few moments. Mr. and Mrs. Denman used to think he was the perfect man for their daughter. Now Allison's stepfather was ready to take him down for mishandling a conversation.

Seth yanked open the paper bag containing his dinner and pulled out the plastic utensils sealed in a flimsy plastic bag with mini-packets of salt and pepper. He hated teeny-tiny convenience packets of seasonings, preferring his pepper out of a mill.

"How dare she make me out to be an abusive fiancé? She was the one who left. Not me." He grabbed the utensils packet with both hands and snapped it in half before tossing it on the counter.

He forced himself to take a deep breath. He needed to get control. This wasn't his problem. It was Allison's. She was overreacting. He'd merely tried to talk to her and make her understand he still loved her, even though she'd hurt him. Embarrassed him.

He picked up the pieces of plastic, tossing them in the trash. He was a calm, rational kind of guy. He pulled out the chicken dinner. So he wasn't crazy about eating takeout. He knew how to make the best of a bad situation. That's how he got ahead in life. So he didn't know where Allison was right now. He'd take his time and find out. By the time he found her, she'd realize how much she missed him.

Eventually, Allison would wish she were here, with him.

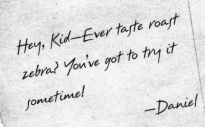

Hey, Kid—Ever taste roast zebra? You've got to try it sometime!

—Daniel

CHAPTER 17

*A*llison ran her fingers through her hair again. The new cut was fun—and *short*. What had she been thinking? In an off-with-the-old-and-on-with-the-new moment, she'd let herself be separated from *ten inches* of her hair. The burnished gold highlights were yet another unplanned change. At least the stylist loved how Allison looked.

"The cut accents your eyes and your cheekbones." The woman had circled Allison, trimming first one side of her hair and then the other. Short. Short. Shorter. Allison's severed ten-inch ponytail was tucked in a plastic bag inside her purse. She'd mail it to Locks of Love, a nonprofit that made wigs for children suffering from hair loss, most because of a medical condition called alopecia areata, which had no known cause or cure.

As Aunt Nita said, what's done is done—and for a good cause. She needed to take a photo and e-mail it to Meghan and get her response. As a cool wind nipped at her newly exposed neck, Allison buttoned her coat and pulled up the collar, glancing at the gray sky. More snow was on the way.

Time to show Aunt Nita and Bisquick and—why not?—the llamas her new look.

Instead of heading home, Allison walked toward the Work in Progress bookstore just down the street. She'd struck up an easygoing friendship with Scoti, the owner. Maybe Susan May Warren's latest novel was in stock. She could grab a cup of tea and read for a while.

Customers crowded the shop. In the back corner, a teen salesgirl recounted the travails of *The Gingerbread Girl* to a bunch of enthralled preschoolers, their faces tilted upward to see the colorful photos on the pages. A book club surrounded one of the café tables, sipping lattes and discussing *The Vanishing Sculptor.* Hadleigh loved that book.

Allison perused the stationery section, looking for a new journal. Only a few blank pages remained in her current one. A watercolor sketch of a sunrise covered one book. She tucked it under her arm and wandered over to the fiction section.

"So many books, so little time—and an even smaller budget," Allison murmured to herself, trying to decide between three different novels. Maybe she should indulge in a cup of tea while she glanced through each one.

Allison moved toward the small coffee and tea bar situated near the front of the bookstore. Scoti had made a wise move when she bought the store from the original owner. Not only had she updated the décor and improved the inventory, but she thought of ways to attract more business.

"Hey, Scoti! Can I have a large—I mean a venti hot tea? Sorry, I never get those fancy sizes right."

"Allison! I can't believe that's you." Scoti shook her head in amazement as she grabbed a white ceramic mug decorated with the letters WIP. "What did you do to your hair?"

"It's tricky tending llamas with long hair. They nibble." Allison touched the edges skimming her jawline. "So, I decided I wanted a change, and I let my aunt's stylist talk me into a drastic one. I can't decide if I like it or not, but it's done. Enough about my hair. Can you order a book for me?" While Scoti wrote down the title, Allison selected a foil-wrapped bag of mint tea and then settled in one of the padded chairs over in a corner.

Blowing on the steaming liquid to help it cool, she picked up the first novel and studied the front cover. The image was washed out. She would have selected something more compelling to attract readers' attention as they scanned the shelves.

Occupational hazard.

She opened the book and read the first page. A gust of cold air blew into the shop as new customers walked in. Allison glanced up and choked on a minty sip of tea when she saw Daniel stride up to the coffee counter with a slender blonde.

Oh. My. Gosh.

She hunched down in the chair, positioning the book so that it covered her face. What was Daniel doing in Estes Park? What was Daniel doing in Estes Park with that blonde? Even with the light instrumental music playing in the background, she heard the deep rumble of his voice when he laughed at something the woman said. Peeking over the edge of the book, she saw The Blonde brush some errant snowflakes out of Daniel's curly brown hair.

Allison longed for another sip of tea to soothe her dry throat but forced herself to stay still. She'd sit there until they left. *Please, please, God, let them order their drinks to go.*

Lowering the book an inch, she watched Daniel pay Scoti and place his hand at the curve of The Blonde's back as he led her to a table by the windows. Dark skinny jeans tucked into creamy white leather boots clung to the woman's petite frame. A belted white coat accentuated her tiny waist. Allison watched The Blonde flirt with Daniel, pulling her seat closer to his.

Between her and the door—freedom—sat Daniel and the overly friendly blonde.

Trapped. Just her luck.

Here she sat. A novel stuck in front of her face. Holding a cup of tea she didn't dare drink. Slumped in a position guaranteed to give her a backache.

Meanwhile, Daniel and The Blonde chatted. The Blonde took every opportunity to lean close and touch Daniel. A hand on his arm. Laugh. A touch of his hand. Laugh.

Allison wanted to throw down the book, march over to Daniel and The Blonde, and dump the contents of her mug over Daniel's head. Or maybe The Blonde's head. It didn't matter. She'd feel better either way.

The Blonde looked out of place in Estes Park, and Allison didn't think that just because she insisted on sitting so close to Daniel, she was almost in his lap. Her jeans were so new Allison expected to see the tags dangling off of them. The heels on her designer boots were ridiculously high. Perfect for hiking around in Rocky Mountain National Park—*right*. Her coat hugged her slender frame but probably didn't offer much warmth. Maybe that was why she looked like she wanted to cuddle with Daniel— to avoid hypothermia.

Allison chewed her bottom lip. How many nights had she fallen asleep replaying Daniel's kiss in her mind? How many prayers had she prayed about her feelings for him? No more. He had told her that she wasn't the last woman he'd kiss. Why hadn't she believed him?

Allison wasn't sticking around another minute to watch The Blonde—obviously the next woman he planned on kissing—fall all over him.

With the stealthy moves of a commando, Allison leaned forward and set the mug on the table. *Put down the book.* She could always come back and buy it later. Pulling up her collar, she stood and walked toward the door, her face turned away from Daniel and his blonde.

"Hey, Allison," Scoti called from behind the coffee counter. "I had one of the sales clerks check on that book you ordered. It will be in early next week."

Busted.

"Th-thanks, Scoti."

Her gaze skittered over to where Daniel sat. Sure enough, he stared at her, ignoring the babbling blonde. Stiffening her back, Allison stuffed her hands in her pockets and walked out of the shop.

Allison Denman. In Estes Park.

Alli. In Estes Park. That unraveled the mystery of Seth's frustrated "No, I haven't seen Allison in a while" during their last phone call.

"Excuse me for a minute, Madison. I just saw someone I know." Daniel bolted from the table, interrupting the woman across from him in mid-stream of consciousness. Did Madison even listen to herself talk? In less than five minutes, she'd verbally meandered from the price of skis to the newest chick flick to her top five favorite restaurants in Denver.

Daniel spotted Alli half a block away, unlocking her car. He sprinted up the street, calling her name. Alli looked toward him, then yanked open the door.

Oh no she didn't.

He increased his speed, coming alongside her Subaru sedan just as she slammed the door shut. He leaned on the hood, resting his forehead on his arms, trying to catch his breath. He half expected Alli to pull away, leaving him sprawled in the street.

A few seconds later, Alli's window rolled down. "Are you going to move so I can leave?"

"Nice to see you too, Kid." Daniel stepped back far enough so he could bend down and see Alli sitting in her car. "If I don't move, are you going to try and run me over like last time?"

"Like last time?" Alli turned to look at him, her hair falling away from her face. "What are you talking about?"

Daniel forced his attention away from how a stray lock of Alli's hair touched the corner of her mouth. Why had she cut her hair? Seth always liked it long. "The day outside your apartment? When you promised to talk to my brother *but you didn't.*"

"You may be older than me, Daniel Rayner, but you are not my boss. I don't have to do things just because you tell me to."

"True. But I thought you were the kind of girl who kept her word."

"And I thought you were the kind of guy who didn't send his best friend on a blind date with his brother's ex-fiancée."

"Still upset about that, Alli?" Daniel couldn't help but see the fire smoldering in her eyes, at odds with her arctic tone. "Poor Jackson may never go on a date again, thanks to that experience."

"Let that be a lesson to him. And to you." She waved her hand as if to shoo Daniel away. "Now move, so I can get home."

"All the way back to the Springs this late in the day?"

"I'm living in Estes Park now."

"Really?"

"Yes, with my aunt Nita. She needed help with her llamas—"

"Her what?"

"Llamas. You know, Daniel, they're South American pack animals."

"I know what llamas are, Alli, I just don't know why your aunt would have any here."

"She rescues llamas—rehabilitates them."

And he thought the conversation with Madison was odd. "So, where does your aunt live? I'd love to meet the llamas sometime."

"We're on the outside of town. She's got property so Kuzko and Pacha can run around."

Kuzko and Pacha? He definitely needed some guy time—with little to no talking. "Seth mentioned your cell number is disconnected. Why don't you give me your new number and I'll call you? Arrange a time to come visit."

"Umm, that might not be a good idea."

"Me visiting?"

"Me giving you my number."

"Come on, Kid, I promise not to call after nine P.M. or make crank phone calls."

"Promise not to tell Seth I'm here, and you've got yourself a deal."

"Secrecy again, Alli?" Daniel placed his hands on the car door. "Déjà vu all over again."

"Cute, Rayner. Your brother is one of the reasons I left. He's having a hard time taking no as my final answer."

"Haven't you heard that absence makes the heart grow fonder?"

"Look, Daniel, I don't need—"

The staccato clicking of heels on the sidewalk should have warned Daniel of the approaching onslaught of perfumed petulance. But it wasn't until Madison interrupted Alli's tirade that he remembered he'd abandoned her in the bookstore.

"Daniel, I've been waiting and waiting and waiting for you to come back. What do you expect me to do? Read a book or something?"

He closed his eyes, his mouth twisting in frustration.

"Want to introduce me to your friend, Daniel?" Alli's voice hinted at repressed laughter.

"Allison Denman, this is Madison Reynolds."

Madison looped her arm through Daniel's. "My parents are opening a new bed-and-breakfast outside of town. Daniel's working with several of the B-and-Bs—ours included—helping us plan out a series of coordinated outdoor activities: snowmobile trails, sleigh rides, that sort of thing. Now I'm showing him around town."

"That's great. I won't keep you." Alli started her car and tapped the accelerator so the engine revved.

"Alli, I didn't get—"

"You don't want to keep Madison standing in the cold, Daniel. I'll see you around."

Daniel followed Madison to the shop, glancing over his shoulder to watch as Alli's car disappeared up the street. She'd see him around.

Yeah, she sure would.

Hey, Kid—One day you need to feed the pigeons in San Marcos Square! I'll spring for the birdseed.

—Daniel

CHAPTER 18

"**G**ot your text, Hadleigh." Allison cradled her cell phone underneath her chin as she finished loading the dishwasher and shut the door. "What's going on?"

"Hey! Thanks for calling me back!"

"No problem. I've missed you." Allison tucked her hair behind her ear. When would she get used to how short it was? "What color is your hair this week?"

"Mom says the red highlights are it for now."

Allison enjoyed the sound of her sister's bubbly laughter. "So, whatcha need?"

"Well, I've got a three-day weekend coming up in a few days, and I wondered if you'd like company."

"Mom and Dad say it's okay for you to drive up?"

There was the slightest pause before Hadleigh answered. "Ummm, no. Evan said he'd drive me."

Uh-huh.

"And was Evan planning on staying too, Leigh?"

"We-ell . . . only if you invited him."

Allison took a deep breath and counted to ten—then added an extra five for good measure.

"You still there?"

"Yes. I was counting."

"Counting? Counting what? Llamas?"

"No, not llamas. Never mind." She paced her tiny apartment, Bisquick monitoring her from his perch on the back of the couch. "Okay, Leigh, here are the rules. Number one: If Evan comes, he sleeps upstairs in Aunt Nita's part of the house, got it?"

"Got it."

"Number two: You guys don't spend any time in the house alone."

"Got it."

"Number three: You don't do anything stupid while you're here. I don't want the 'How could you let this happen?' phone call from Mom."

"Got it."

Allison dug through the cabinet where she kept her emergency stash of mini Milky Ways. She still had some left, didn't she?

"Anything else?"

"I think the 'Don't be stupid' rule covers just about everything."

"Yep."

"Anything you guys want to do while you're here?" She leaned against the kitchen counter and unwrapped two mini Milky Ways, inhaling the rich scent of chocolate.

"Evan wants to visit The Stanley Hotel. He loves that movie with Jack Nicholson. I want to window-shop. And we might try to go snowshoeing."

"When will you be here?"

"We'll come up after school on Friday and head back home on Monday. Does that work for you?"

"I'll check with Aunt Nita, but I think it'll be fine. Oh, and one other thing—I'm sure you'll want to meet Pacha and Kuzko. We'll have the new guy here by then too."

"Sweet. You're the best!"

"Yeah, yeah." Time for another candy bar. Maybe two. "Tell Evan to drive safe."

Great, now she sounded like her mom.

She left her phone on the counter and headed outdoors. Kuzko and Pacha stood at the split rail fence, looking her way. She paused. Considered her options. Turned and headed back inside.

Several minutes later, she snuggled Bisquick in her arms and advanced toward the two llamas. Would she regret this meet and greet?

Kuzko and Pacha maintained their customary stance at the fence line, two tall, furry, four-footed sentries. Bisquick burrowed farther back into the blanket she had wrapped him in.

"It's all good, buddy. Llamas like cats. Now let's just see if you like llamas."

She held her cat firmly, ignoring the angry noises sounding in his throat. Kuzko craned his neck over the fence, and Allison leaned forward so that she and the llama were nose to nose. After a few short weeks, Allison already loved his silly llama face, his white ears tipped with black and a white furry nose overshadowing crooked top teeth and bottom teeth that jutted out. Kuzko blew out, a typical llama greeting. One day she'd get used to the green-grassy smell of llama breath. Or not.

Pacha, all white from ears to nose, sidled over, and Kuzko gave him a warning nudge as if to say "No closer." Pacha turned his face away.

Allison repositioned Bisquick so he could see the tall, long-necked llamas. Pacha and Kuzko stared. The cat stared back. Inch by inch, Kuzko leaned his black-and-white furry face down toward the cat. A warning rumbled in Bisquick's throat. Kuzko paused, his brown eyes with horizontal pupils gazing into Bisquick's yellow-green ones.

Allison took shallow breaths. Maybe this wasn't such a good idea. Maybe Bisquick wasn't a llama-friendly feline. She should go back inside.

But then Bisquick moved out from beneath the blanket. Kuzko remained still as the cat closed the space between them. Within seconds, feline and pack animal were nose to nose. Kuzko huffed a small breath. Bisquick pulled back, shaking his head, but he didn't break eye contact. Then he resumed sniffing the llama.

Allison stroked her cat's head. "Good boy, Bisquick. Good boy. Isn't Kuzko a nice llama? Yeah, he is."

She didn't know how long she stood murmuring niceties to the two beasts before she realized someone was watching her llama-cat antics. She looked to her left. Daniel, all silent-but-grinning six feet of him, waved a greeting. Great, just great. How did he get here?

"Okay, boys, that's enough getting to know you for today." She scratched the soft matted fur along Kuzko's neck. "You can meet Bisquick next time, Pacha."

She turned and headed back to the house, Daniel falling into step beside her.

"Hi to you too." Daniel moved back as she opened the door leading to her apartment. "Thanks, I'd love to come in."

The thought of closing the door in Daniel's scruffy, much-too-handsome face flitted across Allison's mind, but she resisted the temptation. "Make yourself at home."

"Your aunt around?"

"No, she had a shift at the hospital." Allison released Bisquick, who jumped from her arms and stalked down the hallway.

"So Bisquick is a llama lover."

"That was their first meeting. It went pretty well." She'd resisted slamming the door in his face. Now she had to resist the overall temptation of Daniel standing in her living room, appealing as ever.

She stood in the center of the room and watched Daniel. He tucked his hands into the pockets of his brown leather bomber jacket and looked back at her. They could have been Kuzko and Pacha for all the staring going on.

Daniel cleared his throat. "So."

"So."

"How ya been, Kid?"

"Fine. How'd you find me?"

He chuckled, a warm, mellow sound, and moved over to the

couch, sitting and stretching out his legs. "Your friend at the bookstore—Scoti?—told me where you lived."

She'd have to thank Scoti the next time she stopped in at Work in Progress. And tell her to consider Allison's address unlisted.

Daniel's gaze swept the apartment. "You look like you're all unpacked."

"I was unpacked three days after I moved in."

"Always were the organized one."

"Can I do something for you, Daniel?" Allison walked over to the kitchen and opened the refrigerator.

"Water would be great, thank you."

Allison pressed her lips together. She hadn't been offering Daniel refreshments; she'd been asking him why he was there. But she pulled out two bottles of water and handed one to Daniel. She settled on the floor, leaning against the overstuffed chair facing the couch.

Daniel tipped the bottle back, drank, and then placed it on the coffee table. "The question is, can I do something for you?" He pulled a folded legal-size envelope out of his pocket and tapped it against his knee.

Allison fiddled with the label wrapped around the water bottle, peeling it away from the container.

"Aren't you going to ask me what's in the envelope?"

"You're not Ed McMahon, so I know I haven't won a million dollars."

"True, true. But what's inside could be worth some money to you."

"Oh, really?"

"Yep. It's a job offer."

"Who's offering me a job?"

"I am." Daniel held the envelope out to her.

"Y-you?"

"Technically, I'm the liaison. One of the B-and-Bs I'm working for needs some graphic design work done, and I recommended you. The details are inside the envelope, including a contract."

"Why would you recommend me?" And was she crazy enough to take a job that required being near Daniel Rayner?

"The Reynoldses wanted the best. I told them they wouldn't find a better freelance graphic designer than you."

Allison stared at the envelope, twisting a piece of her hair around her forefinger. "I don't understand, Daniel. Why would you help me out?"

Daniel expelled a sigh mixed with a growl of frustration. "Alli, you're perfect for the job. And suggesting you is my way of saying I'm sorry for being a jerk."

Allison's gaze locked with Daniel's, the repentant look in his divergent eyes causing her to look away. Was he sorry for kissing her? Or sorry he'd fixed her up on a covert blind date with his best friend? Or both?

"Consider the job a peace offering." He waved the envelope like a white flag. "Can we declare a truce?"

Allison knew it was her turn to say something, but her brain felt about as intelligent as Bisquick's leftover dried-out cat food.

"I guess it's only fair to warn you that we'll be working together. The owners want me to take you out on some of the snowmobile trails, snowshoeing, maybe a sleigh ride—get the feel of what outdoor activities the B-and-B association plans to offer." Allison looked back at Daniel as he stood and crossed to where she sat. "Bring your camera along. I told them you're a good photographer too."

"I don't know what to say, Daniel." Maybe if he went back across the room, gave her a little breathing space, she'd be able to think clearly.

He knelt in front of her, holding out the envelope. "Take the job. Let's declare a truce. Forgive me, Alli. Please?"

Daniel's intense tone tugged at Allison's heart. But the thought of forgiving him scared her. Better to stay mad. To push Daniel away, to force herself to think of how he infuriated her instead of how he intrigued her.

"Alli?" Daniel rested one hand on her shoulder.

"J-just processing, Daniel." Allison tried to ignore the warmth of his hand radiating through the material of her shirt. "I-I appreciate you recommending me for the job. Truce."

"A truce it is, Alli."

Allison reached for the envelope and closed her eyes. Held her breath so she wouldn't inhale Daniel's clean, outdoorsy scent. She hoped this wasn't another mistake.

"And Alli?"

"Yeah?" Alli looked into Daniel's eyes, the sincerity of his gaze tugging at her heart.

"I realize you didn't say you forgive me yet. I know that takes time." He stood and backed toward the door. "I hope declaring a truce moves us in the right direction."

He needed to be thankful for what he got. A truce with Alli was a start.

Daniel stuffed his sweaty workout clothes into his threadbare gym bag, zipped it shut, and slung it over his shoulder.

It wasn't as if he wanted anything more than Alli's forgiveness and friendship. He'd worked long and hard to obliterate the memory of kissing Alli from his mind, and he'd succeeded. Most of the time. Just because there was no diamond ring on Alli's finger didn't mean she was available to him.

Walking out to his F-150 pickup, Daniel pulled a wool cap over his still-damp hair. If he were more of a praying man, he'd be talking to God about all this. But he and God hadn't talked much since he graduated from high school. They had a casual I-won't-bother-you-if-you-don't-bother-me relationship.

Daniel's relationship with God mirrored his relationship with his father. He didn't bother his dad, and his dad didn't interfere with his life. And why would he? His dad didn't respect the life Daniel had chosen. And that was fine with Daniel. He'd given up any pretense of gaining his father's respect. That hope was shot all to pieces the night during his senior year in high school when he came in from work and overheard his parents talking in the kitchen.

Even all these years later, remembering his father's words caused his heart to pound faster. Daniel had dumped his hockey gear in the garage and moved into the small airlock leading into the kitchen. As he opened the door, he heard his father pacing the tile floor. Daniel could never figure out why he paused with the door only partway opened.

"Now, Seth—there's a boy a man can be proud of. Seth's smart. Motivated. Not like Daniel." His father opened a cabinet. Rummaged around. Probably looking for the fixings for his regular nightcap. "Daniel cares more about camping and hiking than getting ahead in this world."

Daniel held his breath, willing himself to hold the door steady, to not give away his presence.

"He's only in high school, Darrin."

His father barreled over his mother's defense. "He graduates in three months. *Three months.* And where's he going to school? Did he choose any of the schools I suggested? No. He picked some college up north because he could ski! What a waste of his time and my money." Daniel watched his father cross his line of vision, tossing back a drink. "You wait until Seth graduates. I've already talked to a friend who's connected with my alma mater. We'll have it settled before Seth even gets to high school."

Daniel waited for his mother to say something. Anything. The silence in the kitchen seeped into the airlock, stifling him. He slid the door shut and took cautious steps backward. He sat in his car for a good hour and a half. When he finally went inside, his father was hidden away in the den, and the only thing his mother asked was why he was so late.

He *wasted* his dad's money for a semester. Then he paid his tuition and room and board, thanks to a combination of scholarships and part-time jobs. He worked at ski lodges. Guided white-water-rafting trips. Led mountain-biking tours.

He made it home for holidays—some of them. He ignored the hurt look in his mother's eyes. When he came home for Seth's wedding, he waited once again for her to defend him from his father's most recent accusation.

"You don't have a real job, Daniel." His father dismissed his achievements with a wave of his hand. "You've been on vacation since you earned your degree—designing ski resorts is just an excuse for you to travel, avoid any real responsibility."

Degrees, *plural*. His back-to-back degrees—one in civil engineering, another in resort management—never impressed his father.

Daniel wanted to shove his checkbook in his father's face and show him the balance to prove just how real his consulting business was—how successful he was. So what if he preferred to live in a small apartment and dress like a guy who spent most of his time hiking? Daniel didn't throw his wealth around like his dad.

Sure, he'd taken a risk starting his own consulting business, but he'd figured it was now or never. There was no talking to his dad. If a project wasn't built by Rayner Construction, it didn't matter. Why bother? He was thirty-one years old. He didn't need his dad's approval.

Opening the door of his truck, Daniel tossed his gym bag on the seat and climbed in. Let it go. After all these years, why was he even thinking about this? It was ancient, unchangeable history.

Daniel steered the truck toward the B-and-B, ready to call it a night. He'd gotten what he wanted: independence. The freedom to live with no responsibility to his father. And Seth—the favored son—well, he had the life he wanted as second in command at Rayner Construction.

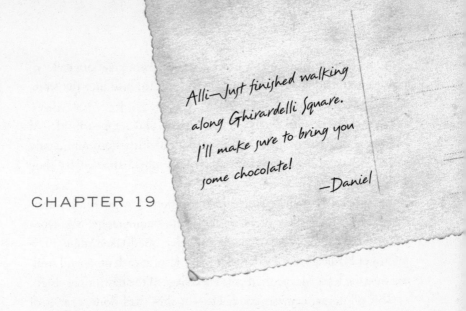

Alli—Just finished walking along Ghirardelli Square. I'll make sure to bring you some chocolate!

—Daniel

CHAPTER 19

*A*llison was done.

She'd followed Hadleigh and Evan up and down the shops lining the main street of Estes Park as if they were a couple of jeans-clad pied pipers. Twice. Stopped in at Work in Progress and introduced Scoti to her little sister and her now-official boyfriend. Evan maintained his best behavior, spending some of his hard-earned money and treating them to lunch at Claire's. He also bought matching gray Estes Park hoodies for him and Hadleigh. The couple wore them as they walked hand in hand, their coats stuffed in a bag.

Allison couldn't remember ever acting that way with Seth, but then he wasn't into being a coordinated couple, at least as far as clothes went. Seth took it for granted that Allison, who didn't have much of an opinion at seventeen, enjoyed the same movies, the same books, the same food as he did. And Allison never bothered to correct him.

"All right, guys. I'm beat." Allison grabbed her sister's hand and pulled her to a stop, thankful they'd driven separate cars. "I'm going to head back to Aunt Nita's and help get the homemade pizzas ready. You can come back when you're hungry."

"Don't you want to go in here? It looks like a great art gallery." Hadleigh looped her arm through Evan's and led him into the store, acting as if Allison would follow her.

"Last shop for me, Leigh." Allison sighed and stepped inside. At least art galleries intrigued her more than T-shirt shops and candy stores. "I have to help with the llamas, remember? The new bad boy arrives tomorrow."

Her sister and Evan explored shelves of pottery while Allison wandered over to a display of black-and-white photography. She repositioned the camera slung over her shoulder. She'd taken quite a few photos of Hadleigh and Evan making silly faces at each other and smiling into the lens. Maybe she'd create a collage of the day for her sister.

This photographer was good. He—or she—had done a series of outdoor city shots. Chicago. San Francisco. New York. Was that Miami? Allison took her time studying the montage. Why had the artist chosen that angle? That lighting? As she came to the end of the display, she stopped in front of a twenty-by-twenty-four color photograph set off from the others.

"Wow, what a cool picture." Evan's voice sounded behind her. "I'd pay some serious money to own a bike like that one."

"I-it's just a Harley." Allison cleared her throat, forcing herself to sound casual. "You've seen one, you've seen 'em all, ya know?"

After a few seconds, Evan turned away as Hadleigh called to him from across the room. Allison's gaze was riveted on the little girl astride the large blue and black motorcycle. She wore faded cutoff jeans, a white blouse dotted with tiny red flowers. Her bare foot dangled. She leaned forward, her face cupped in her hands, glancing sideways into the camera. The wind blew her long auburn hair across her face, obscuring her smile, her eyes.

Allison would have known the girl anywhere.

It was her.

She took one last look at her six-year-old self. In the corner, she noticed the scrawled initials: R.S.

What was her father's photography doing in an Estes Park gallery?

She turned her back on the photo, searching for her sister, thankful Evan hadn't brought Hadleigh over to view the photograph. She found them looking at a case full of turquoise jewelry. "I'm going to head back now. See you soon."

When she pulled up in front of the house, Allison spotted her aunt out in the pasture with the llamas, erecting the temporary wire fence that would separate llama number three from one and two.

No time like the present to confront her past, right?

She zipped her down vest and slipped on her gloves as she approached her aunt, who opened the gate, latching it closed behind Allison. "I think the boys are waiting for a visit from Bisquick. They've gotten attached to that cat."

"He's been an inside cat all his life, and now he's befriended two llamas. I think visiting them is the highlight of his day."

"Moving here has expanded his social circle." Her aunt walked between the two llamas, scratching their necks. "Evan's a nice guy."

"Hmmm."

"We'll need to make plenty of pizza. I figure he's got a typical nineteen-year-old guy's appetite."

"Hmmm."

"He seems pretty interested in Hadleigh."

"Hmmm."

"Will she borrow your wedding gown when they get married?"

"Hmm—get married?" Allison stared at her aunt. "What are you talking about?"

Kuzko and Pacha reacted to the sharpness in Allison's voice, jerking their heads up and stepping away from Aunt Nita, who settled them with a few soft words.

"Thought that would get your attention." Her aunt leaned on the long-handled sledgehammer. "What's on your mind?"

"We stopped in an art gallery today."

"And?"

"There was a series of black-and-white photographs—different cities."

"And?"

"The last photograph was of—"

"You."

Allison met her aunt's sharp blue eyes. "You knew?"

"Yes."

"That's all you're going to say?"

"What else do you want me to say?" Her aunt tried to move the post, nodding when it stood firm.

"Why didn't you tell me that my father's photographs are on display in Estes Park?"

"You may recall posting a no-talking sign on the topic of your father, sweetie."

"Really, Aunt Nita?"

"Yes, *really*. How was I supposed to know there were exclusions to your rule?"

Before Allison could tell her aunt exactly what she thought of her evasiveness, Pacha shoved past and began pacing the fence line. Kuzko stood at alert, his black-and-white ears lying flat against his head as he emitted the llama-on-alert "nerk" noises.

"What's going on?" Allison watched the two llamas, trying to figure out what had set them off.

"They've either seen something—maybe a raccoon—or they've heard something."

A few seconds later, Daniel's old hunter-green truck pulled up alongside the house. What was he doing here? Was there someone with him? And what was jumping around in the truck bed?

The doors opened on both sides of the cab. As Daniel exited from the driver's side, another man exited from the passenger side. Before she could say anything, Pacha paced past her, knocking her aside, eyes glued on the truck. Then the llama let out an ear-piercing screech, body shaking. Allison recognized a large brown Lab watching the two men walking toward them. When the dog started barking, both llamas responded with frenzied cries of alarm.

"Tell Rayner to back his truck up so the boys can't see or smell that dog." Aunt Nita attempted to herd the llamas so they no longer faced the truck.

Giving Kuzko and Pacha a wide berth, Allison exited the pen and ran toward Daniel.

"Hey, Alli—"

"That dog is upsetting the llamas."

"Who, Bailey?" The other man motioned to the barking dog leaning over the side of the truck. "He's a big noisy ball of fur."

"I'm not going to argue with you, whoever you are. But your ninety pounds of noise is freaking my llamas."

"Got it covered." Daniel saluted. "I'll back the truck down the road. Ty, this is Alli. Alli, Ty."

"Good to meet you, Alli." Ty waited with Alli, who watched Daniel sprint to his truck. "I understand we'll be working together."

"We will?"

"I work at the B-and-B. Handle the books." Ty shook hands with Alli and offered her a friendly goateed grin. "Daniel mentioned you're doing some work for them too."

"Some short-term freelance, that's all."

"You're a graphic designer, right? To hear Daniel tell it, there's nobody better than you."

"I like what I do."

"Me too. Some people hate accounting, but I'm all about cash flow, budgets, and financial projections."

What with Ty's goatee and his black hair pulled back in a short ponytail, Alli thought he looked more like a modern-day pirate who plundered sailing ships, not someone who balanced books. All he needed was an eye patch and to trade his dog in for a parrot.

By the time Hadleigh and Evan arrived home an hour later, Aunt Nita had accepted the men's offer to help secure the temporary fence, then invited them to dinner. This despite Allison's frantic charades attempts to tell her aunt not to include Daniel in the pizza-fest. Allison was either a poor communicator or her aunt blatantly ignored her hand signals and grimaces.

Ty announced that he was a pro at making pizza dough, while Daniel commandeered the cutting board and knife and produced a pungent mountain of sliced onions, green and red peppers, and mushrooms. Allison shredded bricks of mozzarella, Parmesan, and cheddar cheese. After pacing inside the house, eager to get outside again and bark at the llamas, Bailey snoozed by the fireplace.

"What can I do?" Hadleigh tossed her coat onto Aunt Nita's couch.

"Set the table." Aunt Nita motioned to the stack of paper plates and plastic cups on the counter.

"Can I use your computer, Allison?" Evan stood at the top of the stairs leading to Allison's apartment. "I want to check some sports scores and my e-mail."

"Sure thing. The laptop's all powered up. Use the PC—I use the Mac for my graphics work. And don't let Bisquick upstairs. He's been hiding on the stairs ever since we let Ty's dog in the house."

"Sure thing. I'll be back up in a few."

"The first pizza will be done in twenty minutes."

"Got it."

"Isn't Evan great, Alli?" Hadleigh watched him disappear downstairs and then tossed plates down on the table.

"Sure, Leigh."

"Mom and Will have been great about him coming over."

"Are you guys still studying together?"

"Yeah. His grades have improved too."

"What about your grades?"

Hadleigh wadded up a napkin and tossed it at her. "They're just fine, thanks. And you are not my mom."

"So what are your plans for tomorrow?"

"We thought we'd go snowshoeing in Rocky Mountain National Park."

"Do you want to go to church with me before you head out? Aunt Nita's invited me to her church, and I thought I might try it tomorrow."

"Ummm . . . Evan's not really into church."

Allison looked up from grating cheese. Her sister faced away from her. What, if anything, should she say, especially in a crowded kitchen? "Hadleigh—"

Daniel dropped the knife on the kitchen counter, slapping his hand to his forehead in a melodramatic gesture. "Alli! I can't believe I forgot I had something for you in my truck. Come on outside with me while I get it."

Allison stared at him. Couldn't he just get whatever it was and bring it back?

"It's hot in here, don't ya think? Walk with me." He winked at her, nudging her to move along.

"S-sure. Let me get my coat."

Daniel meandered to the truck, seeming to ignore how cold it was—and also ignoring Allison. She let the silence stretch between them. Daniel stopped a few feet from his truck and looked up. "Aren't those stars amazing?"

She tilted her head back, her hood falling to her shoulders. The night sky looked as if God had tossed handful after handful of glittering jewels against a black satin cloth.

"This is why I like camping outdoors." Daniel spoke in a near-whisper. "Hate to miss a view like this."

"Aren't you afraid of frostbite?"

"I limit my tent-free camping to the summer months." He moved closer, pointing up at the stars. "How many constellations can you name?"

"Competitive stargazing?" Allison turned her head—and realized she was much too close to Daniel Rayner.

He reached over and pulled her hood back up, tucking a strand of her hair behind her ear before he shoved his hand in his pocket. "Why did you cut your hair, Alli?"

"It seemed like a good idea at the time." Being this close to Daniel wasn't. The last time they were this close, things went wrong. Fast. "And I donated my hair to Locks of Love. They make wigs for people who've lost their hair because of cancer or other illnesses."

"So you got a hairstyle change and a good deed all rolled up in one, huh?"

"It's not just a good deed. I had a friend in high school who had alopecia—unexplained hair loss. She wore a wig from Locks of Love."

"Sorry, Alli. I didn't mean to joke about something that's so important to you. I admire what you did, and your hair looks great. I'm just surprised because Seth always liked it long."

The mention of his brother dumped a bucket of verbal ice water on their conversation. "Yeah, well. You had something for me?"

"Right." Daniel stepped away and reached into his truck, retrieving his backpack. He pulled out a small brown bag and held it out to her. It looked empty. What was going on? She reached for it, but Daniel held on. She tugged and he tugged back, refusing to release the bag. What was this, some kind of game she didn't know the rules to?

"What gives, Daniel?"

"Let me offer you a piece of friendly advice."

"About?"

"Hadleigh and Evan. Don't play the parent. Like Hadleigh said, you're not her mom, she already has one. Be her sister. And don't lecture her about church and God."

"Excuse me?"

"Just because Evan's not into church doesn't mean he doesn't believe in God." Finally releasing the bag, Daniel touched her shoulder, moving them back toward the house. "Maybe he had a bad experience in his last church. Maybe he's looking. I'm no theologian, but I do know I feel closest to God when I'm hiking."

Allison slipped the paper bag into her pocket. "But I don't know—"

"That's just it—you *don't* know. Don't assume the worst, Alli. Your sister's a smart girl."

"I wasn't getting ready to lecture Hadleigh."

"Really? It sure sounded that way."

"I don't need you to tell me how to handle my sister."

"Is our truce over so soon?" Daniel placed his hand over hers before she could open the door. "I was hoping for a longer cease-fire."

Alli slipped her hand away. Daniel needed to stop touching her, distracting her. "Believe me, I'm the last one to lecture anyone about God. I'm still trying to reopen the lines of communication with him. But maybe you're right. I'll try to relax and get to know Evan—inside, where it's warm. The truce holds. Point made and duly noted."

Daniel grinned as he opened the door. "That's what I always liked about you, Alli. You're smart and beautiful."

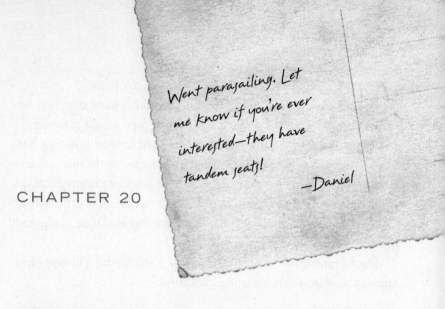

Went parasailing. Let me know if you're ever interested—they have tandem seats!

—Daniel

CHAPTER 20

℧y Monday afternoon Allison wondered how soon she could slip into her pajamas and crawl into bed. First she needed to get some work done and then get her apartment back in order.

Three pairs of long-lashed llama eyes watched Allison as she walked to her apartment. Kuzko and Pacha were less than welcoming to Banzai, preferring to spit and nip rather than play nice when the newest llama with an attitude came near the fence separating them.

She'd just waved goodbye to her sister and Evan. Since Saturday night, she'd focused on avoiding "mom" mode and tried to get to know Evan. When Aunt Nita dug out a well-used Settlers of Catan board game, Allison discovered that Evan and Hadleigh made a good team. The teens beat the other two teams, with her sister handling the cards, reading them aloud to Evan while he plotted strategy.

Allison had decided to stay home on Sunday rather than go to church, but her sister and Evan went snowshoeing. Allison spent the morning making a huge pot of cream of broccoli soup for dinner.

After picking up and starting a load of laundry, Allison settled in front of her computer. Time to catch up on work and e-mail. The bag Daniel gave her two days ago lay beside the keyboard. After she'd slipped it into her pocket, the weekend had been so busy she'd forgotten about it until she wore her jacket again today.

When she tipped the bag over, two postcards slid onto her desk. It had been months since Daniel sent her a postcard. She hadn't received one since Seth announced their engagement.

She picked up one of a stunning sunrise with WISH YOU WERE HERE splashed across it. Allison turned each one over, but there was none of Daniel's familiar scrawl across the back. He'd bought them but never mailed them. Odd.

What to do? What to do? She'd covered her bulletin board with photographs. The original collection of postcards was stashed in her desk drawer. She would toss these. But the sunrise was gorgeous. She mulled over her options and finally tucked the cards underneath the clear plastic desk protector.

There. That would do.

When she accessed her in-box and scanned the list of e-mails, the amount of spam surprised her. Some of the links looked like pornography sites—triple X's and invitations to meet women. She had a high-rated Internet filter. How did this stuff sneak through? Careful not to open any of the e-mails, she deleted them and then checked her filter settings. Everything was the way she'd configured it.

She shook her head and turned her attention to a message from a potential client.

Several hours later, her musical ring tone pulled her attention from the computer screen.

"Hello?"

"Allison?"

She didn't recognize the man's voice. "Yes? May I help you?"

"This is Ty, your Settlers of Catan partner, remember?"

"Hey, Ty." She leaned back in her chair and turned her neck from side to side, trying to ease the tightness that had built up in her shoulders.

"I hope you don't mind me calling. Daniel gave me your number because he thought you could help me with something."

"Sure, I'd be glad to help." She opened a new Word document, preparing to take notes about Ty's project. Why would an accountant need a graphic designer? Business cards, maybe?

"That's what Daniel said." It sounded like Ty shuffled papers and shifted the phone from one ear to the other. "Thanks for making this so easy. Usually, guys have to work up to asking a woman out on a date."

"W-what?" Her hand slipped across the computer keys, leaving a trail of J's and K's on the white page.

"Daniel and I were talking about this wedding coming up next weekend, and I mentioned how I hate to go to weddings alone. He suggested I ask you."

"A w-wedding?"

"Yeah. The son of the guy who built the B-and-B is getting married, and I'm invited. It's no fun going stag to a wedding."

As far as Allison was concerned, weddings were no fun *at all*.

"It's a real casual affair, so don't worry about the what-to-wear part of it."

What to wear was the least of her worries. This conversation had gotten way out of control. She should never answer the phone when she was so deep into work on the computer.

"Oh, one more thing."

Why did Ty's "one more thing" sound ominous? "What?"

"They're doing the reception a bit differently. It's potluck."

"Potluck?" Was this some kind of joke plotted by Daniel and Ty?

"Yeah. I guess it's the new way to do receptions, but hey, I'm no wedding planner. I couldn't figure out what to bring. Afraid I was going to have to go the bachelor's tried-and-true chips-and-dip route."

Allison resisted the urge to bang her head on her keyboard. "Uh-huh."

"But now that you're coming, I figure you can cover this. I'm supposed to bring an appetizer-type dish. I'll let you figure it out."

Enough was enough. Just because she let Ty assume she agreed to be his date didn't mean she'd supply his part of the potluck.

"About that." Allison pressed her fingers to her temples, feeling a headache lurking. "I'll go to the wedding. But since you're the official guest, you can handle the appetizer."

"You won't help me out here?"

"I *am* helping you out. If you don't want to bring chips and dip, order something from a local restaurant or pick something up from a grocery store."

"I guess that'll do." There was silence for a few seconds, and then Ty regained his cheerfulness. "The wedding's on Saturday at two o'clock. I'll pick you up at one, okay?"

"Sure."

"Great. Looking forward to it, Allison."

"Me too."

She hung up the phone, pushing her chair away from the desk. "Sorry, God. I told a major lie just then, because I am *not* looking forward to this wedding." She groaned. "It could be worse. Ty could have e-mailed me the link to the gift registry and asked me to buy the wedding present."

From here on out, Daniel decided he would decline any wedding invitations.

It was for the best.

He may be dancing with Madison, but his eyes followed Alli. She had on the same red dress she'd worn at her rehearsal dinner, this time paired with black leather boots that hugged her long legs. Her new hairstyle allowed him alluring glances of her neck. Did the woman have any idea she was driving him crazy?

The song ended and he walked off the dance floor, steering Madison toward Ty and Alli.

"What say we trade partners this time, buddy?" Even as he made the suggestion to Ty, Daniel thought about stuffing the words back down his throat.

"Sure thing." Ty wrapped an arm around Madison and gave Allison a gentle nudge toward Daniel. "Change partners and dance, right?"

"That's okay, Daniel. You came with Madison—" Alli refused to budge as he clasped her hand and turned toward the dance floor.

Great. She couldn't tolerate a single dance with him. Here he was, fighting his attraction to her, and she didn't want to get near him.

"It's just one dance—probably a fast one." He tried to play it light and easy. But the sound of the band starting a slow romantic song wiped the smile off his face. He eased Alli into his arms, aware that she held herself as rigid as a canoe paddle.

Could the dance be any more awkward?

He concentrated on moving Alli through the couples on the dance floor. Avoided stepping on the bride's train and did a quick two-step around the flower girl, who twirled on the floor, the circlet of flowers crowning her dark curls tipped forward over one of her eyes. Did he dare risk small talk? Alli's posture radiated an I-am-barely-tolerating-you attitude.

"So, are you having a good time?" He looked down at Alli and was surprised by the thunderstorm of anger smoldering in her gray-blue eyes.

"Sure."

"That was a convincing answer."

"Let me put it this way." She leaned away from him and spoke through clenched teeth framed by a pasted-on smile. "I'm attending a wedding. Not my favorite affair these days. With someone I barely know. Who asked me to bring the appetizer that he was supposed to bring. And did I mention Ty the amazing accountant has told me how much money—down to the penny—he's saved his last ten clients? And this lovely occasion is all thanks to you."

Daniel forced his attention away from Alli's mouth, hoping to keep the memory of kissing her at bay. If she knew what he was thinking, she'd slap his face and leave him bruised and alone in the middle of the reception.

"Ty's a nice enough guy. I thought you two would hit it off."

"Who put you in charge of my love life?"

He moved to the outside of the revelers, so the other guests wouldn't overhear Alli's tirade. Okay, so his idea was a bust. He knew it. She knew it. But did she have to ruin a perfectly nice dance? "Truce, remember?"

Allison growled, gripping his arm. "Daniel Rayner, are you going to throw that stupid truce in my face every time you make me angry?"

"If I have to." He tugged her a fraction closer and rested his cheek against her hair. He loved Alli's hair, long or short.

"That's not fair fighting, Daniel." Allison's breath fanned his neck.

"Maybe I don't want to fight with you. Ever thought of that?" He closed his eyes, wondering what perfume Alli wore. Whatever it was, the light citrus scent tantalized him.

Alli's words were spoken into his shoulder. "Then . . . stop . . . making me so mad."

When the band segued into another slow song, Daniel decided he'd slip the lead singer a twenty before he left. He leaned down and whispered in Alli's ear, "I'll work on it. Truce?"

She turned her head and searched his eyes. Nodded.

"Say it."

"What?"

"Truce."

Alli leaned her forehead against his shoulder. "Truce, Daniel."

"Good. And I'm sorry I made you angry." He smiled as Alli rested her cheek against his chest. He tucked their entwined hands up against his heart, resisting the urge to place a kiss on her temple. This was Alli. The Kid. Alli, who'd almost married his brother. Who wanted a nice, safe future.

He'd let himself hold Alli for the rest of the dance and then avoid her—and any further damage—for the rest of the evening.

Sounded like a plan.

CHAPTER 21

*S*eth leaned against his car, scanning the entrance to the high school. According to the district website, classes ended at three o'clock. Which meant teens should come barreling out those doors any minute now. His challenge? To find Hadleigh in the swarm of look-alike high-schoolers.

He couldn't rely on spotting Allison's little sister before she got on a bus or drove off in her car. The minute the school doors swung open and the first wave of bodies hit the stairs, Seth planned on dialing Hadleigh's cell. Until then, he waited.

He couldn't believe he'd been reduced to relying on a teenager for help. One of the men he ran with had suggested talking to a couples counselor. Seth had taken the number; he'd even made the phone call. But after five minutes of answering questions ranging from "Can you explain your problem to me in one sentence?" to "What kind of insurance do you have?" he'd hung up and thrown out the scrap of paper. He'd figure this out himself—but first he needed to find his missing fiancée.

Seth looked up as teens swarmed across the front lawn of the high school. When he dialed Hadleigh's number, she answered on the third ring. The metallic clang of locker doors slamming and kids talking almost drowned out her voice. "Hello?"

"Hadleigh, it's Seth. Seth Rayner."

"Oh. What do you want?"

Not Hadleigh too. She used to joke that she'd marry him if Allison didn't. He needed her on his side. "I was in the neighborhood. Thought I'd offer you a ride home."

"Not buying it, Seth."

In the background, someone yelled, "Call me later, Leigh!"

"What do you mean?" Seth kept his eyes trained on the front of the high school. If Hadleigh came out, he'd intercept her.

"I haven't seen or heard from you since your wedding day. Now you're offering me a ride?"

The girl was too smart. What was he supposed to do, come right out and say he needed her help? Couldn't she play along with him, let him drive her home, work the request into the conversation?

It sounded like Hadleigh was stuffing books and papers into her backpack. "If this is about Allison, you need to know I'm not going to give you her phone number or tell you where she is."

Seth thought of the Starbucks gift card in his coat pocket. So much for subtle negotiation or even bribery. "Come on, Hadleigh, whose side are you on?"

"Nobody's. I'm protecting myself. Dad said if I told you where Allison is, he'd take my car keys and ground me for three months. I've got places to go and people to see, Seth. Can't do it if I'm grounded."

So much for getting any help from Allison's little sister.

"Fine. Forget I asked—because technically, I didn't. But my offer to drive you home still stands."

"Thanks, but I've got my car here."

After ending his unsatisfactory phone conversation with Hadleigh, Seth continued to lean against his car and watch the end-of-the-school-day procession. Groups of teens congregated in the parking lot. Probably making plans for the weekend. When he and Allison dated, they used to meet with other members of the church youth group to discuss upcoming ski trips or lock-ins.

He looked over at the school track. Empty. Before spring tryouts, he used to work out every afternoon, determined to better his time. He had Allison sit in the southeast corner of the bleachers and time him with the stopwatch. Afterward, she'd bring him a towel and a bottle of water. More than once he chased her a few yards on the track before catching her and stealing a kiss.

He found himself analyzing the months leading up to their wedding. Had Allison changed? Any hint she was pulling away from him? There'd been that one night when he'd gotten carried away, when his desire seemed to overwhelm her.

"Stop, Seth." Allison pushed against his shoulders. "Stop."

Seth forced himself to let go of her, to move away and sit on the other end of the couch. He rested his arms on his knees, willing his breath to return to normal. "I'm sorry, Allison."

She sat with her legs pulled up in front of her, arms wrapped around them, her face turned away.

"Allison, I said I was sorry."

"I know."

"Don't you believe me?"

"Yes."

He rested his hand on her knee, hoping she'd show some sign of forgiveness. A smile. Something.

"Come on, babe. I know I, um, crossed a line there." He cleared his throat. "I'm sorry. We've done pretty well, after dating all these years, right?"

"Yes."

"And the wedding's only four months away."

"I know when the wedding is, Seth."

"Can you blame me? I mean, don't you ever think about—"

Allison stood, walking away from him. Then she turned, pushing her hair from her face. She tucked the hem of her green cotton Henley back into the waistband of her jeans. "Sure, I think about it." She tugged at the cuff of her shirt. "But I've always trusted that I was safe with you. That you wouldn't push anything before . . . before . . ."

"You are safe. I wasn't thinking. I love you, Allison. I can't deny I want you too." He saw her eyes widen, her face pale. "But I can wait. We've waited this long. I know it's important to you."

He'd left soon after, following the night with a bouquet of purple hyacinths to say he was sorry. He also made sure they avoided being alone in her apartment or his town home. Allison seemed thankful. Or was she really relieved? Had her feelings for him been changing even then?

Found my campsite ransacked by a bear—or two. He seemed to enjoy my maple syrup the most— not a drop left. Well, he—or she—didn't even leave the bottle behind. That's what I get for not stringing my food up in a tree.

—Daniel

CHAPTER 22

*A*llison glanced at the directions clasped in her right hand as she maneuvered her car along the mountain road, the tires crunching over the loose gravel. According to Daniel, At Ease Bed-and-Breakfast should be just after the bend in the road. The sun dipped behind the mountains, shadowing the tops of the trees and coloring the sky a dusky purple.

Thank God she was almost there. The last thing she wanted to do was try navigating in the dark.

Glimpsing the welcoming glow of lights to her right, she tossed the scribbled notes on the seat and let out a relieved sigh. She moved her shoulders up and down, trying to ease the tension in her neck. How could she make sure things stayed on an even keel with Daniel tonight? As far as she knew, no unplanned blind date waited for her. There would be no unexpected kisses. No verbal tugs-of-war. This was a chance to discuss the brochure. She'd maintain a calm, cool, professional distance.

"I can do this. I can do this." Allison muttered the words over and over like a soothing mantra as she parked her car next to Daniel's hunter-green truck. "It's a job, not a date."

Daniel stood on the rough-hewn log deck that wrapped around

the lodge. Even in the waning light, Allison couldn't help but notice his rugged magnetism. Replace the worn jeans and leather jacket with a suit, and Daniel would be an impressive date.

"Job, job, job . . ." Allison repeated as she stepped out of her car and slammed the door.

"What was that, Alli?" Daniel bounded down the steps and took her laptop and messenger bag from her.

"N-nothing. I'm looking forward to starting the job."

"Me too. Madison's waiting to show you around the place, and then you and I can talk over some of the other details."

"Madison?"

"You remember, she's the owners' daughter—Madison Reynolds." Daniel slung his arm across Allison's shoulders as he ushered her into the lodge. "She handles the reservations and front desk." He motioned to a woman walking across the lobby toward them.

The Blonde.

Okay, then.

Allison noted The Blonde's—*Madison's*—eyes skim over her and then widen when she noticed Daniel's arm draped over Allison's shoulders.

"Madison, this is Alli." Daniel appeared oblivious to the animosity emanating from the other woman. "She's the graphic designer I recommended for the job. You probably remember meeting her several weeks ago in town."

The Blonde's gaze skimmed over her. "Allison. I'm looking forward to showing you around At Ease."

Sure she was.

"I'll put your laptop in the common area, Alli." Daniel headed toward a room off to their left, continuing to talk to her over his shoulder. "You won't need it until you and I talk. We'll take the tour first."

"Let me show you where to put that, Daniel." Madison followed him, her stilettos striking against the polished wooden floors as she tried to match her pace with Daniel's long stride. Madison's Uptown Girl outfit contrasted with her rustic surroundings. Her black leather pencil skirt hugged size-two hips. A bright pink cashmere sweater shouted "Expensive."

As Daniel and Madison walked into a room lit by the glow of a floor-to-ceiling stone fireplace surrounded by couches, Allison breathed out an exasperated sigh. *Puh-leeze. The man is thirty-one years old. He can figure out where to put a computer.*

When Daniel and Madison returned, she stuck to his side like a bleached blonde barnacle.

"Shall we go, Allison?" Madison's chemically enhanced smile gleamed triumphant.

"Sure thing. I'm right behind you."

Which was right where Madison wanted her. Why did she feel as if someone had cut in on her dance at prom?

Job, Allison. Job. Job. Job.

"My parents opened the B-and-B after my father retired from the army. That's why it's named At Ease." Madison walked up the stairs leading to a series of bedrooms. "My father worked closely with the architect and interior designer to get the lodge just the way he imagined it. My mother handles the day-to-day schedule and all the cooking. And each room honors the military in some way."

"Really? How . . . interesting." What would Allison find in the rooms? Weapons? Uniforms draped across the chairs?

Subdued red, white, and blue decorated the first room. An antique victory quilt hung on one wall. "A great-great-aunt made this at the end of World War Two." Madison smoothed the fabric with nails painted to match her sweater.

One room had framed photographs of the different military academy chapels at sunset paired with each academy's song. Another room was decorated in black and white, with a large copy of the famous "Kissing the War Goodbye" photo on one wall.

As they toured the B-and-B, Madison always managed to maneuver herself between Allison and Daniel. Even when he tried to include Allison in the conversation, Madison found a reason to rearrange the circle with an "Oh, Daniel, did you see this?"

Closing the door to the last bedroom suite, Madison led them back to the common room with the fireplace, where her mother had set out dessert, coffee, and tea.

"So, what do you think, Alli?" Daniel stretched out on the couch, a mug of coffee in one hand and two homemade sugar cookies in the other.

"Impressive." Allison sat in front of the fireplace, eager to toast her back. "I wasn't sure what to expect, but I like the military theme a lot."

"When my parents do something, they do it right." Madison slid next to Daniel. "So now that you've seen the lodge, what's next?"

"Well, you tell Alli what you're thinking about for a brochure, and in the next week, I'll take her out for some dry runs on the outdoor activities I've coordinated between the different B-and-Bs so she can experience it up close and personal—get some photos—and then get to work."

"I'd be glad to come along—"

"No need, Madison. You'll be too busy taking reservations and getting ready for your grand opening in a few months. Let Alli and me handle this."

From the way Madison eyed Daniel, Allison knew she was trying to figure out how to be included in anything Daniel had planned.

Allison reached for her computer bag. "The B-and-B has a website, right?"

"Of course." Madison barely glanced at her.

"It'd be helpful to see that before I design the brochure."

"I thought you were going to create something original, not just copy our site."

"I am. But it's always good to have continuity in advertising." Why was she explaining herself to Madison? She wasn't the boss, was she? "I'd like my design to dovetail with the website. I intend to use my own photography."

"Shouldn't we use a professional?"

"Alli's an excellent photographer." Daniel started in on his second cookie. "Didn't you double-major in graphic design and photography?"

"Almost. Seth insisted on it being a minor, not a full major."

"Seth?"

Madison's question caught Allison off guard. "Seth is . . . is Daniel's brother a-and my ex-fiancé."

Not that it was any of Madison's business.

"How interesting." Madison glanced at her cell phone when the faint tones of a jazz tune interrupted the conversation. "Excuse me, I need to take this in the other room. I'll be right back, Daniel."

Allison almost laughed out loud as she watched Madison move past Daniel, ensuring that her suntanned legs slid against his. Daniel, still oblivious to her flirting, stood and walked over to snag a few more cookies. Apparently, dessert held more appeal than the overdressed charms of The Blonde.

Daniel watched Alli position her laptop on the coffee table. She shoved the sleeves of her white fisherman's sweater back and stared at the screen, scrunching her nose and mouth in concentration.

Alli tapped a few keys and muttered, "What is going on here?"

"Problem?"

"I opened my e-mail because I want to add the lodge's e-mail address to my account. And I've got a ton of spam—again. I think a lot of it's X-rated stuff. How's it getting past my filter all of a sudden?"

"Did you adjust the settings recently?" Daniel brushed the cookie crumbs from his fingers, savoring the last morsel of cinnamon-flavored snickerdoodle.

"No."

"Check your browser history."

"Why? I haven't gone to any of those sites."

"Humor me. Check your history."

As Alli clicked through different entries, Daniel moved to kneel beside her.

"Everything is clear—except for . . . what is that? When did someone go there?"

Daniel surveyed the browser. "Looks like Saturday night."

"I didn't go on my computer Saturday night. I was too busy making pizzas and playing board games with Hadleigh and Evan—" Alli stared at the link. "Evan."

"Possibly."

"Who else?"

"Who else has access to your laptop?"

"Aunt Nita, but she wouldn't do something like this."

"I admit, unlikely. What are you going to do?"

Alli closed the page and clasped her wrist, rubbing it back and forth. "I have no idea."

Daniel covered her hand with his. "You do that a lot."

Her hand stilled beneath his. "What?"

"Rub your wrist when you're tense."

"Nervous habit, I guess."

"I guess." He eased her hand aside and ran his finger along a faint white mark on the inside of her wrist. "I never noticed that scar before. How'd you get it?"

She glanced up at him and pulled her hand away, holding her arm close to her body. "It's nothing. Just a scar." Allison rubbed her arm up and down the faded material of her jeans.

What was going on here? Why was she overreacting to a simple question?

"Wait a minute . . . did I see more?" Ignoring Alli's faint protests, Daniel turned her arm so he could see the skin along the inside. Besides the mark on her wrist, several others disfigured her skin farther up her arm.

"Bisquick scratched me. You know how j-jumpy he is." Alli twisted her wrist back and forth, tugging against his grasp.

Daniel refused to let go. "That's odd." He traced each line, the contact causing Alli to shiver. One. Two. Three. Four. "Anytime a cat ever scratched me, it got me on the outside of my arm and the top of my hand."

When Alli attempted to escape again, he caught her right hand, turning it faceup. More scars marred her skin. Alli kept her face turned away from him, staring into the fire's yellow-orange flames.

"Alli—who hurt you?" Daniel whispered, rubbing his thumb across the marks.

At the sound of Madison's steps crossing the front hallway, Alli jerked her hand away.

"Miss me?" Madison's giggle trilled up Daniel's spine like an over-energized jackhammer.

For the next half hour, Alli avoided eye contact with him. From the way she focused on Madison, he would have thought Alli found her the most intriguing person in town, possibly in the entire state of Colorado.

As she packed up her laptop, Alli sidestepped Daniel's attempts to nail down times to get together, suggesting, "E-mail some possible times and dates. Maybe Madison would want to join us."

He stood outside for several minutes after Alli's car disappeared into the night. What had happened in there?

"Are you coming in, Daniel?" Madison stood just inside the doorway. "The fire's so cozy."

"I don't think so, Madison." He zipped his jacket and took the steps two at a time. "I need to go check on a friend."

Hey, Kid, I know it's a local postcard. But the hike up Queens Canyon to the punch bowls is one of my favorites.

—Daniel

CHAPTER 23

Allison sat in her car, the trio of llamas captured in the glow of the headlights. Still odd man out, Banzai paced back and forth on his side of the temporary fence, his dark-furred face highlighted in the white light. Pacha and Kuzko stood facing her, as if waiting for her to come over and say hello.

Allison waved as she walked to the house. "Not tonight, boys. I've had enough conversation for one night."

The cool mountain air surrounded her, the silence enveloping her as she looked up at the stars splashed across the sky.

"Seems to me, God, if you can order the universe, you could help me get back on an even keel." Her breath puffed out in white clouds. "I know, this is all my fault. Maybe I should have said no when Daniel offered me that job. Next time could you just put a big do-not-touch sign on him?"

As she continued to stand with her face tilted heavenward, a star streaked across the sky.

"Some sort of sign, God? Was that a yes or a no?" Allison shivered as a breeze danced through the evergreens. "I'm listening. You just need to speak up."

She stood, waiting for further clarification. Nothing. It could have been worse—something like a bolt of lightning.

She didn't know which was more stressful—putting up with Madison's overt attempts to flirt with Daniel, or Daniel's attempts to find out about parts of her life she preferred to keep hidden. Between the two, she'd felt like she'd ridden emotional bumper cars for the past three hours.

At least Aunt Nita had a late shift at the hospital, so she didn't have to worry about her wandering down for a chat. Allison wanted to slip on her pj's, pop some popcorn, and watch an old movie with a happy ending.

Heaving a sigh, she tossed her laptop on her desk. At some point she'd have to decide what, if anything, she would say to Evan about her discovery. That would be a fun conversation.

She'd just keep telling herself that.

Bisquick followed as she went to her room and changed into a pair of warm pajamas, hanging her jeans with the other jeans and the white sweater in the white section of her closet.

"Men, Bisquick, add too much hassle to my life." She ran a brush through her hair. "Sorry, cat. Present company excluded. But you're the only low-maintenance male I know."

As she walked down the hallway, Allison paused by the new display case she'd bought for her thimbles. She stopped, touching the sterling Christmas tree positioned in the center of the box.

"Seven years. I know I almost tripped up there a few weeks ago, God, but I didn't cut." She slipped the tiny pewter symbol of success into her hand and continued walking. "I can do this, right? I can do this."

Several minutes later, a knock at her door halted her search among her DVDs for a perfect happily-ever-after movie. A glance at her clock confirmed that it was ten-thirty.

"Bit late for a social call." She stood by the door, switching on the outside light. "Who is it?"

"Hey, Alli, it's Daniel."

"No, no, no, no, no, no . . ." Allison banged her head against the doorpost in rhythm with her protest.

She heard Daniel stamping his feet on the ground outside. "I'd open the door and let you in, but I'm standing here on the outside, and it's snowing. How about you open the door and let *me* in?"

With a groan, Allison complied, but stood so she blocked Daniel from coming inside. "To what do I owe this late-night visit?"

"I wanted to finish our conversation."

"And if I don't?"

"Humor me." Daniel took one step forward. "May I?"

"I told you to e-mail me dates for the snowshoeing."

"That's not the conversation I meant." Daniel kicked off his boots and eased past her, moving to the couch.

So much for playing dumb. Leave it to Daniel to zero in on the topic she most wished to avoid.

Allison sat on the floor across from Daniel, pulling a cushion in front of her. They stared at each other for a few moments, the silence as tangible as a third person in the room. Once again, she noticed how Daniel's pair of one-blue-one-green eyes made his face all the more intriguing. What had he said once? *Seth's the purebred Rayner, I'm the mongrel.*

Before she realized his intention, Daniel leaned forward, his hand encircling her wrist. With his fingers, which were cool from the night air, he traced one of the scars he'd discovered earlier. As if afraid he might frighten her away, he spoke in an almost-whisper. "So, about this."

Allison closed her eyes, startled at the way tears formed without warning. Tried to breathe past the ache in her throat. "That is in the past."

"A painful part of your past."

"Yes."

"Alli, who would ever hurt you like this?"

She opened her eyes, found herself caught in the tenderness of his gaze. If he just wouldn't look at her like that, she could find a way to—what? Make light of something that haunted her? Daniel's concern broke past her vow of silence.

"I did."

He shook his head as if puzzled by her reply. "What?"

"I did this to myself, Daniel." She took a deep breath, willing herself to say what needed to be said without crying. "Have you ever heard of cutting?"

"Yes."

"People cut to relieve tension or anxiety. Or because they feel numb and they want to feel *something*. Pain is better than feeling nothing. Sometimes they—*I*—used a razor or a sharp pin or a piece of glass."

Why was she telling him this? Seth didn't even know that she used to cut. She always managed to conceal any suspicious marks on her arms by wearing long-sleeved tops or a hoodie. Allison clasped the pewter thimble in her other hand. How could she end this conversation?

"Why?" As Daniel asked the question, he moved from the couch to the floor, careful to leave some space between them even as he continued to hold her hand and soothe the scar with his touch.

"That's complicated. Long story." She rested her head on her fist for a moment, surprised that Daniel wasn't peppering her with questions. "Okay, long story short. My parents divorced when I was five—*not* amicably. During a weekend visitation, my father abducted me. He then kept me from my mom for two years, moving weekly—sometimes daily. That, ummmm, experience affected me, and in my teen years, I relieved some of the emotional stress by cutting. Just for one year, because a teacher noticed the marks on my arms and encouraged me to get help. I did. The end."

There. She'd calmly told Daniel her sad little story. Her voice hadn't wavered once.

Then why were there tears slipping down her face?

When Daniel tugged her toward him, Allison resisted.

"I just want to hold you, Alli." He knelt and pulled her into his arms. "I'm sorry."

"For what?" With her face buried in Daniel's broad shoulder, Allison's words were muffled.

Daniel ran his fingers through her hair. "I'm sorry life was so tough for you. I'm sorry you hurt so much that you hurt yourself. I'm . . . just sorry."

"It's okay."

"I think God hates it when we say that."

"What?"

Daniel leaned away from her, cradling her face in his hands. "I think God hates it when we say it's okay when we're hurting. I'm not saying it's a sin, it's just not the truth. What happened to you wasn't okay, Alli. Some of it sounds awful. I can't even imagine being abducted—"

"It's—"

Daniel placed two fingers over her lips. "Don't say it's okay, Alli. You were hurt. Don't act like you weren't. You were honest with me tonight—even if I did back you into a corner."

Allison stared at Daniel, aware of him in so many ways. His hands were warm against her skin, and his familiar scent—a touch of the outdoors mixed with no-frills soap—wrapped around her. Not for the first time, the touch of his fingers on her lips caused them to tingle.

"There's just something about you, Alli." Daniel leaned a fraction closer, his eyes searching hers as if trying to find the answer to a question. "Something . . ."

Allison waited for Daniel to bridge the few inches that separated them.

But when he moved again, he backed away from her.

• • •

Was he out of his mind?

Alli trusted him, and all he could think about was kissing her?

Back up, Danny boy. Put it in reverse and keep going.

Daniel sat back on his heels, releasing Alli as if someone set off an alarm that blared, *Put your hands where I can see them. Allison Denman is off-limits.*

"Well. Thanks." He stood and walked over to his boots. Tugged them on his feet. "Thanks."

"Thanks . . . for what?" Allison sat on the floor, watching him.

"For talking to me."

"Oh. You're . . . welcome." Allison cradled her wrist against her chest as if it pained her. Something glinted on the carpet next to her.

"Did you drop something?"

"What? Uh, no. I mean yes. Don't worry about it. It's just a thimble from my collection. I was holding it while we were, um, talking."

Daniel watched her palm the thimble. Continue to sit. Continue to stare up at him, her lashes damp from the tears she'd shed. Waiting. For what? What was he supposed to say?

"Okay, then. I'm going to let you get back to whatever you were doing. Thanks again."

"You said that."

"Right." He backed up, pulled open the door. "I'll e-mail some dates for snowshoeing, snowmobiling, that sort of thing."

"Fine."

"G'night, Kid."

He sprinted to his truck. Once inside, he slumped in the seat. Maybe the frigid air would act like a mental cold shower. Clear his head. Could he have ended the conversation in a more awkward manner?

He wasn't the kind of man Alli was looking for. Alli was all about settling down and home and family. He wasn't a family man.

He needed space and freedom. And he needed to keep away from Alli.

"I need to put up some roadblocks between me and that woman." He groaned and banged his head on the steering wheel. Maybe he'd knock some sense into his head. "And you were the oh-so-smart guy who offered Alli the 'just friends' job."

None of the blind dates had worked out. Did he dare try another one? Alli was cute when she was angry, but he'd worn the hard-won truce pretty thin. It might shatter under another blind-date fiasco.

When his cell rang, he pulled it from his pocket. Seth. Why did his little brother always call so late?

"Daniel here." He leaned forward and started the truck, putting it in reverse.

"Hey. What are you doing?"

"Just heading home." His headlights swept across the llamas. Didn't those beasts ever sleep? "What can I do for you?"

"I can't sleep."

"Insomnia? Drink some warm milk."

"No. I can't stop thinking about Allison."

That made two of them, but Daniel wasn't going to share that information.

"I've tried calling her, but she changed her cell number. She's moved, but she didn't tell me where, and her family isn't telling me, either."

"Seth, you need to move on. Let go of whatever you and Alli had."

"This isn't about getting back what Allison and I had. I want to let her know I've changed."

"What?"

"I've been doing a lot of thinking. I even spoke to a counselor, if you can believe that."

"You don't strike me as the bare-your-soul kind of guy, Tag."

"I'm not. But I love Allison, and I'll do anything to get her back— to make things right between us."

Daniel tapped his thumbs on the steering wheel. Had his brother changed? Did he deserve a second chance?

"But if I can't find her, I can't prove myself to her. I'm at a dead end."

Dead ends. Roadblocks. Maybe Daniel could help his brother and himself at the same time.

Decision time.

"Seth, I can tell you where Alli is."

Hey, Alli—Went hippo-
watching tonight. Sat
on the top of a jeep and
watched them romp in
Lake Naivasha near our
campsite.
                    —Daniel

CHAPTER 24

*D*aniel handed his boarding pass to the attendant and then strode down the passageway onto the plane. He shifted his backpack onto his shoulder, stopping to wait while a man stowed his carry-on in an overhead compartment. Flying the red-eye never bothered him. He'd turn on his iPod, pull his hat down over his eyes, and sleep all the way to Vermont. He'd sleepwalk through the terminal in D.C., where he switched planes.

The unexpected invite to visit the resort where he'd updated the layout of the ski area two years ago provided a timely exit stage right. He postponed his get-togethers with Alli. Seth had time to make an appearance. When Daniel came back in ten days, maybe Alli and his little brother would be well on their way to reconciliation.

Daniel lifted the brim of his cap and turned down the volume on his iPod when someone tapped him on the shoulder.

"Excuse me, would you mind switching seats?" A stocky young man holding the hand of the woman standing next to him waited in the aisle. "We—my wife and I—just got married and we'd like to sit next to each other."

Terrific. Newlyweds.

"No problem." Daniel moved his backpack from under the seat in front of him. "I'll take the window seat, okay?"

"Thanks."

As Daniel slid over, the new Mr. and Mrs. stowed their luggage and settled in their seats.

"I'm Connor. This is my wife, Tess." The new husband shook his head. "Wow. Can't believe I'm saying that. *My wife.*"

"Daniel Rayner. Congratulations."

"We're going to England for our honeymoon. Tess always wanted to visit London."

"London's a fun city."

"You've been?"

"Several times."

"Married?"

"Me? No. Single—and happy that way."

"Yeah, me too. Or so I thought." Connor clasped his wife's hand and rubbed his thumb across her wedding band. "We dated on and off for five years. Finally, she said I needed to choose—marrying her or being independent. I chose independence."

"Then how'd you end up on a honeymoon?"

At this point, Tess leaned around Connor and joined the conversation. "As much as I loved Connor, I knew I had to move on. About six months ago, I started seeing someone I knew from college. Connor heard I was dating—"

"I heard she was getting married. I knew she was marrying the wrong man." Connor kissed his wife's hand. "She was supposed to marry me."

A light sheen of pink dusted Tess's cheeks. "That's what he told me the night he showed up at my house. 'You're supposed to marry me.' I asked if he was proposing, and he said yes."

Daniel chuckled. "Sounds like one of those chick flicks."

Connor waved the thought away. "I hate those things. Give me a good *Die Hard* movie any day. This was my life, my future. And I couldn't see it without—"

Daniel was thankful when the attendant's voice broke in on their conversation. Listening to preflight instructions was better than listening to this. "Like I said, congratulations."

He shifted in his seat. So the guy changed his mind. Good for him. What was Daniel doing, getting all chummy with Mr. and Mrs. Ain't Love Grand? Daniel made his choice and Connor made his. There can be two right choices in life for two different people.

Time to get some sleep and ignore the couple savoring their dream come true. Daniel cranked his music back up and pulled the cap back down over his eyes.

"I'm fine, Meghan." Allison walked among the bookshelves at Work in Progress, browsing while chatting on her cell phone.

"If you keep repeating that, maybe we'll both believe it."

"I like living with Aunt Nita. The llamas are beasties, but they're Bisquick's new best buds." Alli stopped in the travel section, perusing titles. "I had a good visit with Hadleigh and Evan last weekend."

"And?"

"And what?"

"How's the older Rayner brother?"

"Oh, him."

"Said with just the right amount of a you-could-care-less-about-Daniel-Rayner attitude. And I'm not buying it. Any more kissing— or are you not telling?"

Apparently, the man had no intention of ever kissing her again. She confided her ugly scars to him, and Daniel was so disappointed in her that he'd gone missing in action.

"You still there?"

Allison pulled a travel book about Greece off the shelf. She wanted to visit the islands one day. "I'm here. That kiss between Daniel and me was some sort of unexplainable mishap. Blame it on the moon. Was it a full moon the week before the wedding?" She added a book on Ireland to the one on Greece.

"But you're working with him, right?"

"I'm not sure anymore. I mean, I have a contract to design the brochure. But Daniel was supposed to set up times for us to do some outdoor activities—snowshoe, snowmobile—and he's AWOL."

"What do you mean?"

"Madison said he took an impromptu trip to Vermont."

"Who's Madison?"

"The owners' daughter—a teeny-tiny Barbie-doll blonde who has a most definite thing for Daniel." Allison moved on to a book about Venice, another one of her must-see locations.

"Life is more than men, my friend. Let Madison have Daniel."

"I couldn't agree more."

"Sure you do."

"Listen, how about if we meet in Denver for dinner some night soon?"

"Sounds good."

"I'll check my planner and get back to you with some dates. Let me know what works best for you." Allison tucked the cell into her messenger bag and continued daydreaming her way through the travel section. She gathered an eclectic assortment of dream vacations—Venice, Greece, England—and decided to indulge in a cup of hot tea and some imaginary trip planning.

She walked to the end of the aisle and turned left, heading to where Scoti stood behind the coffee counter making lattes and mochas. As she looked in her purse for her wallet, she bumped into a man facing away from her. The books in her arms shifted, and he turned to steady her.

"Hello, Allison."

Seth.

Alli, took a train through the Alps. Even at night, it was an amazing trip.
—Daniel

CHAPTER 25

Allison would not run.

No dropping the travel books like a discarded bridal bouquet and sprinting past Seth and out of the bookstore.

Seth held out his hands. "Carry your books for you?" A sheepish grin crossed his face. "Reminds me of when we were in high school."

Allison clutched the books to her chest like a nervous teenager. "No need."

"Okay, I'll just walk with you, then." Seth shrugged. "More high school. Can I get you something to drink?"

The last thing she wanted to do was sit and sip tea with her ex-fiancé. What was he doing here? How did he figure out she'd moved to Estes Park?

"S-sure."

She moved to the coffee bar, berating herself. She should have said "Thanks, but no thanks." She placed her order and sat down when Seth insisted on paying. He introduced himself to Scoti as an "old friend," and Allison didn't correct him. It wasn't like she could explain her past with Seth while Scoti frothed a Frappuccino.

"Planning a trip?" Seth settled into the chair across from her.

"More like daydreaming." Allison shoved the books to the side. "I hope to travel. Someday."

Seth flipped through the pages of the book on top of the pile. "Greece. Looks beautiful, doesn't it?"

"Yes. I think a cruise around the islands would be fun."

"Me too. Where else are you thinking of going?" He looked at the other books. "England. Venice. You've always wanted to go to Venice."

Allison traced the outline of the gondola with a bandaged finger. She'd suggested Venice for their honeymoon, but Seth vetoed it. She had thought the final decision was fine, it just wasn't where she wanted to go. It didn't even figure in her "top ten places to go on your honeymoon" list.

Seth touched her injured finger. "What happened?"

"Umm, llama bite." Allison tucked her hand in her lap.

"Llama bite?"

"Banzai didn't mean to bite me. He was aiming for Kuzco, and my hand was in the way." Allison stopped talking, realizing Seth sat staring at her. "I'm not making sense, am I?"

"Not much."

Before she could explain herself, Scoti arrived with their drinks. She paused by the table. "Hey, Allison, I still want to display some of your photographs in the café section. Say yes, please?"

"I'm not a professional—"

"But you're good. I loved the ones you took when we went hiking the other day." Scoti deposited a mug of tea on the circular table along with two packs of Splenda. "Promise me a few prints. I'll pay to have them framed."

"I'll think about it." Allison stirred her tea and then looked up to find Seth watching her.

"So?" He leaned back in his chair, waiting, tapping his signet ring against the side of his coffee mug.

"So?"

"You were explaining about your injury."

"I'm living with my aunt Nita—you remember her?—and she's caring for llamas."

"I wouldn't think there's much money in that."

"There's no money in it. She likes doing it." Allison realized she was scratching her wrist and wrapped her hands around the mug of tea.

They sat in silence for a few moments. If Seth wanted to talk, let him. He'd come looking for her. Which reminded her, how did he know she was in Estes Park?

"Seth, who told you I was living in Estes Park?"

Scoti's reappearance interrupted Seth's answer. "I apologize, but I just realized I shortchanged you. I only gave you change for a ten, and you paid with a twenty." After handing Seth his change, Scoti winked at him. "And your next drink is on the house. Sorry for the inconvenience."

Allison considered her friend as she walked away. Had Scoti just flirted with Seth?

"You cut your hair." Seth reached over and touched the ends skimming her jaw.

"Um, yes. I mean, *I* didn't cut it myself. Obviously." Allison took a gulp of her tea, preferring a burned tongue to sounding like a babbling fool.

"I've always liked your hair long, but this is cute too." Seth nodded his approval. "So, Allison, can I take you to dinner tonight?"

Allison watched him pocket the change and fold the bills into his wallet. "W-what?"

"I promise to be on my best behavior. No talk of engagements or what-might-have-beens." Seth held his hand up like a scout reciting a pledge, though Allison knew he'd never gotten past the first year of Cub Scouts. "I'm only in town for one night."

"I've got to go back and take care of the boys—the llamas. Finish a project."

"That's fine. I'll check in to my hotel and go for a run. I'll pick you up whenever you say."

"Let's just meet somewhere later."

"I don't mind picking you up—"

Allison stood. "It's easier to meet at the restaurant."

Seth held up his hands in surrender. "What restaurant do you recommend?"

Allison shrugged out of her coat and hung it on the antique stand by the door. Only ten—not that late. But she ached with exhaustion. Since meeting Seth in the bookstore, she'd run an emotional marathon. Seth had run the event like a pro. True to his word, he hadn't talked about their past, keeping his focus forward on the finish line.

Which was—what?

She collapsed on the couch, grabbing the remote control, hoping to override her brain with something, anything. The handsome face of Mark Harmon, aka Jethro Gibbs of *NCIS* fame, filled the screen. Could she ever love a man who spent most of his time solving murders?

Jethro Gibbs, hero.

Asset: Loves kids.

Liability: Only attracted to redheads.

Asset: Confident.

Liability: Fills his basement with handcrafted full-size boats (and how does he get them out?).

Asset: Has a soft heart under that gruff demeanor.

Liability: Imaginary man.

Sigh.

"May I join you? This is one of my favorite episodes." Aunt Nita's upside-down face, framed with her tried and true but definitely no longer natural red curls appeared over Allison's head, causing her to gasp and cover her eyes.

"Make a little more noise, please." Allison hit the mute button.

"Sorry." Her aunt sat on the other end of the couch. After a few moments, she patted Allison's leg through her corduroy pants. "You're quiet tonight."

"Tired."

"Out with Daniel?"

"No. Seth."

"You don't say."

"I feel like I'm in some alternate universe. Daniel disappears and Seth shows up."

"Well, as my doctor friend likes to say, that could be 'true, true, and unrelated.'" Her aunt reached up to stroke Bisquick as he walked across the back of the couch.

"Translation, please."

"Seth's appearance and Daniel's disappearance may not be connected."

"I'm not saying they are." Allison pulled herself into a sitting position. "Daniel wouldn't tell Seth where I was, would he?"

"You'd have to ask Daniel that question." Her aunt turned toward her while pulling Bisquick into her lap. "So why did you go out with Seth?"

"He asked."

"Ah."

"He asked *nicely.*"

"No explanation needed, sweetie."

"I don't *know* why." Allison got up and began pacing the living room.

"Old habits die hard."

Allison watched her cat snuggle closer to Aunt Nita as she scratched behind his ears. A faint purr indicated his satisfaction. "Meaning?"

"It may be easier to say yes to Seth."

"Really, Aunt Nita?"

"Or maybe there's no reason not to have dinner with Seth. Not for old time's sake, but just because." Her aunt shrugged. "Not a date. To prove to Seth—and to yourself—that you've moved on."

"I like that reason better."

"Then take it. No charge." Her aunt stood and deposited Bisquick into Allison's arms. "Now, if you and Jethro will excuse me, I need to get my beauty sleep. I have a lunch date tomorrow."

"You don't say. With whom? Another llama lover?"

"My doctor friend. He says he makes an amazing guacamole."

After her aunt left, Allison walked to her room, where Bisquick jumped from her arms and curled up on the pillow.

"You're going to have to move. Soon."

She halted just inside the closet, stopped by the sight of her wedding dress encased in the plastic bag embossed with the bridal store's initials. Will had packed it on the truck with all her other clothes. She needed to get rid of it, but it was easier to leave it in her closet and ignore it.

She unzipped the bag, her fingers touching the smooth ivory-colored lace. For weeks the dress hung in her closet, a silent reminder complete with a five-foot train of what might have been. A wedding. A marriage. A groom. A husband. Everything she'd thought she wanted. Whom she thought she wanted to be married to for all the days of her life. Look what she ended up with. Her aunt. Three misbehaving llamas. And all her belongings crammed into a basement apartment while she telecommuted and freelanced.

So much for dreams come true.

"How long am I going to hang on to this?" She turned her back, changing from her clothes into her pajamas and slipping into bed. One more night with the reminder of the wedding gone wrong hanging in the closet wasn't going to change anything.

"But I'm changing, aren't I, God? I'm different." Allison rolled over onto her back and stared at the ceiling. "Aren't I?"

She reached for her barely used Bible, the one the youth pastor had given her at summer camp the morning after the bonfire. Shifting to sit up, she turned through the pages. She'd tried to follow Meghan's advice to focus on one verse but found herself flipping back and forth, looking for something to anchor her.

"Same song, second verse, God. Little help, please."

She searched until she noticed where she'd underlined several lines on a page. What had her fifteen-year-old self found so important?

> *Light, space, zest—that's GOD!*
> *So with him on my side I'm fearless,*
> *Afraid of no one and nothing.*

She stared at the passage. Is that how she thought of God? Light? Space? Zest?

Hardly.

More often than not, she felt as if he were watching her, waiting for her to make her next mistake, shaking his head in disappointment when she did, but not at all surprised. God knew her, right? If there was one thing Allison did, she made mistakes.

But here God was being described as *light* and *space*—room to breathe, not somebody who hemmed her in with rules. And not someone who kept track of how many times she broke them.

And *zest?* God was zest? Like passion? Or enthusiasm? She didn't know that God. But it seemed like knowing him would give a person confidence—the ability to face anyone unafraid.

Allison read the words over and over, a prayer forming in her heart and finally breaking out as a hesitant whisper. "God, I'd like to know you like that—as light—as someone who gives me breathing space. And to be able to face other people and not be afraid of them. Most of all, I'd like to be able to look in the mirror and not be afraid of who I see."

CHAPTER 26

*H*e needed coffee.

Halfway through Boulder, Seth pulled into the Starbucks parking lot, debating the drive-through or going inside. Getting out of his car won out.

He inhaled the bold fragrance of coffee as he stood in the haphazard line. Baristas scrawled orders on the sides of insulated cups, their voices overwhelmed by the sound of milk being frothed and beans being ground.

Looking around, Seth realized most everyone wore typical college clothes—faded jeans, hoodies, backpacks slung over their shoulders. And there he stood, starched and pressed in a dark suit, white dress shirt, and tie. He looked like a younger version of his father, even though he was only a few years older than some of these kids. He should have dressed more casually this morning, grabbed some Dockers and an oxford shirt. But he'd been on autopilot once he decided to take the day off and visit Allison. He'd showered and put on a business suit. Habit.

Minutes later, he placed the cup of house blend in the cup holder but continued to sit in his car. Even on a weekend, Boulder felt like a college town. Overflowing with teens and twentysomethings. Busy.

He'd considered coming here for college, but his father vetoed that. He'd given Seth his top-three list, and good son that he was, Seth applied to all three. Thanks to his father's good ol' boy network, Seth was accepted to all three. His father wanted MIT, but in a minor fit of rebellion, Seth opted for Stanford.

It was all a means to an end. Undergraduate degree. Master's degree. Climbing the ladder at Rayner Construction.

Marriage.

Allison's flight of fancy derailed that goal, but Seth knew he could win her back. He'd use the rest of the drive up to plot the next step in his plan of attack. First, to analyze his assets and liabilities.

Liability: Allison thought they started dating too young.

Asset: He and Allison had been together for six years. They had a history together. He'd help her focus on the fact that they'd grown up together and knew each other so well because of all their time together.

Liability: He'd blown it with Allison before Christmas—coming on too strong, possibly scaring her off.

Asset: He was in the perfect position to play the repentant fiancé. He could do humble. He could play nice.

Liability: Allison now lived in Estes Park with her aunt Nita.

Asset: Absence made the heart grow fonder, right? He was proving how dedicated he was by driving back and forth to visit—almost three hundred miles round-trip. He'd start sending her cards; flowers were obviously out for a while. And they'd keep trying new restaurants.

Liability: Allison's best friend probably was encouraging her not to get back together with him.

Asset: He had Daniel on his side, and Daniel was in Estes Park, at least for a little while.

Seth drained the last of the coffee. All in all, things looked pretty good. He just needed time, patience, and a few tanks of gas, and he and Allison would be sending out brand-new save-the-date cards and planning a romantic destination wedding.

Hey, Kid—Nothing like
stuffed Rock Cornish hens
roasted over a campfire
under the heavens. Now,
that's a five-billion-star
meal!

—Daniel

CHAPTER 27

"Meghan, I don't want to shop for lingerie." Allison stopped outside the store, trying to ignore the photographs of scantily clad models filling the windows. If she could, she would dig in her heels, but her winter boots didn't have any. "I want sushi."

"Shop first, raw tuna and eel topped with wasabi later." Meghan held the door open and ushered Allison in with a wave of her hand, fuchsia nails flashing. "In the store now."

"Why can't we shop for jeans like normal people?"

"I'm indulging myself. I need a pick-me-up, and nothing lifts my spirits like a new matching pair of panties and an underwire bra."

"Something wrong?" Allison sifted through a multicolored assortment of boyfriend briefs tossed like confetti in a bin. She didn't need lingerie. She'd stocked up on all-new undergarments right before the wedding that wasn't.

"Just bored. With my job. My life. I'm even thinking of dyeing my hair a different color." Meghan ran her long fingers through her short brown curls, which she'd caught in a wide purple headband. "What do you think about red?"

"My only advice? Stay away from the blond section of the hair-color aisle. You don't need a repeat of the high school hair disaster."

Allison followed Meghan as she threw assorted panties and bras into a store basket. After a while, her friend moved on to sleepwear, eyeing coordinating tops and bottoms.

"Have you thought about switching jobs?" Allison shifted hangers, selecting a lemon-yellow-and-white-striped set she thought Meghan would like.

"Sure, I've thought about it. But as much as I hate my same-old-same-old routine, it pays the bills."

"What would you do if you didn't have to worry about money?"

"Downsize. Go back to school. Totally change the direction of my life." Meghan glanced at the overflowing pile of clothes. "Let's go try things on."

"You're the one shopping, not me. And please resist the urge to ask me what works and what doesn't."

Meghan snorted. "Deal. Just talk to me while I do the whole slip-on-slip-off routine."

"Did I mention Aunt Nita is dating?" Allison collapsed onto a stool outside Meghan's dressing room.

"No. Nice guy?"

"I have no idea. She hasn't brought him home for my approval. He's an ER doc."

"Ah. Overworked and overconfident."

"I'll pass your opinion along. Banzai's finally got full access to the pasture. Kuzko and Pacha tolerate him, but he's low llama on the totem pole. If he gets out of line, they spit on him."

"Ewww." The door to Meghan's dressing room swung open. "Pajama check. Yes or no?"

"I vote yes—and I told you, I don't want to be asked to vote on what you're trying on."

"I vote yes too, and I won't ask you to weigh in on the bras and panties." The door clicked shut. "How are the two-legged men in your life?"

"Daniel e-mailed me to say he'd be in town this weekend and that he'd touch base about a sleigh ride."

"Nice of him."

"Seth called a couple of times." ,

"Again? How many times is that?"

"No big deal. He just wanted to say hi. I'm keeping it casual."

"Okay."

"You don't believe me?"

"I believe you want to keep it casual. Seth—I'm not so sure." Meghan moved around the dressing room. "No peeking, just tell me: flowers or basic purple?"

"Both."

"You love to spend my money."

"I just want to make sure you feel better."

"I do have nail polish that exactly matches this purple set."

"That settles it, then." Allison stood and paced the dressing room hallway. "Can we get dinner?"

"I've got a few more options here. So, back to Seth. Why are you talking to him?"

Allison leaned against the wall. "You sound like my aunt."

"Thanks, I think. What did you tell her?"

"I told her 'because.'"

"Very mature."

"Aren't I being mature, Meggie?" Allison stopped in front of the dressing room. "Things ended badly between Seth and me—*I* ended them badly. Wouldn't it be better if we could be friends?"

"But Seth's stated objective is still to marry you."

"That was weeks ago. I'm sure he's accepted my decision by now."

A store worker led a customer to the room next to Meghan's, instructing the woman to let her know if she needed anything.

Allison rapped on Meghan's door. "I'll be browsing the robes."

"I'll be done in five. And just so you know, I think you and Seth have different goals for each other."

"Thanks, Meggie."

"What are friends for?"

Allison rested her head in her hands, closing her eyes and trying to will away the ache building in her temples. She had a deadline to make, headache or no headache. She was only on page twelve of a thirty-two-page e-zine spread. The editor had pulled the theme article, substituting one with a completely different slant and throwing off Allison's roughed-out layouts. That's what she got for having a lingerie-and-sushi day with Meghan.

She needed some caffeine and some serious inspiration. She'd wander upstairs, chat a few minutes with her aunt, and then come back and finish the project.

Aunt Nita's main floor was empty, all the lights turned off. Allison had forgotten that her aunt had volunteered to cover someone's shift tonight. She'd indulge in her aunt's not-so-secret chocolate stash and head back downstairs.

She walked through the open family room and stopped at the sight of an easel set up in the room. She'd also forgotten about her aunt's latest hobby. When Aunt Nita had come home last week loaded down with an easel and a box of oil paints and brushes, Allison had said she didn't realize her aunt painted. Her aunt had laughed and said, "I don't. But someone at work was throwing all of this stuff out, and I've always wanted to try!"

Allison stood in front of the easel, staring at the still life her aunt had started painting, a crude rendition of a purple glass vase, a bowl of Granny Smith apples, and—was that a stuffed llama?—arranged on a card table draped with a red-and-white-checked tablecloth.

She fingered a brush laying on the easel's edge, remembering her college art class. The instructor had pushed the students to move past the fundamentals of lines and shapes and colors and explore what would happen if they experimented—*dared to be dangerous with art,* he'd said. At first Allison resisted. But then one day in class she'd stopped caring what grade she might get or what the other students might say, and had fun mixing colors, blending bold, broad strokes across the canvas, like sweeping streaks of an unleashed rainbow.

She'd brought the canvas home at the end of the semester and hung it up in her bedroom at her parents' house. Looking at this painting tugged at a neglected part of her heart. Where was her painting now? Probably stashed in the attic.

She glanced around the room and found what she was looking for—a blank canvas. Did she dare? She knew Aunt Nita wouldn't begrudge her a piece of canvas. But painting again . . . could she recapture that girl who was willing to open her eyes wide enough to see past the boundaries of have-tos and shoulds and let color spill into something more than all the right places and shapes? Maybe it had been too long.

Allison walked around the back of the B-and-B, enjoying the quietness of the mountains and the light-falling snow. The scent of evergreens hung in the air, blending with the faint fragrance of a wood fire.

It shouldn't be that difficult to find a sleigh and two horses, especially since Daniel, Ty, and Madison were waiting for her. She adjusted her camera bag on her shoulder, glad her first meeting with Daniel since the cutting confession included other people, even if the other people weren't her closest friends.

The sound of Madison's laughter invaded the stillness, an additional aid in helping Allison find her way to the group.

"Hey, Kid. Right on time." Daniel stood beside the horses, adjusting the traces.

"I try to be punctual, big brother."

"That's tr— What did you call me?" Daniel rocked back on his heels, a bemused expression marring his handsome face.

"You called me 'kid.' I called you 'big brother.' You *are* eight years older than me, Daniel, and you were almost my brother." Allison set her camera bag in the back of the sleigh.

"Brother-*in-law*."

Allison walked beside the horses, allowing the bay to nuzzle her hand. "Same rules apply to both positions."

Madison perched on the front seat, a furry white jacket coordinating with the hat pulled over her long blond hair. Equally furry boots covered her feet. Allison coughed into her hand, hiding a gurgle of laughter. She could hear her stepfather's commentary on Madison's outfit: *Some hunter would love to get that girl in his sights.*

Ty stood in the back of the sleigh. "Daniel talked the regular driver into letting him handle the horses, which leaves the backseat to you and me."

"I'm the photographer on this trip, so leave me plenty of elbow room, please." Allison forced a smile. Just because she and Ty had gone on a date didn't mean she had to be rude. She positioned her camera supplies between them, declining his offer to share the worn southwestern-print wool blanket.

"I'll be taking lots of pictures." Allison took a few test shots of the surroundings. "You three try and forget I'm here."

That shouldn't be too difficult for Madison, who linked her arm with Daniel's, telling him that he could keep her warm.

The horses maintained a lazy pace through the woods, their hoof beats muffled by the snow-packed trail. Allison took several shots of Daniel and Madison, who requested copies.

Within forty minutes, Daniel drew the sleigh to a stop alongside a campfire surrounded by seats hewn from logs. A large metal pot and ladle, along with Styrofoam cups and a plastic bag of mini-marshmallows, sat on a portable table. As they approached, Allison noticed a figure on horseback ride off a trail that paralleled theirs back toward the B-and-B.

"I got the fire ready earlier. Couldn't leave it unattended, so one of the kitchen staff was watching it for me." Daniel jumped down, offering Madison his hand to help her from the sleigh. "The

Reynoldses will be offering hot chocolate to their guests who go on sleigh rides, so I figured we ought to experience that too."

Allison moved around the area, trying to determine what photos to take. She watched as Daniel moved the pot over to the fire, stirring the chocolate mixture. When Madison and Ty joined him by the fire, Allison took a few pictures of the trio.

Once the hot chocolate was ready, Ty brushed the snow off the log and sat, stretching his legs in front of him. "A sleigh ride and hot chocolate. Nice touch." He saluted Madison with his cup as she moved to sit beside him, cradling her cup in her gloved hands.

Allison turned her camera on Daniel, who crouched in front of the fire. After adding extra logs, he settled on his heels again. Despite the presence of Madison, Ty, Allison, and a team of horses, he seemed lost in thought. His elbows rested on his knees, his hands loosely clasped as he stared into the flames. Daniel's dark curls, dusted by snow, touched the collar of his jacket. That was the comfortable, outdoors Daniel Rayner that Allison knew.

She took one photo of Daniel beside the fire and then zoomed in on his face and took a close-up. Daniel looked over at her, a half-smile turning up one corner of his mouth. Allison clicked the shutter again. Perfect.

"Daniel, come sit with me and Ty." Madison's voice broke through the stillness. "Get a group shot, Allison."

"Sure thing, Madison." Allison looked away from Daniel. "That's what I'm here for."

Daniel eased to his feet and went to sit beside Ty.

"Oh, don't be silly, Daniel!" Madison squeezed herself between the two men. "This is a much better picture."

"Say 'money.'" Allison knelt in front of the group.

Madison held her hand in front of the camera, blocking the picture. "Don't you mean 'cheese'?"

"Actually, smiles look more natural when people say 'money.'"

Ty threw his arm around Madison's shoulders. "Works for me. I'm an accountant. Money."

The snowfall thickened as the trio sipped hot chocolate. Allison moved away, taking photos of the horses, clouds of cool air puffing from their velvety noses. She captured images of Daniel checking the harnesses and Ty tromping through the woods on a "bear hunt."

"Not the kind of excitement I'm looking for." Daniel bagged the trash and tossed it into the back of the sleigh before making sure the fire was extinguished. "Everybody ready to go?"

On the way back, Daniel offered to let Ty handle the horses, slipping into the seat beside Allison. The faint scent of smoke clung to his jacket. After taking a few more photos, she opened the case to put the camera away.

"All done?"

Allison wiped off the lens and put the cover on. "It's starting to snow harder. I think I have plenty of photos to choose from."

"We didn't get any of you."

"I'm *designing* the brochure. I'm not supposed to be in it."

Daniel reached over and took the camera from her hands. "Say 'money.'"

"That's ridiculous, Dan—"

"I'll keep taking photos until you say the word."

"Give me my camera."

"Wrong words."

"Now."

"Still the wrong word." Daniel angled the camera and took another picture.

"Rayner."

"I am getting some great shots, but you still haven't said the word. M-o-n-e-y."

Allison gritted her teeth. "Money."

Daniel lowered the camera and winked. "Now say it like you don't want to hit me with a sack full of gold coins."

Allison sighed. She looked straight into the camera and smiled.

"Beautiful—and you didn't even have to say the magic word." Daniel handed the camera back and faced forward.

Allison couldn't help but notice how Madison's shoulders stiffened at Daniel's words. The Blonde didn't need to worry—Daniel didn't mean anything by his offhand comment. She dried off the lens again and stowed her camera. When the horses pulled up near the barn, she hopped down and headed back to her car.

"Alli!"

She turned at the sound of Daniel's voice.

"Snowmobiling next, okay?"

"Fine. Just let me know when."

"Will do."

She marched to her car. Why had she ever said she would work with Daniel Rayner? The man made her crazy.

"Crazy, crazy, crazy." She shook her head. "But I need the money, money, money."

Alli, stuck in D.C., thanks to a snowstorm. It's not the same since they barricaded all the monuments. My favorite is the Vietnam Memorial. Some of my dad's friends are listed on the wall, but he doesn't talk about that.

—Daniel

CHAPTER 28

"*J*ust like old times, isn't it, Allison?" Seth guided her into his car, shut the door, and then strode around to the driver's side. The lights from the Stanley Hotel illuminated his erect posture, trim haircut, and satisfied smile.

Just like old times? Well, yes. And no. Allison tried to remember when and how she had indicated she wanted the old times back.

Seth slid behind the steering wheel of his maroon Lexus sedan, clicking the seat belt in place. "Did you enjoy dinner?"

"Very much."

Of course, if she'd ordered for herself, she would have chosen the soup, not the salad. The fish entrée, not the game. And she would have ordered dessert, not cappuccino. But just like old times, Seth took charge of their evening and handled everything from the appetizer to the after-dinner drinks.

Allison sighed, watching the darkness glide by outside. She'd make herself a cup of tea when she got home. She shouldn't criticize Seth. He wasn't controlling. This was Seth Rayner's brand of consideration, ensuring everything went smoothly for them. For her.

"Remember some of our dates in high school?" Seth turned the car toward Aunt Nita's house, the lit image of the historic Stanley

Hotel illuminated in the rearview mirror. "Back then we usually split a burger and fries at Red Top. It's nice to be able to afford the finer things in life."

"I still like a good burger every now and then." Allison reached over and turned on the radio, searching until she located a favorite country station.

"Since when do you listen to country music?" Without even touching the radio, Seth switched to one of his favorite jazz CDs using the control feature on the steering wheel. "Where did I take you for dinner when we went to homecoming?"

She'd listened to country music—Keith Urban, Rascal Flatts, Lady Antebellum, and Sugarland—for years. Just never around Seth, who preferred Stéphane Grappelli. "We went to Olive Garden. Back then that was pretty high-class."

"Now I remember. I ordered lasagna and you ordered ravioli. You wore a pale green dress and were the most beautiful girl at the dance."

"Hardly."

"Well, you were to me. You always have been." He reached over, resting his hand on hers.

Seth's walk down memory lane led them out of "just friends" territory faster than Allison realized.

"This is a fun song." Allison pulled her hand away, adjusting the volume, and then hummed along with Susannah McCorkle singing "Night and Day." That managed to stop the handholding—at least for the moment.

Seth drove in silence for a few minutes. Allison hoped he'd picked up on her not-so-subtle cue to back off. Seth needed to remember she wanted to be his friend—and that was all. "Are you going back to the Springs tonight?"

"No. I've got a room at The Stanley. I'll head out right after breakfast tomorrow." Seth glanced over at her. "Want to meet me for breakfast, say about nine?"

"N-no, thanks. I promised Aunt Nita to help her with the boys."

"The boys? Your aunt is working with kids now?"

"No. I call the llamas 'the boys.' They're like a bunch of rambunctious middle-school boys."

"Ah." Seth drummed his fingers on the steering wheel. "I'm traveling for the next week or so, but I'll call when I can."

What could she say? *Don't bother? It's not a big deal? You don't have to call me?* "Okay."

They drove the last twenty minutes to Aunt Nita's in silence. Allison could just make out the faint images of evergreen trees lining the road, patches of snow on the ground glinting in the moonlight. As Seth parked the car, Allison opened the door and stepped out. "Thanks again for dinner, Seth."

"Let me walk you to the door."

Allison watched the llamas watch Seth coming around to meet her. The trio lined the fence, four-legged, silent witnesses to the end of her date.

Wait. This wasn't a date.

She and Seth were establishing a *friendship*, not renewing a romance.

Seth walked alongside her, his hand resting on the small of her back. He made no attempt to hold her hand. But Allison tucked both hands into the safety of the pockets of her green pea coat.

Seth cleared his throat in an uncharacteristic nervous gesture. "Allison, one more thing before you go inside . . ."

She turned, leaning against the door, trying to establish some sort of do-not-cross-this-line personal space. Surely Seth wasn't maneuvering for a good-night kiss.

"I have something for you—a gift." He pulled an all-too-familiar black velvet jeweler's box out of his coat pocket.

"Seth, what—"

"It's not what you think." He opened the lid, the soft click causing Allison to jump, revealing the diamond earrings he'd given her months ago as a wedding present. "I know you're not ready for an engagement ring. Yet."

As she stared at the brilliant gems nestled against the soft black material, Allison almost missed his whispered "yet." But she did hear the one small word and understood Seth's unspoken intent. "I can't accept these."

Seth held up his hand, palm out. "Hear me out, please, Allison. I bought the earrings for you. I can't return them. I don't want to sell them." He held the box out toward her. "Originally, I gave them to you as a wedding present. But now I'd like to give them to you, well, just because. Wear them and remember all the good times we had."

Allison looked from Seth's earnest face to the jeweler's box and back again, trying to decipher his sincerity.

Seth closed the box. "No strings attached." He pressed the box into her hand and closed her fingers over it, exerting a gentle, insistent pressure as he bent to kiss her cheek. "Please. It's just a gift—friend to friend."

"What is wrong with me, Bisquick?" Allison threw her coat onto the rack, listening to Seth's car disappearing down the gravel road.

She clutched the once-upon-a-time-wedding gift and paced the living room. "When Seth offered me the earrings, all I had to do was say no. Even a polite 'No, thank you.' Aaargh!" She threw her hands in the air, careful to hold on to the jewelry. "But nooooo. I take the stupid gift. Why is it so hard to say what I want to say to that man?"

Bisquick jumped down from the couch and, with an "It's your problem, not mine" swish of his tail, meandered to the bedroom. Allison followed, unclasping her necklace and taking off her gold bangle bracelets.

"Now I'm the proud owner of one barely used wedding dress and an equally barely used wedding gift from my ex-fiancé." She tossed the black box onto her dresser and pulled out a pair of sweats. "And

Seth has me so stressed out, I'm talking to myself. Well, talking to my cat. I don't know which is worse."

After brushing her teeth, Allison picked up the box again. Opened it. Seth said to wear the earrings and remember all the good times they'd had. She turned the box so that the emerald-cut diamonds glinted.

"We did have some good times, didn't we?" She dropped the box back on the dresser, picked up a brush, and ran the bristles through her hair. "It wasn't all bad with Seth."

When had their relationship changed? Seth seemed happy, never once having second thoughts about getting married. He had a plan and was sticking with it. Marrying Allison was part of that plan. How many times had she heard him tell someone they were the perfect couple?

When did she stop thinking that?

At first she liked Seth's take-charge attitude. She felt protected, cared for. When she didn't know what to do, Seth did. But over time, she realized Seth's idea of being the perfect couple meant doing things his way.

His vetoing her desire to double-major in graphic design and photography still stung.

Midway through sophomore year, she'd met up with Seth at the campus coffee shop after talking to her college adviser. She still remembered how the thought of pursuing photography excited her. Her professor's encouragement bolstered her confidence.

Seth dismissed the idea after listening to her plan for less than five minutes. "It's a waste of time and money." He folded the papers containing her projected class schedule for the next semester.

"But I'm applying for a scholarship. My professor thinks I should get it. And it will only be an extra semester and some summer classes." Allison sat back, stunned by Seth's vehement reaction.

"We're already planning on getting married after we graduate. I don't want to postpone that."

"I-I can continue classes after we're married—"

"I don't think it's a good idea." Seth stood, acting as if the conversation were over.

"But my adviser said this would actually benefit my graphic design degree."

"Allison, we've got our plan. This . . . photography hobby of yours isn't part of it." Seth gathered the college catalog and her papers and tossed them in the trash can near their booth, along with his empty coffee cup. "Look, I'm late. I'm supposed to meet up with some other guys for a run."

He'd bent down, kissed her, and left. End of conversation. And end of her dream.

Allison shut the velvet box, opened the top drawer, and dropped the gift in among her socks.

Maybe that interaction with Seth had been the start of Allison's doubts. How could Seth, the man she loved, the man she was going to marry, not support her dreams?

The buzz of her cell phone alerted her to a text. Seth? No, he didn't text. A quick glance revealed Hadleigh's name.

hey sis you up?

Allison curled up on her bed and typed a quick affirmative back.

Yes what's up H?

nothing much just wanting to say hi

Well, hi to you little sis How's school?

good aced my last test

And how did Evan do?

okay i guess

You guess? you and evan have a fight?

Allison waited for her sister's response, surprised when several minutes passed.

H? You okay?

Allison almost resorted to calling, but then a text came through.

we didn't fight just haven't talked in a couple of days

You want to talk about it H?

maybe later

Allison sighed, disappointed that Hadleigh didn't want to talk. Did her sister suspect that Evan was into porn? But then, texting wasn't the best form of communication about something serious.

Want me to call?

no its late maybe i will ask mom if i can come visit

Sounds good I can come get you if you want

great

Call me and tell me when OK?

ok love you sis

Love you too

ttyl

Goodnight

Allison tossed her phone to the end of the bed and pulled the cat into her lap. "Honestly, Bisquick, I don't know which relationships are harder—high school ones or adult ones. It's a toss-up."

She was too frustrated to sleep. Too frustrated to be productive at work. With an apology to Bisquick for abandoning him, she climbed the stairs to her aunt's family room and stood in front of the easel. After one look at her painting, Aunt Nita had retired the still life, giving Allison carte blanche with the oil paints. Despite Allison's insistence that she was just playing around, her aunt proclaimed the art supplies were now hers.

Allison stared at the canvas. There was no rhyme or reason to her art. She chose the colors that appealed to her and alternated brush sizes. She loved the deep colors of the oil paints, the way she could pile on colors to create a sense of depth. Sometimes she found herself muttering her college professor's mantra: "Be dangerous."

For some reason, she was drawn to shades of blue and green. She selected her favorite playlist on her iPod, then prepared the paints she wanted to use. As she painted, somehow her instructor's words and the verse she'd parked her brain on this week became intertwined. *Be dangerous. Zest. Enthusiasm. Fearless.*

That's what she loved about painting. It wasn't so much that she was dangerous as she explored the dance of colors. It was that she was becoming *less afraid*. Painting tapped in to a hidden vein of enthusiasm in her life . . . she just needed to give it space to come to life.

CHAPTER 29

Hey, Alli, just hiked part of the Appalachian Trail. Tell Seth we'll do Pikes Peak again one of these days, okay? He can run it and we'll walk.

—Daniel

Allison stared at the photos she'd taken during the sleigh ride with Daniel, Madison, and Ty. Everything looked good. There were several Allison could use for the brochure, and she could even give a few to Madison to use on the website.

She scrolled over to the trio of photos of Daniel. For being such impromptu shots, they'd turned out well. Of course, Daniel was in his element: outdoors. He looked relaxed, content, and as appealing as ever. Yep, she'd captured the Daniel she knew and lo— Allison cut off her thought. She was *not* going there. She'd captured the Daniel she *knew*.

What to do with the photos? It wasn't like she could turn them into a screensaver for her computer. Maybe Daniel would want them.

Did she dare?

She'd spent weeks avoiding Daniel. Sending him the photos would be a step toward him, initiating contact instead of continued evasive action.

Why not? She would send him the photos along with a casual, friendly e-mail. It would show him that she was happy with the way things were—willing to let the truce stand. Nothing more, nothing less.

• • •

"Thanks for the invitation, Seth." Allison glanced out the window at the four-legged boys. Things were quiet in the pasture. "I'll let you know if I can go."

As she ended the phone call, she realized her aunt stood just inside the apartment.

"Sorry, sweetie." Aunt Nita shrugged, not moving any farther into Allison's space. "I knocked. Didn't realize you were on the phone."

Allison motioned her aunt to come in. "Just talking to Seth."

"Seth, huh? He calling a lot?"

"Not really. Couple times a week."

"You're okay with that?"

"Sure. Nothing to worry about." Maybe if she kept saying that, she would convince herself. Allison stretched her arms overhead, arching her back to ease her stiff muscles. "He's just a friend."

"A friend you were going to marry a few months ago."

"I haven't forgotten that."

"Do you think Seth has?"

A memory of the earrings Seth insisted she take—friend to friend—flashed through Allison's mind. "I doubt it. But I'm hoping he'll see it's better if we're just friends."

"Correct me if I'm wrong, but you moved up here to put distance between you and your ex-fiancé, right?"

"Right."

"Then why are you dating him again?"

"I'm not *dating* him. I'm just trying to . . . to . . ."

"You went to dinner, right? And didn't I overhear an invitation somewhere else?"

"Seth was given two tickets to a Broadway show." Allison carried her mug to the kitchen, stashing it in the dishwasher. "He asked me to go with him."

"How *friendly* of him."

"It's dinner and a show, not a proposal. And I'm not sure I'll accept the invitation."

"Be careful. Seth may be hoping you'll fall in love with him again."

Her aunt's caution echoed Meghan's warning during the lingerie shopping spree. And the word "yet" that Seth had whispered when he gave her the earrings. Maybe she should heed her aunt's and best friend's warnings. But Allison was trying to do things right, not to make any more mistakes with Seth. She didn't want to hurt him again. She was trying to be mature—to show Seth and everyone else that they could be friends. She knew what she was doing.

Didn't she?

"So, my dear aunt, besides eavesdropping on my conversation, did you have another reason for coming downstairs?"

"Point taken." Her aunt stood beside the couch and scratched behind Bisquick's ears as the cat lounged across the cushions. "I did want to talk with you about someone—about something. But I don't know if now is a good time."

"Well, now you have to say something. I hate those 'I was going to say something, oh never mind' conversations."

"Okay, then." Her aunt took a deep breath and then expelled it, her words flowing out on the exhale. "Your father is coming to town and would like to see you."

Allison let the words settle into her brain one at a time, separating the key ones. *Your. Father. Would. Like. To. See. You.*

That wasn't going to happen.

"I'm getting all sorts of invitations tonight, aren't I?" She picked up the stack of mail on her desk and began sorting through it, tossing items in the trash. "I'll decline this one."

"Won't you even consider seeing him, Allison? Pray about it?"

"No."

"It's been—"

"I know how long it's been." She threw the envelopes down, scattering them across her desk. "What is he waiting for? Some sort of expiration date on my decision not to see him?"

"For you to forgive him?"

Allison stalked across the room and yanked her coat off the rack, pulling it on without looking at her aunt. She opened the door. "I think the no-trespassing sign that I posted about the topic of my father must have fallen down. Let me put that back up for you." She ended the conversation by slamming the door.

Allison marched across the yard to the llamas. Where else did she have to go? Upstairs to Aunt Nita's? Down the unlit, unpaved driveway? She'd visit the boys and cool off. Then she'd apologize. She wouldn't change her mind. Just apologize for her rude behavior. Aunt Nita loved her, and she also loved her brother. Allison's father.

Unlatching the gate, she stepped inside, not surprised when Kuzko approached her, followed by Pacha. Banzai stood watching. Allison had a decided preference for the newest llama, intrigued by his dark face sitting atop a long neck covered with curly reddish-brown fur. But he still kept his distance.

She leaned forward until she was nose to nose with Kuzko's white face, his mouth rimmed with licorice-black fur. Her secret nickname for him was Licorice Lips. The huff of breath he exhaled in her face as a greeting no longer surprised her.

"Good to see you too, boy."

Pacha nudged Kuzko out of the way, wanting his turn to say hello. Banzai watched the other two llamas.

"All right, boys, one at a time. No need to fight." She scratched Pacha's rump, causing the llama to twist his neck and rub his face against her shoulder. When Kuzko moved in again, she pushed back. "Wait your turn."

Banzai paced closer, agitated by the jostling between Allison and the other two llamas. In one swift move, he nipped Pacha, causing the white llama to jump and twist, pushing Allison against Kuzko. When Allison knocked into Kuzko, the llama moved away. Allison lost her balance and landed on her backside in the hard, cold dirt.

She scrambled to her feet, afraid of being trampled by a trio of rowdy llamas. She sprinted to the gate, slipping to safety on the other side. Brushing off the seat of her jeans, she watched as Banzai rammed his chest into Kuzko, who shoved back. Pacha circled around and came at Banzai from the other side.

"And people talk about catfights." Allison leaned her arms on the fence. "You boys are being ridiculous. No different from any of the guys in my life. Kuzko, you're bossy, like Seth. And Pacha, you're crowding me, like Daniel."

Banzai spat at the other llamas, refusing to back down, despite being outnumbered. "And Banzai, you're no better than my dad. You just won't go away, no matter how much you're ignored."

Allison had delayed talking to her aunt long enough. She'd loaded and started her dishwasher. Refilled Bisquick's water bowl. Changed into her pajamas. Flossed and brushed her teeth. Sorted her laundry. Checked her e-mail.

All the while she thought. About Daniel. About Seth. About her father.

Two hours later, she didn't have any decisions, and she still owed her aunt an apology.

Her aunt meant well. She just didn't understand. Allison ran her fingers through her hair and exhaled. "I know I won't sleep until I talk to her, Bisquick."

Her cat yawned and kneaded the pillow. "I'm tired too." Allison shrugged. "But I've got to do the right thing. Keep the bed warm for me, will you?"

She found Aunt Nita sitting at her dining room table, flipping through cards as she played a game of solitaire, a pair of paisley-printed readers on the tip of her nose.

"Not asleep?" Allison stood at the top of the stairs, feeling like a misbehaving middle-schooler facing the principal.

"Nope." Her aunt lifted a mug and waved it. "I'm having some warm milk and honey. Care to join me?"

"That's okay. Can we talk?"

"Anytime, sweetie."

"Even this late?"

"I'm not asleep. You're not asleep." Aunt Nita gathered the cards and shuffled them. "Interested in a game of crazy eights?"

"I've never beat you at cards. I doubt I'll start tonight." She sat, folding her legs underneath her, and watched her aunt shuffle the cards with the skill of a Las Vegas blackjack dealer.

Allison reached over and covered her aunt's weather-worn hand with her own. Waited for her aunt to look up. "I'm sorry I was so rude tonight."

"No need to apologize—"

"Let me do this." She squeezed her aunt's hand. "Aunt Nita, I know you love me. And I love you too. In some ways, you understand me better than anyone else. Please forgive me for walking out tonight. I'm not usually a door slammer."

"All's forgiven, sweetie." Her aunt patted her hand and then went back to shuffling. "What are you thinking?"

"So many things." Allison rubbed her wrist. "All I have to do is the right thing. That should be easy." She watched her aunt cut the deck and then resume shuffling the blue-and-white patterned cards. "But why does doing the right thing always have to be the hardest thing? Why is the right thing all about the have-to?"

"I'm not sure I'm following."

"If I do the right thing with Seth, I'd let my yes be yes and go through with my original commitment and marry him." Allison paused, waiting for her aunt to argue with her. When Aunt Nita said nothing, she continued. "If I did the right thing with Daniel, I'd ignore . . . well, things like how I feel most like myself when I'm with him. I'd remind myself that you can't be attracted to your fiancé's brother."

"Ex-fiancé."

"Whatever, Aunt Nita." Allison waved the comment away. "And if I did the right thing with my dad, I'd forgive him."

"For what?"

"For abducting me. For how much I loved being with him. For teaching me to live life out loud for two years. For saying 'This was a mistake,' then walking away. For breaking my heart."

Allison, dismissing her aunt's offer of a napkin, pretended there were no tears streaking down her face.

"Why does doing the right thing cut off my breath? It's like . . . like someone hands me an outfit and says, 'Put this on.' And then I shove myself into this dress two sizes too small. Cram my feet into shoes that pinch my toes and scrape my heels. I go and stand in front of the mirror and try to convince myself it looks fine. That I look fine. I tell myself to just buy the outfit. And the whole time, I want my yoga pants, cotton top, and flip-flops."

Allison sat, waiting for her aunt to say something profound. Something that would make everything all better. "Nothing to say?"

"Just a question." Her aunt set the deck of cards aside.

"Only one?"

"Yes."

"Okay, what is it?"

"Is the hardest thing always the right thing?"

Hey, Alli—Spent a few days scuba diving in the Bahamas, where they filmed the old TV show _Flipper_. Remember when we watched that marathon of reruns while Seth studied for finals?
—Daniel

CHAPTER 30

Daniel gathered up his workout clothes and tossed them on the straight-back wooden chair in the corner of the room. Grabbing his laptop, he turned it on and stretched out on the bed while he waited for it to power up.

Living at the B-and-B was manageable because someone picked up his room every day. Since the lodge didn't officially open for another two months, there was a skeleton staff. That meant an unknown, overworked someone made his bed and wiped the hair out of the sink. He needed to be neater.

What he needed to do was wrap up this job. Pack his duffel, head to his apartment, do a few loads of laundry, pay some bills, and then start the next job. If time allowed, maybe he'd manage a few days of camping. Where was he heading next? Canada? He needed to check his calendar. First he needed to find his calendar.

Daniel scanned his e-mail, stopping when he saw Alli's address in the in-box. A brief note with a PDF attachment.

Daniel,
I sent the photos for the brochure to Madison, figuring she'd get

them to her parents. They'll let me know which ones they like and
then I'll put together a proof.

I've attached several photos I took of you. I don't think you realized I had the camera pointed in your direction—not until the last
photo.

I looked at these and thought, *Daniel Rayner, in his element.*
They show who you are—a man who's comfortable outdoors and
with himself.

Anyway, enjoy a glimpse of yourself through my camera lens.

Alli

He opened the document, surprised to see Alli had designed an
eleven-by-fourteen layout of three photos against the faint image
of Pikes Peak. Two smaller close-ups of him—one staring into the
campfire, one smiling into the camera—set off a larger photo of
him crouched in front of the fire. The caption, DEFINITIVE DANIEL
RAYNER, ran across the bottom of the page.

How did Alli do that? With a few point-frame-and-shoot decisions,
she captured who he was. Daniel stared at the photos. Ever since he'd
met Alli, she'd expressed interest in who he was, what he did. She'd
listened to his stories, exclaimed over some of his more harebrained
escapades, thanked him for every silly postcard he sent her.

His parents didn't get him. Seth didn't understand his fascination
with hiking, climbing, camping, white-water rafting. He was the odd
man out in his family.

But Alli accepted him for who he was.

Too bad he didn't have a printer; he'd run off a copy of the photo
montage. He closed the e-mail, a smile playing across his lips. He'd
do that when he got home. Print out the collage and tack it up over
his desk.

"Daniel, do you realize what time it is?" Allison watched Daniel
rummage through the bed of his truck. What else could he be

looking for? He'd stuffed his daypack with an absurd amount of un-essential essentials. Parachute cord. Rope. Several bandanas. An extra pair of gloves. And all the while, he'd lectured her on safety precautions: protecting herself from frostbite, safe driving tips for snowmobiles, how to survive if she got lost.

"I dunno. Nine-thirty?" He held up a small metal shovel and set it on the ground at his feet.

"I thought you wanted to leave at eight-thirty—nine at the latest."

"I did." He turned and gave her a quick grin. "But the bottom line is we'll leave when we're ready."

Allison slumped against the bumper. "I'm ready. I've *been* ready."

"And I'm almost ready." Daniel fastened the shovel to the side of his pack, tossing it into the back of his truck. "And since I'm leading this little expedition today, I get to say when we roll out."

Pulling her knit cap off her head and stuffing it in her coat pocket, Allison ran her fingers through her bangs. "We *are* going sometime today, right?"

"Quit complaining, Alli." Daniel slid to the side and gave her shoulder a gentle nudge. "If you don't, I won't let you drive the snowmobile."

"Hey, I get my own snowmobile, Daniel Rayner. I don't need you chauffeuring me around."

Stepping forward to open the door, Daniel motioned her to the front passenger seat. "Aren't we the bossy one today? I suppose you want your own pair of snowshoes too?"

Warmth heated Allison's face when Daniel winked, a teasing look lighting his eyes. She needed to get a grip. Daniel wasn't flirting with her. They were just two friends—coworkers, really—out for a fun day of snowmobiling and snowshoeing. Nothing more. Nothing less.

Resting in a grove of mountain cedar, Allison had to admit she'd enjoyed the slow pace of the sleigh ride a few days ago, even though it had included Madison and Ty.

When Daniel had arranged the job for her, he'd mentioned a sleigh ride, snowmobiling, and snowshoeing. It figured he would opt for snowmobiling *and* snowshoeing on the same day.

Four hours later, exhaustion had slowed her pace. Earlier the trees had protected her, but the wind had increased in the past half hour. Her legs ached from snowshoeing all morning. She needed to get to the gym and restart her workout routine. Or invest in a treadmill.

The wind whipped so much snow around, it was useless to try for any more photos. With awkward steps, Allison turned toward the snowmobiles, thankful she had plenty of photos for the brochure. As she tucked her camera into the side pocket of her backpack, Allison heard the static crackle of the walkie-talkie strapped to her belt. She unhooked the radio and brought it close to her mouth. "Yeah, Daniel?"

"I don't like how—winds—worse—" Allison held the receiver to her ear, straining to hear what Daniel said. "Head back—snowmobiles. Waiting—"

"Already doing that!" she shouted into the receiver. "I'll see you in just a couple of minutes."

Tightening the ties of the hood under her chin, she started back down the slope to where they'd left the snowmobiles. It sounded as if Daniel wanted to play it safe and head back to town before the weather got worse.

"I'm all for that. Hot chocolate, here I come."

As she cleared the trees, she looked down the mountain slope and saw Daniel off to her left, packing the snowmobiles. He waved and motioned her to move faster. She was only halfway between the trees and Daniel when she heard the drone of an airplane overhead.

That was crazy! Why would someone fly in this kind of weather?

Still moving, Allison looked up at the sky.

No plane. What was that noise?

Only when Allison felt the tremors under her feet did she look behind her. At first she couldn't comprehend why the small grove of trees she'd just been in had disappeared. It had been obliterated by an advancing massive white cloud.

Avalanche!

Even as Allison's snowshoes hampered her efforts, she realized the futility of trying to outrun something moving eighty miles an hour.

"Daniel! Avalanche! Avalanche!" Allison would *not* look back. "No way I'm getting out of this. God, help!"

Daniel turned from strapping his pack to the snowmobile. He screamed her name just as a wave of snow engulfed her, sucking her under like a riptide at the beach. Only this was so much colder than any ocean she'd ever been in. She tumbled over and over. Snow filled her mouth, and she sputtered and clamped her lips shut. She fought to draw air into her lungs through her nose, but cold, wet snow surrounded her.

What had Daniel told her to do? Swim . . . Daniel expected her to *swim* in this?

She flailed her arms like a drowning woman.

Snow, rocks, and tree branches torn off by the avalanche's assault pelted her body as she tumbled down the mountain. In desperation, Allison covered her face with her hands.

God . . . help Daniel find me.

"Alli!" Daniel screamed her name as he half ran, half fell down the slope. "Alli!"

He trained his eyes on the avalanche plummeting down the mountain, trying to estimate Alli's location. With wind-driven snow thrashing his face, he fought to keep his eyes open. The horror of watching Alli disappear in a raging mass of snow stole his breath.

Fumbling, he pulled his goggles down over his face, straining for some glimpse of her red cap. Her red gloves. For an instant, Daniel saw Alli's arms, and he knew she was fighting to stay on top of the snow, as he'd instructed her that morning.

Precious seconds ticked away with every beat of his heart.

Think. *Think.*

Alli had a beacon. Hands shaking, Daniel switched his beacon to receive. He slipped and slid, trying to figure out how unstable the terrain was. He had to stay safe; he was Alli's only hope for survival.

Reaching the area of trees that had stopped the avalanche's onslaught, Daniel used the beacon to gauge Alli's location underneath the snow. He grabbed the folded aluminum avalanche probe from its sack, assembling it to its full length of almost nine feet and securing the locks. Even with the limited shelter of the trees, the wind whipped the tree limbs in his face.

How many minutes had gone by? How badly was she hurt?

Using the probe, he broke through the layers of snow, trying to determine how deeply Alli was buried. Within a few moments, he caught a glimpse of something red.

Blood?

Dropping the probe, Daniel fell to his knees. His fingers shook as he brushed away the snow. What would he find? A few seconds later, his hands touched the ice-encrusted fabric of one of Alli's crimson gloves.

He clasped her hand for a moment, relief overwhelming him. Now to determine Alli's position. He grabbed the compact shovel tied to the lower section of his backpack.

"So much for being overprepared." He shoveled the snow, trying to be quick but careful, not wanting to cut Alli with the blade. "God, please, please . . . help me get to her before . . . before . . ." He couldn't put words to the fear gnawing at his heart. Alli had to be alive. He was not leaving the mountain with her in any other condition.

Five minutes later, Daniel knew he was close enough to abandon the shovel. He knew that for Alli to be so near the top of the snow mound, she must have fought to swim through the out-of-control slide.

Throwing the shovel to the side, he scooped away handfuls of snow until he saw Alli's face. Her eyes were closed, her skin as white as the snow still burying most of her body. Tears threatened to further blur his vision.

"No time to lose, Danny boy. You know what to do. Do it."

He shoved his goggles up on his forehead. Alli's lips were a dull blue, her hair caked with ice and pine needles. Scrapes marred her forehead and cheeks.

Brushing the snow away from her face and neck, Daniel put his face up against hers, trying to feel her breath against his skin. Nothing. Pulling off a glove, he placed his fingers against her neck. Searching for a pulse, he found a slow, thready beat. While her heart hadn't stopped, it probably wasn't pumping sufficient blood to keep Alli alive for long.

Daniel placed his hand underneath her neck, tilting her head back as best he could. Leaning in again, he placed his mouth over her icy lips and began to breathe for her.

$\mathcal{H}$e was losing ground with Allison, not gaining.

Seth waved at a runner coming down the incline as he strode up, his breathing steady. Off in the distance, he detected the faint image of a climber scaling one of the rock formations scattered throughout the Garden of the Gods. The orange-red structures seemed out of place in the Colorado foothills.

Seth's feet pounded against the asphalt, his legs stretching out, propelling him past a couple of women out for an early-morning walk. Since traffic was light this time of day, he mostly had to watch for other runners, walkers, or cyclists and the occasional overfriendly, undercontrolled dog.

He ran in the Garden of the Gods several times a week, so he set his body on autopilot, allowing him to focus on his relationship with Allison. Or rather, his lack of a relationship with Allison.

She treated him like a friend—and a casual "see you when I see you" one at that. Go out to dinner? Sure. Talk on the phone? Fine—but she often left the TV on in the background and then made some excuse to end their conversation after five minutes. Go to a Broadway show? Maybe. And he'd almost had to force the earrings on her. That heartfelt gesture earned him the right to kiss her cheek. Her cheek! She might as well have been his great-aunt Tillie.

Should he admit defeat and move on? Find someone else? There were plenty of other women who would be thrilled to date Seth Rayner, the soon-to-be vice president of Rayner Construction. Michelle, his assistant, gave off not so subtle hints. Lingering by his desk. Wearing perfume that almost slapped him across the face and said, "Hey! Notice me." But he wasn't interested in a cougar relationship.

He glanced at his watch, monitoring his heart rate and time. He needed to pick up the pace.

Was Daniel back from his latest trip? Seth could never keep track of his big brother. He'd call later today, get advice on how to handle a skittish woman. Ask him to put in a good word, tell Allison he'd changed. Did she even notice how patient he'd become? How he wasn't forcing her engagement ring back on her finger? He was doing things according to her timetable, not his, no matter how frustrating it was.

Was there some subtle way to remind Allison of his good qualities, the reasons she fell in love with him? She always liked to let him lead, make the decisions for her, take care of her. Seth was ready to do that again.

The road curved, giving him a panoramic view of varied rock formations, evergreens, the sun set in a brilliant blue, cloudless sky. Seth set his sights on the hill rising ahead of him.

When Seth launched his campaign to win Allison back, he'd never imagined failure. Being Seth Rayner, he was used to getting what he wanted. He wasn't afraid of hard work, and he didn't expect life to be easy. But he did expect his hard work to pay off.

He reviewed his pursuit.

Carefully timed visits—check.

Appropriately friendly cards—check.

Phone calls beginning with a casual "was thinking of you"—check.

Get the diamond earrings back into her hands, with just the hint of the engagement ring—check.

Increase the physical affection—bust.

Allison seemed determined to keep him at arm's length. Could there possibly be somebody else? Had Allison met someone since moving to Estes Park? Was that why she cut her hair—for some new guy? The thought brought him up short. Allison and someone else. Allison dating someone else. Allison falling in love with someone else, marrying someone else.

Impossible.

He shook his head, clearing away the image of Allison kissing some unknown man. If what he was doing wasn't working, he needed to figure out what would bring her back. Veering off the road, he headed for the Scotsman Trail. His body was up to a challenge today. He'd add an extra mile or two. Maybe by the end of his run, he would figure out some way to get closer to his goal of winning Allison back.

Alli, I'll be guiding white-water rafting trips on the Arkansas River this summer. Try and talk Seth into bringing you up here in between some of his marathons. I'll introduce you to some Class 5 rapids.
—Daniel

CHAPTER 32

They'd never make it off the mountain by nightfall.

Daniel cradled Alli in his arms, watching the shadows deepen on the mountain as the sun disappeared. Snowmobiling out in the dark was foolhardy at best. He doubted anyone would search for them when the winds were this high. His cell phone wasn't picking up a signal, so he had no way to tell anyone where they were.

While he wanted to get Alli somewhere warmer than the side of a mountain, he didn't see how he could do that with darkness falling.

He'd stopped the bleeding from a huge gash across Alli's palm from her thumb to her pinkie finger. Best as he could tell, she'd broken her left wrist when the avalanche slammed her against a tree. Using her wool muffler, he'd bound her swollen forearm against her body, zipping her coat closed over it to hold the bone still. He couldn't rule out a concussion, what with the way Alli complained of dizziness and nausea while he'd tended to her injuries.

"Gotta get moving." He needed to put together some sort of shelter for them. But he continued to hold Alli wrapped in two emergency blankets he found stashed in the snowmobiles.

"Alli, sweetheart." Daniel brought his lips close to her ear and whispered, "I need you to listen to me."

She turned toward his voice, trying to open her eyes. Their faces were a mere breath apart. Daniel pressed his lips against her skin. She still felt so cold. "Alli, I need to leave you for just a bit. I've got to get us some shelter."

"Wh-what? Leaving me?" Alli's lids fluttered open, her eyes hazy with pain and panic.

"No. I'm not *leaving* you." Daniel pulled her closer, running his gloved fingers down the side of her face. "But I need to put together a shelter of some sort. A snow cave to keep us warm until the morning."

Alli's breath came in halting gasps, telling Daniel without words how much pain she felt. Even with her wrapped in his arms, shivers racked her body.

"You know best." She tried to smile through chattering teeth. "Don't have much say . . ."

"Not this time. You can boss me around all you want when we get back to town. Deal?"

"Deal, Danny boy." When he gave a start of surprise, she tried to laugh, and then bit back an exclamation of pain. "Talk to yourself when you're worried."

"I guess it's better than 'big brother.'" Instead of getting up, he continued to hold Alli.

"I gotta admit, Daniel . . ." Alli buried her face against his shoulder. "Don't really think of you as a big brother . . ."

"You don't, huh?"

"No . . . not supposed to know that." Alli shook her head and then groaned. "My head. Hurts. Not thinking straight."

"If we're going to be honest with each other . . ." Daniel rested his gloved hand on her cheek. "I don't think of you as a kid. And I don't have a concussion making me say that."

"Daniel—"

"Don't talk. You're exhausted." He needed to focus on caring for Alli's physical needs, not their mixed-up feelings for each other. "Okay, I've got to build that snow cave." He pulled the blankets closer around her. "I don't want you walking around, but you need to keep warm. Move your good arm and both your legs as best you can." When she groaned again, he gave her a gentle hug. "Sorry. Besides huddling together, it's the only way to stay warm. While I work, I'll talk to you. You have to stay awake, Alli. No Sleeping Snow Beauty."

"Sure, Daniel." Alli rested her head on his shoulder, her eyes closed. "Tell me what you were like when you were younger."

"That'll put you to sleep. Okay, sweetheart, I've got to get busy, and you've got to keep yourself warm."

Holding Alli in his arms, Daniel positioned himself on his knees. Until now his body shielded her from the wind. Once he stood up, the bitter cold would steal any warmth he'd provided her.

After positioning her on the ground, he formed a berm of snow to protect Alli from the wind, packing the snow about a foot high. "I'll work as fast as I can. Just keep moving. And don't forget to drink some water."

"That's the way it's going to be." Alli clutched the silver solar blankets. "You doing most of the work."

Daniel remembered reading in one of his favorite outdoor magazines that once you built a snow cave, you needed to wrap up in a blanket, sit on your pack, light a candle, and remember your best jokes.

"Too bad I never remember any punch lines." With one last look around, he crawled out of the snow cave and headed back to Alli.

As he'd worked, he heard Alli moving her arm and legs in slow motion, thanks to the metallic crinkle of the solar blankets. Every time it got quiet, he called out to her to keep moving.

"Tyrant. Can't you let a girl rest?"

"All in good time." A little over two hours later, he knelt beside her. "I've just got to punch a couple of ventilation holes through the top of the cave, and then we can crawl inside. It'll be a lot warmer in there, away from the wind."

As it was, he felt plenty warm, despite wearing only his Gore-Tex pants and his base-layer shirt. He'd tried not to work too fast, wanting to avoid working up a sweat. His anxiety about Alli had driven him to dig faster. He didn't care about himself, but he had to be able to take care of Alli.

"Okay, sweetheart. Home sweet snowy home awaits. It's not much, but it was the only place with a vacancy. Come on, I'll help you in."

Alli remained silent. Daniel bent and lifted her into his arms, careful not to jostle her injured arm.

"Daniel, don't. I can walk."

"And I can carry you. It's no big deal, Alli." He shifted her weight so she rested more securely in his arms. "I just wish I could carry you into the cave too. But I've got a plan."

He looked at Alli as he walked back to the bank that he'd judged was safest for the snow cave. Her head lay against his shoulder. Her eyes were closed, her lashes a stark black against her cheeks. Her lips had a blue tinge.

"Once we get in the cave, I'll get you some more water and something to eat. I've got the granola bars and nuts we packed. Not much, but it's calories."

"Always prepared. Boy Scout?"

"Yep. Eagle Scout."

But there was no way he was prepared for this.

"Okay, I'd like to say ladies first, but the only way this is going to work is if I go ahead of you. I'll lay you down inside the opening— just stay there. That's all you've got to do."

"Got an escalator?" Alli offered the hint of a smile.

"No, that wasn't in the plans when I constructed our accommodations. My oversight." Daniel knelt as close to the entrance as he could and laid Alli in the snow. "Give me just a second to get in, then I'll pull you up."

"Sorry I c-can't . . . crawl . . ." Alli's teeth chattered. "Not c-coordinated with one arm . . ."

"Sweetheart, I'm the one who's sorry. I suggested this whole stupid day trip."

"Not stupid . . . d-didn't plan . . . avalanche."

"Well, we could sit out here in the wind and cold and argue all day, or be warmer inside the cave. I'm for being warmer."

Daniel scrambled up the entrance. Within seconds, he reached down, grabbed hold of Alli's hood, and eased her up the slope and into the cave. Once she was inside, he gathered her in his arms. He'd already lit the candle before getting Alli. Now all he needed was to come up with some jokes.

The emergency candle flame cast dim light on the sides of the cave. He'd pulled the cushions off the snowmobiles, figuring they'd provide insulation from the snowpacked ground. Sitting with his back against the snow wall, Daniel positioned Alli on his lap, trying not to jar her arm again. He reached for the emergency blankets and pulled them around her shoulders. "Comfortable?"

"Sure." Allison's reply was muffled against his coat. "Can I sleep now, boss?"

"For about four hours. I couldn't let you sleep earlier because I wasn't sure how bad a head injury you had. I think you've got a concussion, so there will be a few wake-up calls during the night, Miss Denman."

Allison groaned in protest and moved restlessly in his arms.

"Am I hurting you?"

"Just getting comfortable . . . That's better." Allison curled against him like a young child. "I'm sorry, Daniel."

"What are you sorry for? Keeping me up past my curfew?"

A yawn swallowed her faint giggle. "You haven't had a curfew in years." Allison yawned again but couldn't quite hide her tears of pain. "Sorry I can't help."

Daniel brushed her face with his fingertips. "Let's just concentrate on staying warm and you getting some sleep."

He leaned against the cave wall. The way his head ached meant he probably was dehydrated. Leaning a little to the left, he snagged one of the water bottles and helped Alli drink before taking a swig.

"They were expecting us back in town by now. I'm thinking they'll send out a search party first thing in the morning."

Alli kept her eyes closed as she spoke. "Not sooner?"

"Not with the winds the way they are. More than likely, that's what triggered the avalanche. The snowpack was unstable to begin with, and then the winds set off the avalanche." Seeing Allison beginning to nod off, he stopped talking.

"It's okay, you can keep talking . . ."

"Putting you to sleep?" Daniel chuckled and shifted his weight. His arm was going to fall asleep at that angle.

"No . . . that's not what I meant. Glad I'm not by myself. I'd be too scared. But I know I'm safe with you." Another yawn interrupted her words. "You're not afraid of anything, are you?"

Just afraid to admit he loved her.

"So, are you?"

"Am I what?"

"Afraid of anything?" Allison snuggled closer to him, a contented-looking smile playing along the corners of her mouth. Daniel thought about tracing the outline of her lips but forced his hand to hold tighter to his bottle of water.

"Sure. Everybody's afraid of something, Alli."

"What are you afraid of?"

"O-kay. When I was a little kid, I was afraid of jumping off the high dive at the pool."

"But you did."

"Sure did. I hit my head on the board and ended up with four stitches."

"Oh, so that's why you have that scar . . ." Opening her eyes, Alli slowly lifted her free hand and traced the mark near his temple. Daniel took her hand in his and tucked it between them.

"It's not my only scar, Alli. I've got plenty."

"None self-inflicted."

Daniel didn't know how to answer. He knew what she meant.

"It's okay, Daniel. I brought it up. Talk too much when I'm tired . . ."

"I'm not sure what I'm supposed to say right now."

"Nothing . . ." Alli's eyes closed as her voice trailed off.

Daniel sat watching her for a few moments, realizing from her even breathing that she'd fallen asleep.

Probably for the best. They were both too tired for that conversation.

Trying not to disturb Allison, he set the alarm on his watch to wake him every two hours just in case he fell asleep. He'd give anything to get some rest too, but doubted he'd take even a catnap. He had the night shift—and no backup.

Alli, went to Cozumel to get my Scuba Divemaster rating. Let me know if you'd ever like to learn to dive.

—Daniel

CHAPTER 33

Allison struggled against the remnants of sleep tangling her thoughts. Why was her room so chilly? And why couldn't she move her arm? Had she rolled over and slept on it all night?

And her hand *hurt*.

When she twisted to the right, her face brushed against something cool. Soft. When she moved her right hand, it scraped against— what?

Allison forced her eyes open and realized her hand rested against Daniel's scruffy face.

Make that *whom*.

Watching him, she remembered how he'd held her all night, waking her several times to ask what her name was, what his name was—once he even asked her to sing "The Star-Spangled Banner." She'd declined. He'd hummed a few off-key notes as she sipped some water, and then he eased her back into a comfortable position again.

"All good, Alli?"

"All good."

Yeah, too good to be true. Months ago she'd been engaged to his brother. She'd imagined waking up next to Seth, not Daniel. Now here she was, her gloved fingers touching his solid jaw, wishing . . . what?

Without warning, Daniel's eyelids lifted, and his at-odds-with-each-other eyes skimmed her face.

"G'morning." He touched her cheek, a crooked half-smile tugging at her heart. "You okay?"

"Y-yeah. Just woke up."

"In a lot of pain?" Daniel pulled off his knit cap, raking his fingers through his hair. "I'm sorry the first-aid kit only had ibuprofen. Didn't realize you were allergic to it."

"The pain's not too bad."

Daniel yawned and then glanced at his watch. "Five-thirty. You're not a late sleeper."

"Never got into the habit."

"Me, either. Why waste daylight?" He tugged off his glove and scratched at the stubble darkening his jaw. "I prefer to start the day at the gym, followed by a hot shower."

"Not gonna happen today, I'm afraid." Allison closed her eyes, trying to ignore the throbbing in her wrist.

"I've been thinking about the game plan for today."

"In the two minutes since you woke up, you devised a game plan?"

"I was awake most of the night. No ESPN. I'm sorry you caught me dozing." His voice was hushed inside the ice cave. "Here's what I'm thinking. Someone's going to come looking for us, because folks at the lodge will report we didn't come back. They know our general location, although I confess I veered from it a bit. Not too much. Hey, you awake?"

Allison opened her eyes. "I've heard every word. My head still hurts, so it's easier to keep my eyes closed."

"I'm sorry, Alli." His concern wrapped around her like a warm hug. "I need to hike up the mountain to try to pick up a cell tower. That way I can contact someone using my phone—let them know exactly where we are. Speed up the rescue effort."

"Why don't we just snowmobile out of here?" The sooner she got someplace where she could get some pain medication, the better.

"I thought about that. You can't drive your own snowmobile anymore. And I'd rather an EMT look at you before I put you on a snowmobile again."

"I'll be fine."

"It's a couple of hours back to the lodge, Alli. You're hurt. They might decide it's better to take you out on a stretcher."

"Can I go with you—" Allison struggled to sit up.

"No. I can't let you walk around outside." Daniel's arms tightened around her. "Your risk of hypothermia is still high, and I don't want you to fall and further injure your arm. The best thing is for you to stay here."

"Daniel—"

"Alli, I hate to leave you even for a little bit. But I have to do everything I can to get us off the mountain and get you to a hospital as soon as possible."

Allison fought against the desire to cry. If she weren't here, Daniel could just snowmobile off the mountain.

His whispered words seemed to echo against the snowpacked walls. "We're in this together, Alli." He tilted her face up, forcing her to look at him. "Don't go thinking how much easier it'd be for me if you weren't here."

"What are you, a mind reader?"

"I wish." Daniel repositioned the blankets around Alli's shoulders. "We've known each other for six years. I know how your mind works, at least a little bit. You take responsibility for entirely too much."

"Do not."

"And while you often let other people—for example, Seth—take the lead, that doesn't mean you don't like being right." He shifted to reach the water bottle. "This time I need you to let *me* be right. Let me take care of you. Please?"

Daniel delayed her response by holding the water bottle to her mouth. After she finished drinking, he lightly pressed his thumb against her bottom lip and wiped away the lingering moisture. At her quick intake of breath, he glanced at her, their gazes entangling.

Daniel stroked her lip with the pad of his thumb. "Alli . . ."

Even in the dim light of their shelter, Allison recognized Daniel's conflicting emotions. He seemed to debate the wisdom of kissing her again. She watched him take a slow breath, move his hand away. Then he pressed a kiss against his fingers and placed them against her lips.

"You, my sweet Alli, are one tempting woman." His fingers remained a warm pressure against her lips. "But while I hope to kiss you again, The Code says a guy doesn't take advantage of a woman with a broken wrist and probable concussion."

"Th-The Code?"

"Yep, it's a guy thing." The warmth of Daniel's touch made her forget all about her aching arm. "But let this be a warning to you, sweetheart. I'll be asking for another kiss one day soon."

He said he'd be back in an hour.

Allison squinted at Daniel's Swiss Army watch. He'd strapped it to her good wrist, kissed her cheek, and said, "I'll be back in an hour, easy. Take a nap. And don't worry."

She'd dozed off with the echo of Daniel calling her "sweetheart" in her mind, even though she wanted to stay awake until he returned. She woke up because she'd slipped down so that her face rested against the cold material of the snowmobile seat cover. She'd managed to push herself back up with one arm. Now she struggled to remember what time Daniel headed out. Six-thirty? Seven-thirty? She stared at the watch face again. Either way, it was almost ten o'clock now.

Allison chewed on her chapped bottom lip and winced. "'Don't worry,' he says. What else am I supposed to do when he disappears and I'm left all alone on a mountain?"

Faint sunlight filtered down from the ventilation hole. Using her good arm, she pushed herself away from the icy wall of the snow cave, the solar blankets slipping off her shoulders. The dull ache in her head increased once she sat upright. She shook the water bottle. Almost empty. She took a small sip and considered her situation.

Asset: She was warm.

Liability: She was alone. In a snow cave. On the side of a mountain.

Asset: She had shelter.

Liability: She was alone. In a snow cave. On the side of a mountain.

Asset: If she stayed inside the snow cave, she'd keep Daniel happy.

Liability: If she stayed inside the snow cave, Daniel—who wasn't here—would be happy. And she would still be alone.

She could wait for Daniel inside the snow cave. Or figure out how to get outside and go looking for him. Daniel would want her to stay inside.

"What do I do, God? A little help, please?"

What if Daniel was hurt? What if he'd been attacked by a bear? What if there'd been another avalanche and he was buried out there? *Stay inside? Look for Daniel? All this thinking makes my head hurt.*

Daniel wanted to get to the top of the mountain to try and reach a cell tower. He'd taken his cell. Her cell phone was— where? She rubbed her palm against her forehead. Unremitting dull pain clouded her thinking. Why couldn't she move her other hand? She stared at her arm, encased in her coat. If she gave herself a minute, she'd remember . . . Daniel thought her wrist was broken. Okay. And her cell phone was . . . was . . . stored in the snowmobile? Maybe she should try to get to the snowmobile, find her cell, and head for the top of the mountain. And Daniel. And a cell tower.

Allison twisted over onto her knees and one-arm-crawled to the entrance of the cave. Should she be on her back or her stomach? She couldn't lie on her stomach without hurting her arm. Her back it was, then. She positioned herself feet first and half slid, half squirmed out of the shelter.

The brightness outside caused her to close her eyes even as she grimaced against the cold. She had underestimated how warm the snow cave was. Why hadn't she thought to bring a blanket with her? And the goggles Daniel left with her?

She lay against the snow, trying to catch her breath. Then she pushed herself to a sitting position. Glancing around, she noticed Daniel had spread out a bright orange tarp. He must have found it in one of the snowmobiles and was using it as some sort of signal banner against the backdrop of the snow near their shelter. Up to her right, the snowmobiles sat where they'd left them yesterday afternoon.

She determined the path of the avalanche, her stomach somersaulting as her mind filled with images of being tossed and turned by the out-of-control snowslide. Shaking her head to dispel the memories only increased her nausea.

With tears threatening, Allison thought of crawling into the cave again. How would she do that without help? Daniel said not to worry. He said to wait. But he was so, so late. What if he needed her help?

Okay, what was her plan again? Find her—what? Her cell phone. Head to the top of the mountain. Find Daniel. Signal for help. Find Daniel.

With a weary sigh, Allison forced herself to stand. She could do this. One step at a time, she'd get to the snowmobile. One step at a time, she'd get to the top of the mountain.

Allison sat back down. Her head hurt. Her arm hurt. Increasing roils of nausea caused her stomach to protest any unnecessary movement.

What was I thinking? Daniel's going to kill me when he gets back and finds out I didn't stay inside the cave. She leaned her head against her knees, her body shaking with cold.

Could she manage to get back inside?

Strong hands gripped Allison's shoulders just when an enticing dream of Daniel fulfilling his promise to kiss her lulled her to sleep.

Someone yelled. Shook her. Who was that, and why couldn't he just let her sleep?

"Alli! Alli, wake up!"

Someone lifted her, pressed his rough face against her chapped skin.

"Come on, sweetheart, you're scaring me."

"Your face . . . scratchy . . ." Allison mumbled a protest into a man's broad chest. She should know him.

She heard him mutter something. He needed to be careful about his language.

"What did I tell you? Wait *in the cave*. Take a nap."

"I did . . . I did." If only he'd stop talking, she'd take a nice long nap. Maybe then he wouldn't be so angry with her.

The man—*Daniel*—knelt in the snow and laid her down, the ground cold against her back. Uncontrollable shivers ran through her body.

"Okay, you know the drill. Give me a minute to get inside, and I'll pull you up. Don't move."

By the time Daniel had her back inside the snow cave, her sobs were causing her body to shake even more.

"Sweetheart, don't cry." Daniel took her in his arms and wrapped her with the solar blankets.

"W-where were you?" A loud hiccup punctuated her lament.

"At the top of the mountain, trying to contact our rescuers."

"You said an hour . . ." Allison buried her face in Daniel's chest, knowing she'd soak his coat with the salty tears burning her skin.

"I'm sorry. I took both our cell phones, but they were so cold I couldn't get them to work right away. I had to wait for the batteries to warm up." Removing his glove, he caressed the nape of her neck with a cool hand.

"I thought you were hurt . . . or lost . . . or . . . or that there'd been another avalanche. I was afraid you'd never come back."

"Alli, look at me." Daniel waited until she looked at him. "I will *always* come back for you."

For some reason, his words caused her to cry even harder. Murmuring soft words of comfort, he held her until she'd exhausted herself.

"All cried out?"

"I-I think so."

"Good." He wiped her face with a folded red bandana. "Don't worry, it's clean. Can't have those tears freezing on your beautiful face. Okay, you ready to hear about being rescued?"

"We're getting rescued?"

"Yep." Daniel brushed damp tendrils of hair away from her face. "As much as I've enjoyed having you all to myself, you need to get to a hospital. Turns out the rescue teams headed out at first light. After I contacted emergency services, the dispatcher radioed our location. The team will be here with snowmobiles or a snowcat by lunchtime."

"What do we do until then?"

"Until then I expect you to follow my orders." He winked at her. "I intend to hold you while you rest. Don't even have to wake you up for any impromptu solos. When the team gets here will be soon enough. Sound good?"

"Sounds good, Daniel." She sighed and snuggled into his arms, savoring how his warmth chased the cold from her body. "Very good."

CHAPTER 34

*W*as Alli finally alone? Daniel pushed the door to her hospital room open a few inches. No sign of her parents or Hadleigh. Maybe they were getting something to eat or had gone to Aunt Nita's to rest.

As he stepped into Alli's private hospital room, Daniel tucked the overstuffed orange cat with crazy-curled whiskers under his arm. Orange wasn't her favorite color, but the selection in the hospital's gift store offered the cat, a purple hippopotamus, or teddy bears—pink for baby girls or blue for baby boys.

He hesitated just inside the doorway, surprised to see Alli taking a few wobbly steps into the bathroom.

He should have knocked. No woman wants to be caught parading around in a faded blue hospital gown paired with another gown in the back for modesty.

Alli's muted voice stopped his retreat. "An easy twelve steps . . . now to see how bad I look before that nurse comes back . . ."

Allison was talking to herself? Not good. And unless there was a magic mirror in that room, Alli wouldn't like what she saw reflected back at her. Being thrown down a mountain by an avalanche had left her with bloodshot eyes rimmed in black and blue. Additional purple bruising discolored her swollen face.

When he checked on her last night, she looked like a prizefighter who'd gone fifteen brutal rounds and lost.

"Oh, no . . . no . . . this is bad . . ." Alli's words ended on a muffled sob.

Daniel imagined her leaning closer to the mirror to inspect her face. She should just turn out the light and shuffle back to the bed. He took three quick strides toward the door. To give her fair warning he was nearby, he rapped on the door and called, "Alli, you in there? Or have you gone AWOL?"

"Daniel! Wait—give me a minute! I was just, um, brushing my teeth."

Daniel couldn't prevent a chuckle when he heard Alli turn on the faucet. Would she actually go through the whole rinse-and-spit ruse? "Shouldn't someone be helping you get around?"

Alli appeared in the doorway, keeping her head turned away as she walked back to the mechanical hospital bed. "They just took out my IV, and I-I didn't want to bother the nurse again."

"Let me help you, since you disobeyed orders." Daniel resisted the urge to pick Alli up and carry her the rest of the way. Instead, he moved ahead of her and set the stuffed animal on top of her pillow before pulling the blankets down. "What's the best way to do this?"

"The best way to do this is for me to do it myself." Alli pointed to an uninviting white vinyl chair at the foot of the bed. "You go sit there and let me get settled."

"Oh, I get it. I did promise you could boss me around once we got back to town, didn't I?" Daniel knew Alli didn't see his grin, because she refused to look up.

He sat back in the chair and kept his eyes focused on the speckled white tile floor as Alli eased herself into the bed. He peeked once he saw her feet underneath the blankets. Her left arm was splinted from her fingers to above her elbow, her hand bandaged to cover the laceration stretching across her palm. Only her fingertips were evident outside the blue sling supporting her arm. As Alli struggled to get comfortable, he jumped up to help her.

"I can do this, Daniel—"

"No, you can't. Hold Morris." Daniel placed his gift in her good arm, effectively stopping her from doing anything. He straightened the blue hospital-issue blankets that matched the gowns she wore, positioned her pillow higher behind her head, and wondered why Alli wasn't asking why he dubbed the cat Morris.

When he risked a glance, he realized she'd buried her face in the stuffed animal. Tiny sniffles hinted that she was crying.

"Sweetheart, what's wrong?"

Alli shrugged.

"Are you in pain? Do I need to call the nurse?"

Alli shook her head, still refusing to look at him.

"Come on, help me out here. I can't fix the problem if you don't tell me what's wrong." Daniel sat down on the edge of the bed, the plastic mattress liner crinkling in protest, and rested his hand on her shoulder. "We survived an avalanche and a night in a snow cave. Nothing can be worse than that."

"I-I look like somebody beat me up!" Alli sobbed her complaint into the garish orange fur of the gift-store offering.

"Yeah—like a hundred tons of snow beat you up. You look pretty good, considering your opponent."

"I looked in the mirror. It's awful . . ." Alli hiccupped and cried all the harder.

Being careful not to hurt her arm, Daniel pulled Alli close. "Sweetheart, you're *alive*. Let's be thankful for that." He pressed a swift kiss to her temple. "Your bruises will fade. If people ask who beat you up, tell them the other guy looks worse."

A giggle found its way in between Alli's sobs.

"I'll go get you a pair of those gigantic sunglasses all the Hollywood stars wear, how about that? What color do you want? White? Black? I'll buy you a red floppy hat too. If someone tries to take your picture, act like they're paparazzi and threaten to sue them."

"You hate to shop." Alli kept her face buried in his chest, but he heard a smile in her voice. "And you have no fashion sense."

"If it'll get you to stop crying, I'll hit every store in the mall. Or you can make it easy for me and tell me your favorite place to shop." Daniel hugged her to him, being cautious with her arm. "Besides your face, how are you feeling?"

"I feel like I wrestled the Abominable Snowman. I ache all over. My head hurts, and my hand still hurts where that awful doctor scrubbed it out . . . and I'm whining like a baby, aren't I?" Alli glanced up at him between Morris's fluffy ears.

"You're allowed five minutes out of every hour to whine." Daniel smoothed strands of hair away from her face. "I saw it written in your medical chart."

Alli giggled again. "Thanks for my cat, by the way. Nice bright orange. Why'd you name him Morris?"

"Think about it—Morris, the cat from the old 9Lives commercials? I figure after our mountain adventure, you have eight lives left. Morris and Bisquick will be buddies."

"You watch too many old TV shows. Bisquick will probably throw Morris to the llamas."

"But llamas like cats." Despite her injuries, he couldn't deny he enjoyed the chance to hold her. "I'll just have to come by and make sure Bisquick behaves himself."

Allison liked the sound of that—almost as much as she liked it when Daniel called her "sweetheart." His coming by for any reason would give them a chance to figure out what—if anything—was happening between them. Surely now that he had promised to kiss her again, he was done setting her up on blind dates.

She gave a guilty start when she heard someone push open the door to her room. The nurse wasn't going to like Daniel sitting on the bed. He was probably violating some sort of hospital cleanliness regulation.

She tried to avoid a confrontation with a whispered warning to Daniel. "Move! The nurse is going to order you to go sit in the chair—"

Before she could finish her sentence, Seth appeared at her bedside, carrying an overflowing bouquet of pink roses.

Allison wished she could pull the blankets up over her head. Impossible to do with Daniel's arms around her and Morris snuggled with them. She'd make a bad situation look absurdly worse. Warmth flushed her swollen face.

"Hey, Seth. Didn't know you drove up." Daniel settled Allison back against her pillows and stood to greet his brother. He acted like it was no big deal that Seth just walked in on him holding her. Okay, she could do the "act natural" routine too.

Seth ignored Daniel as he placed the bouquet on the bedside table, the roses' fragrance mingling with the antiseptic odor of the hospital. He seemed ready to play the "no big deal about Allison being in Daniel's arms" game too.

"Allison's parents called me last night after they got to her apartment." Seth placed a hand under her chin and surveyed her face. "Her mom told me that she was pretty banged up. I'm sorry to see she was right."

Allison turned her face away with a jerk. She knew how bad she looked. She didn't need Seth's assessment.

Daniel straightened his shoulders and moved closer to Allison. "Real smooth there, Tag. That's what every woman wants to hear."

"Allison and I were together six years, Daniel. I never gave her false flattery then, I'm not about to start now."

"It's no big deal," Allison insisted as she used her uninjured hand to smooth her blankets over her legs. "My bruises will fade."

"I always liked that about you, Allison," Seth said. "You're not a complainer. Why whine about things you can't change?"

"You're right there." Daniel seemed to be squaring off with Seth from the foot of the hospital bed. "Why fuss about little things like a broken wrist or a concussion or being buried alive in an avalanche? Hypothermia's no big deal—or the fact that Alli wasn't breathing when I dug her out. All's well that ends well, right?"

Seth cleared his throat. "I'm certainly relieved you're okay, Allison."

Daniel interrupted him with a harsh laugh. "Certainly relieved she's okay? That's big of you, Seth. God forbid you get upset about Alli's accident."

"I don't see how my getting upset is going to help—"

"Enough, both of you." Allison sat up in the hospital bed, clutching Morris to her chest. "I appreciate your concern for me. But the doctor says I need a nap before lunch. So I'd like both of you to please leave—and take your concern with you."

With those words, she lay back down, pulled the covers up to her shoulders, and rolled onto her side, hugging Morris as if she were a preschooler. She continued to face away from Daniel and Seth as they mumbled apologies. She kept herself rigid when Daniel placed his hand on her shoulder, promising to stop by later. Not until she heard the door open and close did she realize she'd been holding her breath and let out a sigh of relief.

She'd felt like the overstretched rope in a tug-of-war between Daniel and Seth.

The man's not in the room for five minutes, and I'm letting Seth Rayner dictate how I feel—or how I should feel. I did that all the time when we were dating. I am tired of being controlled by him! Why did I think being friends with him would ever work?

Was her prayer making any difference? Or were her mistakes—past and present—building an impenetrable barrier between her and God?

Why am I even considering getting involved with Daniel? I was engaged to his brother! That could never be the right thing, could it, God?

Seth used to be her security, but she gave that up months ago when she ran out of the church. For years Daniel and his adventurous life beckoned Alli past her comfort zone and into unknown dangers, even during her engagement to his brother.

Did she really want to allow herself to fall completely, hopelessly in love with Daniel? At what cost? Was it worth ruining Daniel's relationship with his brother? Could she live with herself?

She rubbed her uninjured wrist against Morris's fur. How long would it take before she stopped responding to emotional tension by thinking about cutting?

"What do you think, Morris? What should I do?" Allison tucked Daniel's gift against her side. "You're right. I can't go back to Seth. But do I dare get closer to Daniel?"

Silence.

"Not talking, huh? Some help you are."

She closed her eyes against the pain building in her head. How desperate was she, talking to God one minute and a stuffed animal the next?

"God, I'm listening. I'm listening the best I know how. I'm so afraid I'll make a mistake. Please, please help me."

Faint noises of the busy hospital—the nurses walking past her door, the elevator's ping, machinery monitoring a patient's bodily functions—invaded the silence in her room. Maybe that nap was the best thing. She opened her eyes again, looking for the call button. She needed to do one thing before she went to sleep—ask the nurse to put up a NO VISITORS sign.

Hey, Alli, was thinking about you and saw this postcard while I was running around the Springs the other day. Go, Air Force Falcons! You do like football, right?

—Daniel

CHAPTER 35

Allison settled at her aunt's kitchen table, watching Meghan and her sister finish prepping for an evening of homemade sushi.

Allison lifted her bandaged arm. "Sorry I can't help."

"You picked up the tab for the groceries." Hadleigh laid out a pile of blanched and sliced carrots, cucumbers, and spinach leaves. "Meghan and I don't mind being the sushi chefs."

"Make your selections, and we'll custom-make your sushi." Meghan arranged the pot of white sticky rice next to a clear bowl of warm water and a package of paper-thin crinkly sheets of green seaweed.

Allison surveyed the other ingredients spread out on the white Formica counter. "What do I have to choose from?"

"Avocado, tuna, salmon, imitation crab meat, and the vegetables." Meghan ticked off the items, her neon-orange nail tips distracting Allison. "I also made up some spicy mayo that I like to use with the tuna. And, of course, there's always ginger slices and wasabi."

"Meggie, you are a recipe junkie." Allison dipped a finger in the spicy mayo and tasted it, enjoying the tang of it on her tongue. "I think you have more cookbooks than you do bottles of nail polish."

"Not true. I counted once, and my nail polish collection definitely outnumbers my cookbooks—but not by much!"

Hadleigh picked up a small bamboo mat, a puzzled expression scrunching her thin eyebrows. "I have no idea what to do with this thing, but I'm game to try."

"That is a *makisu*. A sushi-rolling mat." Meghan placed the bamboo mat on the table in front of Hadleigh. "Sit and learn. And while I instruct you in the ancient art of sushi, your big sister can tell us about Daniel putting Seth in his place when he visited her in the hospital last week."

"What? Trouble between the Rayner brothers?" Hadleigh watched Meghan spread cooked rice on top of a sheet of seaweed. "Do tell, Allison."

Allison nibbled on a piece of carrot. "That experience is not worth talking about. And if that's my sushi, I'd like crab and avocado."

"Not until you give us details. Lots of them."

"What, trading food for information?" Allison tried to ignore the itch marching its way up her arm inside the cast. "What can I say? I was upset because, well, you know how bad I looked right after the accident. Daniel showed up with Morris the Cat and tried to make me laugh. Seth came in with the perfect floral bouquet and said I looked as awful as he expected."

Hadleigh snarled under her breath. "Wasn't that sweet of him?"

Using a chopstick, Allison tried to scratch the annoying itch. "Then they faced off like I was a ticket to a sold-out Broadway show. I told them to leave so I could nap. The end."

"Why would Seth be upset about Daniel comforting you?" Hadleigh focused on Meghan's careful rolling of the sushi as she asked the question.

Did Allison really want to get into this with her little sister? "No reason."

When Meghan opened her mouth, Allison silenced her with a quick shake of her head.

"Can I try to make one this time?" Hadleigh positioned herself next to Meghan, ready to create the next sushi roll. "I've decided guys aren't worth the trouble."

Meghan placed the first roll on a rectangular glass platter near Allison. "All guys or one particular guy—as in Evan?"

"Him especially, yeah."

"Why Evan especially?"

Hadleigh dipped her fingers in the bowl of water, then began spreading the white rice on the dried seaweed. "He's a jerk."

"What happened?"

Hadleigh worked in silence for a few moments, concentrating on smoothing the rice and selecting slices of spinach, cucumber, and tuna. "Here I am, liking the guy. Helping him with his grades. Telling him he can graduate, go to college, be more than a bagel boy." Hadleigh's bottom lip quivered. "And then he . . . he . . ."

As Allison started to say something, Meghan mouthed the word "wait."

Her little sister exhaled a shuddering breath. "He sent me a text. He didn't mean to. He was forwarding it to a bunch of his guy friends and added my name by mistake. It was a picture of a-a girl. A naked girl."

"Oh, Leigh."

"What happened?" Meghan helped Hadleigh arrange tuna and slivers of cucumber on the rice, adding an extra layer of her special sauce.

Hadleigh motioned to the unrolled sushi. "Can you help me do this too?"

Meghan guided Hadleigh's hands, helping her form an eight-inch-long sushi roll. After she placed it next to the first one, Hadleigh started talking as she assembled another one. "The next night he came over to study, I-I confronted him about it. He said it was no big deal. All the guys look at that kind of stuff."

"You're right. He is a jerk." Meghan eased Hadleigh's sushi roll from her hands. "Careful, there. Don't take your anger out on our dinner. You're mashing it all to pieces."

"Sorry." Hadleigh sniffled. "When I opened that text, I thought Evan was setting up our next date. And then I saw . . . saw . . . I just can't understand why he would want to look at disgusting stuff like that."

Allison wished she could fast-forward the conversation with her sister, but she knew that wouldn't be fair. "Who knows how Evan got into porn."

Meghan nodded in agreement. "Even girls are getting into X-rated stuff these days."

Hadleigh winced. "I'm not naive. I just didn't think . . . I mean, I don't look at that kind of stuff. I didn't think Evan would, either. I feel stupid."

Meghan put her hand up, the line of her mouth grim around her lip piercing. "Whoa, you're not stupid. Evan is. Right now I am more concerned about you."

Meghan's words brought the hint of a smile to Hadleigh's face, but she looked so vulnerable. Allison wanted to wrap her arms around her. Protect her.

"So what are you going to do, Leigh?"

"I told Evan I didn't want to see him anymore."

Allison clasped her sister's hand. "That was smart. Do you still have the text?"

"No, why?"

"If he sent it to you at school, you could report it to the principal. Let them handle it."

"I never thought of that."

"Too late if you deleted the text."

Hadleigh sighed. "Mom keeps asking me what's bothering me. She wants to know why Evan isn't coming around. What am I supposed to say?"

Allison rapped her sister's forehead. "The truth?"

"I couldn't. Will would kill him."

"So let him."

Hadleigh giggled. "Maybe I should."

"You're not in the wrong here, Leigh. Don't let Evan convince you differently."

Meghan finished arranging the sushi on the platter. "There is one more thing you can do for Evan, you know."

"What?"

"You can pray for him—we can all pray for him." She rinsed her hands off at the sink. "I had a friend who got caught with porn. She felt so guilty about it—she'd be okay for a few months, and then she'd get tripped up again. It's addictive. Evan may be caught up in it too."

"I hadn't thought of that. I've just been mad. And hurt. But if you two will pray with me, I'm game." Hadleigh pushed her spiky black hair off her forehead. "And then is anybody else ready to eat sushi? I don't want to talk about this anymore."

"I'm starving." Allison held up the chopstick. "I'm going to need a new one of these. I've used this one as an arm scratcher."

Meghan grimaced. "That's disgusting."

"It would be more disgusting if I ate with it, Meggie."

CHAPTER 36

"That's all for today, Michelle." Seth slid the laptop into his dark brown leather satchel and buckled it closed. "I won't be back until Monday. You can reach me on my cell."

"Yes, sir." His assistant hovered by his side, holding the papers he'd signed so she could fax them.

Seth checked the time: two-thirty. Later than he liked, but he might get out of town before weekend traffic backed up too much on Monument Hill. "If you need anything, just call—" He stopped as his father walked into his office.

"Leaving early, son?"

"I'm heading to Estes Park."

"I figured."

"Is there something you need to talk about before I head out?"

"If you can spare the time."

Seth nodded to his assistant, who moved past his father with a murmured "Good afternoon, Mr. Rayner."

His father settled into one of the matching leather chairs positioned in front of the desk. "Going to see Allison again?"

"Actually, I'm having dinner with Daniel in Denver before driving up to Estes Park."

His father pulled out a pair of nail clippers, opened it to the file, and began cleaning his nails. "What's the occasion?"

"We're brothers—do we need an occasion?" Seth came around to the front of the cherrywood desk and leaned back, bracing his hands on the glass top.

"No. I just didn't realize you and your wander-the-world brother met for dinner that often."

"We don't. Daniel suggested dinner tonight. Denver's on the way to Estes Park, so I figured why not?" He watched as his father began to cut his nails shorter. He hadn't realized his office had become a beauty salon. "So I'd like to get on the road ahead of rush hour. Is there something I need to finish up—the hospital construction hit a glitch?"

"I'll get to the point." His father stood and folded the clippers together, tucking them back in his pants pocket before depositing his nail clippings in the wastebasket. "Seth, you're being considered for the vice presidency, but it's not because you're my son."

"And your point is?"

"There are plenty of people who will assume that's exactly why you got this promotion—if you get it."

"So let them."

"I would prefer you give people no reason to think you don't deserve this position."

Seth pushed away from the desk. "Are you suggesting I have?"

"This is *Rayner* Construction. You have to work harder than anyone else on the payroll, son—because you are my son. You have to come in early." He tapped the clock on Seth's desk. "And you have to stay late."

"You know I'm committed to this company. I'm the one who got us involved with energy and environmental design. And look at all the business that brought us."

"Lately, all you seem to care about is that unstable girlfriend of yours."

"Allison is my *fiancée*."

"She walked out on you on your wedding day."

Seth walked away from his father, putting the desk between them. "I know that. I was there."

"She's not good enough for you, son."

Seth picked up his satchel, moving past his father to the door. "Is there anything else?"

"No. I've said all I wanted to say."

"Then let me say something before we end this conversation." Seth paused with his hand on the door and turned to face his father. "I am going to marry Allison Denman. And when I do, you will be happy about it."

"Your personal life is your business. But when it affects business, then I stop being your father and I become your boss. Keep the two separate. And that's your boss talking, not your father."

"Understood." Seth opened the door and stood aside to let his father leave. "I'll see you on Monday."

"Have a good weekend."

"You too, sir. If any work-related problems come up, my assistant knows how to reach me."

Alli, ate a very unhealthy
waffle cone on the Santa
Cruz boardwalk—but
it was after the Wharf
to Wharf run. It's only
six miles. I'll leave the
marathons to Seth.
                        —Daniel

CHAPTER 37

*D*aniel shifted in his chair, glancing at the restaurant entrance to see if Seth had arrived. Normally, he'd relish the idea of feeding his inner carnivore by sampling the various meats roasting in the kitchen at the Rodizio Grill. Not tonight.

Is honesty really the best policy when it comes to Alli?

He'd debated being truthful with Seth ever since they'd squared off like a couple of prizefighters in Alli's hospital room. If he ever hoped to pursue a relationship with her, he needed to be honest with his little brother.

No time like the present, Danny boy.

Daniel watched waiters carrying sword-length skewers of sizzling pork, beef, and poultry from table to table. Despite the delectable aromas, anxiety ruined his appetite. He'd rehearsed what to say to Seth on the ninety-minute drive from Estes Park to Denver. He figured a restaurant in LoDo filled with couples and families was a neutral location for their conversation. The Brazilian grill in the lower historical district of Denver was one of his favorites. If he was going to have a difficult conversation with Tag, he might as well enjoy dinner.

When Seth entered the restaurant, Daniel leaned back in his chair, forcing himself to at least *appear* relaxed. Only when Seth stood across from him did he stand and reach out to shake his brother's hand.

"Good to see you, Daniel."

"You too. Thanks for meeting me."

"Sure, although I don't see what all the urgency is about." Seth realigned his place setting. "What's this about?"

Daniel ignored the questioning look Seth threw his way. He motioned for the gaucho. *Order first. Talk later.* Why couldn't he shake the feeling he was setting Seth up—wining and dining him before confessing he was in love with Alli?

Guilt and relief warred in Daniel's heart. Guilt about what he'd kept hidden from Seth; relief that he was finally being honest with his brother. People always said you were only responsible for your own actions, not someone else's reactions. That statement had never been truer.

After ordering drinks, he followed Seth through the salad bar line, loading his plate with quail eggs, hearts of palm, and Greek salad. Back at their table, Daniel watched his brother season his food with salt and pepper. Seth looked the same as ever. Fit. In control. He wore his trademark dark dress pants, tailored white shirt with a red power tie, and a dark navy blue blazer.

"So, Seth. Have you seen Alli since she left the hospital?"

"No."

A vest-clad gaucho walked over, placing two loaded skewers points-down onto a pewter serving plate on the table. "Ham and pineapple?"

Seth nodded before continuing the conversation. "Every time I went back, there was a NO VISITORS sign on the door."

"Know what you mean." Daniel spoke around a mouthful of chilled quail egg. "Those nurses know how to protect their patients."

"You okay after the avalanche?"

"I'm fine. Alli bore the brunt of it."

"Would you care for Brazilian sausage?"

Both brothers sat back while the waiter carved chunks of spicy meat onto their plates.

"How long had you known Allison was in Estes Park?"

"A few months." Daniel shoved aside his salad plate, concentrating on the main course, inhaling the aroma of spices and grilled meat. "Pretty much since she moved there. Why?"

"Why didn't you tell me sooner?"

Daniel stopped chewing. Swallowed too big a bite. "I figured it was Alli's call. I tried to respect her decision."

Seth's words were clipped, precise. "I never understood why she didn't inform me that she was moving. Why she asked her parents not to tell me where she was. Some nonsense about a clean break being better for both of us."

"You didn't agree with her?" Daniel looked around, motioning a server to bring him another glass of iced tea.

"Of course not. How could we work on our relationship if I didn't know where she was?" Seth cut his meat into equal-sized pieces. "I figured I just needed to be patient. That she'd contact me when she was ready. Thanks for telling me. I was getting tired of waiting."

"I figured you deserved a chance to see if you and Alli had a future."

"Brisket?"

Daniel waited while the server piled more meat on their plates before continuing the conversation. The restaurant was busy tonight, the room filled with a constant hum of voices and laughter against the backdrop of clinking cutlery.

"You've had some time with Alli. Do you still think there's a chance for you two to get back together?"

"We're talking on a regular basis. We've gone out to dinner. Before the avalanche I had just invited her to see a Broadway musical. We may have to get tickets for a show later in the season."

"Seth, have you ever slowed down your pursuit of Alli long

enough to consider her perspective? That you aren't right for each other?"

"I've spent six years with Allison. We're perfect for each other. I just have to convince her."

"Convince her? Is that what a relationship is?" Daniel sliced into a thick piece of ham, topping it with a sliver of sweet grilled pineapple. "Convincing someone how right you are for each other?"

"Have you been talking to Allison?" Seth's posture was rigid, his jaw clenched.

Three gauchos converged on their table at the same time, postponing Daniel's reply. After adding spicy chicken, pork loin, and Brazilian pot roast to his plate, Daniel looked at his brother again.

"Of course I've seen Alli. She's working on the project with me—that's how we got caught on the mountain." Daniel gulped down half a glass of tea. "One of the B-and-Bs I'm helping needed a brochure designed, and I recommended Alli."

Seth's eyes narrowed. "Can you give me one good reason why you didn't tell me sooner Allison was in Estes Park?"

Now was Daniel's chance to come clean. But he felt as if he were jumping out of a plane without a parachute. "I can give you two reasons. Alli said your relationship was over, and like I said, I figured it was her choice to let you know where she was."

Seth shook his head, dismissing Alli's assessment. "And the other reason is?"

"I'm in love with Alli."

A muscle twitched in Seth's jaw. "What did you just say?"

"You heard me."

"Would you like to try some roast boar?"

Seth declined the offer but requested a second serving of the ham and pineapple. Then he resumed the conversation, his tone suggesting they were discussing business.

"Does Allison know?"

"Yes, Alli knows I have feelings for her—"

Seth held up his hand to stop Daniel from saying anything else.

"Feelings. Don't be vague. Do you want a serious relationship with my fiancée?"

"No." Daniel locked eyes with his brother. "I want a serious relationship with Alli, your *ex-fiancée*."

"Chicken hearts?"

"No!" The men's shouted reply almost caused the waiter to drop his offering and sent him scurrying to the next table.

Daniel ran his hand across his face, blocking out the anger in Seth's eyes. "Let me explain all this to you, Seth. I know it sounds crazy, but I've been attracted to Alli for years."

When he paused, Seth sat and waited. No comments. No questions.

"I didn't pursue her because you were there first. I wasn't going to go after your girl. Besides, Alli's eight years younger than me. So I backed off. I let you win."

"You *let me win*?" Seth threw down his fork. "I don't think so, Daniel. There was no competition."

"I didn't mean to say that, Seth. Don't make this harder than it already is."

"You expect me to make it easy for you to go after Allison?" Seth leaned across the table and lowered his voice. "Allison's confused. You're taking advantage of her mixed-up emotions."

"Whatever you and Alli had is over. How many times does she have to tell you that? She walked out on your wedding day. She kissed me—"

"Allison kissed you? When?"

"Forget it. It's not important."

"You owe me an answer."

Daniel sat back in the chair, wishing he'd never started the conversation. "A week before the wedding."

Seth jumped to his feet, shoving his chair back. "Do you mean to tell me you—you seduced Allison?"

"Sit down. Don't be melodramatic."

"Melodramatic?" Seth placed his fists on the table, glaring down at Daniel. "What would you do if you were me? How would you feel if you just found out I was in love with your fiancée?"

"I came here tonight to talk to you about all this because I feel bad about it." Daniel placed his hand on Seth's arm, trying to force him to sit back down. They were attracting an audience. Several waiters hovered in the background, holding meat-laden skewers.

"I bet you feel bad. So bad you want my fiancée."

"Ex-fiancée, Tag."

"Let me tell you something, Daniel. You have an odd sense of family if you go after Allison."

With that, Seth turned and strode out of the restaurant, almost knocking over a waiter carrying a skewer loaded with bacon-wrapped turkey.

Having a great time swimming with the manatees in Florida. Impressive lightning storms in this state.

—Daniel

CHAPTER 38

*A*llison scanned the shelves of books. Since Scoti was surrounded by a horde of caffeine-deprived customers, she couldn't see whether the book Allison wanted was in stock. And with so many multi-hyphenated-named drinks for customers to choose from, Scoti wouldn't be available anytime soon.

Did she really need another book? Her to-be-read pile teetered like a literary Leaning Tower of Pisa. Maybe it was time to invest in an e-reader.

There it was—*Happily Ever After*. Allison pulled the novel off the shelf, knowing she wouldn't be reshelving it. She'd given her last copy to Hadleigh and the copy before that to a coworker. Standing off to the side, Allison flipped through the book and found one of her favorite passages.

Within minutes, she was so engrossed in the romantic conflict that she didn't notice Daniel's presence until he leaned over her shoulder and whispered, "Whatcha reading?"

He laughed out loud at Alli's yelp of surprise, wrapping one arm around her waist to pull her up against his chest, and catching the book she dropped with his other hand.

"That is not funny, Daniel Rayner."

His unrepentant chuckle against her ear sent a tingle down her spine. "I beg to differ."

After maneuvering to face her, Daniel continued to hold her next to him. "Your book, ma'am." He read the title before handing her the book. "*Happily Ever After.* Good book?"

"One of my favorites." Allison resisted the temptation to lean back into Daniel's arms. But that meant she was pressed against his broad chest, so close she could see the flecks of gold in his eyes.

"You've already read it?"

"More than once."

"Then why are you reading it in the bookstore?"

"I keep giving my copies away." Allison shrugged. "I need to replace it."

"So you can give it away again?"

"Probably." As another customer walked down the aisle toward them, Allison attempted to move away from Daniel. "You do realize we're in a bookstore, don't you?"

"Yep." He tightened his arms around her, while his mischievous grin indicated he didn't care. "But this is better than the last time I got to hold you—we were on the side of a mountain and you were mostly unconscious."

Allison stifled a nervous giggle. She was anything but unconscious. Unlike her "being friends is nice" reaction to Seth the other night, she found herself hoping Daniel might do something ridiculous, like kiss her in public.

"I don't read much romance." He took the book from her, studying the back cover and somehow managing to open to the end of the book with one hand.

"I doubt you've ever read a romance novel, Daniel." When she went to take the book back, he held on to it—and her hand.

"Except for the required high school reading of *Romeo and Juliet,* guilty as charged. I'm more of a techno-thriller kind of guy." He read the last page as if it contained the secret to some unexplained mystery. "Humor me. Why is this one of your favorite books?"

"It's a great story. The heroine's looking for her happily ever after. And she finds it."

"That easy, huh?"

"No, it's not easy." Hearing someone on the other side of the bookshelf, Allison dropped her voice to a whisper, as if they were in a public library. "But she and the hero decide loving each other is worth the risk."

Daniel nodded. "I understand that."

"Y-you do?"

"A good romance has a happy ending."

"Of course."

"And that's risky, because you don't always know if the other person wants the same happily ever after."

"Right."

When he looked at her again, Allison was caught by the warmth in Daniel's contradictory-colored eyes. "Alli, I'm not saying I'm a perfect-hero kind of guy."

Allison would argue that point. In his hiking boots, jeans, and white sweater, Daniel was the all-too-tempting hero who invaded her dreams every night.

"And I'm not saying I know how to make all your dreams come true." In one easy movement, Daniel set the book on the shelf behind them and drew her closer. "But I want you to tell me your dreams, and I'd like to imagine some dreams—together."

"What are you saying, Daniel?"

"What I should have said years ago. Alli, I love you."

"What?"

"I love you, Allison Denman. I watched you plan your happily ever after with my brother—and walk away from it. Ever imagine a happily ever after with me?"

Alli exhaled his name on a whisper, leaning in and resting her head on his chest. She inhaled Daniel's familiar scent, listening to the steady beat of his heart.

Daniel nuzzled her ear. "I haven't read any romances, but isn't the woman supposed to say something at this point?"

"You surprised me."

"It's not the first time I've surprised you, sweetheart." He traced the curve of her jaw with his knuckles, then rested his hand at the nape of her neck. "Alli."

"Yes?"

"I promised to ask the next time."

"The next time?"

"The next time I kissed you—I said I'd ask." Daniel's warm breath caressed her ear. "May I kiss you?"

Alli's eyes closed as she whispered her answer. "Yes."

Daniel didn't rush this kiss, despite the fact that they were in Scoti's bookstore. Allison couldn't stop a mental comparison to Seth, who was all about the right moment, the right place. Sometimes their kisses felt choreographed.

Allison's eyes flew open. This was no time to be thinking of Seth. "Daniel—"

"Alli." His hands cradled her face, his eyes searching hers. "Falling in love with you is the last thing I expected—and the best thing that ever happened to me."

The gentleness of Daniel's actions overwhelmed Allison. He kissed the corner of her mouth and then brushed his lips over hers in a tender prelude to completing the kiss. His lips tasted of mint Chap-Stick. Even as he coaxed a response from her, his hold tightened, as if he were afraid she'd slip away from him.

"What do you think you're doing?"

Daniel let go of Alli as someone grabbed his shoulder, yanking him around. As he fought to regain his balance, he heard Alli stumble against the bookshelf.

Seth.

"Hey, Tag." Daniel shrugged, straightening his sweater.

"Don't call me Tag. What are you doing with my fiancée?" Seth stood with his fists clenched at his sides.

"Ex-fiancée, Seth. Ex." Daniel positioned himself between his brother and Alli. "And it's obvious what we were doing."

With a roar of frustration, Seth launched himself at Daniel. Seth's first punch connected with Daniel's jaw, while the second went wide. Daniel rammed into shelves on his left. Hardcovers and paperbacks scattered across the floor.

Allison screamed for Seth to stop, but Daniel nodded at him, motioning him forward. "Ready when you are."

When his brother came at him again, Daniel sidestepped and hit Seth in the gut, causing him to double over and stumble into the bookshelves behind Daniel. Seth straightened, turned, and charged again, stomping on the books littering the carpet. Before Daniel could move aside, Seth's fist grazed his cheekbone. Daniel lunged forward, pinning Seth's arms against his rib cage with a bear hug. The two of them struggled against each other.

"Get. Out. Of. My. Shop." As Daniel looked over his right shoulder, Scoti rushed toward him, a salt-and-pepper-haired avenger brandishing what looked like a Klingon weapon.

Whoa.

A searing pain coursed through Daniel's side, buckling his knees. With a groan, he dropped to the floor, Seth on top of him. What had just happened?

Allison knelt beside them. "Did you just *Taser* them?"

"You bet you I did." Scoti pointed the weapon at them again. "This is a bookstore, not a bar."

Daniel lay on the floor, feeling as if he'd just danced with a lightning bolt. He shook his head, trying to clear his thoughts. "Get off . . . of . . . me . . ."

"I would . . . if . . . you'd let . . . go."

Daniel pried his stiff arms loose, trying to push his brother off. As he lay on the floor with his eyes closed, he felt Alli move away.

Where was she going?

If she'd wait a minute, he'd get up and apologize. He just needed a minute. Or two. Or five.

When Daniel opened his eyes, he saw the bookstore owner, a curious crowd of onlookers, and finally, his brother, lying on his back next to him.

But no Alli.

Where was she?

Allison wrapped her arm around her waist, trying to control her trembling. The chilly April wind bit at her skin and tossed her hair across her face, but she wasn't going back to Work in Progress to get her coat. Or her messenger bag. Scoti would keep them behind the counter until she came to pick them up.

She looked over her shoulder, but there was no sign of either Rayner brother following her up the street. She closed her eyes, trying to block out the sight of Daniel and Seth brawling in the bookstore. Over her.

"Hey, watch out!"

Allison's eyes flew open as she stumbled into a group of teen boys. Pain shot up her arm. "Sorry. I didn't see you."

"Open your eyes, lady."

What was she doing, walking around Estes Park with her eyes closed? She ducked into the closest shop before realizing it was the art gallery she had visited with Hadleigh and Evan.

She moved among the displays of pottery and stained glass. She wasn't surprised to find herself standing in front of her father's artwork. She studied the black-and-white city montage photograph by photograph until she stood in front of the photo of her little-girl self astride the motorcycle.

She and her dad had traveled around the country for almost two years in a beat-up Jeep. They slept in motels, sometimes for weeks at a time, sometimes for a night before they packed their bags and moved on.

Allison loved every unpredictable, free-as-the-wind minute. Sure, she missed her mom. But her dad was a larger-than-life hero conquering the world—and Allison took on the world too, her hand tucked safely in his. Even at a young age, part of her embraced the risk of it all.

The motorcycle belonged to one of the many friends her father made along the way. She rode behind her dad, clinging to his waist, and imagined them together like that forever. After the ride, he pulled the helmet off her head and smiled down at her, brushing the hair out of her eyes.

"I love you, Allison."

"Love you too, Dad."

He grabbed his camera and took her photo, telling her that one day she'd grow up and get her own motorcycle.

Her mom found them the next day. Took Allison back home.

Allison closed her eyes, shutting out the photograph of a much younger girl. A much more trusting girl. The day her father turned his back on her and walked away, she turned her back on adventure and risk. She preferred things black and white. Safe. That was why she fell in love with Seth—he made her feel protected. Daniel appealed to the part of her heart that, to this day, missed her father.

But look what loving both of the Rayner brothers had done: They ended up brawling in a bookstore. What was she thinking, saying yes when Daniel asked to kiss her? She had no future with him. They were too different. He lived life out loud, and her desire for a risk-free life would hold him back.

Allison opened her eyes and stared at the photo. There was no going backward. No recapturing that trusting, carefree little girl.

"Nice photograph, isn't it?" A man stood behind her, just off to her left.

"Yes, it is."

Allison continued to look at the picture, not wanting to engage in small talk with a stranger intent on discussing art.

"It's one of my favorites."

"You know the artist's work?"

His chuckle snagged a corner of Allison's memory. "You could say that."

Allison held her breath as she turned to face the man.

"Hello, Allison."

Allison closed her eyes. Breathed in. Out. Opened her eyes and confronted the image of an older version of her father in faded jeans, a Hard Rock Cafe T-shirt, and worn cowboy boots.

"Still here." He smiled a rueful half-smile, his arms spread wide, palms out.

"I can see that."

"When you came in the gallery, I couldn't resist the chance to see you again." He motioned toward her cast. "How's your arm?"

"Fine."

"Nita told me about the accident. She even snuck me into the hospital after hours so I could visit you."

She'd have to talk to her aunt about breaking the hospital's visiting hours—and Allison's no-trespassing policy. Again. "I don't—"

"You were pretty sedated after surgery." Her father rubbed the back of his neck. "Can we get a cup of coffee or something? Talk?"

"There's nothing to say."

"There's too much to say while standing around here, Allison."

"I am not getting into this with you." Alli backed away from her father, rubbing her wrist up and down her jeans. "I heard what you said to Mom when she came to pick me up. 'This was a mistake.' I get it. Our two years together were nothing but a mistake to you." She swallowed, willing herself not to cry even as the first hot tears seared her skin.

"That's not true." Her father gripped her wrist, preventing her from moving past him. "I loved those two years. I remember every last minute."

"Don't lie. I heard you."

"The mistake—*my* mistake—wasn't in spending two years with you. It was in taking you from your mother." His voice broke. "Your mother didn't find us, I *told* her where we were. It killed me to let you go, but what I had done was wrong."

"You *told* Mom?"

"Yes. Nita convinced me to call her and tell your mom where we were. Your mother agreed not to press charges if I gave her full custody of you and left you alone."

Allison pulled against her father's hand on her wrist. "I get it now. Abandoning me was your get-out-of-jail-free card."

"That wasn't it at all." He released her. "What was I supposed to do, Allison? What kind of life could I offer you? Living city to city, motel to motel?"

He could have taken her with him. Couldn't he? If he loved her, wouldn't he have found a way?

Her father's words interrupted her thoughts. "I had to let you go. It seemed like the best thing at the time—letting you have a normal life. Your aunt kept me updated. I thought of contacting you, but I'd promised your mother I wouldn't. I can't tell you how much I regretted that promise . . ."

"I have to go." She backed away from him.

"Will you think about talking? Your aunt knows how to contact me. I'm here for a while longer."

"Maybe."

That was all she could promise her father. Maybe. Maybe not. None of her relationships with men began or ended well. So why bother talking?

Alli, a friend of mine competed in the rodeo in Elko, Nevada. Forgot to make motel reservations, so I slept in my truck.

—Daniel

CHAPTER 39

"Sorry you had to sit in the lobby until my shift was done." Aunt Nita parked her battered red Jeep in front of the house.

"Better than a return visit to the bookstore." Allison had refused to go back to Work in Progress. She'd described the brawl between Seth and Daniel, skipping over her run-in with her father. Her aunt agreed to pick up her coat and messenger bag while Allison hid in the car.

"You want to come upstairs while I get us some lunch?"

"I'll walk around and check on the boys and be up in a few minutes." Allison paused, realizing if she was going to talk with her aunt about her father, now was the time. "Aunt Nita, wait."

Her aunt sat back in the driver's seat. "What's up, sweetie?"

"I-I wanted to tell you that I saw my father today."

"You did? Where?"

"I was in the gallery that's showcasing his photography, and he was there. He talked to me."

"Just to clarify things, is the no-trespassing sign up or down right now?"

"Let's say it's moved aside for the moment, okay?"

"Okay. What's on your mind?"

"He said you convinced him to call my mom and tell her where we were."

Aunt Nita pursed her lips, nodding. "That would be correct."

"Why?" Allison was surprised by how her voice cracked on the one syllable.

"Because it was the right thing to do, Allison. Your mother had been looking for you for months. Even with Randy calling her, letting her know you were fine, she was a wreck. I loved my brother, but he didn't have the right to hide you from your mother."

"I was happy, Aunt Nita."

"Were you? Randy told me there were nights when you woke up crying for your mom."

"I don't remember that."

"You were five years old!" Her aunt clenched the steering wheel. "I've never had children, but even I know how strong a bond there is between a mom and her child."

Cold seeped into the car, causing Allison to curl her toes up in her boots. She stared through the windshield, noticing a tiny crack running along one side of the glass. Her aunt needed to get that fixed before it covered the entire windshield.

"I guess you did what you thought was best for me . . ." Allison spoke as if to herself. "All this time I thought my father just got tired of having me around, that he thought I was a mistake, slowing him down . . ."

"Randy fought me for weeks. Wouldn't return my calls. He said he had to choose between two broken hearts—his or your mom's."

"Three."

"What?"

"Three broken hearts—his, my mom's . . . and mine."

"I'm sorry, Allison. I'm sorry."

Aunt Nita reached out to touch her hand. For a moment Allison hesitated, but then she clasped her aunt's trembling fingers.

"I could only see it from my child's perspective . . . I'm trying to understand it now . . . as an adult. How my mom felt. How my dad felt. How you felt. It's such a new way to look at the past." She squeezed her aunt's hand. "Give me time to get used to the change of view, okay?"

"Sure, sweetie. All the time you need. I love you."

"Love you too."

After her aunt jumped out of the Jeep to start boiling water for pasta, Allison rounded the corner of the house, her coat slung over her shoulders. Kuzko, Pacha, and Banzai grazed in the field, having finally managed a rocky-at-best three-way friendship. Maybe she needed to take notes. Write a book called *The Rocky Mountain Llamas' Guide to Reconciliation*.

When the boys stood at attention and started nerking, Allison tried to determine what upset the beasties. A stray dog? A bear? She hoped it was a dog. Within seconds, the sound of tires crunching on gravel foretold the appearance of Daniel's truck.

"Go away, Daniel. Go away, go away." Instead of muttering to herself, she ought to stand her ground and insist he leave. She debated ducking behind the fence, putting the pasture and the llamas between her and Daniel, or making a run for her apartment.

She pressed her back against the fence, watching as Daniel parked, jumped out of the cab, and advanced toward her. He stopped with a foot separating them. His brown curls were tousled, as if he'd raked his fingers through them while driving. This close, she could see the angry purple bruise forming along his jaw where Seth had hit him. His green eye was set off by a red welt on his cheekbone.

"Oh, Daniel, you're hurt." Allison reached out and touched his face.

He clasped her hand, turning it so he could press a kiss on her palm. "I'm fine. No big deal. I've been worried about you."

"Me? I wasn't the one throwing punches."

"I'm sorry you saw that. I know you're upset."

Allison pulled her hand away and turned to greet the boys, thankful for an excuse to break contact with Daniel. He came to stand beside her, their shoulders touching.

"Alli, we need to talk."

Banzai nudged his way past Pacha and Kuzko, intent on saying hello. Allison closed her eyes, willing herself to be strong. To do the right thing. "No, Daniel, we don't."

She forced herself to meet his eyes when he turned her face toward his. "How can you say that? I love you. I want to figure out how we can make a relationship work."

God, help me do the right thing—not make any more mistakes. Not everyone got their happily ever after.

"We can't have a relationship, Daniel. It's crazy to think we can."

"It's crazy not to try, Alli. We can make this work. I'm willing to change." He grasped her shoulders, turning her to face him. "I'm talking to Jackson—seeing if he's interested in working for me so I won't have to travel as much."

"This isn't about you doing something different. Traveling more or traveling less." Allison wanted to close her eyes again, blocking out the hurt darkening Daniel's eyes. "This is about who I am—my past. I dated Seth for six years. I was engaged to him. Until a few months ago, I thought I was going to marry him."

"But you realized you didn't love him."

"I loved Seth, but I couldn't marry him. I was doing it for all the wrong reasons—for security. Safety." Even as she fought to stand her ground, Banzai nipped at Daniel's shoulder.

He ignored the pushy beast. "So what does that have to do with us?"

"*You're brothers.* Don't you get it?" Allison gripped Daniel's arms. "I can't fall in love with my ex-fiancé's brother."

Daniel's laugh was harsh. "Don't let that worry you, Alli. I haven't had a close relationship with Tag for years. He's the favorite son. I'm not. Besides, he's already told me if you and I get together, we're no longer brothers. I'm good with that."

"When did Seth tell you that?"

"I talked with him about us after the hospital standoff, Alli. It was time."

Allison wrenched away from Daniel, turning and gripping the rail with her unbandaged hand, the wood rough against her skin. "Don't you think you should have talked to me first?"

"You were in the hospital—you'd almost died in an avalanche!" Daniel leaned forward again, taking Alli's hand and lacing his fingers through hers. "I was trying to protect you."

"Another Rayner brother protecting me. First Seth, now you."

"It's not like that."

She shoved Banzai's furry face away when he tried to go nose to nose with her. He was some sort of ill-timed comedic relief.

"You just said you were protecting me, Daniel. What else is it?" She pulled her hand away, tucking it against her body. "Seth took care of me for six years. Now you want to take care of me. I need to be by myself—*be* myself—for a while."

"Alli, look at me." He stood in front of her, palms out. "Don't you know that I want you to be yourself? Pursue your dreams? I'd never get in the way of that."

"And I don't want you to change for me. I love how you live life, Daniel. It's who you are." Allison bowed her head in defeat, the words burning her throat. "But it's not me."

Alli's rejection shadowed Daniel as he drove over the mountain road to the B-and-B.

Not good enough. Same old, same old.

Daniel pulled into the parking lot, rocks spewing under the wheels of his truck. After climbing out, he leaned against the bumper and stared off into space.

It wasn't that Alli picked Seth instead of him. She just hadn't picked him at all.

His fists clenched and unclenched. *Get a grip, it's not the end of the world.*

Just the end of a long-buried dream.

"Daniel! Daniel, are you ready to go on our little hike? You're late!"

He glanced up to see Madison running down the porch steps, looking as if she fell out of an REI catalog. Her khaki shorts were pressed, her denim top covered a pristine scoop-necked white T-shirt, and her hiking boots looked as if they had been out of the shoe store for an hour, tops. Her blond curls were pulled back by a crisp red bandana. Had she starched it?

"Hike?"

"Yes, our hike." She looped her arm through his and smiled up at him, pulling him close. "We're supposed to hike up to the waterfall today—explore it as a day trip for our customers, remember?"

No, he didn't remember. And the last thing he wanted to do was take a tricked-out, transplanted city girl hiking. What he wanted to do was head for Canada. Or California. Anywhere away from Alli.

"I forgot. Got tied up in an—an appointment. Can we do this another day?"

"Daniel, you sent me a text saying you're leaving tomorrow. There is no other time. You're not going to keep me waiting and then cancel on me, are you?" Madison formed her lips into a pout and pleaded with what Daniel guessed was her best "aren't I too sweet to say no to" face.

"No." Daniel shrugged and forced himself to smile. He pulled his faded blue Cabela's cap out of his back pocket and positioned it backward on his head. "No, I'm not going to cancel. Let's grab some provisions—some water, a couple of other necessities—and head out."

Within twenty minutes of starting up the trail, Daniel realized Madison was not a hiker. She tended to traipse along beside Daniel, chatting about her plans for decorating the lodge's dining room. Nodding, Daniel let her drone on. He wasn't hearing a single word.

Should he go back and try to reason with Alli? Maybe kiss her senseless? Yeah, that would do it. Or not. She'd probably smack him—with her cast.

Forty-five minutes into the hike, Daniel stopped long enough for them to down the bottles of water. Well, he chugged his. Madison took several sips as she snuggled next to him on a boulder. At least she couldn't talk while she was drinking.

"Make sure you're well hydrated, Madison. We're still about thirty minutes from the waterfall." Daniel tucked the water bottles into his backpack. "The trail gets rougher from here on. We've got to criss-cross the river a few times. Watch out, because the wet boulders are slippery."

"I'll just hold extra tight to you, Daniel. You'll keep me from falling." Madison tightened her grip around his arm as if he were a human life preserver.

They managed the first crossover without a problem. Farther up, they needed to climb over several tall boulders to reconnect with the trail.

"I'll go ahead. Just follow my lead."

"I'm right behind you, Daniel." Madison increased her grip on his arm.

"You don't need to hold on—it's better if we both have our hands free to help get over the boulders."

"But I don't want to slip." Madison refused to let go.

"I don't want either of us to fall, so let's get over these boulders—"

The next moment, Daniel's right foot slipped off the boulder he was trying to climb. As he balanced on his left foot, it slipped out from underneath him. He fell, all his weight crashing on his left knee.

He heard the sickening *thwack* as his kneecap fractured—a sound similar to that of a cantaloupe hitting concrete and splitting apart. Odd, he didn't feel any pain. But he had no ability to straighten his left leg, either.

"Daniel, are you okay?" Madison stood over him. "You pulled on me so hard I almost fell."

"No, I'm not all right." He stared at his deformed kneecap, which looked like two twin peaks with a valley in between rather than a solid piece of bone.

"What do you mean? Let me help you get up."

"I *can't* get up, Madison." Daniel stopped himself from adding *Thanks to you hanging on me.* With the sleeve of his T-shirt, he swiped at the sweat forming along his forehead. "I've broken my kneecap."

"Are you sure?"

Daniel gritted his teeth. "Yes, I'm sure. Do you want to look at my knee?"

"No! No—if I see blood, I faint."

"There's no blood, Madison." Using his right leg, he maneuvered down to a flat area beside the boulder.

"What are you doing?"

"Trying to get comfortable so I can figure out what to do."

"We need to get help."

"Well, I can't do that. And I'm betting our cell phones don't work, thanks to all the surrounding rocks." Gripping his calf, Daniel straightened his leg and probed his injury. "You're going to need to head back down and notify search and rescue."

"I can't hike back by myself!"

"Madison, listen to me." Daniel pulled her down so they were face-to-face. "I have a serious injury. I can't walk. My quad muscle is no longer connected to my kneecap—"

He stopped when he saw Madison's face pale. *Okay, no need to get detailed.* He didn't want her to pass out.

"Never mind. Listen, just head back down the trail the way we came." He dug his cell phone out of his backpack. "Try using my cell every few minutes. Call 911 if you get a signal. Tell them I'm injured and I'm on the eastern trail to the falls."

Madison choked back a sob. "What if I get lost?"

"You won't get lost. There are bound to be other hikers coming up this trail. It's well marked. The sooner you get started, the sooner search and rescue will get here." He smiled up at her. "Do me a favor before you leave."

"What?"

"Let me have your headband."

"What? Why?"

"I may need it."

"But it keeps my hair off my face—" Madison fingered the red bandana.

"Here, take my ball cap." Daniel pulled his hat off and threw it to her, trying not to laugh at the look of disgust on Madison's face. "One more thing. Two, actually. Can you find me two tree branches?"

"Tree branches?"

"Yep. About three feet long and as big around as two fingers."

"What are you going to do, rub two sticks together and build a fire?"

"No, that's not how it works." He slung her bandana around his neck. "I may try to support my leg with them."

After Madison found some branches and left, Daniel shifted his weight so he could pull another bandana out of his back pocket. He zipped open the side compartment of his backpack and pulled out a bundle of parachute cord. He never left home without it. The two bandanas served as padding near his knee. Then he positioned the tree-branch splints on either side of his leg, securing them with the parachute cord.

Not professional, but it would do.

Gripping the boulder, he pulled himself to a standing position, testing his weight on his left leg. Not too bad, as long as he kept his knee straight. If he took it slow, maybe he could meet the rescue team on their way up the trail.

Who knew how quickly Madison would get back down? He wasn't going to sit here and wait to find out. Maybe he'd meet another hiker who'd help him.

He took two steps. His leg buckled and he fell. He rolled onto his back and sat up again, laughing out loud.

"What a day," he muttered. "First Alli. Now this. One for the books."

He brushed himself off and stood, tightening the cords above and below his knee to ensure it wouldn't bend again. His knee was starting to swell.

His father may not have made it to his Eagle Scout ceremony, but the training sure had come in handy.

Time to start back down. No one would say Daniel Rayner was a quitter.

Alli, just hiked the upper part of the C&O Canal with Jackson. Reminded us of old Boy Scout camping trips—only this time we didn't forget matches and fuel.

—Daniel

CHAPTER 40

"I cannot believe I am back here."

Her aunt gave Allison a gentle push in the direction of the ER. "But this time you're walking in instead of being wheeled in on a stretcher by a couple of hunky search-and-rescue guys."

"I was *unconscious*, Aunt Nita." Allison refused to budge. "I didn't notice what the guys looked like."

"It's an unwritten rule that all search-and-rescue guys are drop-dead gorgeous. Same with EMTs. Let's go."

"They're going to laugh me right back into the parking lot when I tell them why I'm here."

Aunt Nita placed her hands on Allison's shoulders and propelled her through the sliding glass doors. "True. But ERs are such gloomy places. You'll be the comic relief. Move."

Great. She'd been reduced to comic relief.

The harried woman sitting behind the admittance desk nodded at Aunt Nita but didn't look even slightly amused to see Allison. She gave her the once-over before asking, "May I help you?"

Should she apologize for *not* bleeding all over the paperwork?

Allison leaned in close, lowering her voice as if confiding a secret. "I . . . I need to have my cast replaced."

"Excuse me?"

"I need to have my cast replaced." She raised her arm and waved the bright purple cast in front of the woman's frowning face. "I tried to reach an itch with a plastic cat toy, and it . . . it broke off inside my cast."

"This is an *emergency room.*" The woman glared at Allison. "Make an appointment with your family doctor."

"I called my family doctor. He's on vacation—"

"Then call your surgeon."

Allison gritted her teeth and spoke slowly, ignoring her aunt's muffled giggles. "My doctor's on-call service already suggested that, but Dr. Osborn is in surgery all day. Her office told me to come here."

"Well, you're going to have a long wait. We're a small emergency department." She handed Allison a clipboard loaded with paperwork. "Fill these out. No rush—as you can see, we're swamped." She motioned to the chairs filled with bona fide emergencies.

Allison turned and walked toward a pair of seats, positioned across from a mother holding a toddler who looked—and sounded—miserable. "Wanna go home, wanna go home, wanna go home!"

"Me too." The exhausted woman tried to comfort her child, looking as if she wished someone would come and comfort her.

Just as Allison settled in the chair, she heard the wail of a siren getting louder and louder.

"Looks like you just got shoved farther to the back of the line." Her aunt sat in the chair next to her and pulled a book and a pair of fire-engine-red reading glasses from her expansive purse. "Glad I brought some reading material. Maybe I should have brought the sequel."

"Got anything in there for me?" Allison leaned back, resting her head on the wall. "I didn't think to grab anything to read. And I'm sure all these magazines are from the last century."

Aunt Nita dug in her purse again and pulled out another book. "Here, read this—*after* you fill out your paperwork."

"Who are you, Mary Poppins? What else do you have in that bag?"

"Some people keep their reading materials by their bed. I keep mine in my purse."

Allison flipped the book over to scan the cover copy. Why did she think she'd distract herself with reading? The fiasco with Daniel earlier in the day still wrenched at her heart. Had she made the right decision? Rethinking it wouldn't help—she couldn't go back and change anything.

Just focus on something else, like all this paperwork.

Shoving the book aside, Allison anchored the clipboard with her cast and began filling out the forms. Name: Allison Rayner.

What? She was single, and her name was still Denman.

With an exasperated shake of her head, she drew a line through the incorrect last name and wrote Denman. Halfway through writing her address, she realized she'd written her previous address in the Springs.

She'd moved on—literally. Maybe she should just dictate the answers to her aunt.

She looked up when the sliding glass doors whooshed open. A petite female EMT strode through the doors.

There went Aunt Nita's hunky-guy theory.

"We're bringing in a hiking accident." The woman leaned on the admissions desk. "Got an empty bay?"

"How bad?"

"The guy broke his kneecap, but he hiked halfway down—met the rescue team coming up to get him. They were concerned about shock, so we brought him by ambulance." She laughed. "We used the sirens 'cause we were bored."

Allison didn't know if the accident victim was brave or stupid. She would have waited for the rescue team to carry her down the mountain. That's what they were trained to do.

She watched as two men who looked as if they spent a considerable amount of time at the gym pushed a stretcher into the ER. The guy lying on the stretcher probably wasn't bad-looking either, with his dark wavy hair and muscular build. As a matter of fact, he reminded her of . . .

Daniel?

Allison pulled the book out of her aunt's hands. "Do you see what I see—or rather, *whom* I see?"

"What? Who? Where?"

"On the stretcher. That's Daniel."

"*Your* Daniel?"

"Not *my* Daniel. Just Daniel. But yes, it's him." Allison fiddled with the papers on the clipboard and watched at the same time. "I heard the EMT say something about a hiking accident."

Aunt Nita tucked her reading glasses on top of her head. "Go over and see if he needs anything."

"No."

"Oh, come on, Allison. I'm not suggesting you offer to kiss his boo-boo and make it all better." Her aunt took the paperwork. "Just offer to call somebody or something. The man saved your life!"

That would be the adult thing to do. The friendly thing to do. Besides, she wasn't going anywhere anytime soon. Allison watched the admissions clerk direct the EMTs.

"Wait for me! Wait for me!" A shrill voice invaded the waiting room. "I'm with that man on the stretcher. I helped rescue him!"

She knew that voice.

All eyes turned to watch Madison charging into the waiting room as if it were Nordstrom at a "get it before it's gone" sale. She waved her bright yellow Dooney & Bourke handbag. As she tried to follow the stretcher, the no-nonsense nurse barred her way. Thanks to the small waiting room, Allison heard the heated exchange.

"Are you the patient's wife?"

"No."

"Are you a family member?"

"No. We work together." Madison tried to sidestep the nurse. "I told you, I helped rescue him."

"You'll have to wait here while he's examined."

"I'm sure he'll want me to be with him. We're dating."

Oh, really? Is Daniel aware of that? Allison pressed her lips together and shifted in her seat, turning away from Madison. Maybe Madison thought if she said Daniel and she were dating, that would make it come true. After several minutes, Madison admitted defeat. As she passed in front of Allison, she pulled out her iPhone and texted someone.

Allison buried herself in the insurance forms. Halfway through page three, Allison heard the nurse call her name. "Miss Denman? Would you come here?"

What happened to people saying "please"?

As she walked to the desk, the nurse turned to discuss something with another employee. Allison stood to the side and looked toward the back, surprised that she could see into several medical bays, separated by slate-blue curtains. Daniel lay propped up on one, a huge ice pack covering his knee. He chatted with several medical personnel, including the female EMT who'd brought him in. He said something, and the entire group laughed.

Typical Daniel. Charming no matter where he was or what shape he was in. By the time he was discharged, both the EMT and Madison would be offering to take care of him.

"Miss Denman?"

Allison jerked her attention back to the nurse. "Yes?"

"I called Dr. Obsorn's office. It turns out she canceled her last surgery of the day and is willing to meet you in her office and replace your cast."

"Oh . . . okay, then. I guess I can stop filling out the forms you gave me." She hesitated, watching Daniel chat with his new friends.

"Is there anything else I can help you with, Miss Denman?"

"I-I know the man who just came in—the guy who broke his leg?"

"Yes?"

"Would you ask him if I can do anything for him? Call anyone? Get him anything?"

The nurse heaved a sigh. "Someone came in with him—his girl-friend, I think. I'm sure she can help him. You need to get your arm recast."

"Would you just ask, please? Tell him Alli would like to help him. If there's anything I can do."

It was the right thing to do. The adult thing to do. She'd keep telling herself that.

The nurse strode to Daniel's bedside and motioned to where Allison stood. Daniel looked up, his eyes locking with Allison's for several seconds. She lifted her hand in a tiny wave, waiting for Daniel to respond. Instead, he looked back at the nurse, exchanging a few brief words with her.

The nurse's face was sympathetic when she came back. "Mr. Rayner said he's fine, that he can handle everything himself."

"Um, can I just talk to him for a moment?"

The nurse's expression conveyed her opinion of Allison: *Idiot.*

"I know he said he's fine, but I-I just want to talk to him. It'll only take a minute."

With a disbelieving shake of her head, the nurse motioned for Allison to follow her into the back. "You've got a visitor."

Daniel's laughing banter with the small group of new friends ceased. "Allison."

"H-hey, Daniel. What happened?" The tension in Allison's head eased a little when the group dispersed, leaving her alone with Daniel.

"I fell. Broke my knee."

"How awful." Allison noticed streaks of dirt on Daniel's clothes. Sweat soaked his shirt. An ugly scrape ran up his arm. "Are you sure I can't do anything to help you? Call someone?"

"I'm good. Used to handling things myself." Daniel repositioned the ice pack on his leg.

Allison threw a quick glance over her shoulder and then lowered her voice. "I hope you know I'm sorry about . . . about earlier—"

"Hey, no worries. My mistake." He shrugged off Allison's apology. "Really, it was a mistake."

A mistake.

Daniel's comment echoed Allison's father's assessment of her. A mistake. Why was she surprised that yet another man in her life had come to that conclusion?

A nurse stepped up beside her. "Excuse me, but he needs to be taken to X-ray."

"Sure. Sure. I'll get out of your way." Allison forced herself to act as if nothing were wrong. And nothing was wrong. She had made the right choice, and Daniel confirmed it. She had other things to do besides trying to make things right with Daniel Rayner—like getting a scratchy piece of plastic out of her cast.

And getting on with her life.

CHAPTER 41

*T*his was his last chance.

Seth sat in his car outside Allison's basement apartment. He'd spent most of last night awake, trying not to replay the image of Daniel kissing Allison. He'd abandoned his bed and sat in his den, thinking over his six years with her. Trying to figure out how they ended up here. All he'd ever wanted to do was love Allison. Take care of her. Protect her. Was that so wrong?

If he had it to do over again, would he do it differently?

No.

Maybe.

If there was something he could have done or said that would have assured him that Allison said "I do" on their wedding day, rather than running out of the church, he'd do that.

Enough thinking. He was a man of action.

Seth exited the car and walked to the front door, rapping on it with his knuckles. He shifted his feet and straightened his shoulders, waiting for Allison to answer the door. He ran exploratory fingers over his jaw. Daniel was the one with the bruised face, thanks to yesterday's bookstore brawl. Seth's ribs ached where his brother had hit him, causing him to ram into a shelf, but other than that, he looked pretty good.

He tried to ignore the three pairs of eyes watching him from the pasture. Why would anyone rescue llamas—and problem ones at that?

"S-Seth." Allison opened the door, holding a bottle of pink nail polish.

"May I come in?"

"I guess." She stepped back, balancing the open bottle of polish. She wore a Rocky Mountain National Park sweatshirt with a pair of gray sweatpants, her bare feet peeking out from beneath the frayed hems. The toes on one foot were painted pink; the other foot still needed a coat of polish. Her cat watched from his preferred spot on the back of the couch, tail twitching.

If things had gone according to his plan—their plans—Allison would have been curled up on the couch in his town home, reading a book while he watched TV. Or painting her toes. They would have enjoyed six months of married life and settled into some sort of routine. Instead, he'd spent the past few weeks driving back and forth from the Springs to Estes Park, hoping to convince Allison again to marry him.

"Do you want something to drink?" She took a few careful steps toward the small kitchenette, as if the polish on her toes wasn't quite dry.

"No, I'm fine." He glanced around the room. There were no pictures hanging on the walls, no mementos at all except her thimble collection. Silly things to collect. Thimbles and postcards from his brother, that's all Allison ever saved. She bought the thimbles for herself once a year and, up until the week before the wedding, kept every single WISH YOU WERE HERE postcard Daniel ever sent her.

Of course. Why hadn't he seen it sooner?

He watched her cap the nail polish, sit it on the kitchen counter, and then perch on the arm of the couch.

"I came to apologize for yesterday—for the fight with my brother. I'm sorry I lost control like that." He rubbed his forehead as if he could erase the image of Allison in Daniel's arms. "I just didn't expect to find you kissing my brother in a bookstore."

Allison refused to make eye contact with him, her fingers twisting the cuff of her sweatshirt.

"I've been hoping that all these weeks, all our time together, meant we were working things out between us."

"Oh, Seth, no . . ."

"Why not? You have to know I still love you, Allison. That I want to marry you."

Allison closed her eyes, seeming to weigh her words. "Seth, you don't even know me."

"What are you saying? I've known you since you were a junior in high school."

"What's my favorite kind of music?"

"What?"

"Answer the question."

"You like jazz, like me."

"Who's my favorite author?"

"You like to read Grisham, like me."

"What's my favorite movie?"

"We both like mysteries."

"Favorite thing to do on Saturdays?"

"You like to cheer me on when I run a marathon." Seth threw his hands up in the air. "What's this all about, Allison?"

"I like country music, Seth. I like to read Susan May Warren and Rachel Hauck—and you've never read any of their books, believe me. My favorite movie is *The Magic of Ordinary Days,* and since you took some sort of crazy vow to never watch anything on the Hallmark Channel, you don't know what that is, either." She took a deep breath and smiled, despite the tears causing her eyes to shimmer. "And my favorite thing to do on Saturdays is to get up early and grab my camera and photograph the sunrise. Or sometimes I stay home and paint."

Seth stared at her. "How come I didn't know this?"

"You never asked me."

"Okay, you've made your point. We like different things."

"That's not my point."

"Then what is?"

"My point is that we are *two different people*." Allison took a deep breath and twisted her fingers together, but hoped she met the question in his eyes with a look of confidence. "It's like I said months ago, Seth. If we got married, we'd both be unhappy."

"I wouldn't be unhappy."

"Yes, you would. Can't you see that we outgrew each other?"

"I can fix this, Allison. I know I can."

"You are one of the smartest, most capable men I know. But this isn't something you fix. This is something you accept."

Allison watched Seth pace her apartment. After a moment, he stopped and knelt in front of her. "Allison, I can't believe I've lost you. What can I do?"

"Let me go, Seth."

His earnest brown eyes searched hers as he covered her hand with both of his. "But I love you."

"You love who I *was*. I met you when I was sixteen, when I needed someone to take care of me. I was lonely and hurting, and you were . . . wonderful." She touched the side of his face, almost catching a glimpse of him as he'd been back then—everything she wanted.

"I haven't changed."

"I have. That's the problem. You still want to take care of me. To be in charge. Have our relationship be like it was in high school. I'm not that girl anymore." Allison stood and moved away, resisting the urge to apologize for growing up.

"This is my fault, then?" Seth followed, turning her to face him. "Everything happened because I didn't recognize—didn't accept you were changing?"

"Does it have to be about blame?" Allison rested her hand on his chest. "It's my fault too, for not saying something sooner. That was my mistake—I was too afraid to be honest with you. I did love you, Seth. You were my first love."

"But not your forever love."

"No."

"That would be Daniel."

Allison pulled away. "What?"

"Daniel told me about you and him—"

"I'm not with your brother, Seth."

"What's stopping you?" Seth jammed his fists in his pockets and stared at her, demanding an answer.

"He's your brother."

"And that kiss in the bookstore?"

"It was a mistake."

"The kiss before our wedding—a mistake too?"

Allison turned away from Seth, unable to look at him. So Daniel had told his brother. Her response was a mere whisper. "Yes."

"Are you telling me you don't love my brother?"

She wanted to hurl words into the pause that lengthened between them. But she couldn't lie to Seth.

"I see."

"It doesn't matter." Facing him again, Allison raised her hands as if warding off more questions. "Nothing is going to happen between me and Daniel."

"That's supposed to make me feel better? If Daniel were anybody but Daniel—if he weren't my brother—you'd admit you love him—"

"Seth, we were talking about us."

"But there is no us, is there, Allison? Because you love my brother." He bracketed her face with his hands. "And I . . . I love you. I wish I didn't, but I do." She watched as Seth closed his eyes. Clenched his jaw, as if trying to hold back the words he spoke next. "I admit it. This *was* my fault. I took our relationship for granted. I just expected you to always be there . . . to be my Allison. My mistakes ruined everything."

"No, Seth—"

"Yes. I'm man enough to admit it. I wish I were man enough to say go and have a wonderful life with Daniel, but I can't. Don't ask that of me."

CHAPTER 42

Alli, the sunrise on the Riviera Maya was stunning. Wish you were here to see it with me— and had your camera so you could capture it.

—Daniel

*A*llison snuggled underneath her comforter, cell phone tucked to her ear.

"You heard me, Meggie. It's snowing."

"It's blue skies and sunny down here in the Springs." Her best friend's husky laugh warmed Allison all the way down to her cold toes. "You've got to love Colorado weather."

"Aunt Nita's out with her doctor friend. The boys are huddled in their shelter. And Bisquick and I are bedded down for the night."

"Already? It's not even nine-thirty." Meghan muted the television. "No dinner with Seth? Or Daniel?"

"I think it's safe to say I won't be hearing from either Rayner brother anytime soon."

"What happened?"

"You mean besides Daniel kissing me in the bookstore? And Seth finding us? And the two of them pounding on each other like a couple of middle-schoolers?"

"Oh, Allison, every girl dreams about guys fighting over her."

Allison rolled over on her back and stared at the ceiling. "Not this girl."

"Hold on a sec." Allison heard muffled sounds for a few moments. "Sorry. Just needed a root beer while we talked. You talk, I'll listen. So, what happened?"

"I told Daniel I couldn't get involved with him because he was Seth's brother."

"How did he take that?"

"The next time I saw him? He said it was all just a big mistake."

"Ouch."

"He's right, Meg. It's not like anything could have worked out between us."

"What about Seth?

"He came by today."

"And?"

"I think he finally accepted that we're over. He says he still loves me, but he's not pursuing me."

"How do you feel about all this—losing both Rayner brothers?"

"Resigned. There's no other way it could have ended." Allison moved her feet for Bisquick to walk across the bottom of her bed.

"So what now?"

"It's me, myself, and I—and one barely used wedding dress."

"Finally."

"What's that supposed to mean?"

"Remember when I found you hiding out at my parents' cabin?"

"Ye-es. I've thought about it a lot."

"And?"

"My mistakes have ruined my relationship with Seth and Daniel. I keep thinking, how could God love someone like me?" Allison sat up, pulling the comforter around her shoulders.

"He made you, Allison. He loves you because you're his . . ."

"I'm sure when he looks at me, God thinks, *Can't you do any better than that? I'm so disappointed.*"

"That is not how God talks to us, girlfriend. Listen closer—I think it sounds a lot like something *you'd* say."

Allison huddled under her blankets, seeking warmth. "You know how you said to concentrate on one verse? Well, I found this one that talked about God being light and space and zest—like passion and enthusiasm. I don't know him like that, Meggie. I wanted all of that when I was five or six, but not anymore. And if that's God, it scares me."

Meghan was silent for a few minutes. Had she dozed off? Then her voice came across the phone, soft but sure. "God can be scary, Allison, but in an 'isn't he amazing' way, not in a 'you better watch out' way. Look past that one verse . . . read a little farther and see what else God might want to say to you."

Allison crawled out of bed, dragging the comforter with her, and went to stand beside the window. Moonlight caused the falling snow to glitter like tiny crystals. Or maybe frozen pieces of her shattered heart.

Meghan broke into the silence. "May I make a suggestion?"

"No?"

"As heartbreaking as all of this has been, maybe it wasn't a mistake. Maybe you aren't supposed to run from Seth right into a relationship with Daniel."

"Oh."

"I've known you since middle school, Allison. You've always wanted a strong man in your life. First it was your stepdad. Then it was Seth. Now it's Daniel."

Allison opened her mouth to argue, but Meghan plowed into the silence.

"Hear me out. God's stronger than any of those guys. Stop trying to figure out things on your own and listen for God's voice. Don't assume you know what to do. Run from evil and run to God instead."

"I don't think wanting a relationship with Daniel is evil, Meghan!"

"You're missing the point. You ran from Seth. Then you seemed ready to run straight for Daniel. Why not run to God instead?"

"What do you mean?"

"Stop focusing on whether you should have had a relationship with Daniel. Don't worry about having a relationship with anybody. You were in a six-year relationship with Seth. Take a hiatus!"

No Seth. No Daniel. No guy at all. Run to God instead. Could she do it?

"Any suggestions for how I do that, Meggie?"

"As a matter of fact, I have a great idea—but you're going to need to wear that wedding dress gone wrong one last time."

"Thanks for the water break, Meggie." Allison wiggled her toes inside her hiking boots. "I cannot believe I let you talk me into this."

"We haven't gotten to the really fun part yet." As Allison stood, Meghan rearranged the billowing skirt flowing around her legs. Then she cinched the hip pack around Allison's waist, positioning it so the water bottle didn't tip over.

Allison tried to ignore the incredulous stares of the other trekkers passing them by. So she was slightly overdressed for hiking the thousand-foot incline to Mills Lake. She tugged the lace at her wrists, thankful she'd waited to undertake this oddest of odysseys until the doctor removed her bright purple cast. The tight sleeves never would have fit.

Allison paused a moment longer, taking in the view around her. She ignored how the hem of her gown dragged in the brown dirt of the trail, focusing instead on the blue sky, the sound of the mountain jays flitting from tree to tree and calling to one another, the muffled whisper of the mountain stream.

Meghan shrugged on the backpack containing Allison's veil. "Ready to go? We're over halfway there, so we'll be at the lake in about forty minutes."

"The photographer's going to be there, right? I better not be hiking up this mountain in a wedding gown for no reason."

"He said he'd head out early and be all set up by the time we arrived. Let's get a move on."

"That's easy for you to say—you're wearing jeans." Allison picked up the hem of the gown and sidestepped in front of her best friend. "Grab my train, like a good bridesmaid."

"You do realize this is absolutely the last time I'm helping you with this dress."

"This is absolutely the last time I'm wearing this thing. You packed my change of clothes, right? I don't want to hike back down the mountain in this getup."

Meghan trudged behind her. "Where's your sense of adventure?"

"My sense of adventure is going to be thoroughly exhausted by the time I am done with this idea of yours." Allison moved to the side of the trail to let a runner pass by. "The photographer knows there's no groom, right?"

"Yes. Stop worrying. I explained this is a 'trash your dress' photo shoot—that you want some fun photographs in your wedding gown before you lay it, and your past, to rest." Meghan gathered up more of the material. "I even brought some props."

"What kind of props?"

"Don't worry. We'll have fun with it—them—when we get there."

By the time Allison teetered across the rocks stretching out before the lake, she no longer thought trashing her dress was a brilliant idea. She was tired of traipsing up a mountain in a dress that weighed as much as a week's worth of clothing. Tired of dodging runners who stepped on her train. Tired of being asked, "Who's the lucky guy?"

"Okay, Meggie, where's this photographer you've been raving about?"

"Right over there—with the llama."

"The *what*?"

Allison stopped, the gown swishing around her legs. Standing next to a camera set up on a tripod stood her father—and her aunt holding a lead rope connected to Banzai.

"Me-ghan."

"All-i-son."

She turned and faced her traitorous friend. "What have you done?"

"I got the best photographer I could find to take your pictures. And I got a prop—but the llama isn't the only prop. Come on, your dad is waiting."

"I'm not even talking to my father."

"You don't have to. All you have to do is pose, smile, and say 'Cheese' when he tells you to. And watch out for Banzai. Your aunt told me that he still likes to spit."

Aunt Nita walked toward her, leading Banzai. "Great day for a photo shoot, isn't it?"

If her aunt was going to act all nonchalant, Allison would play along. She'd think of her dad as a photographer, nothing more. She wasn't going back down the mountain without the photos. "Couldn't be better."

"What kind of photos were you thinking of, Allison?" Meghan's voice was muffled as she searched through her backpack.

"A mix of close-ups and shots with the mountains and the lake in the background." Allison pulled the hem of her gown up a few inches. "And it won't hurt to show my hiking boots."

"Want some of you barefoot?" Her father came to stand beside Aunt Nita, giving Banzai a wide berth.

"Why not?" Allison would treat him like any other photographer making suggestions. "Meghan made sure I got a mani-pedi."

Meghan held up a red bow tie and matching cummerbund with a flourish. "Here's Banzai's outfit! I thought about a boutonniere but was afraid he'd eat it."

"Smart girl. Although he prefers pink lemonade." Aunt Nita motioned to Allison's father. "He can put those on while I make sure Banzai doesn't get antsy."

"And I brought these!" Meghan knelt beside the backpack and pulled out a white shoe box. "Something special for the occasion. Glass slippers!"

"Are you kidding me?" Allison knelt beside her friend and lifted the lid. Nestled inside the box was a pair of faux-glass high heels. "How did you find these?"

"You can find anything online." Meghan pulled the shoes out of the box and held them up. "These symbolize that you're still hoping for that happily ever after."

"Let me start with a picture of Allison sitting over there, holding the glass slippers." Her father pointed to a large flat rock jutting out over the lake.

For the next hour and a half, Allison posed. Wearing hiking books. Holding glass slippers. Wearing glass slippers. Barefoot. Wearing her veil. Not wearing her veil. Standing next to the bad-boy Banzai, who tried to snack on her veil. Lounging by the mountain lake, with her dress spread out around her. While she posed, Aunt Nita let children come up and pet Banzai. When several little girls volunteered to be flower girls, Allison posed with them. Meghan got their addresses, promising to send their mothers copies of the photos.

After the first several groups of people gathered to watch the trash-the-dress celebration, Allison forgot about them and, for the first time, enjoyed wearing the gown. The dress in no way reflected her personality. But after today she'd hand it to Meghan and never, ever see it again, except in a series of totally unexpected photographs.

"Are you game to try one more shot?" When her father arched a bushy eyebrow at her and grinned, Allison couldn't help but grin back.

"Sure, why not? You didn't bring a motorcycle with you, by any chance?" Did she just joke with her dad?

"I'm sorry to say I didn't. That would have been perfect." He pointed to the lake. "How about a picture of you standing in the water?"

"Are you kidding me? It's freezing!"

"I said standing, not swimming. I brought along a pair of waders in case you were willing to try a water shot. You only have to stand there for a few minutes. Then we'll head back down the mountain."

"Why not?"

Aunt Nita handed Banzai's leash to her father. With Meghan managing the dress and Aunt Nita helping with the waders, Allison

wrestled her body into three feet of dark green rubber boots. "I'm
gonna need your help, Meggie."

"Me? Why me? And don't you dare tell me this is some sort of
maid-of-honor duty!" Meghan backed away from Allison.

"This has nothing to do with being my maid of honor and everything to do with being my best friend." Allison motioned her aunt
to grab hold of her friend. "Just roll up your jeans and help me get
out there."

Meghan sat on a rock, pulled off her shoes, and began rolling up
her jeans. "If I get pneumonia . . ."

"Once you get me out there, you can come right back on shore."

They waded into the lake, the gown floating up around Allison's
knees. Meghan pretended to arrange the five-foot train one last time.
"How's this?"

"Perfect." Her father stood on the shore. "Let me get one shot of
the two of you."

Allison wrapped her arms around Meghan and leaned back.

"Don't. You. Dare. I don't have a change of clothes." After giving
her a hug, Meghan dashed back to dry land.

"Okay, Allison. Look at me. Smile. Now turn away from me and
look back over your shoulder. Smile."

Allison couldn't believe how much fun she'd had trashing her
wedding dress. She'd bought the gown to please everybody else.
She'd worn it for a wedding ceremony to marry Mr. Right, who
was all wrong for her. These photos made the dress her own. Put
her past in the past—and gave her the freedom to claim her future.

"Hey, Meggie. Hand me those glass slippers one last time."

"I am not coming back in that water, girlfriend."

Allison sloshed closer to the shore. "Just get close enough to hand
them to me. I need them for the last shot."

While she waited for Meghan to retrieve the high heels from the
backpack, Allison whispered, "It's gonna be okay." She thrust her
arms up in the air and shouted, "I'm gonna be okay!"

Then she took the shoes from Meghan and clasped them to her heart, wading back into the water and turning to face her father. "Last picture."

While her father framed her in the camera lens, Allison dared to believe she'd be brave enough to follow her happily ever after—someday.

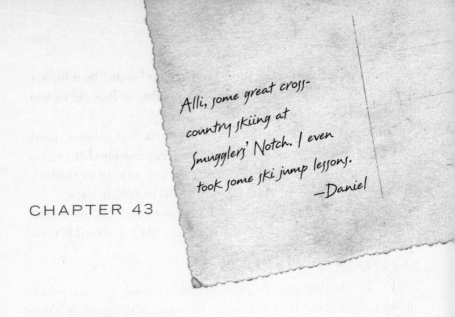

Alli, some great cross-country skiing at Smugglers' Notch. I even took some ski jump lessons.
—Daniel

CHAPTER 43

Daniel eased himself into the deep end of the pool, the cool water soothing the ache in his knee. Joel, his physical therapist, was part skilled healer, part legalized torturer.

Yesterday Joel had commented on how well he was doing three months after the hiking accident—and then proceeded to work on an area of scar tissue. Daniel had walked into Joel's office relatively pain-free. He'd hobbled out to his truck, praying he had a bottle of Motrin stashed in the glove compartment.

He positioned his goggles and dove underwater, determined to ignore the bum knee and swim hard for a good thirty minutes. At six A.M., he had the lap lane to himself and set a steady pace, concentrating on breathing.

For the first few laps, he counted strokes, alternating between freestyle and butterfly. As he found his rhythm, his thoughts turned to Alli.

He hadn't seen or heard from her since their last meeting in the hospital. The memory of the hurt clouding her eyes still caused his chest to constrict. However, she'd said "Thanks but no thanks" when Daniel said he loved her.

He flipped, twisted, and turned, pushing off from the wall in a burst of pent-up frustration, his feet scraping the concrete. What was he supposed to do, chase after her?

Yes.

He should have gone after her. Talked some sense into her.

His arms sliced through the water, his legs kicking in tandem, while his thoughts tried to keep pace with his increasing speed.

If he'd forced Alli to listen to him, he could have made her realize they could make things work. If he'd pursued her . . . refused to quit, no matter what she said, he'd . . . he'd . . .

He'd be just like his brother.

The force of the truth brought Daniel to a complete stop in the middle of the lane. He treaded water, the shock of the realization hitting him with the strength of a tidal wave.

If he hadn't let Alli go, he would be no different from Seth.

Daniel resumed swimming, his strokes slow and sure.

The truth was, Alli walked away from him. Held back by pride, he hadn't run after her. And now, he was no better than his little brother, trying to figure out how to get Alli to realize they were meant to be together.

As much as he hated to admit it, Alli had the right—the freedom—to choose or *not* choose him. That's what a relationship was: a choice.

Daniel stopped at the end of the pool, tugged his goggles up to his forehead, and rested his arms on the cement ledge. The chlorinated water stung his eyes, but not as much as the truth singed his heart.

His dad never accepted him for who he was. Never accepted his choices. Not his choice of college. Career. Even his choice to drive a beat-up old truck and a motorcycle, for that matter.

Alli had always believed in him. She'd listened to his travel stories. Saved every one of his postcards. Understood that his love for the outdoors was as much a part of him as his one-green-eye-one-blue-eye genetic makeup.

She loved him—she just wasn't *in love* with him.

He repositioned his goggles and pushed off from the wall.

How many times had he told Seth to accept the reality that he and Alli weren't meant to be? Daniel needed to accept the same reality: He and Alli weren't meant to be.

How many more disappointments, how many more rejections, were waiting for him? He'd managed to barricade his heart after his father's emotional rebuff, but his love for Alli battered his heart as if she'd flung it off the high dive into an empty pool.

Later that day, Daniel parked his motorcycle at the trailhead of Blodgett Peak. He needed to think, and the best place to do that was outside.

The November afternoon was unseasonably warm. He grabbed a water bottle and his fleece vest, shading his eyes with a worn ball cap. He'd take it slow or his knee would keep him awake tonight.

It appeared he was the only person hiking so close to dinnertime. He scuffed along the dirt path, enjoying the stillness. The scent of firewood drifted through the air. Someone insisting on treating the day like an autumn afternoon despite the warm temperature.

He followed the winding trail, letting his thoughts free-fall until they formed into the looming question: What next?

Work. And more work.

The thought exhausted him.

For so long, work had been enough. He loved the travel, yes, but he also relished the challenge of designing ski resorts and recreation sites—places where people like him could come and enjoy the outdoors.

He'd told Allison he felt closest to God outdoors. As close to God as he'd let himself get. He didn't doubt God's existence, not after seeing so many different magnificent examples of his creation. An icy expanse of glaciers. Breathtaking views from countless mountaintops. Deserts that could bury a man alive in suffocating heat but still lure him to trek across their dunes.

Ever since his dad had shoved him out the door and given Seth his time, attention, money—his love—Daniel had held his father at arm's length.

He'd done the same thing with God.

How could he let God get close? If his own father could reject him, how long would it take before God realized Daniel wasn't going to live up to his standards? Before God had a chance to shove him aside, Daniel had stiff-armed God.

This close but no further.

Belief but not trust.

Daniel's bitter laugh broke the silence of the late afternoon. Who was he to tell Allison anything about God when he'd kept him at arm's length for years? He'd assumed God was no better than his father.

That couldn't be right, could it?

He'd never given God the chance to prove anything different.

Allison opened the top drawer of her desk in search of a pen—and found the notes Seth had sent her months ago when he'd barraged her with bouquets.

The stack of six miniature white envelopes lay in a pile, unopened. She lifted them out of the drawer, sitting in her chair and fanning them out like a hand of playing cards. Her name had been written on the front by the florist. One by one, she broke each seal, removing the card inside. They all contained the same message: *I love you. Seth.*

"I love you too." Allison gathered the cards and envelopes and then watched them slip through her fingers into the wastebasket beside her desk. "Just not enough to marry you."

She stood, giving herself a shake as if she could toss off the melancholy threatening to overtake her. She'd made her choices, but sometimes the loneliness made her wish she'd made different ones.

"Hey, Bisquick." She scooped the cat into her arms. "How about we go visit the boys?"

The cat stretched up, rubbing his face underneath her neck. As they walked toward the corral, the llamas jostled for position by the gate.

"Back up, Banzai. You too, Kuzko." Allison unlatched the gate and slid in sideways. "Good boy, Pacha. Nice to see one of you has manners."

Bisquick mewed a greeting as the trio of llamas surrounded Allison, snuffling her face.

Allison shouldered her way out of the group. "One at a time, guys. You know Bisquick doesn't like to be crowded."

Kuzko nipped at Banzai, who backed up, acknowledging the other llama's position as alpha llama. Pacha sidled up beside Allison but let Kuzko touch his nose to Bisquick's.

Allison reached over and scratched the fur along Banzai's back. For some reason, she liked him best. Maybe she naturally rooted for the underdog.

When the rumble of a truck interrupted their feline-llama get-together, Allison couldn't stop herself from hoping Daniel's truck would appear. Instead, a delivery truck lumbered up the gravel driveway. A few minutes later, a man hopped out, carrying a large package.

"You Allison Denman?"

"Yes." Allison maneuvered herself through the llamas and headed for the gate.

"Package for you."

"I'll meet you at the door."

After signing for the package, Allison examined the return address. No hint, since it had been packed by the delivery company. She slid the box to the center of the room, hurrying to the kitchen for a knife to cut through the packing tape.

She reached into the box and lifted out a bubble-wrapped rectangle. What was this? Who was it from? Setting the box to the side, she leaned the package against her couch. As she peeled away the protective covering, she gasped when she saw the framed photograph of a stunning mountain sunrise.

Allison knelt, her fingers brushing the frame. "Oh . . . who sent this?"

She pulled away the rest of the bubble wrap and noticed a white envelope taped to the front of the packing. Once again, her name was scrawled in unfamiliar handwriting. Inside was a notecard with a familiar nature photograph. She turned the card over. Thomas Mangelsen. She loved his work. She looked at the framed photograph again, realizing that it was one of his pieces too.

Her fingers trembled as she opened the card.

Dear Alli,

Only Daniel called her Alli. Daniel sent this?

Dear Alli,

You are looking at one no longer appropriate wedding gift. I've kept this for months, debating what to do with it. The reality is, I bought the photograph for you, knowing how much you love sunrises.

I hoped things would end differently for us, but I'm learning I'm not in charge of my life, no matter how much I try to be. I won't lie and say I'm content with that—yet. But God and I are having lots of conversations about what happened—and what's next.

Anyway, back to the gift.

When you look at this, I hope you remember not what happened between us. Not what could have been.

Just remember I love you.

And I'm praying you find the life you're looking for—the life you deserve.

Love, Daniel

Allison read and reread the note, her eyes torn between the beauty of the gift he'd sent and the words he'd written.

She loved two very different brothers, and both loved her. Seth had loved her too much to let her go. Daniel loved her so much, he was willing to let her walk away.

CHAPTER 44

*H*e should have called first.

Seth stood outside his brother's apartment, not sure Daniel was home. And if he did open the door, would he slam it shut when he realized who waited to talk to him? Maybe Seth should forget the whole thing, get back in his car, and leave things as they were.

When the door swung open and Daniel leaned against the frame, Seth forced himself to stand his ground.

"Seth."

He took a step forward. "May I come in? I've got something to say. It won't take long."

Daniel ushered him in with a nod. "Be my guest—unless you're planning to finish off what we started in the bookstore. In that case, maybe we should go outside."

"All that got us was Tasered." Seth stepped over a pile of shoes—running shoes, cycling shoes, climbing shoes—left in a jumble by the front door. He moved toward the couch, stopping when he saw it was covered with at least a week's worth of unread newspapers.

"You want something to drink?" Daniel stood beside the couch, his hands shoved in the pockets of his cargo shorts, his shoulders tense underneath his ROCKING R VERMONT T-shirt.

"I'm good." Seth twirled his key ring around his forefinger, staring out the sliding glass doors, then clasped the bunch of keys in his fist. "This won't take long."

"Yeah, you said that."

Seth watched his brother for a few seconds, wondering how their relationship had come to this—struggling to talk to each other. Loving the same woman, and yet neither of them having her.

"I've realized a few things. And I've made a few decisions." Seth resisted the urge to pace the room. "As much as I love Allison, I have to face the fact she doesn't love me. I can't change that. God knows I've tried. I wanted to blame you, but I can't. The only person I can blame is me. I thought I knew what was best for both of us. I put my wants, my preferences, ahead of Allison."

"Seth, I—"

Seth held up his hand. "Let me finish. I know for some reason Dad bestowed the favored son status on me. I don't think it's because I did something right. I think it's more because of something you *didn't* do. I admit, at first I liked being his favorite. But you know what? Favored son status came with a price. I had to choose between being me and being who he expected me to be, and too often I went with what he wanted. I think the only thing I ever challenged him on was trying to get Allison back after she left me standing at the altar. I couldn't lose Allison. We'd been together for six years. Our relationship was the one area where I got to lead—Dad wasn't in control.

"Don't get me wrong." Seth couldn't resist walking a few steps around Daniel's apartment. "I love what I do. But I hate the fact that Dad's constantly watching me. Telling me what to do and how to do it. You want to know the funny thing?"

Daniel stood silent.

"The one person's approval I really wanted? I could never get it."

"Whose was that?"

Seth took a deep breath. Was he ready to be completely honest with his brother? "Yours."

"What?"

"To you, I was always Tag, the little brother. Nothing more. And to me, you were always this amazing guy who managed to break away from all the had-tos Dad put on us. You lived your own life." Seth huffed out a breath. "See, this is why I don't like talking to counselors. They always insist you drag up the past. What a waste."

Daniel seemed ready to interrupt, so Seth determined to finish what he'd started.

"Okay. Getting back to the reason for my visit today. I realize I've lost Allison. I put too many other things before her. Before our relationship. She's asked me to let her go, and I'm going to. I don't know if you're the man to make her happy, but I want you to know I'm stepping away. I just won't be around to watch if you and Allison do end up together."

"What do you mean?"

"I've decided to follow in your footsteps, big brother. I'm going to travel. Well, as much as I can with Rayner Construction."

"Does Dad know?"

"He will when I tell him." Seth rocked back on his heels. "We've got sites all over the country. Surely some of them require hands-on attention. I'm the man to do it."

Daniel stepped forward and extended his hand. "Truce?"

Seth clasped his brother's hand. "Can we do better than that? Can we forgive each other?"

"Yes."

"All I ask for is time." He released Daniel's hand and stepped away. "If you and Allison . . . if you are the man for her, then so be it. You'll know when I'm ready to know. Deal?"

"Deal."

One down. One to go.

Seth scanned the interior of the bookstore. Thirty minutes before closing, there weren't too many people in the shop. A mom wandered the children's section with her two daughters. A couple of teens scanned the magazine racks. Allison's aunt said Allison would be here; now all he had to do was find her. He moved toward the tables clustered near the coffee bar, wondering if Allison could be there, sipping her customary tea and reading a book.

He spotted her hunched over a photography magazine, a half-full glass of iced tea sitting on the tabletop. Scoti, the owner, sat curled up in the other chair. As he approached, she leaned over and said something to Allison, probably warning her of his presence.

Allison sat up, closing the magazine and tucking her hair back behind her ear. Seth raised his hands, palms out. "I come in peace—and I'm unarmed."

"Fine." Scoti excused herself, motioning for him to take the seat she vacated. "Then I'll leave you two to talk."

"How are you doing, Allison?"

"I-I'm a bit surprised to see you, Seth."

"I decided to take my chances and drop in. Do you have a minute?"

"Sure." Her eyes asked a dozen different questions.

"I came to say I'm sorry—and to say goodbye."

"W-what?"

"I've had a lot of time to think about our last conversation. At first all I wanted to do was find a way to prove you wrong—to be able to come back and show you I was the right man for you, even if I'd made mistakes." He reached over and removed the mangled straw from her fingers. "But I can't. And I'm sorry. Sorry I hurt you. Sorry I've lost you. I still love you—still see you in my dreams, walking toward me in a wedding gown. And then I wake up and realize that's all it will ever be—a dream."

He looked away when tears filled her eyes. Saying all this was harder then he'd expected. He'd gotten the words out with Daniel, but talking to Allison caused his throat to tighten. He knew as much as Allison might be hurting, she wasn't going to change her mind. And he wasn't going to ask her to. He took a deep breath, waiting until he felt strong enough to continue.

"I've talked with Daniel, so I'm telling you what I've already told him. I don't know if he's the man to make you happy, but . . . I'm stepping away so you can find out. If he is, so be it. I won't interfere."

"Seth—"

"Allison, I know you love him. I know he loves you. It's a question that needs to be answered sometime. But like I told my brother, I . . . I don't want to be around to watch."

He couldn't.

Allison's words were a whisper. "What do you mean?"

"I'm going to follow in the footsteps of my adventurous older brother." He paused, then forced a smile and a lighthearted tone. "I'm going to travel a bit. See the world—at least the fifty states."

"Are you changing jobs?"

"No. I love what I do. I'm going to oversee some of our out-of-state construction projects." He found himself hesitating, wondering how to say all he wanted to say. He stood, pulling her up to stand with him. "I want you to know . . . I love you, Allison Denman. You'll always be in my heart. They say it's better to have loved and lost than never to have loved at all." He traced the contour of her face with a gentle touch. "I will never regret loving you. Losing you, yes. Loving you—never."

When a single tear slipped from the corner of her eye and trailed down her cheek, Seth erased it with a brief kiss. "And I am sorry for every tear I ever caused you."

"I'm sorry too, Seth." She wrapped her arms around his waist and held him in a tight embrace.

"I know, Allison. I know." He closed his eyes, allowing himself one last moment to savor holding her close. Would the ache in his chest ever go away? He forced himself to let her go. Stepped away. "Take care of yourself, love."

"I will. You too."

"I will."

He turned and walked away from what he'd thought for so many years was his future, refusing to look back. He tapped the ticket in his jacket pocket. He had a plane to catch.

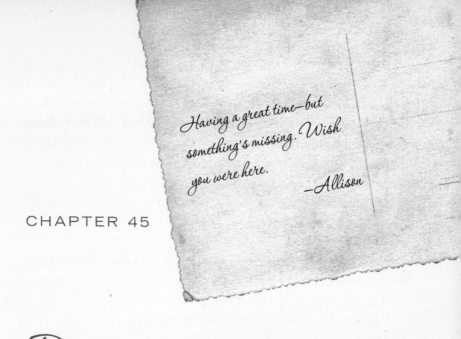

Having a great time—but something's missing. Wish you were here.

—Allison

CHAPTER 45

$\mathcal{D}$aniel stared at the view of Estes Park on the front of the postcard. The words WISH YOU WERE HERE arced over a sunrise view of Longs Peak. He turned the card over and, even though he'd memorized the note, read the twelve-word message one more time:

> *Having a great time—but something's missing.*
> *Wish you were here. —Allison*

Time to unravel the mystery of the postcard.

He'd debated the wisdom of this two-and-a-half-hour trip to Estes Park. Once he'd hit I-36, he'd thought about turning around. He knew what Alli's postcard *could* mean. Knew what he *wanted* the message to mean. But until he talked with her face-to-face—read the truth in the depths of her gray-blue eyes—he wouldn't know why Alli sent the postcard.

Jackson had positioned the postcard on top of a small stack of mail he'd collected for Daniel while he'd tested his rehabbed knee skiing in Germany in January. His best friend had even attached a neon green sticky note that said: *Read this first.* Daniel had read the card several times a day for the past two months.

After that, Daniel kept the postcard on his refrigerator under a
SKI VAIL magnet. He'd seen it every time he opened his refrigerator—
from the short, cold days of January through the snowiest March
that Colorado had seen in years.

A week ago, Jackson waved the postcard in front of his face like a
man signaling the final lap of a car race. "So?"

Daniel concentrated on his mug of hot-and-sour soup. "So what?"

"What are you going to do about this?"

"Nothing."

His friend slapped the postcard down on the table. "I never knew
you were a coward."

"I'm not a coward, Jackson. I'm also not stupid."

"You are an incredibly stupid coward if you don't go ask Alli what
this note means."

"Maybe I'll call her—"

"Maybe?"

Daniel stared at the remains of the soup like a tea-leaf reader trying to divine a message.

Jackson wasn't backing down. "Really? That's it?" Jackson slid the
postcard under his nose, flipping it so Daniel could read Alli's message. Again. "Don't be a fool, Daniel. If you love her, now's your
chance."

So here he stood on a Saturday morning, outside Alli's basement
apartment. Things were oddly quiet. No llamas paced the fence, eyeing him through their long lashes and dark horizontal pupils. Alli
had to be home, because he'd parked beside her Subaru sedan, but
her aunt's red Jeep wasn't around. Then again, maybe Alli had gone
into town with Aunt Nita.

Daniel shifted his weight from foot to foot, hesitant to knock on
Alli's door. Once he did, there was no going back. Just as he lifted his
hand, the door swung open, and Alli barreled into him.

"Ooof!" She placed her hands on his chest, grabbing the collar
of his coat. Surprise and pleasure danced across her upturned face.
"D-Daniel?"

"Hey, Alli." He resisted the urge to lock his arms around her. Pull her close. But he didn't step away.

"I-I didn't hear you knock." She hadn't moved. A faint blush stained her skin. "What are you doing here?"

"I came to ask you about this." Daniel held up the postcard.

"You got it."

"I got it." This time he allowed his fingers to brush a few strands of hair away from her face. Then he curled his hand into a fist before he did anything that betrayed his feelings—like trace the curve of her jaw with his fingertips. "It came while I was out of the country. Skiing."

"S-so your knee's all better?"

"Not a hundred percent. And if you tell my physical therapist I was skiing, I'll deny it."

"Why am I not surprised?" Alli seemed to realize she was in Daniel's arms. She let go of his coat. Stepped back into the apartment. "D-do you want to come in?"

"Sure."

He walked into the living room. Surprise jolted him when he found it crowded with packing boxes. "Going somewhere?"

"I hope so." Alli stood by a stack of boxes marked BOOKS in her careful handwriting.

"Excuse me?"

She waved off both her cryptic comment and his question. "Aunt Nita's getting married. Seems James the doctor friend was more than a friend." She shrugged. "She sold the house—closing in three days. The llamas are already enjoying their new home."

"I wondered what happened to the hairy beasts." Daniel surveyed the room. "So, your aunt's husband-to-be loves the llamas and all?"

"Yep."

"When's the wedding?"

"They're having a small ceremony next weekend. Just family and a few friends. Then they're off on a honeymoon."

"Ah." Daniel tapped the postcard against his palm. At least some-one was getting a happily ever after. "Where are you heading?"

"Me? Back to my parents' house for now. Bisquick's already there."

"Looking forward to that?"

"Some." Alli hesitated, looking around at all the boxes. "It'll be fun to have some time with Hadleigh before she heads off to college. I'm not ready to sign a lease on anything permanent. She's gotten over Evan pretty well."

"Dating anyone?"

"Who, Hadleigh?" Allison rubbed her wrist, giving away her ner-vousness.

"Sure. Let's start with her."

"Nobody serious."

"What about you?"

"No, I'm not dating anyone." Alli traced the letters D-V-D-S, not meeting Daniel's eyes. "But I have met someone."

"Really?" Daniel willed himself to act casual. This conversation wasn't going like he'd planned. "Who's the lucky guy?"

She turned and walked over to her messenger bag, rummaging through it for a few seconds. She came back, holding something out to him. "Maybe it'd be a little clearer if I gave you this."

Her passport?

"What's this for?"

"Put your postcard and my passport together." She moved closer, clasping her hands over his so they covered the two items.

"I'm not following, Alli."

"Daniel, months ago when you said you loved me, I got it all wrong. I should have told you that I loved you." She closed her eyes, appearing to search for the right words. When she looked at him again, her eyes lit with an unreserved emotion he'd never seen before. "Loving you was too risky. I'd barricaded myself in this safe zone. Your life is nonstop adventure. As much as I wanted to follow my heart, to follow *you*, I couldn't. And then you said it was all a mistake—"

Daniel clasped the postcard and passport in one hand, caressing her face with the other. "I didn't mean that . . ."

"I tried to convince myself you did. I'd told myself for so long that I was only the sum of my mistakes . . . how could I be anything but a mistake in your eyes too? I knew I broke your heart—and your words broke mine. The only good thing out of all that heartache was that, with Seth gone and you gone, it was just me. And God."

"And?"

"And without the distraction of . . . other things, I was finally able to hear God. He got through the voice in my head that kept telling me I was nothing but a long succession of mistakes and wouldn't be anything else. And he dared me to embrace him and to embrace life, risks and all.

"I started painting again. I'm taking photography classes. I even tried snowboarding because it scared me. I found out I don't like snowboarding . . . but I tried it. And day after day, week after week, I missed you." Allison leaned in to his touch, turning her face to place a gentle kiss on the palm of his hand. "I dug out all the postcards you sent me over the years and read and reread them. I realized I didn't just love how you lived your life—I love *you*, Daniel Rayner."

The urge to kiss Alli kept getting stronger, but Daniel meant to clear things up between them first. "So this postcard is a love letter?"

"I didn't know how to tell you how I felt." A mixture of shyness and hope tinged Alli's smile. "I sent a postcard, hoping you'd get the hint. And then . . . nothing."

"The postcard arrived while I was out of the country. To be honest, I tried to ignore it. I felt like I needed to let you go, no matter what my feelings said." Daniel tapped Alli's nose with the postcard. "Actually, Jackson insisted I come up here and talk this out with you."

"Tell him the blind-date fiasco is all forgiven."

Daniel leaned his forehead against hers, savoring how Alli's perfume teased him closer. "Besides realizing you love me, what else have you been up to these past few months?"

"Besides the photography classes and the failed attempt to snowboard, I've been trying to make peace with my past. I'm hoping Seth will forgive me, but that has to be his choice." Bittersweet emotion shadowed Allison's eyes. "My dad and I are talking some. He's traveling again. I know I'll always have scars, but I don't want what happened in my childhood to be the defining moment of my life."

Daniel traced the faint marks marring Alli's wrist. "We all have scars, Alli—some external, some internal." He pressed his lips to her skin. "I think with God's help, we can find healing—love each other, scars and all."

Allison buried her face in his chest, but not before he saw tears glistening in her eyes. He pulled her close, the blue passport brushing against his hand. One more question needed an answer.

"What's the passport for?"

Allison giggled, twisting to retrieve her passport. She flipped open the shiny cover to show him the blank pages. "Mine's empty. I can't think of anyone better to help me fill this with stamps."

"Now I'm nothing more than a glorified travel agent?"

"I was hoping for something a bit more long-term than that."

"Allison Denman, are you proposing to me?"

"No. I sent a postcard. Got a passport. But I will *not* propose."

"I hate to disappoint you, but I am not proposing, either."

Alli pulled away from him. "Y-you're not?"

"Not without a ring. And I have no idea what kind of ring you like. Or when you want to get married. Or where you want to go on our honeymoon."

"Those are all things we can talk about."

He settled her back into his embrace. "Sounds like we've got some planning to do, sweetheart."

"First things first."

"Did I forget something?"

Alli tapped her lips with her forefinger. Her voice dropped to a seductive whisper. "I . . . wish . . . you . . . were . . . here . . ."

He stopped her words with a kiss. Alli's lips were soft, and he followed the first kiss with another, not wanting to rush the moment. Alli's hands rested on his shoulders, her fingers curling into the cloth of his shirt, pulling him closer. Daniel deepened the kiss, holding nothing back. He buried one hand in the softness of her hair, wrapping his other arm around her to draw her closer against his chest. She tasted as sweet as Daniel remembered, but this time he was free to delight in her response. Their first kiss had been a mistake. Their other kisses had been clouded with uncertainty. But this kiss—

"Perfect." He whispered the word against the curve of Alli's jaw.

"What, Daniel?"

"Everything's perfect." He traced the hint of a smile along Alli's lips with a succession of light kisses. "Just perfect."

ACKNOWLEDGMENTS

For many years I said I would never write fiction, so it's almost surreal to be writing acknowledgments for my debut novel. I have many people to thank, and most of them believed in me as a novelist before I did.

My family: Only you know the truth of how many dinners weren't cooked, how many loads of laundry languished in the dryer, how many conversations remained truly one-sided while I wrote and rewrote and rewrote this book. Thanks for not keeping track. And thanks for loving a wife and mom who is also a writer. I love you too, even though I sometimes let the writing world trump the real world.

Roxanne Gray, aka "Rocky": You were the first person to whom I confessed my "I'm trying to write a novel" secret. Thank you for not laughing—and for reading through the early scenes. You are a forever friend. I know one day I'll be holding your novel in my hands!

Donita K. Paul, Evangeline Denmark, and Mary Agius: My first-ever fiction critique group—thank you for reading my chapters no matter how many times I revised them. Thank you for luring me to the Dark Side (the world of writing fiction) with the promise of cookies, and for ensuring they were gluten-free.

The Ponderers (Alena, Amy, Delores, Ginger, Heidi, Jennie, Jenness, Jennifer, Marie, Melissa, Lisa, Pat, Paula, Reba, Roxanne, and Teri): Who knew what God had planned when he brought us all together at a My Book Therapy (MBT) writers retreat? What blessings we've received: community, unceasing prayers, encouragement, and unity in the spirit. You are my writing friends who stick closer than a brother—um, I mean *sister*.

Susan May Warren: Your faith in me as a writer helped me believe in myself. Thank you for being my mentor and my friend.

Rachel Hauck, aka "Madame Mentor": Thanks for challenging me to go deeper when I write. Though I appreciate your insights, I appreciate your prayers even more.

Rachelle Gardner, my agent: Little did we know where this partnership would end up, eh? Thank you for all you've done to make this unexpected dream come true. You are the best of agents!

Holly Halverson and Jessica Wong, my editors, and Linda Sawicki, my production editor: I'm used to wearing the title of "editor" and wielding the red pen. Thanks for answering all my questions and ensuring *Wish You Were Here* improved on its way to print—and for encouraging me even while pointing out needed rewrites.

Howard Books: Thanks for saying yes to my dream of seeing *Wish You Were Here* in print.

Bruce Gore, Howard Books' art director (and all who were involved): Thank you for going the extra mile (and then some) to produce a beautiful cover for my debut novel.

Sonia Meeter, aka my "preferred reader": Thank you for taking the time to read my manuscript and give me excellent feedback. You caught some needed corrections that the professionals missed!

Discussion Questions

1. In *Wish You Were Here*, Allison Denman is a bride-to-be having second thoughts about the dress she'll wear for her wedding in five days. The dress is actually a symbol of Allison's uncertainty about marrying her fiancé, Seth Rayner. Why do you think she allowed things to progress so far without expressing her doubts? How could she have talked to Seth about her doubts? Do you think he would have understood?

2. Allison shares an unexpected kiss with her fiancé's brother, Daniel, which causes her even more confusion about marrying Seth. Should Allison have told Seth about the kiss and that she was having second thoughts? Was it best for her to try to forget about what happened and focus on the wedding? If Allison were your friend, what would you advise her to do? Have you ever done something impulsive and regretted it? Did you confide in anyone?

3. Allison makes it almost all the way down the aisle on her wedding day, and then she runs away. Should she have said "I do," based on her six-year history with Seth? Have you ever found yourself confused about what to do in a relationship? Is it possible to be attracted to two men at the same time? What truths does God offer us when we are uncertain about our choices?

4. Seth is determined to marry Allison even after she returns her engagement ring and says they wouldn't be happy together. While Allison's best friend, Meghan, tells her that Seth isn't a villain, were his actions those of a man who truly loved Allison? Did they demonstrate another motive? What do you think he could have done to win Allison back?

5. Allison suspects her sister's boyfriend, Evan, looked at X-rated sites on her computer. Should she have talked to Hadleigh about it before her sister brought it up? Should Allison have confronted Evan with her suspicions? What should she have said? Have you dealt with the issue of pornography, maybe with a family member or a friend? How did you approach the topic? What scriptural truths did you share?

6. Daniel believes he's not the right man for Alli, so he sets her up on blind dates and then tells Seth where she's living, even though she doesn't want Seth to know she's moved to Estes Park. Was that the right thing to do? Or was Daniel thinking only of himself?

7. Seth knows he's always been his father's favorite son, and Daniel knows he's never been. Should parents have favorites? Have you seen this happen in families, maybe even in your own? Consider the biblical example of Jacob and Esau (Genesis 25), in which parents chose favorites. What problems were caused because Rebekah favored Jacob and Isaac favored Esau?

8. After running away with Allison for two years, Allison's father returned her to her mother, agreeing to walk away from his daughter. Allison tells him doing so was his "get-out-of-jail-free card." Her father insists he was trying to let her have a better life than he could give her. Did he do the right thing by staying away from his daughter all those years? Should he have gone to jail for abducting Allison from her mom during their divorce? If he served time in prison, could he then try to have a relationship with his daughter later?

9. Struggling with how to handle her feelings for Daniel and her attempts to be friends with Seth, Allison believes the right choice has to be the hardest choice. Her aunt Nita challenges her by asking, "Is the hardest thing always the right thing?" What do you think? Have you ever made a decision under the assumption that it was the right thing to do just because it was the most difficult choice? What helps when you are faced with difficult choices?

10. Allison's view of God has been shaped by her relationship with the men in her life—first her father, then both of the Rayner brothers. When she finds a Scripture passage that says, "Light, space, zest—that's God!" (Psalm 27:1, *The Message*), Allison admits that's not how she sees him. Who or what has shaped your view of God, and how would you describe him? Is your view based on what others have told you or on what Scripture reveals about him?

11. Do you think it's possible to have a romantic relationship with the brother of the man you were going to marry? Was Allison right to reject Daniel at first because he was Seth's brother, even though she loved him? Did you understand why, months later, she sent him a "Wish You Were Here" postcard? What—or who—had changed to allow them to have a relationship?

12. What was your favorite scene in the book? Which character in the book are you most like?

Author Q & A

Wish You Were Here is your first novel. What kind of challenges did you face? Did your original plans for the novel differ from what you ended up with?

Challenges? How do I choose? Maybe alphabetically? The transition from writing nonfiction to fiction was, at times, painful. My mentors—and I am blessed to have several—had to talk me down off the ledge several times. Why? I had a lot to learn. Storyworld—excuse me? I'm a trained journalist. I write tight. If I say my heroine walked into a room, figure it out. Four walls, a floor, and a ceiling. I learned that style of writing doesn't work on the "Dark Side" of the writing world.

I wrote and revised *Wish You Were Here* for three years. *Three.* I had a lot to learn, remember? At one point, I thought: *I need to increase the tension in this book.* So, I turned the novel into romantic suspense. I went to an advanced My Book Therapy (MBT) writers conference with fifty-plus thousand words. During the weekend, author Susan May Warren told me, "Beth, you don't write romantic suspense. That's not your voice." Susie was right. The suspense angle was a beginner's attempt at ramping up tension. I went home and deleted all the suspense scenes. I had twenty thousand words left. I still had a story left too. And the desire to keep going.

Wish You Were Here has a recurring theme of doing things for the right reasons and, more important, doing them for yourself. Have you had any experiences that informed this theme?

Several years ago, I identified myself as an "Accidental Pharisee." I wanted to be all about God's grace, but really, law is so much easier. Just tell me what to do or what not to do—I can handle those kinds of directions for life. God's grace, which he says he lavishes on us, is scary. It's limitless—no boundaries. I want to embrace the truth in Romans 5:2 (*The Message*): *We find ourselves standing where we always* hoped we might stand—out in the wide open spaces of God's grace and glory.

So, yes, I've done things for the wrong reasons. I wanted to make sure I was getting all good marks from God and that I was keeping everybody in my life happy. In doing so, I wasn't being true to who God created me to be.

What kind of role has faith played in your writing? What kind of messages do you hope to convey through your characters?

I write because I believe God created me to be a writer.

Olympic champion Eric Liddell said, "God made me fast. And when I run, I feel his pleasure." I believe God made me a writer. When I write, I feel his pleasure. At a few precious times, there has been a tangible sense of God's presence as I sat at my computer working on an article or a story. My "writer's verse" is Psalm 90:17 (NIV): *May the favor of the Lord our God rest upon us; establish the works of our hands—yes, establish the works of our hands.*

I thought long and hard about Allison's and Daniel's relationships with God and decided I wanted them to both believe in God, but to have mixed-up ideas—wrong ideas, really—about who God is. That was true in my life and I think it's true for other believers. Many people have a relationship with God that is based on error. They don't yet understand who he is and what he offers us. Why? Maybe they've been taught something wrong or maybe they've been wounded by life, and that hurt causes them to believe something untrue about God.

Seth's and Daniel's treatment of Allison could not have been more different: Her relationship with Seth was borderline abusive, but her relationship with Daniel was accepting and supportive. These differences seemed especially intriguing given that Seth and Daniel are brothers. What were you trying to illustrate with their contrasting personalities?

My main goal with Seth and Daniel was to highlight what can

happen when one child is favored over another child. I'm *not* saying the favorite child grows up to be abusive. I want my readers to step back and look at what happened to Seth and Daniel long before they met and fell in love with the same woman, and then see how it affected the brothers. Daniel knew he wasn't the favorite son, and he knew Seth was. Daniel chose to distance himself from his father—and in some ways, found freedom to be himself. Seth, however, accepted the mantle of favoritism and found that it weighed heavily on him.

Aunt Nita is a particularly multifaceted, passionate character who possesses just the right measure of wisdom and doubt. Did you have any inspirations for the characters in Wish You Were Here? *Who is your favorite character? Why?*

We all need an Aunt Nita! She is a wonderful mixture of all the friends who have offered me encouragement and wisdom when I've doubted myself or faced struggles. At times I wove in actual bits of advice others gave me. (You know who you are!) And the name "Nita" is based on bestselling Christian author Donita K. Paul, who invited me to join a fiction critique group at her house when I was a trembling novice.

My favorite character? I've seen other authors say they can't choose a favorite character; that's like choosing a favorite child. And I certainly am against that, aren't I? Can I say Banzai, the llama?

If I had to choose, I would say I love how Allison changed through the story. She embraced who she was, grew closer to God, made the choices of her heart, and dared to risk loving the right man—no matter how wrong it seemed.

Allison's mistakes ultimately lead her to finding true happiness. Has anything like this ever happened to you?

Now there's a funny story . . . I met my husband, Rob, about five weeks after I broke off an engagement. No, I didn't leave the guy at the altar. There was no frothy dress. Everyone told me I was crazy for letting this "perfect guy" go. When I met Rob, I was so not interested in getting romantically involved—and I told him so.

And yet, God used Rob to lead me to my faith, and he also used Rob to show me what romance really can be like—thirty-one years and counting!

Are there people in your life who help you get through difficult times, the way Allison's best friend and aunt helped her?

My husband was in the military for twenty-four years. We moved more than I ever planned on. One lesson I learned: Friendships have seasons.

The benefit: I have been blessed with a worldwide circle of friends. I do not know what I would do without my girlfriends. As my daughters were growing up, I taught them that you need your girlfriends.

Two quick stories: When we lived in Florida, I was experiencing some extreme heartache because I was working through my childhood sexual abuse. At one point, I left my house for the day, looking for a place to go to rest (hard to do with three small children). Where to go in a small town? McDonald's? The local mall? I drove around and around and got the impression to drive to my friend Fran's house. When I drove up, she was standing in her doorway, looking out. I walked up to the door and she said, "Rob called and said you were having a tough day. I prayed you would come here."

Second story: Our move to Colorado was tough because I left behind close friends, and it took a while to make new friends. I had an unexpected pregnancy and, after some complications, was told I needed a hysterectomy. In tears, I called my friend Pamela, who lived back in Florida, to share the news. Five minutes after we finished talking, she called back and said, "Faith [another friend] and I have decided you need your girlfriends. Can we come out before your surgery and help?" The tears flowed again. They came out and we had a girls' weekend before the surgery, and then they took care of my toddler and filled my freezer with meals before they left.

I'm thankful to say I've developed close friends in Colorado too—ones who know the real me.

Do you have a special place you like to write?

I have my own office in our home. Well, it's mostly mine. There's another desk in the room where my husband works some and where our daughter does schoolwork and continually asks if I'll help her browse Amazon.

But it's painted according to my preferences: one bold red wall, and then the others are a warm harvest yellow. I have my favorite sayings or photos on the walls, including the cover of *Baby Changes Everything,* my first book. I invested in a new desk, a red ergonomic chair (yes, I have back problems), and two computer monitors—an editor's delight! My daughter and her BFF just made two signs for my door. One reads: *Yes, I can talk.* The other states: *BRRR! It's Cold in Here! Enter If You Dare!* I'm not divulging who made which sign.

How have your past nonfiction works affected the way you craft fiction? How are they similar and different from each other? Which do you enjoy writing more?

There's that "more" question again. In some ways, nonfiction is easier because it's what I am trained in—it's what I know. It's like breathing. Write a lead. Be short. Concise. Beginning, middle, end. Breathe in. Breathe out.

Some people will see my name on *Wish You Were Here* and think, "She's arrived! She knows what she's doing!" I know what I'm doing—and I know what I still need to master. In my next book, I am focusing on storyworld and weaving in spiritual truth.

The truth is, I enjoy writing both—and I enjoy editing. But my focus is now on writing fiction. I write fiction like a journalist. I write tight. My chapters tend to be shorter than some authors' chapters. My journalism training is part of my voice.

What are you working on now? It felt like the story of Allison Denman is just beginning. Can we expect to see her again in a sequel of Wish You Were Here?

I will never say never to revisiting Allison and Daniel's story—or possibly a closely related story. My agent, Rachelle Gardner, and I talked about whether Seth could ever have a healthy relationship with another woman. And then there's the story with the Air Force helicopter pilot and the female family physician who has never been "picked" . . . and the one that popped into my head when I walked out of a bank and saw an armored car and thought, "I've never been in a bank holdup. What if . . ."

Any teasers you'd like to share?

Oftentimes, I distill my stories down to questions. Ones like:
- Do opposites attract or combust? (Answer: Yes!)
- What if your attempts to be yourself reveal your deepest fear: You're nothing but a failure?
- Does life only start after the "I do"?
- Where do you run for refuge?